TURPENTINE

TURPENTINE

SPRING WARREN

Black Cat
New York
a paperback original imprint of Grove/Atlantic, Inc.

Published simultaneously in Canada
Printed in the United States of America

FIRST EDITION

ISBN-10: 0-8021-7036-6
ISBN-13: 978-0-8021-7036-1

Black Cat
A paperback original imprint of Grove/Atlantic, Inc.
841 Broadway
New York, NY 10003

Distributed by Publishers Group West

www.groveatlantic.com

07 08 09 10 11 12   10 9 8 7 6 5 4 3 2 1

For Louis

CHAPTER 1

April 1871
    Dear Brill,
    The solicitor does not respond. The three letters I sent to Mother have been returned.

                                   Edward

    Dear Edward,
    Perhaps, in this country that requires more and more travail from its citizenry each day, it is no longer three but four that is the charm.

                                       Brill

B uffalo, some yet kicking and bawling into death, others still as boulders, soughed the plain. A cadre of skinners laid open hides, steam curling into the freezing air. The skinners were burly men; browned from weather and dirt, and fast. I, Edward Turrentine Bayard III, was picket, pallid, and slow. I sat on my heels shivering beside a mountain of a buffalo, keeping low to escape sharp wind blowing over the hump. Blood and hair matted my hands, arms, and coat.

Two months earlier I'd been in Connecticut, boarding the train. Plum blossoms framed my mother as she waved a handkerchief bidding me goodbye. She was my only relative, my grandmother having died three months before and my father dead when I was seven. So it was my physician, Dr. Bateman,

1

who lifted me onto the train west. I was to be treated in a small private sanatorium promising miracle cures for the lungs.

The only miracles I suffered, however, were the transformation of the sanatorium into a rickety outpost on the Nebraska plain. The doctor who sent the advertisement was a scoundrel with a printing press.

The greatest miracle was that the West had not yet killed me. Nebraska, being good for cold the way the south side of houses was good for lilacs, was yet covered in icy mud. After seventeen years avoiding dust and drafts like poison gas, I was now ever chilled, never clean, and with no choice but to push on. I picked up my knife, the sizable blade honed to wicked sharpness, and began the divorce of hide from meat.

Tilfert Slade stood at my elbow. Overseer of the hide production, he'd taken on my western education to please my landlady, Avelina, whom he was courting. He was a huge man with tree trunk limbs and woolly hair that crested the neck and cuffs of his grimy shirt onto his face and over his knuckles, but he was elegant as silk at work. He sailed his blade between muscle and hide, sliding the steel from the tail, around each leg to the brawny neck, discharging hide from head, then turning to sheet his knife across the next beast in line.

The pay was twenty-five cents a hide, but for every quarter I earned, twenty cents went to boots, to biscuits, to liniment. Today I'd torn my pants from crotch to knee. Resolving to work faster, I rowed my knife through the hide. When I began the southern descent around the horn to the leg, however, I punctured the entrails, loosing a belch of stink. I flung back retching, to the delight of Tilfert, who was entertained by emetics. I didn't stint on his pleasure. Whereas life in civilization was scented and borne in pretty containers, in the West it oozed, poured from orifices, wriggled, stunk, and I was indisposed to it.

"Ned." Tilfert wiped his eyes delicately with his hairy paw. "You're somethin'."

I nodded and took up the knife again. "I could do with neither seeing nor smelling another buffalo as long as I live."

Tilfert squinted. "Shaggies everywhere. Sometimes a man can't see grass for the skins. That don't just disappear."

He slapped my back, nudged me over. He put out a hand for my knife, took the buff's ears, cut around the neck, and finished my course around the legs. I noosed the neck hide with a rope gathered around the pommel of Tilfert's saddle. Tilfert clicked his tongue and the horse strained forward, peeling the buffalo's skin from the fatty corpse. Tilfert asked, "What would you eat, if there wasn't buffalo?"

I imagined we'd starve. The meal I'd lost was buffalo tongue fried in tallow. We ate buffalo hump for breakfast, boiled rib for supper. Biscuits were buttered with marrow pushed out of the buffalo's hip bone. As variety: the clod pieces cut from the shoulder; buffalo liver, eaten raw and sprinkled with gall; or steaks, which, when seared over a buffalo chip fire, required no pepper.

"How about a chicken?" I thought of my old cook and the roasted capon she lovingly prepared with spring potatoes and parsley.

Tilfert was insulted. A buffalo disciple, he admired the animals as if he'd invented them himself. "Buffalo *shit* bigger'n a chicken, Ned." The horse took another pull, the hide gave way from the carcass with a pop, and I retrieved the rope and left the hide for the pegger. Tilfert adjusted his coat, the curly buffalo hair on the shoulders seamless to the pelt on his head. "Can't *wear* a chicken, neither."

I slogged to the next animal apprehensively. They sometimes flinched with the first poke of knife. Tilfert followed.

"Buffalo feed you. Buffalo wood to burn." He put a foot on the haunch of the buffalo I'd knelt beside and leaned on his knee. "Ran out of water'n came so near to dyin' a thirst, I cut my mule's ears for the blood. Killed a buffalo, punched a hole in the stomach. They carry extra water like a camel. Comes out jelly but good 'nuff."

Disappointed in my lack of affect, Tilfert added, "Caught in a blizzard? Clean out the gut and crawl in, they're a goddamn dugout!"

I glanced at his expectant face and though my stomach roiled, agreed. "Room and board. What more can you ask?"

"That's it, Ned. What more?"

I began the rip from the neck.

"You hear from your people?"

The last time I'd heard from Mother was on that Connecticut station platform two months ago. It was not like her. Though she was a timid woman, she was devoted to me, even indulging me in many ways my formidable grandmother disapproved of, once gathering bones from the kitchen so that I, in my bed, could assemble an entire chicken skeleton for my studies.

Sawing desperately through hide and ligament, I gasped, "Nothing. Note from my tutor, Brill, but he's teaching in Pittsburgh now."

When I left Connecticut, Brill, as much friend as tutor and only four years my senior, handed me "The Prairie Prince" from the *Post* and told me I was on my way to great things. This, though my vision blurred and I could barely speak through my labored breathing. Now his letters and my father's watch were the only things that reminded me of who I had once been, if not who I was.

Tilfert shook his head. "Shame. Usually it's the fella goin' west that lets go."

I put my weight on the knife, but my arms trembled, my breathing was ragged.

Tilfert, embarrassed at my puniness, looked away, gauging the trajectory of the afternoon. The skinners were getting fractious; tempers often failed an hour from supper and it took no little peacekeeping to conserve his crew's numbers. "I don't think you got the finish of this one in you, Ned. Why don't you head back?"

Quitting was a fine idea, though I could hardly sit a pony and my sense of direction was as laughable as my taxidermy. But Tilfert gave me a leg up onto the nag that toted pegs, who knew the way back like a homing pigeon. Tilfert slapped her haunches, and the mare and I began the plod to the fort.

It wasn't as far as it could've been, and the horse was warm under me. I clutched my ripped pant closed against the wind and relaxed into the horse's rolling gait, closing my eyes with few qualms. If it took any skill on my part to get home, we were lost anyway.

After some time I roused when the horse stopped altogether. I opened my eyes and saw what I initially took for fever: a woman. She sat not sidesaddle but astride a palomino, holding a hand to her brow as if she were a man surveying a piece of property. There was nothing else of a man about her. She was small, maybe five feet tall, with dark curls lifting her hat, and wore a red dress that was too fine both for riding and for the newly minted state of Nebraska, appearing of another texture and pigment than the dun life of leftover winter.

She asked, "Are you alive?"

Tongue-tied, I nodded.

"Lost?"

I found a thin voice. "The horse knows the way."

She smiled and danced her horse toward mine. "Lill Martine."

I shook her hand with mired fingers. "Edward Turrentine Bayard the Third."

She inclined her head. "My, my." Wheeling her horse, she looked me over once more and called, "Good day!"

My nose was dripping, my toes numb, but when Lill passed I felt a rush of warmth.

As I had extended winter by my ride on the train, Lill pulled spring behind her. A warm breeze sighed, combed branches free of dead leaves, stirred grass to tender, sap to rise. The blood returned to my extremities. Agog, I watched her spark diminish across the plain. I roused the horse into a turn and followed as though Persephone herself were fleeing the world.

The horse quickened into a brain-thumping trot, pegs rattled from the paniers as I shouted, "Miss Martine!" biting my tongue half through. Nebraska bumped up and down around me. I spit blood and fell farther behind by the jog. Lill Martine disappeared; my horse lathered; my privates screamed. Still I hung on, kicking the mare into motion, racing across a world that grew nothing taller than a stunted cedar, sagebrush, or prickly pear. Yet the land rolled like folds of fabric. Lill Martine could be a half mile away, she could be five, and not only did I not know her location, I would not have know my own. If I'd realized, I certainly would have panicked.

A resident of Nebraska for just under two months, I'd already seen how many ways the prairie could do harm to a man. A horse could fall on him, a sudden blizzard take away his toes, fingers, his sensibilities, his life. There were rattlesnakes, rabid skunks, bad water, no water, and starvation threatening at every turn. The Pawnee were generally accepting of the whites, but the Sioux were not and I feared earning a nickname like Noseless (and earless) Joe Means at their hand.

The horse had better sense than I, however, and, having turned from one destination, circled to the other. Rising from one of those soft folds, hopeful I would espy my fugitive spring, I, instead, found myself back in the cold company of skinners as though I hadn't traveled at all. I wondered if Lill and my flight toward her had been a dream, but Tilfert ran to me from the wagon, horror on his face.

"Ned, goddamn, what's happened to you?" My shirt was spattered with blood. He helped me off the horse.

I hesitated for only a moment, spoke through my thickened tongue. "Raddlesnake. Damned horse panicked."

I reclined in the wagon on a bed of buffalo hides, barely registering the fleas jumping my ship, as we returned to the low ranges of barracks, officers' bungalows, and stables of and around Fort McPherson. McPherson was a ragtag place, serving not only as a military post but also as a locus of free enterprise. Drovers stopped along their routes. Pioneers passed through toward free land. Tourists rode in on the train to take a look at all the West at the end of the line, before racing back to tell their stories of shoot-outs and wolves. All these passing citizens had great needs, if varying amounts of money, to trade with McPherson's entre-preneurial residents for lodging, tobacco, whiskey, bread, enter-tainment, or, perhaps, a new pair of trousers.

My thoughts paused not on my need for trousers, however, but on the beautiful Lill Martine. I reexamined each word she spoke, cringed over what she must have thought of me. What had that "My, my" meant? It was possible she didn't *believe* that I was Edward Turrentine Bayard the Third.

No one had questioned my identity when I arrived at the fort in linen trousers with a trunk of useless shoes and ascots, fleeting sweets and plasters, and a pocketful of money. Yet my cash and cookies were soon gone, and with a whiff of imposter about me, the solicitude the officers at the fort had shown evaporated. The men addressed me as My Lord Turpentine. My syphilitic land-lady put me out of the closet I'd rented, claiming she wouldn't risk a lunger in her house any longer. If it weren't for Avelina, I suppose I might have frozen to death.

A rawboned woman with a face mottled in freckles the color of her Irish red hair, Avelina had a house on the river side of the fort she'd built herself, digging into the swell of earth for part of it and fashioning the rest from logs she'd driven her team a good distance to cut and haul. She was a phenomenon of energy: ro-bustly sweeping the dust that rose from the continual drilling of soldiers on hardpan, hoeing a garden three men would not man-age, lifting a barrel of flour onto a buckboard with a coarse groan, or splitting enough wood for a week's baking in an hour. She could turn the wringer all washday without effort, her flat back-side shifting like bellows boards beneath her skirt. When introduced, Avelina had pinched my arm and stated, "Eat. Wimmin like rat better'n mouse."

I wondered what Tilfert saw in Avelina. Though corpulent and rough, he was high-toned in comparison. I decided the draw was Avelina's agreeable house and palatable meals, for the fellow who ran the squalid mess hall served bread green with saleratus and docked with flies, poisonously greasy doughnuts, and charred buffalo. These meals told on the men with damaging effect until, like arsenic, they built up a tolerance. Tilfert put so much away at one sitting that one disastrous supper could have been his undoing, even with his rock-ribbed constitution.

Avelina also had an uncanny ear for rumor and—through similarly gifted friends cast like seed corn throughout the forty-one states and the Wyoming and New Mexico territories—she always had information to trade. Gossip was an art form at Fort McPherson, as assiduously practiced and deeply appreciated as any piano étude in a New York drawing room. And so, on my return, it was Avelina who told me about the beautiful Lill Martine.

Known in Georgia as Lyllith Hays, she had been affianced to a surgeon of some repute. Lill's family, fallen on hard times, had brokered their future on the marriage. When informed the man was affianced to another in Louisiana, Lyllith rode to her fiancé's house and, from astounding distance, shot the surgeon through his cheating heart.

The Hays family fled law, rumor, a flood of debt and took a new name. They headed west, where Lill might avoid the noose by dint of distance and discretion. For in the West, prostitutes might become innkeepers and an Irish brawler turn cattle baron.

Negroes magicked their indenture to freedom. Though there was the murmur of gossip to live out, it was understood here, the past was nobody's business. Lyllith the murderess expired, giving birth to Lill Martine, pioneer. And so the ruined rose from the flames. What this meant for My Lord Turpentine, I wasn't sure, except the journey between pan and fire went both ways.

From the other side of the curtain Avelina hung for privacy, I heard Tilfert burst into the house. He shouted, "Woman!" Avelina shrieked and cackled. There was a thump and a crash. The two of them would be wrestling and bussing their exuberant welcome, titans testing their strength.

Tilfert roared with laughter; Avelina threatened his life and called him sweetness. I remained moused in my corner until it was decided. Then we sat for dinner.

CHAPTER 2

Dear Mother,
Why do you not write? I contemplate petitioning the neighbors as to your circumstances and risk mortifying our good name.

Dear Brill,
I have met the most astounding woman.

"Turpentine!"

I ignored Tennessee. The scout, nicknamed for his opaque drawl, had a love of practical jokes of which I was often the brunt.

"Got a job for you, Turp, good pay."

"Then why aren't *you* taking it?"

"I would. Plum job drivin' supplies," he whined. "But *I'm* out with Captain Ellmore. Goddamn settlers at Wolf Point stirring up the Sioux again."

I shook my head. "Unfortunately, my vast ignorance extends to horses. It was only last week I figured out the difference between the front end and the back."

Tennessee brightened. "That explains the constipated horses. Anyhow"—he motioned behind him where a gigantic dapplegray horse was harnessed to a wagon—"all you gotta do is drive out that lumber. She's a plug horse. She'll plod along till you say stop. Fourteen miles there, fourteen back."

I eyed the horse, who stood switching her ashy tail. She didn't look plug, with a deep chest, powerful legs, and arched neck.

The horse looked me over as well, the long ears quirking my way, keen dark eyes below a wide forehead. Now in desperate need of both new pants and shirt, however, I could not help but ask, "What's the pay?"

"The horse. The fella what owns it is backin' to New York."

I was yet dubious. Tennessee took off his hat. "You know what a big Percheron like that is *worth*, Ned? Five dollars at least. Sell the animal to one of these farmers green off the train and, *bang*, ten bucks in your pocket. If it weren't for the damned Indians, I'd be makin' the money myself, and afore noon too."

It was tempting, but for Tennessee offering. He sweetened the pot. "Get a look at that redbird just moved in."

"That's Martine's load?"

Tennessee nodded. I was crazy to see Lill again, more intrigued than nervous over her dangerous past, and would likely have ridden a wolverine if that's what it took. But my experience with horses had taught me that getting *on* in no way ensured getting *to*. I looked again at the Percheron, who'd hardly moved a muscle. She had a smile, the way some dogs had grins, that didn't mean anything except more of a letdown when they bit. "You *sure* the horse is all right?"

"All right? You could sell 'er for sausage and make a pretty penny." He put the hat back on his head. "Look, the horse is a wind-up toy, moves like molasses. Tell the truth, I can't handle watchin' a big horse like that waste my time."

For two miles, at a satisfyingly decelerated pace, I decided Tennessee wasn't so bad, while anticipating ball-hawking social interaction with Lill. The horse, Chin, walked with a low easy stride along the crushed grass trail leading to the Martine homestead.

About the time I was polishing highlights of droll conversation, however, Chin strayed from the path. I jerked on the reins, to no effect. I pulled with all my might to turn her head, but Chin shook her head free of the pressure, burning the leather along my palms. I levered back and shouted "Whoa!" until my voice was gone. I jumped out of the wagon and stood in front of her, windmilling my arms. Had I not leapt aside, she would have run me over. Chin was an engine chugging on an invisible track, a hungry engine. She stopped at one of the little creeks that ran to the Republican River to eat the water-tender grass that grew there.

I climbed into the wagon and waited, but Chin ate as slowly as she walked. After watching her big jaw rise and fall for some time, I exited the wagon and meandered along the little creek.

Had I not had the worries of my own lunch, the specter of Tennessee's Indians on my shoulder, and a clamorous anticipation of seeing Lill, I would have been happy in the pretty place. Wildflowers dappled the grass, and birdcalls wove through the whisper breeze.

At a soft bank, where a raft of sand had fallen away, my heart commenced pumping so that my very vision wavered with the cadence. I put out my hand and caressed the raw cut of earth where the ancient remains of a turtle jutted. Its great beaked capitulum agape, the ridge of fore shell thick as my wrist, it would best me in height had we stood carapace to spine. My agitation was not only of discovery. The sight of the giant past was sobering.

One expects small things to die away, to be weak and unable to fight. But this primeval king of turtles—what could have happened that it and all its giant progeny had shrunk to the plate-sized modicums that now existed? If only Brill were there to discuss the beautiful monstrosity.

I took my notebook from the wagon and painstakingly drew the orbital brow of the fossilized turtle, feeling a confusion of proportion I partially ascribed to having spent the morning staring at Chin's oversized hind. When I finished the drawing, I stepped back and searched for the horse. Chin was back on the trail.

How I wished for a train, some engined conveyance for reliable safe transportation, rather than being tethered to the fractious nature of horses. Instead, I rode spindleshanks, and by the time I caught up with Chin I was gasping, drenched in perspiration, and the three canvas tents of the Martine homestead were in sight. I hurriedly picked a bouquet: lamb's quarters, lupine, chamomile, and anemone. The stink had not dried on me before we were there, my blouse marked with dark moons under each arm, my hair yet plastered to my head. Chin gave a long-winded sigh and stopped neatly at Lill Martine's side.

Lill was once again dressed for high society, though her hair was loose and tumbled as if she'd been riding in wind. She waved as I rode up and, to my chagrin, didn't remember me, putting out her hand and introducing herself as I presented her with the prairie flowers.

I took her hand and gave a stately if aromatic bow. "Edward Turrentine—" I began.

She interrupted, delighted. "My Lord Turpentine! Sleeping on the horse!"

I made the best of it. "Call me Ned."

Lill's father ambled out of one of the tents, a man of bully chest, gat legs, and the furuncular nose of the habitual drinker. We unloaded the lumber and nails until Mr. Martine waved me off. "Take a rest."

I crouched, mopped my face, and, breathing hard, thanked him. Lill hooked her arm in mine and drew me upright. "Now, the palisade."

Her tent was on the crest of the hill. A triangle of red fluttered from the pinnacle of the white canvas, looking suspiciously like the fabric of the dress in which I first espied her. Lill pulled aside the flap and I peered in. The smooth floor was covered with a striped rug. Buffalo robes piled into a couch reclined on one side, her rifle and pistol hung from one of the tent posts, and some rough shelves fashioned from a wood box held about two dozen books.

"Rude, but of no little romance, don't you think? A story cannot be writ without . . . grit." She smiled and took a leather-bound book from the shelf while I stammered agreement over grit. She sat on the robes, patted the spot beside her. "I have had some success in the world of words." When I was seated she fanned her hand and pointed at the gold ring on her finger; it was inscribed POETICA. "This was an award for my entire body of work, but I could read a mere selection if you'd like."

I would happily have listened to a shipping roster if she had read it. "A selection . . . your entire body . . . either one," I blushed and added, "Body of work, I mean."

Lill raised an eyebrow. "Of course."

She read me a poem that I hardly followed for the music of her voice; her perfect rose lips freed gossamer words into prairie air. Her dark lashes fluttered on pale cheeks that dappled with a diamond tear at a particularly moving passage. Everything about Lill Martine was fine. With every sigh she breathed, every word spoken, every graceful kick of her tiny feet, I was further enraptured.

Lill closed the book.

"Beautiful," I murmured.

"It was published in the *Georgia Mercury*. I did poetry readings around the state and into Louisiana to *full* houses: sitting rooms filled with ladies in feathered hats, gentlemen in white gloves." She sighed. "I fear my career as a poet has been upended, but eventually, I imagine, an audience will grow even here." She gave me a sidelong look. "Does my calling shock you? Is a female auteur distasteful?"

"Not at all." I cleared my throat. "*Women are the civilizers of mankind. Let the laws be purged of every barbarous impediment to women!* Ralph Waldo Emerson."

"Impressive." Lill slowly placed the book back on the shelf, then spun around. "Enough of me, I hear you are *ever* writing in a book. Are *you* a poet, an essayist . . . a *spy?*"

I laughed, pleased she could think me capable of espionage. "I do scientific studies." I proudly showed her my sketches of grass varietals, a diagram of a grasshopper's jointed craw, and my examinations of handwriting styles with which, I tried to explain, I had once solved a minor household crime by identifying a maid's false signature. But Lill pointed to a page on which a giraffe was drawn.

"Lamarck." The great French scientist was a hero and gave me faith in my improvement. I would be as the giraffe, stretching my neck to survive. I thought perhaps Lill might share my hopes. As beautiful as she was, as an exterminator of fiancés, temperament would be a point she'd hope to improve on.

She merely nodded and turned to the page on which the turtle was drawn.

I was thrilled to share the discovery with her. "The monster was enormous."

She laughed. "Perhaps not. Perhaps it is we who are small." Before I could comment, she shut my book and demanded, "Tell me your story. I hear you've been abandoned."

"I wouldn't say abandoned." I didn't want to seem like an unwanted puppy, no matter how often I felt so, and therefore skirted misery and told her about my luxurious past. The house in Cornwall, Connecticut, with an acre of cutting gardens around. Linen sheets, a private physician, a voluminous library, and a string of tutors.

She nodded. "And how did you get here . . . and to these circumstances?"

Without lying, I could not hedge about that. And so I described my journey west to convalesce in what proved to be a wild outpost. I paused, then admitted that I did seem to have been, if not abandoned, then marooned in Nebraska. I hadn't heard from my doctor, my solicitor, or my mother in months.

She took my hand. "I felt there was something special about you, Ned."

I blushed, intensely aware of the pulse in her fingertips. "Nothing special about me."

"There *is*. You are . . . pure. Unsullied. You have lived your formative years free of the corrupting influences of men: their desires, their *weaknesses*." She hastened to assure me. "I know it is hardship to be lonely and, worse, to be forsaken—yet, lucky you." She laughed at my shocked face. "Look at you, Ned. *Unique*, and while not *exactly* hale and hearty, no consumptive either. At this rate, the Lilliputian will be a giant at year's end."

Mr. Martine interrupted our tête-à-tête, shouting from outside, "Lill! Company!"

Lill jumped up and peeked out the tent. "Joe and Jim!"

17

My heart sank at the announcement of what I thought must be suitors. Lill spun from the tent flap and reached for her pistol. "Do you shoot?"

I replied I had never held a gun in my life.

"Pshaw. You cannot be giant, much less Western, without knowing how to shoot." She flourished a hand. "Come meet my friends."

I followed Lill out of the tent, wondering not only about her visitors but also about the wisdom keeping company with her and a firearm, yet unable to marshal my feet in any direction but hers.

Outside, two Indian men stood staring at Chin, who dwarfed their stocky ponies. Lill waved. "How! How!"

I was confused. "*Joe and Jim?*"

Lill whispered. "I cannot fathom their real names." She motioned toward me and announced, "This is *Ned*."

I waved at the men; they nodded back. Lill sang out, "Good!" patting a young mule deer carcass slung over the back of one of the Indian ponies as Mr. Martine arrived with a two-pound bag of coffee. Mr. Martine handed over the coffee, hoisted the venison onto his shoulder, and tipped his hat.

As Mr. Martine departed, one of the Indians pointed to Lill's firearm.

Lill grinned, whispered again. "I think this is why they *really* come." We wandered a ways out to the prairie, the Indians following close behind. Lill loaded shells into her pistol as she walked with as much attention as one would give to scratching an itch. She stopped, pried rectangles of dried mud from the earth, and threw them into the air, shooting them as they began their descent with so little concentration and such great success it was as if her glance itself obliterated them. Dirt rattled onto our heads as I whooped in thrilled admiration. The Indians roared with laughter, then returned to solemnity as Lill smiled and curtsied.

The show over, the Indians mounted and rode away. I brushed my hair clear. "You are marvelous!"

"Thank you. I *do* love an appreciative audience."

"How could there be any audience *other* than appreciative?"

Lill gave a sharp laugh and snapped her fingers. "Enough of me. Your turn."

Ignoring my protests, she showed me how to grasp the gun and sight down the bead on the barrel. I forgot my fears, inhaling the scent of violets from her hair. She put her hand over mine and I could hardly think. Could hardly discern the words in her soft voice as she instructed me not to pull but embrace the trigger. I took a faltering breath, let it half out as instructed, and, drawing my attention finally to the endeavor, envisaging the bullet's parabolic journey, I fired.

Magic! I hit the target! I fired again. Wood splintered. *This* was what power felt like. The charge expanded my gangly frame. Gun muscle masked my feebleness. Lilliputian, indeed. I had only to work a small steel lever for the bullet to speed to remote and thrilling destruction. Gun in hand, I equaled any man. I would shoot forever. Lill herself faded from my consciousness as I fired over and over, reloading with haste, hitting the face of the stump face until it was punky with holes.

Lill finally took the gun from me. "You are a surprising marksman, Lord Turpentine."

I took a few breaths and regained my composure. "I am nothing in comparison to you and your many talents."

She waved her hand. "My talents are generally regarded as hindrances, to put it mildly, the writing perhaps the greatest drawback of all. Turns my head, you see." She regarded the pistol in her hand. "At least this is useful." She glanced at me. "Pot hunting."

I hurried to draw the conversation to a safer arena. "What good is feeding the body if the spirit cannot find sustenance? The work you do is important."

Lill tilted her head to the side. "I believe you truly see it that way, and I cannot tell you what a relief it is to be appreciated." Lill made a face. "It is an anomaly of late. Perhaps entirely of the past."

"Not as long as I am by your side." When she smiled again I asked, "I've told you my sad tale; what is your story, Miss Martine?"

She arched one perfect eyebrow and gave me a long measuring look. "Suffice to say abandonment is not unfamiliar to me either, Lord Turpentine." She gazed down the barrel of her gun. "My past is not a pleasant one, I regret to say, and before we progress further, I must insist you, as I do myself, leave history to ashes. If that cannot be, we must terminate our friendship now." She returned her gaze to me. "It is the one request I cannot have any but full agreement on."

If I doubted the rumors of murder before, I did no longer. Nor did I care, however, and hastened to assure her in my most aureate speech. "The present and the future render yesterday superfluous in all our lives. We must leave fresh footprints and ignore chasms cut by the roiling past."

Though she smiled and nodded agreement, she looked a bit rattled—pained, even—still suffering, I imagined, the betrayal of her betrothed. Did she pine for him, regret her action?

We wandered back toward the tents. Lill shot three heads of prairie flowers from their stems and announced, "I am thinking we two lost souls should band together. You are a natural marksman but not yet a crack shot. Some practice, however, and we could offer shooting exhibitions, poetry readings, and scientific rumination for the cultivation and entertainment of the western pioneer. The world is passing by our doors, Ned. Emptiness, such a draw, is perpetually killing itself. In its wake, a hunger for *spectacle*!"

The savor with which she spoke intimated the abandonment she'd spoken of was not only by the surgeon but by the crowd. Lill pined for the public gaze. She sighted on a pine tree. "What fun we should have. You practice, Ned, and we will perform as . . . India and Omar, the shooting twins." She shot and bounced three cones from their high perches to the earth. She looked at me, my disappointment at being cast a sibling certainly on my face. "No one will cluck over your hand on my arm."

Lill grinned luminously at me, then shot once more. The fourth cone recoiled in a long arc onto the canvas side of Mrs. Martine's tent.

Mrs. Martine appeared at the tent's flap, a cuttlebone woman with prominent teeth behind tight lips, which tightened further still when she saw Lill with the pistol. She took a breath as if she would speak, felt the bare finger on her left hand that, I surmised, a ring had adorned in better times, then turned abruptly away.

I imagine all mothers harbor seeds of enmity for their children. Understandably. Children ruin their parents from the moment of conception. Ruin their romance, their health, their composure, their figure and freedom. Children are weeds in the garden of Eden. Yet mothers opened the Pandora's box of baby, and so it is their duty to keep the resentment buried, to make the child believe in a pure love, when there is nothing untainted about it.

My first inkling of this came at eight years of age, when Father had been dead a year. My room reeked of menthol and mustard as I wheezed painfully through the night. I shammed sleep against my mother and grandmother's worried scrutiny. Mother cried, "I cannot *stand* this suffering!" Grandmother snapped, "You've made your bed, and because of it that poor child must bear this misery and you will do the same."

I couldn't fathom then what it meant, but in the months after my grandmother's death I came to understand I stood between my mother and a shadowy gentleman who waited for her nightly in the parlor. I wondered now if it was to this shadow's arms that she'd fled, having cut herself free from me and my illness. Yet, when I took leave of her at the station, I felt her sorrow like a knife.

Dr. Bateman had taken special care that morning to bleed the toxins from my body and administer tincture of arsenic and opium in the hopes it would keep me until I arrived in Nebraska. He lifted me from my chair and into the red train seat, admonishing the ancient attendant to contact him immediately if there was any trouble. He trickled a rejuvenating nostrum into my mouth and tucked the blanket around me as I wheezed and shivered, clutching Brill's *Saturday Evening Post*. I stared desperately out the window and saw my mother wave her handkerchief. I could not discern her face. But I could feel my mother's fear and met it with my own, thinking we would never see each other again. Not because I ever imagined she would flee, but because I thought I would die; indeed, I felt so badly I wished I would.

Did the dark man comfort her when the train departed? I felt a shade of forgiveness. If she loved him the way I already loved Lill, she'd been heroic to tarry so long.

The strip of prairie circling the tents was weightless in comparison to the arena of blue sky overhead. I stood a moment with my hands at my brow, then turned and looked at Lill. She'd holstered the gun and now turned slowly, her hands out as if it were raining sunshine. She smiled, caught me in her circle, and sang:

> *"Who will catch and who is caught?*
> *Who is head and who is heart?*
> *Who can stop and who will start?*
> *Will you love or will you not?"*

She laughed. "We are too old for kissing games." She pecked me on the cheek and spoke, so close I could feel her breath on my skin. "It is hard to have lost so much, isn't it? Come again, soon. I've been long from a kindred spirit. *How* I need a destination to aim for."

CHAPTER 3

Dear Brill,
You would not know me. A gun in one hand, an ax in the other.
I have not vomited in two weeks. I am in love.

Dear Omar,
We have met an age before, perhaps in Ceylon. You were riding
an elephant. I believe you saved me from a tiger with a single shot.

Dear India,
You wore saffron and indigo silk and recited odes as flutes sang.
Monkeys jumped through the trees against purple hills, and we
dined on mango and mongoose.

Dearest Omar,
Will you create the posters for our splendid concern? Reds and
golds with the words OMAR AND INDIA: EAST MEETS WEST.

Dearest India,
I insist our convocation shines as INDIA AND OMAR, DERVISH TO
PIONEERS. An epic journey suitable for the poet's hand?

Dear Ned,
The boys in my charge are thick as pudding, the young ladies a
delight, burgeoning in the lavage of education. Be wary of love.
An untried heart is tender, rising with little yeasting.
                                                        Brill

Aweek before her own death, my grandmother, murmuring into my ear as I reclined on the pillow, foretold my good blood would tell. I would be as Peter the Great. Peter had been sickly, usurped and exiled to the wilderness. There he did not molder but hewed logs into a great garrison. Worked his small muscle into tremendous strength, returned to Moscow, and retook his empire. He built, with his own hands, the first heroic ships of Muscovy, the greatest shipyard ever known. Peter broke the boundaries of his private world, traveled widely, and learned more trades, skills, and sciences than a hundred men of his time, bringing culture and knowledge to the wild Russian steppes. He was made great by the wilderness and he did the same for it.

I was not hewing logs, but I could split kindling. Though catching sight of myself in the rare pane of window glass, my hair dank and shaggy, my clothes ill-fitting, I worried the robust backbone of the prairie was working on me not only to good effect. After all, spitting was a Nebraskan sport, handkerchiefs unheard of, bathing an elective summer pastime. My time with Lill reminded me of my breeding, however. Upon my return to the fort I begged a haircut from Avelina.

She pulled out the scissors and told me to sit down. "Steer clear of that Lill, she's got a hundred years on you."

I glared from under the shower of hair clippings. "She's three years my senior, which is nothing. Lill's perfectly nice. Better than that, she's *wonderful.*"

Avelina sighed, and an alarmingly long chunk of hair fell into my lap. I picked it up. "What are you *doing?*"

"Slipped. A wonderful girl won't mind *that.*"

"Avelina! Please!"

"Don't get cramped. Hardly shows."

I kept my decision to make Lill mine to myself. Instead, I regaled Avelina with my newly discovered talent as sharpshooter. She trimmed calmly until I revealed my plan to, with luck, make a trade of Chin for a firearm. Avelina shook the towel from around my neck and said, "If you're planning on getting anything for that horse other than a kick in the pants, you're in need of more than luck, Turpentine."

I didn't want to believe it. Chin had behaved herself on the way back to the fort. Admittedly, she had sidetracked for another bite of grass on the journey, but I'd decided that wasn't unreasonable. She was a big horse and in need of constant refueling.

Others had a different opinion. Though there was some controversy over her name—either the horse had been named Chin, short for Chink, because she was obstinate, lazy, and not to be trusted, or it was short for Chinchilla, an animal useless until dead—the regard was much the same. Sausage was too good for her. No one would waste lead on shooting what was certain to be unpalatable.

Chin had, in fact, been wandering the prairies for months. Some other rube who had been fooled into a tortured ownership set her adrift into a snowstorm back in November. Tennessee stalked her for a week and struggled through three days to hook her up to the wagon, all for the pleasure of saddling me with the joke. I supposed, if I played my cards right and was patient, the right greenhorn would show up and I could pass on the favor. But I could not wait that long to secure a gun.

Lill and I had exchanged letters, delivered by anyone going between the fort and the Martine homestead. I opened the delicate envelopes with a shudder of pleasure. Yet as the violet-scented letters multiplied under my pillow, my eagerness for my own firearm mounted into a panic. There was no question that our relationship was predicated on my sharpshooting skills. If I, a penniless young man, patched and of impeached social standing, wished to have any chance at all with the beautiful Lill, I was going to have to win her heart with a well-placed bullet.

And so when a homesteader came through, desperate for cash and offering a silver .22 pistol with a burled walnut handle for sale, I spent what I'd so painfully saved for a ticket home with barely a regret.

I proudly showed the pistol to Tilfert. He turned it over, handed it back. "Tell you now, Ned, if you was to shoot me with that gun and I was *ever* to find out about it, I'd kick you from one end of the prairie t' the other."

Tilfert was in a foul mood. Breaking up volatile skinners who still embraced Union and Confederate colors as if the war weren't over but only relocated to Nebraska, he'd had the lobe of one ear sliced almost from his head. As Tilfert bellowed, Avelina cut the hanging flesh from its mooring, too far gone to sew up. She threw the piece of skin out the door, handed Tilfert a cloth to hold to his head, and shouted, "Men will fight, no *thought* to what's left after, *who* they leave behind. Worse than animals. But I won't have the 'news carried home to Mary' on Tilfert Slade." She slammed tin plates on the table. "No, they can find their bloody way without taking *my* man's ears. Send 'em packing, I got another idea."

27

I was unsettled by Avelina's pronouncements. *I* was one of the skinners Avelina was so callously sending packing. If Tilfert didn't pay me, certainly no one else was going to. I'd starve to death at the cusp of my growth spurt, my love affair withering on the vine.

I cleared my throat. "I'm out, then?"

Avelina looked surprised, then frowned and slapped the table. "You ain't goin' nowhere till you pay the *sizable* back rent you owe me . . . good and well worked it off, Turp. Got it?"

Tilfert snorted. "Work it off? Came with two dollars in his pocket and now he owes *me* three." He shut up at the violent look from Avelina.

And so I entered into my second employment in Tilfert Slade's Wild Western hunting and scouting services, catering to the adventure-hungry dudes who came west on the train (more numerous every day!). If all went as planned, we would certainly be rich by season's end.

The new concern seemed, however, employment only for Avelina and unpaid at that. She raised the tents where the dudes were to sleep, stretched buffalo robes to lay over each cot, and prepared large-scale meals.

When she was ready, Avelina wagged the filaments of her gossip web, brushed Tilfert's hat, hung a gold medallion around his neck, and pushed the shy man to stand on the platform when the train came in. His aim: to snag dudes in search of adventure like trout on a line.

Tilfert suffered. He could hardly say hello to a stranger, much less reel one in. "Cain't *you* do the talkin', Ave?" he muttered, staring at the platform like Satan was going to rise from the buckled pine. She would have none of that, but after days of Tilfert standing red-faced and salt-mute beside the tracks, I was enlisted to provide narrative.

Tilfert made a great effort to look wild and monumental as I hiked my thumb in his direction and made up outrageous lies. "That's *Tilfert Slade*." I spoke conspiratorially as though I were blowing Hickok's cover. "Part bear, part Pawnee, part buffalo. Goes through bullets like peppermint candies. Killed more buffalo than any man on the planet and got that gold medal from President Grant himself for civilizing the prairies. Won't be any wild left much longer. I spose Tilfert will have to go to Argentina or Black Africa, because a man like him can't be contained. Still, he's got a *few* hunts left." I'd cross my arms and the dudes and I would stare and nod while poor Tilfert would try to contain his embarrassment and look savagely toward the lion-filled savannahs of his future.

"He's off on a hunt tomorrow. I'm goin' along to get some adventure before *he's* used it all up." Then I'd start, like an idea just came to me. "Say, *you* look like an adventuring kind of man. Would you be interested?"

Still, we had no takers. Tilfert's savage silence looked more like simple-mindedness as he reddened and sweated throughout my narrative, rolling his eyes at the bullshit. For my part, I was skinny as a bean and looked as disposed to adventure as a walking stick.

Though I worried what would happen to me if Avelina and Tilfert went under, there was a benefit to unemployment: the freedom to practice sharpshooting to my heart's content.

I headed out to the prairie, as anyone in sight laughed themselves silly. Chin, predictably and to the amusement of the fort company, refused to let me cinch her up to the wagon again:

bucking, flirting out with her hind legs, rearing like a goat, and biting when any attempt to curtail her freedom was made. Her broomstick teeth and pie-plate hooves terrified me, so I gave up and traipsed about on foot.

That would have, in itself, been bearable. But Chin, though disinterested in being useful, was loath to be left behind. By the time I wandered ten yards from the fort in any direction, and no matter how carefully I crept away, Chin would espy my crouched form in the grass, commence neighing like an equine banshee, jump any fence or gate in her way, and follow at my heels like an enormous hound. It was hard to take.

On top of my horse problems, I found my beautiful little gun hopelessly out of whack, the barrel bent ever so slightly, the sights off-kilter. I couldn't hit a dog if I were standing on its tail. I was truly alarmed. Omar would let India down. If I couldn't be twin brother, could I hope to be lover?

I set my jaw. I would not give up. I practiced with that crooked firearm for hours, for days, my ears ringing, hands and shoulders stiff and sore, desperate to impress Lill. I used up my ammunition, spent the pennies I had left to buy more, used those up, then, unbeknownst to Avelina, begged more off the softhearted Tilfert.

Finally it came together. My muscles strengthened, my acuity sharpened, I could hit any stationary target with absolute regularity, though I couldn't hit a moving target worth beans. Tilfert was sufficiently impressed that he agreed to hold a playing card at arm's length for me to pierce with a bullet. If Avelina hadn't burst from the house howling, "Are y' *completely* soft in the head?" I think I would have done it.

I also spent no little time imploring Chin to behave like a real horse. I cleared Avelina's garden of carrots, bribing Chin to allow the traces, the bridle, the harness to be, initially, just alongside her, then to be lifted toward her, finally to be placed on her person. I sluiced carrots into the horse's maw while holding long conversations, impressing Chin with my desperate need of transportation. She seemed to take my desires into consideration, nodding as I spoke. Whether it was my debating skills or she was made sluggish by the volume of carrots, by week's end she allowed me to tether her to the wagon.

Avelina, far from congratulating me on my accomplishment, came after me with the hoe. "A winter of stew you fed that no-good animal, a spring of breaking sod and a goddamn summer of toting water to ruin her good and embarrass you both!"

Probably true, I morosely figured, and by acclimating to the bent pistol I'd likely ruined myself for shooting any decent gun on top of it. While worrying over a future handicapped from regular guns and steeds, and figuring that my plan to get more money for powder and lead from Avelina was now defunct, it occurred to me that at least I could make some use of my dubious experience.

I searched out Tennessee.

He grinned at my arrival. "Hey there, Turpentine."

"Tennessee."

"You teach that horse to fetch yet?"

I laughed. "You really caught me on that one."

"Can't take much credit for it, you being dumb as shit, Turp."

"Yeah, and you're a clever guy: savvy, even."

Tennessee looked wary. I hastened to camouflage the compliment. "I need some help. I want to impress that Martine girl with my new gun, and I can't hit anything. You being such a sure shot, I wondered if you'd give me a tip or two."

He took on a paternal air, nodded toward his rifle. "Sure. Let me get Henrietta, there."

We shot for a while. I aimed wild. Initially, Tennessee swelled like a toad every time I missed and he hit, patting the breech-loading repeating rifle he'd been issued at Shiloh like a faithful pet. After a time, however, he grew irritable with my poor showing, then out and out frustrated. I acted the good sport for a while until Tennessee exploded, "You ain't gettin' it at *all*. I hate to tell you, Turp, but you better learn to bake, 'cause at this rate you ain't *never* gonna shoot worth *beans*."

I let on like I was mad. "I can shoot just fine. It's harder to shoot with a pistol, and you know it."

"Aw, hell. It ain't *that* much harder."

"It is. You sit there with a rifle making easy shots and putting me down. I'll bet you couldn't hit *half* as good as I'm doing with *my* gun."

Tennessee hooted. "Now that's rich, comin' from a cloud-watcher like you!"

I crossed my arms. "Rich, huh? I'm willing to put three dollars on it, it's so rich."

"Are you nuts?"

"Are you scared?"

"Shit, I'm not scared, but I ain't gonna take calico money." He grinned at my idiocy.

"You're scared, and I'm goin' back and tell everyone so."

Tennessee squared his shoulders and lost the grin. "All right, I'll take your money and teach you a lesson, you moronic greenhorn guttersnipe. Give me the goddamn pistol."

I handed him a bit of paper and a pencil. "Write it down, first. I'll do the same and the winner will keep the notes."

Tennessee looked at me with that wary look on his face again, but took the paper and put down his mark.

I nodded. "I'll go first." Four shots into the target center.

Tennessee took the gun. He looked down the barrel. "I 'spect I hardly need to make the attempt, do I?" Still he sighted, shot four times. He snorted at his poor showing. "Yup. You got me, Turp. Greenhorn no more."

Avelina forgave me for the garden debacle when, with Chin's help, we finally managed to snare half a dozen dudes to take part in the Wild Western Adventure. Instead of standing awkwardly on the station platform available for close inspection, Tilfert sat astride Chin, who, when plied with oats, would stand immobile. The sight of the titanic man on the gigantic horse was impressive indeed, as if western adventure itself pushed humans into monumental proportion.

The dudes stared, slack-jawed, at the spectacle. Each and every one was already in the grasp of the greenhorn disease, "buckskin grippe," which symptoms included leather coats and pants finished with fringe cut as long as possible and enough silver conchos to periodically blind one another with the sunlight winking off them, eventually progressing to include moccasins gaudy with porcelain beads.

I, wearing a shirt Avelina padded in the shoulders, complimented their bang-on costuming, and referred to Tilfert as "Zeus of the plains," and the dudes tumbled over themselves to purchase a breath of his Olympian atmosphere.

We herded the prospects into the tents, and Avelina fed them buffalo stew and rotgut as they chattered like schoolboys. They talked big talk into the night, sweating under the heavy buffalo robes, so full of excitement, whiskey, and the roles they were playing as to make sleep almost impossible. At dawn they arose from their cots looking a decade older than the night before, drank coffee, and pushed bacon around their tin plates.

The hunt itself was an embarrassment.

Tilfert, finally managing something to say, addressed the group of five shooters from the top of a small ridge. He motioned toward the dark smear near the horizon and mumbled, "There they are. We's gonna ride to 'bout there"—he pointed to a freshet a small distance from the ridge—"where we're gonna shoot. Don't jump too soon. You'll jes' spook 'em, make th' job harder."

The dudes pushed back their hats, jingled their spurs, and rearranged their leather doublets, wearing looks of fierce concentration. Tilfert mounted his horse, the dudes followed suit. Tilfert began the approach, then turned and cautioned. "If the herd looks like it's comin' right on you, anythin' you can do not to be caught in the middle of 'em is a real good idea."

I waved good luck, and Tilfert rode up close. He tossed me his hat and nodded toward the dudes, jingling and shifting in nervous anticipation. "If anything happens to me, that hat's yours, Ned. Good and broke in, prob'ly put on two pounds since the day I bought it."

Tilfert rode out, the dudes jouncing on their horses to keep up. Before they reached the stream and the appointed shooting sight, however, anticipation proved too much. At the report of a gun behind him, Tilfert ducked low over the pommel of his saddle.

At that distance from the buffalo, the dudes had an icicle's chance in hell of hitting anything, but once a bullet was spent, the dudes, absolutely unconcerned over Tilfert's being in their line of fire, discharged rifles with abandon. The buffalo bolted. Tilfert urged his horse into a gallop, either to catch the herd or to escape the dudes' fire, I couldn't know. By the time Tilfert galloped abreast of the herd, the dudes were still struggling to calm horses spooked by the whooping and shooting. Tilfert did the only thing he could to save the hunt. He shot a big cow in the haunch to slow her up, then turned the limping animal back toward the dudes. When the hunters spied the wounded cow, now the only buffalo in sight on the wide prairie, they kicked their horses into action, pursuing the maimed cow like the furies.

All in all, it was Tilfert's life that was in the greatest danger, as the dudes attempted to bag their trophy. Watching Tilfert duck an unremitting whine of lead overhead while the buffalo strained, tongue out and eyeballs rolling, overheated from the protracted run, it occurred to me that it would be safer for my friend, and provide a quicker death for the buffalo, if the dudes were to target Tilfert instead. Or Tilfert could have allowed the dudes to shadow the cow all day until the animal died of exhaustion. Yet he kept patiently turning the animal, giving the dudes one chance after another to make their target. The men shot off a horn here, a piece of hide there, fired into the dirt and over the animal's head, enraged her by peppering haunches, slowed her with unwitting hits in a torturous farce of hunting.

I clutched Tilfert's hat, ducking and dodging in sympathy, wondering how I was going to tell Avelina her man was gunned down by men who that morning hadn't even known how to put bullets in a rifle.

Finally Tilfert'd had enough and delivered a fifty-caliber coup de grâce. The cow rolled into the dirt. The men dismounted and emptied their rifles into the dead animal.

Tilfert got off his horse and fell to his knees. I ran to him, terrified he'd been hit. His face was raised to the heavens. He whispered into blue sky, "I'm *alive!*" He looked at me, thunderstruck. "If I never thought there was a God afore, Ned, I can't say I don't think so now." He jammed the hat I offered him back on his head. "Let's get to it."

There wasn't much reason to skin out the carcass, riddled as it was with holes and the meat rank from the steam she'd built up. Tilfert would send the men home with robes we'd skinned previously, so I wielded the knife at the hunt site merely as theater.

In spite of their poor showing, or perhaps because of it, the dudes had the audacity to berate *my* skills. They gathered around, having close to exhausted themselves whacking each other on the back in congratulations. One fellow nudged me with a silver-toed boot, speaking in an Easterner's idea of a Westerner's drawl. "Knife's bigger 'n you are, young buck. Get yourself something your own size, maybe you'd do better."

I looked up, incredulous. "*I* should do better?" No less than twenty bullet holes slubbed the hide. "You've got nerve—"

Tilfert hurried over. "There, there, Ned. You jus' leave that be. I'll finish it myself." He ushered the men away, his near-death experience having loosened his tongue and warmed him to his part. "Don' mind 'im, orphaned by Indian attack, had 'is hair half lifted, now's not altogether there."

Furious and disappointed, I strode away. Some distance off, I pulled out my notebook. I'd entertain Lill with a drawing of the gaggle of dudes: the outlandishness of their costumes, puffed hair, and smirks.

As I sketched, I considered the buffalo. Out on the plains they were majestic, awe-inspiring. Once you were close enough to smell them, they ceased to be kings of the prairie, but vehicles for lice and worms, fur-matted, shit-spattered. From afar the wealthy sparkled, and I thought once again of Peter the Great.

My grandmother didn't tell me—perhaps she didn't know— that the boy Peter, within his log garrison, killed two hundred and forty children in the jejune war games he conducted there. She didn't tell me that the man Peter conducted himself like a sophomoric ogre, not so much wearing his welcome out as ransacking it in one country then another at the cost of thousands of lives. Peter ordered his own son, who had fled the penalty of rule and his terrible father, to be beaten until he agreed to follow his father's footsteps. The boy died before he would do so. If Peter was great, how terrible was Ivan? What are the men who back our wars, our hungers, our progress?

"What's this?" One dude wandered back to look over my shoulder. "Damned fine drawing." He shifted back on his heels and patted his pockets for a cigarette. "I'll buy the portrait— Turpentine, isn't it? How much do you want?"

I stiffened. "My name is Edward Turrentine Bayard the Third."

The dude smiled and raised an eyebrow, lit his smoke, and held out his hand for my book.

I watched him flip through the pages, noted his ivory cigarette case. "Five dollars," I told him.

He blew smoke in the air, turned another page. "Steep." He looked at his likeness on the paper. "Exceptionally well done, however. I'll take it, if you'll make a copy to go along with it."

He reached in his jacket for a wallet, handed me a card and a five-dollar bill. "I'm off tomorrow, but send the original and the copy to this address."

The card read MONTGOMERY ELIAS, SOLICITOR. HARTFORD, CONNECTICUT. My heart jumped. Though I'd struggled to contain my imagination, I worried that my mother's mysterious visitor had done her in. Why else her silence? Only foul play could explain it. It was a classic plot: The innocent stalked for her wealth. I could hardly bear thinking about it. But here, in front of me, was a man who could ferret out the details, bring justice to bear.

Mr. Elias closed my book and walked with it toward the tents. I trotted behind, waving the money. "No charge, after all, Mr. Elias. But I would appreciate if you'd do me a favor."

Mr. Elias ignored me and handed the book to the portly man who had fired the hunt's first shot. The fellow was slumped at the table, suffering, I expected, from the heat. He wore a high-collared blouse and a vest, jacket, and trousers of beaded and fringed doe hide. He carried plenty of his own insulation as well, the kind of girth prone to gravity. He was likely in his mid-forties, but his chest had slipped to belly and his belly to ass. His wide cheeks drooped to jowl, which, at the moment, flamed crimson to match an upper lip protruding in a rabbity overbite.

Elias pushed the book at him again. "You'll want to see this, Quillan."

Quillan waved him off, smoothed back his sparse oiled hair, and mopped his temple, glaring at Elias.

Elias chuckled. "I promise this is no prank."

Quillan took the book as if worried that it might bite him. When he deemed it safe, he pinched a pair of spectacles onto his nose and opened the pages with a smirk. If I hadn't been so frantic to engage Elias, I would have removed the sketches from Quillan's condescending pink grasp.

Almost immediately upon opening the book, however, Quillan began murmuring in a pleased sort of way. When he arrived at the illustration of the turtle he out-and-out yelped, drumming the paper with a fingertip. "Where did you see this? You *must* show me. Right away!"

Yet trying to get Elias's attention, I ignored Quillan and repeated, "No charge, but the favor, *sir*?" I brokenly detailed to Mr. Elias what little I knew of my missing mother as Quillan continued to tap the paper like a telegraph.

"Boy, do you hear me? Tomorrow, I said!" Quillan took my arm but I shook him off.

The solicitor laughed at the round man. "Edward Turpentine, I think you'd better pay attention to this gopher before he has a heart attack."

The man reddened. "*Gopher*! I am Wallace Quillan. Chief paleontologist at the Peabody Museum in New Haven, Connecticut. Perhaps you have heard of me."

I had heard of Wallace Quillan. I had even briefly visited the Peabody during a spate of passable health and had seen his display of fossils. I was agog that he stood before me but was that desperate to dig up information on my mother, he had to wait. I begged the great man. "Sir, one moment please. Mr. Elias?"

Mr. Elias agreed. "Certainly, I will investigate, Ned." I pushed the five dollars at him, but he refused it.

The professor folded his arms, irritated. Elias patted him on the back before leaving, advising me, "Take care with this one. He is round and soft, but gophers have long sharp teeth."

Quillan glared. "Business has no feeling for science, only money. And unfortunately, scientists have no feeling for money. If the two came together, what *progress* might be made." He put out his hand and I shook it. He held up my sketches. "I must see the fossils!"

CHAPTER 4

Dearest Omar,

It is no less than tedious here without you. Come to me and we shall picnic and shoot. When may I expect you?

Yours, India

Dearest India,

Seeing you is ever on my mind. I have much to show you and tell you as well and could not anticipate our visit any more if the Queen were pouring tea. I will come, if it is convenient, day after tomorrow. Regards to your family.

Yours ever, Omar

I spent a long night, though pleasantly filled with the riant phantoms of prospect: Montgomery Elias returning my name, my fortune, and my mother; Wallace Quillan recognizing me as a fellow scientist; Lill, adoration brimming in her eyes. It was hard to sleep. It was hard to say what I anticipated more keenly, the morrow with Quillan or the day after with Lill, so agreeably were the two entwined. I'd finally drifted to dreams when I was roused by the squeak of the door. A shuffling toward my corner, the curtain drawn aside. Through the dawn I saw Quillan. "Time's wasting, Edward," he whispered. "Wake up!"

Before I could nod, Avelina descended on the professor, taking him by the collar and shaking him like a rat. Quillan howled.

Tilfert roared from his bed, stumbled over, sized up the situation. "Hey now! That's our little round man, woman! Lay off there!"

Avelina dropped him and shot back to bed, so far under the quilt that not even the berserk nimbus of her hair was in evidence.

Quillan fell to his knees struggling to regain his composure, though it must have been difficult. He not only had his marbles shaken loose, but Avelina was a beauty queen by day in comparison to how she appeared in the night hours.

Tilfert scratched his woolly chest. "Sorry 'bout that, perfessor. You shouldn't be sneakin' around. Avelina likely thought you was Indians."

I put my boots on as Quillan waved Tilfert off, gasping. "No harm. . . . Ned . . . let's get out of here."

By the time the sun rose, Quillan was in full torment with the delays. I was used to chasing Chin around, wheedling, to get a bit in her mouth and harness around her casklike belly, but with Quillan shouting over and over that the horse needed to be taught a lesson, I thought Chin would never let me hook her up. I finally insisted that Quillan wait out of sight for forty minutes of begging, petting, oating, and pledging my undying gratitude to Chin before I was able to drive her and the wagon round and pick Quillan up from behind the officers' quarters.

Chin had run herself low on obstreperousness, apparently, for once we were on the way she behaved admirably, not even stopping to refuel. The day brightened over the sea of grass, the morning air soft. Chin plodded along. I was in the company of an eminent scientist and my girl waited for me on the morrow; I was the prairie prince indeed.

Quillan was not as happy. He was still grousing a full hour after leaving the fort, rustling like an irritated bird, complaining about Chin and squawking over Avelina. "She's not a woman, she's an *ape*." He cheered greatly once we arrived at the turtle site, however.

A punctilious man, squeamish about dirt except when in company of fossils, Quillan jumped from the wagon and slogged through the small creek in order to run his hands over the ancient turtle's skeleton, murmuring happily, "*Archelon ischyros,* great turtle of the Cretaceous!" He turned to me, aglow. "This monster swam the muddy waters of the western interior seaway over seventy million years ago, Edward." He ran his hand over the beaked head. "The heavy mandible and the thick palate gave him a bite like a guillotine, my boy. See these huge paddle-like legs? Not only the appendages of a swift hunter, but one swiftly hunted. What eats a nine-thousand-pound turtle? A forty-foot mosasaur!"

My very vision was altered, the prairie before me transformed into a giant sea pregnant with soupy beginnings. The turtle that I'd drawn so painstakingly weeks before fattened and swam in the world Professor Quillan described.

He broke off his musing. "Ned, fetch the kit in the wagon."

He handed me brushes, small picks, needle tools, paint in a canvas bag. He ferreted out a notebook of gridded paper and demonstrated drawing to scale. "One square for every inch of measure."

When he was certain I understood, Quillan took measurements of the fossil. As he called out numbers, I sketched. It took an hour to complete the drawings, after which we set to work incising the fossil from the bank. We removed the fractured

43

bones with the tiny picks and needle tools, cataloging as we went, numbering, wrapping, and packing them into giant rolls of burlap. We loaded the bundles into the wagon.

The day was a dream; the sun ran its track far too quickly. Before I'd even begun to weary, Quillan was griping over his fugitive dinner, throwing tools back into his bag and demanding my sketches.

He clapped me on the back. "Edward, you have a *gift*." He turned page after page of drawings. "Would you consider a career in science?"

I laughed. "It's my dream."

He crossed his arms over his chest, scrutinizing me from my worn shoes to my stained shirt, walking behind, making me acutely aware of the ragged haircut Avelina had delivered. Still, he announced. "I will train you in paleontology as my *personal* assistant. Scientific illustrations, cataloging, research. Interested?"

I felt as though I would pop. Lill's song was in my ear: "You will catch and I am caught." How would I tell her? What would she say, what would she do? Perhaps she would throw her arms around my neck, once again kiss me. Should I ask her to marry right then or wait until I'd procured a ring?

Quillan harrumphed. I returned to the world and stammered, "Interested? I am *very* interested, Professor Quillan, *very*."

"A young man like yourself could be instrumental in the progression of science, Ned."

The sky was aglow. I would use just those words. "Lill, I am to be instrumental. . . ."

I tried to look serious and wiped the smile off my face. "Are you offering me a position, Professor Quillan. A *paid* position?"

"Of course. Paid handsomely. Partially with a small stipend and the rest, more importantly, in education. I will be your mentor, the great Yale University your classroom! You have only to pack your bags and it will be yours. We depart on the morrow."

"Depart?"

"For New Haven, my lab at the Peabody."

The glow damped. Of course he would want me to return east. But tomorrow? Lill was in the palm of my hand. I thought of her lips on my cheek, the courtship just begun. It was ludicrous to think I could knock the future together in the hours I had left.

I stared at the ground at my feet. The clay was dry and checked, the grass sparse. A grasshopper methodically mowed down a beige slip of timothy as I made my decision.

"Professor Quillan, I can't go with you tomorrow. I have personal business to attend to."

He frowned. "Personal business? In this backwater? No, young man, you have a future, but it is not here under these brutish conditions with brutish people flown from civilization and likely the law." Quillan shook his finger at me. "You spend enough time out here, and a pigsty will look like a castle. It is time to go, young man."

I spoke quickly, snatching at the sherds of my dreams and trying to piece them together midair. "I could meet you in New Haven, after I've made my arrangements." When Lill was mine and would venture there with me.

Quillan slapped his thigh in exasperation. "I need you now, damn it all." He glared at me. "There are dozens of young well-educated Yale scholars banging on my door begging to have this experience I offer to *you* . . . a *buffalo skinner*! I have a mind to rescind my offer altogether!"

I slumped but stared straight ahead. I couldn't give Lill up.

Quillan looked through the drawings again. "You do have promise. All right, I will leave money for your ticket east. If you do not board the train in one week, I give the job to someone else."

A week? I figured feverishly. Thoughts I would never have entertained outside the laws of daydreaming now seemed not only possible but plausible. My luck had turned. I wouldn't be surprised if there wasn't a letter for me from my mother in the mail, clearing up the entire disappearance of herself and my money. But a week? It was still too soon. The circuit preacher was due in three weeks, when Avelina and Tilfert were to be wed. If I could ingratiate myself with Lill's parents, Lill and I could make it a double wedding, then honeymoon all the way to Connecticut. "A month, sir. Please."

"Of all the *cheek*!"

"I know of other fossil beds," I blurted out. "I would put the time to good use here, gathering and recording what I find."

He rubbed his chin. "You know of others?" He looked behind him, as if someone shadowed us, narrowed his eyes, and apparently made his decision, for he handed me a clear notebook. "Record the finds *exactly* as I showed you. I will see you—"

I shook Quillan's hand, my change in fortune singing like meadowlarks. "In a month, sir. One month."

CHAPTER 5

Dear Brill,

Walter Quillan has offered me employment! Further, the next you hear from me, I hope to be affianced. How the world can tip on and off its axis.

Ned

The next morning I woke late, my arms and thighs tight from the digging of the day before. Nothing would dampen my spirits, however. This was to be the day my tepid life burst into flame. I jumped from bed to find Avelina sitting in her rocker, taking stitches in her wedding dress. She held it up. "A shame to wear just once."

With the voluminous skirt, tiny tucks, and froth of ruffles, the dress had a circus tent's worth of fabric in it. Avelina pointed with her needle to the stove. "Stew's on."

I ladled out a bowl. Avelina asked, "You get the bones that man wanted?"

"Yep." I sat down and took a huge bite of stew. "Offered me a job."

"He say anything about me scarin' him like that?" She glanced up at me and stitched quickly.

I shook my head, amazed she was thinking about herself when I had my whole life flowering in front of me. "You want to hear about the *job*? I'm going to be a scientist. He's paying my way back east."

"Good for you, Ned, you can clear up the situation with your mother while you're at it. How long you going to be gone?"

"Forever, I guess."

She stopped sewing. "Forever?" The froggy lines of her face drew down. "Don't tell me you're going to miss the wedding, Ned, it's gonna be a real callathump."

"Of course I won't miss it. He wanted me right away, but I said I couldn't go until after the wedding. He almost took back the offer too, but I stood firm."

She nodded but still looked troubled. Frankly, I was thinking more of my own wedding than hers. Seeing Avelina's cheerless face, however, reminded me I was leaving behind more than Nebraska proper. Avelina, Tilfert, even Tennessee: Would I ever hear from those friends again, or would they disappear as resolutely as my mother?

I shook off my fears. Of course I would stay in touch. I would be an important man in Connecticut. I would have status and money. I would not be trapped there as I was here. "I'll come back on fossil expeditions in the summer. We'll see each other every year," I assured her, and she perked up. I shoveled in stew and spoke with my mouth full. "I gotta get going, need to tell Lill."

Avelina nodded. "It's for the best. She's just not for you, Ned."

I shook my head. "Oh, she's for me, all right. I'm going to ask for her hand in marriage."

Avelina dropped her sewing into her lap. "Are you addled? The last fiancé is feeding worms, Ned."

"The last fiancé *cheated* on her."

"Fer lesser crimes, she gonna charge your nose, take yer scalp?" I glared at her. "I would think, as a woman, you'd understand."

"Phaw! I understand plenty. That fiancé of hers was likely not worth the cotton he was stuffed with, but what's someone worth what decides to kill a man?"

"She was young," I argued.

"You're young yerself, and she ain't grown up *yet.*"

In the corral I dropped turnips and carrots into a cloth bag while Chin looked on. "These are for *you,* girl, as soon as we arrive— as soon as we both arrive, *together*—at Martine's." Chin corked her head, pummeling me with her felted nose. As soon as I pressed my backside to the buckboard seat, Chin was off, no need of direction or rein, leaving my hands free to compose a sonnet by which I would profess my love and ask Lill's hand.

My thoughts were scattered, to say the least, and trying to write legibly in a wagon on a rutted track was close to impossible. Within ten minutes I decided I was no poet after all. The best I could do was a limerick, and even that didn't go well.

> *There was a young man named Ned*
> *and Lill he said he would wed,*
> *then take her away*
> *to write poems every day*
> *and forget that she'd shot a man dead.*

I laughed, then sobered. Lill would not think it humorous but a betrayal, and rightly so. I had pledged to leave her past behind. Her very happiness and her safety depended on it, and I would keep that pledge. Lill was more than a mistake she'd made, as big as that mistake might have been. I balled the limerick and put it in my pocket. I would simply ask her, *Will you marry me?*

Chin earned her lunch, stopping only when we reached Martine's. Taking her tractability as a portent of the day's success, I leapt joyfully from the wagon, dumped Chin's vegetable payoff on the dirt, and took up Lill's hand. "It is a pleasure to see you again." She gave me a small hug and kiss, took my hand, and led me to the house.

The Martine house had been almost entirely framed. Mrs. Martine stood inside the skeleton house watching Mr. Martine swing his hammer from a rafter. I looked at them now as in-laws and wondered how it would be to have a father again. Mr. Martine, as if he'd read my thoughts, waved enthusiastic greeting from the roof, his sot's floridity diminished or disguised with tan. Mrs. Martine looked, if not well, better. She smiled shortly and gestured to the wall. "The sitting room, Mr. Bayard. At some point we will offer you tea, but I'm afraid we are as yet indisposed."

I was anxious to be alone with Lill and happy to assure Mrs. Martine I would anticipate a future cup but could wait for the environs to catch up to the lady's admirable standards.

Mrs. Martine inclined her head and glanced at the pistol at my hip. "I trust we will not have a repeat of last visit's gunplay, Mr. Bayard?"

I must have looked crestfallen. Lill took my arm. "We are going for a ride, Mother, a picnic. I did tell you."

Mrs. Martine worried her fingers. "Don't go far." She looked me over. "And watch for wolves."

Lill whistled for her palomino. I climbed into the wagon and protested. "We'll drive."

She laughed. "Bump over the prairie in a freight wagon? Unhitch Chin and ride your elephant, Omar."

I gauged Chin's mood. She had finished her vegetable kickshaw and dozed, head drooped to her knees. I desperately wished I'd kept turnips back for just this sort of emergency. "Chin's a wagon horse, I've never ridden her. I don't have a saddle or bit . . . and even if I did, I doubt she'd let me on."

Lill swung up on her own horse bareback. "Grip the mane, it's easy."

I stood beside Chin, not wanting to disappoint Lill, either with the day or with me, certain one was inevitable. Chin woke to look at me with an obstreperous look in her eye. The mesa of her back formidably high. "She's a *mountain*. I can't possibly reach."

Lill took hold of one of Chin's ears, led her to a stump from which I could mount, and held her there with a sharp grip. I suspected Chin would let me on only to throw me when Lill released her sensitive hold. I flopped belly first onto the big beast, groaned a leg over, and held tight. Lill let go to remount her own horse and Chin acted as if I weren't on her back at all, embarrassed, perhaps, at her Achilles' ear being publicly pulled.

Chin's back was so incredibly broad, my legs pokered from her sides like a five-year-old's. My knuckles whitened around a fist of mane. I couldn't possibly propose in this condition. Further, while Lill's palomino trotted, Chin sailed along with the motion of an ocean freighter, making me somewhat queasy on the inland sea. Lill, unaware of my distress, spoke nonstop, reciting poetry she had written since we'd last seen each other, regaling me with her miserable attempt at ironing, and the barely edible meal she'd put on the table but cooked western style over an open flame.

"I am keeping a diary, Ned. At least when the occasion disappoints, the story is the beneficiary."

I grunted agreement, jarring on Chin's back some paces behind Lill, "As—you—said. Grit."

After what seemed like ten miles, she pulled her palomino up, announcing, "Perfect." Lill slipped off her horse. I tumbled thankfully from Chin, thighs chafed, feeling permanently bandy-legged.

A vast settlement of prairie dogs stretched before us, neat mounds and winding avenues, mown and tidy as any eastern burg. The gopher-like animals sat on their hind legs, sentinels on their roofs, chirping in consternation. I wondered if they had seen the like of us before.

"Lill." I took her hand. "I have something to discuss with you."

She grinned at me. "Lovely." Then dropped to her belly and patted the ground beside her.

I settled myself alongside and Lill began the colony's eradication.

I could not begin my romantic essay with a backdrop of gopher potting. They were timid things, startling with a jerk of the tail, somersaulting into their holes. Tennessee told me the Indians called the animals *wish-ton-wish*, after their soft cries. Chin in hand, I watched one after the other recoil and die, trying to quell the dolorous mood the fallen dogs put me in. Lill finally stopped and looked at me askance. "Didn't you practice? No one will come if only India can shoot."

"Softhearted, I guess."

Her face grew tender and she leaned over and kissed my cheek for the second time—"That is *so* sweet"—then continued to lay prairie dogs low. "*Have* you practiced? I talked to one of the scouts at the fort. He cuts a fine figure and says he is a crack shot."

I felt a surge of jealousy. Was she replacing me?

She fired again. "He is taking a western show on the road, Ned, and we must be competitive."

Relieved at the *we,* I interrupted her next salvo. "Lill, I've been offered a job."

She stopped. "A job?"

"By *the* most famous man in all of paleontology, head of the Peabody Museum himself, Wallace Quillan. He's offered to train me as a scientist."

Lill squinted down her barrel but didn't shoot, her face unreadable. "That's wonderful, Ned." She held the gun still for so long I was uncomfortable. Finally she put the gun down and fixed a grin on her face. "And how does this bode for Omar and India?"

I was certain that prestigious employment trumped theatrical fantasy. Now looking at her crestfallen demeanor, I wasn't so sure. "This will be *better* than Omar and India, Lill." I fiddled with the walnut handle of my gun. "Professor Quillan wants me to go to New Haven with him."

She looked shocked. "Right away?"

"No, not *right* away. I have some time left."

She got to her feet slowly. "Some time. Well, that's good, at least there's *some* time." She looked around her as if she were lost and searching for a landmark. "Let's ride."

I had to talk to her. "Let's walk."

We strode along for some time, silently. I could see she was upset, but I could not make out if she was angry, mournful, or heartbroken . . . and I was afraid to say the wrong thing because of it.

Finally she turned to me. "Edward Turrentine Bayard, you promised me Omar. I won't have you throw away what we have together. What job is so important to take you away?"

"It is not only a job but an education. Professor Quillan has promised I will attend *Yale University*. It's an astounding opportunity, a chance to regain all I've lost, my name, my fortune, my honor, a promise for a real future."

She sighed. "Oh, Ned." Our hands brushed. I took her hand, her palm cool, mine hot and sweating. My heart hammered in my ears.

She twined her fingers with mine. "I was fortunate to find you, Ned. I knew it the first I saw you, a callow begrimed Don Quixote on his horse. To lose you now . . ." I began to protest. Lill put her finger to my lips. "Such is the way of the world. But I insist on your loyalty, Edward Turrentine Bayard the Third."

I again tried to speak but she held a staying hand and continued.

"No matter what happens, wherever we find ourselves, we will care for each other, defend each other, the remainder of our days."

I pulled my hand through my hair, trying to parse her declaration. Lill looked rapt. I could see Nebraska in her limpid eyes. She blinked slowly. "Do you agree?"

"I do," I croaked.

She tucked her hand in my arm and leaned her head on my shoulder. I wasn't at all sure if I had been turned down or accepted, or even if I had asked. Had I made my intentions clear?

I cleared my throat to spell it out, but Lill straightened abruptly. She took her hand from my arm and shaded her eyes. She pointed. "Horseman."

In the distance, the peg of a solitary rider. We watched the apparition's approach for some minutes, straining to distinguish the rider as friend or foe, but the heat waves dancing over the grass contorted the image so that it was impossible. The rider came on. I put my hand on my pistol and wished Lill had not murdered so many of the prairie dogs. A mean price for craven gopher killing was to die for want of defensive ammunition.

Lill waved. "Halloooo!"

I stopped her hand. "Don't draw attention!"

She slapped me away. "He's a white man, Ned, don't be silly."

The horseman pulled out of a shimmer. He was a big man with a chiseled countenance, swathed in buckskin and astride a sleek ebony horse. I knew him from the fort: not someone I wanted as a third when courting. When he swept off his wide-brimmed Montana hat, Lill dimpled like all get out.

"Hello, Buck," I said.

He gazed at Lill even while addressing me. "If it isn't Lord Turpentine."

I halfheartedly introduced them. "Lill Martine, Buck Mason."

Lill lowered her eyes a bit, her lashes resting on pale cheeks. "Mr. Mason and I have met."

I narrowed my eyes. I should have guessed the fine figure of a scout Lill referred to was Buck Mason.

Lill demurred. "But he likely doesn't recall."

Buck showed canines like wolf fangs. "On the contrary. That meeting was a flower in the desert of my life."

"What a distressingly dull life you must lead then, sir," Lill said.

"I can imagine ways to enliven it."

"Then you must." Lill seemed to remember I stood beside her and took my arm. "Ned and I have been adventuring. He is a marksman to be reckoned with and hardly picked up a gun a fortnight ago."

Buck rested gloved hands on the pommel of his saddle. "Ned, I imagine, has many hidden talents."

I ignored the emphasis on *hidden* and nodded toward Lill. "Miss Martine puts what little talent I have to shame."

Lill thanked me with a charming little curtsy, then addressed Buck again. "I've heard, Mr. Mason, that you are no slouch with a firearm yourself." Buck inclined his head and Lill laughed. "Now that we have thrashed each other with compliment, shall we show our cards?"

This was not at all how I had hoped things would go; so far from it, in fact, I felt dizzy. I would have chosen anyone other than Mason to ride up and interrupt my proposal. And now to have to shoot against him. I would have more of a chance at gluing feathers to my pants and vying for Lill like a peacock. From horseback, Buck could shoot the heads from prairie hens as they ran through the grass.

Buck dismounted, took a bandanna from his saddlebag, and stretched it between two juniper sticks stuck into the ground at some distance.

The three of us eyed the flag. I was somewhat confident I wouldn't embarrass myself with a miss. Still, I wasn't eager to begin. I extended a courtesy. "Ladies first."

Without hesitation, Lill shot a hole through the cloth.

Buck and I took turns offering the next turn to the other until Buck acquiesced. He looked steadfastly through the sights of his gun toward the red flag. I grew hopeful at his delay. Perhaps he wasn't the marksman he was reputed to be; he would be humiliated, leave, and I could finish my golden business.

He still didn't shoot. I smiled broadly at Lill. "Buck, you going to shoot or sleep?"

Buck put up a hand to silence me, spoke quietly. "We have company."

I scanned the grassland. Sure enough, a span of horsemen milled in an eerie puddle on the horizon and then individuated into six riders as they drew closer.

"Sioux. It's trouble."

I felt suddenly sick. Young Sioux men roamed the Platte River country, meting out retribution for land and lives taken, broken treaties, and white greed. Every terrifying Sioux story that had circulated and inflated at the fort now ran through my head. Lill looked not alarmed at all, imagining, I supposed that any Indian would be Joe and Jim, ready to admire her marksmanship and trade for coffee. She demanded, "How do you know they're looking for *trouble*? Maybe they're just traveling through."

"Painted. Army horses tethered behind. Somebody's come out on the dead end of the stick."

She looked a little more alarmed but still shrugged. "Maybe they traded, bought them."

Buck looked at the Indians again, judging the distance. "If we're lucky, they've gone some distance and are sapped." He strode to his horse and holstered his rifle. "Ride hell for leather, maybe they won't follow."

Lill, finally catching the dread in Buck's voice, swung onto her horse with haste.

Buck looked at me. I croaked, "I might need some help onto my horse."

Buck shoved me up on Chin, then swept onto his own mount. Lill was already flying for home; Buck thundered behind.

Chin plodded reluctantly.

I quickly lathered into panic. "Chin, go! Go! Yaaaaaaaaaw! Go! Chin!" I kicked her ribs, I slapped her neck, I pleaded. "Please, Chin, for the love of your own skin, you've got to hie! Lose me and who will you talk to?" She continued her easy plod. I kicked; I was practically jumping up and down on her back; I shouted. "All right, you miserable evolutionary blunder! Atavistic pile of shit! Put me through all the humiliation you want, but if you get me killed I'm going to pull every last one of your teeth, how about that?" Chin stepped up from plod to slow lope.

Growing ever more distant, Buck looked behind, then wheeled his horse. When he was close enough to be heard he shouted, "*Get a move on!*"

"*Tell the horse!*"

Buck circled back and swung leather at Chin's backside with a whistling *thwack*. Chin got the message and lunged into a gallop. Buck flew ahead; Chin caught up, then passed with her ten-foot stride.

Unfortunately, I wasn't on her. Within four of Chin's now-spirited strides, I'd lost my feeble grip on her mane, slid sideways off her pumping flank, caught a rear hoof in the chest, and landed on my head in the prairie dirt, rendering me insensible.

When the stars cleared, six Indians on horseback, three with rifles, were shouting at me. I put up my hands as though involved in a burglary. An Indian with a lance prodded me, piercing the skin on my hammering chest. With one look at the roses blooming on my blouse, I jumped to my feet, blacked out, dropping like a sack of potatoes.

When the dark cleared again, only one Indian was mounted, while four Indians bent over me as though I were a clockwork curiosity. I was prodded again, to see, I imagine, if I would repeat the performance. I gritted my teeth and this time sat up slowly, waiting for the whirling to slow. Another few jabs and one of them spoke to me. I shook my head. "I only speak English." A trickle of blood tickled my stomach. Another Indian brandished his knife at my face, and I almost fainted with the fear he'd take my nose or eyes. Instead, he used his knife to lift the glasses from my nose as if he were disgusted to touch me, then put the glasses on and strutted around repeating, "Cheeekin, tobaccy, moove out, it is time to be hungry," to the delight of the others. They suddenly straightened, and the one wearing my glasses flung them to the ground.

Buck Mason crested the hill. While the Indians watched his approach, I reached for my glasses. The Indian with the lance drove it into my arm, pinning my forearm to the earth. I jerked back, leaving a goodly piece of meat behind, but I had my spectacles.

At the same moment, Buck called out something in Lakota, repeating it as he drew near. Once close, he instructed, "Stand up, Ned."

I slowly pulled myself upright. The Indian with the lance charged forward again but only waved his blade. Buck hissed,

"Don't move." He walked his horse closer until I could clutch the saddle blanket.

The mounted Indian addressed Buck in English. "You ride with women and dogs. What does that make you?"

Buck shrugged. "A better man than you are."

"Deader man, maybe." One of the other Indians motioned toward the prairie.

Lill sang out, "Hellooooo!"

Buck swiveled and groaned through gritted teeth. "Damn."

Lill came forward, speaking gaily as if she were being introduced at a debutante's ball, but an octave too high. "Hello, hello, hello, how."

Buck barked, "Stay back!"

The mounted man grinned. "You *are* a sad man. We do you a favor to end it now."

Buck made a motion with his heel and his horse stepped backwards, as well trained as a circus performer. Lill had a smile frozen on to her face. "What do we do?" she whispered, still smiling.

Buck smiled like an animal baring its teeth, whispering back. "Not do—*don't*. Don't talk. Don't shoot. Neither a horse nor an Indian. If you do, they *will* kill us."

Lill lost her grin momentarily. Then smiled woodenly again.

Lill's arrival had plunged a horrifying situation into one so terrifying as to be intolerable. The pressure of my lungs and the throbbing of my arm and head were bringing some moisture to my straining eyes. I straightened my back the best I could, however, and put on what I hoped was a proud and fearless expression. The Indian gestured to the west, shouting in a mix of Lakota and English, then pointed at Lill and me. "This ugly

60

woman and boy are not worth even one toothless old woman of the people we have lost, but it is a start. We will take them. Tell your army what we are owed will be paid."

"I'll take the message, but not without these two. If you try to stop us"—Buck pointed toward them nonchalantly with his pistol—"we'll take at least three of you with us."

The Indian considered Buck. "Do you fear death?"

Buck smiled. "Kill me if you like."

The Indian stood silent for a time. "I will let you go"—he smiled—"because I am a kind man." He said something more to his men, and they turned their horses and trotted away. He called over his shoulder, "Tell your army that a kind man is one to be feared when he sees his people brushed away like dirt." The horsemen kept up a quick trot and soon disappeared into a rift. For some time we watched the spot. When there was no sign of return, Lill jumped from her horse.

"Ned, oh, Ned, you're bleeding!" I looked at my shirt and thought how curious that, both times I had pursued her, I'd ended up ruining a shirt with my own blood. Except for the gash in my arm, the other wounds were surface abrasions. Buck took Lill's kerchief and wound it tightly around the deep cut. "You must treasure those glasses, Ned."

I nodded. "Long way to get another pair." I caught a movement in my peripheral vision. Beyond Lill and Buck a rifle barrel slid from behind an outcropping of eroded sandstone. I pulled the pistol from my holster and shot as the Indian and Buck fired as well. There was an explosion of dust between Lill and me and a ping of metal against metal as the Sioux's rifle was knocked out of his hand by the bullet's impact. The Indian leapt onto his horse and fled the way of his compatriots.

We whirled again as a thunder of hooves approached from the opposite direction.

Chin, galloping as though she'd circumnavigated the globe and only just noticed I wasn't on, barreled over the hill.

CHAPTER 6

My dear Lill,

I raise my glass to the song that is you, to your beauty, to your grace that spurs a man to be more than he thought possible. For this is certainly the case with me. What little that I have done that may be called heroic was a mere reflection of the strength I see in you. You are a light in my life, a dream in waking hours, a dream I wish forever to dream. And so I ask you to be my wife.

I'd entertained myself with daydreams of the sort. Lill hanging on my arm, telling of my daring exploits, her eyes shining. The men of the fort clapping me on my back, shouting, "Goddamn, Ned!" Even Buck Mason giving me my due.

To tell the truth, I hadn't been so sure I'd done anything at all. It was only after Buck lifted Lill from the path of the engine of Chin, and I'd pitched to one side as the big horse skidded to a stop, that Buck whistled.

"You saved our necks, Ned. Goddamn, you did."

I stared at him, trying to figure what he was talking about and how I was going to kill him for holding Lill in his arms for far longer than safety required.

Lill stammered, "Thank God you were here." She gazed into Buck's face while she said it. I didn't realize she was referring to me.

63

Buck put her down and shook my hand heartily. "Never seen shooting like that. If you hadn't pipped that Indian's gun, I'd be a goner for sure. You saved my life. Hell, you saved us all."

I was eating off the topmost canopy.

Back at the fort, the dudes ambled out of their tents to hear the news. Avelina told them a gilded-lily version of events, which included not six but ten Indians, three of them lying dead in the dust by story's end.

Lill leaned on my arm, she kissed my cheek. "Ned's my champion."

I squeezed her hand. "Lill, I have something to ask you. We need to talk."

Lill gave me a small hug. "I must go now, but ask me tonight. There's to be a pitch-in in your honor!"

"Really?"

"I'm baking my special biscuits and expect the favor of your arm."

Buck inclined his head. "Ready?"

I frowned and Lill explained. "Buck is going to escort me home. My poor parents are likely swooning."

While I was thankful I wasn't going to have to face Mrs. Martine and her sharp white fear, I didn't like the idea of Buck escorting my girl. Lill smiled. "I won't be long." She pointed playfully to my shirt. "Don't forget to change."

This was going to be a problem. I didn't *have* another shirt. I was certainly the most ragtag hero that ever came down the pike: crooked gun, obstreperous horse, stained shirt. I looked at Lill. "I left the wagon at your place."

Buck inclined his head. "Allow me, if you will, to pick up the wagon for you. The least I can do for the man who saved my life."

I smiled, but not much. He was too helpful. He grinned back as if he knew what I was thinking.

I didn't have much time to worry. Avelina rebound my arm and commenced tailoring one of Tilfert's shirts so I would have something to wear at the fete that night. Watching her cut great swaths of linen from Tilfert's enormous raiment I observed, "You're cutting off more than you're leaving in."

"I sure as hell am leaving a lot more than I would've two months ago."

"You think?"

"Oh, sure, don' you, Tilf?"

Tilfert strode over and lifted me slightly from the floor. "Half again heavier, at least. Lessen you got rocks in yer pockets."

Avelina grinned. "A course he got rocks in his pockets; proved that today, didn't he?"

Tilfert roared with laughter. I blushed and hoped they were right. Tonight I would ask for Lill's hand and would need all the rocks I could get. Leaving Avelina stitching the trimmed shirt, I retired to my corner, sat on my bed, took pad to lap, licked my pencil, and began to write.

It took hours to produce a few lines. I agonized over each word, erasing with a ball of gum rubber until the paper thinned. Avelina finished my shirt. The sun dipped low. Tilfert stuck his head through the curtain and cautioned it was time to go and they would meet me there.

I nodded and waved him off. Another ten minutes and I'd finished my proposal of marriage to Lill Martine. I was pleased with the effort. Poetic without being effusive, elaborate but not too long. It was as perfect as this imperfect man could make it. And now I was late. I pulled on the now beautifully fitted shirt, brushed down my pants, buffed my tired shoes, and headed out.

Captain Ellmore's house was lit, illuminating the crowd inside. I could see Lill's mother, looking amazingly animate within the yellow windows, Mrs. Ellmore in a pastel dress, and Tilfert, scratching his beard and looking uncomfortable in the social situation. Piano music issued from the parlor; the pulse of conversation murmured out into the cricket choir night. I smoothed my hands over my hair and walked circuitously toward the house in order to sidestep mud in the path.

Between the captain's quarters and the enlisted men's bunk I heard surreptitious noises. Initially I thought it was another Indian attack: the Sioux returned, whispering and readying their knives. Then I heard a small giggle. Sighs and murmurs. I edged closer and heard Buck Mason's husky voice. He had some woman in that dark alley, likely a Pawnee. The scouts were notorious for taking their pleasures with Indians. I peered around the corner. He had the girl backed up against the bunkhouse. It was so dark the only thing I could see was the white of her blouse, his hands dark against it. They kissed. The woman pushed him. "Mr. Mason, how dare you presume?"

I stumbled back, horrified. It was Lill and, truth be told, it sounded to me like she knew very well how he dared. I blazed with fury. That was *my* girl Buck was fondling. After I'd saved his skin, he was pressing it against the woman who would be my wife. Trust, indeed!

I stumbled away and slumped against the mess wall. What should I do? There was only one thing to do. I ran back to the cabin, retrieved my gun, and strode back to the dark alley, trying to keep my fury ascendent over the sorrow that was lifting like the tide.

The alley was quiet now, Buck and Lill gone I refused to think where. I walked the length of the alley with my pistol drawn and shaking in my hand. Out the other side, a group of newly arrived Easterners smoked cigars in the moonlight.

They looked up but didn't blink at the gun in my hand. Perhaps they thought all Nebraskans walked around ready to slay someone. A fellow with a ten gallon hat gestured with his cigar, drawing red lines in the dark. "Say, are *you* Bayard?"

I nodded and one of them reached out, requiring me to holster my pistol before pumping each of their hands in turn.

"All we've heard since we came in is your story. What an adventure, eh? Keep shooting a dozen Injuns a day and the West will be civilized in no time." They waited for me to elaborate, but I stood mute.

The tale from their mouths was preposterous; *I* was preposterous. Buck crowing over my valor was something else entirely. The shot that hit that Indian's rifle could just as well have been his, and he was sure quick to deflect that honor. I'd been involved in a swap and not even known it. Buck took my girl and was giving me some sort of false heroism in trade.

I wilted with the realization, then squared my jaw. Well, I wasn't going for it. Lill Martine was *my* girl. And it *was* just as damn likely that I was the one that saved our skins as it was him. Buck Mason could go to hell, and I was pleased to help him. I fingered my pistol.

The men on the porch glanced at each other, almost as disgusted with me as I was. To break the silence one reported, "They're looking for you in there."

Inside, Lill rushed forward. "Here you are! My paladin!" She gave me a verbena-scented hug and scolded, "I've been waiting an hour, shame for making me worry." She pointed. "What am I to do with you? A pistol in the parlor? My goodness, your manners."

I put my hand to my gun as Buck strode forward and put out his hand. "Ned."

My hand tightened on the pistol's burled handle. I would shoot Buck through the absurd fringe on his buckskin jacket. In this country a man who shot another for taking his woman would as likely be given a shot of whiskey as a jail term. I hated Buck as deeply as I wished him dead, as deeply as I had loved Lill an hour ago, as deeply as I loved her now.

But I couldn't shoot him. I wavered only a moment, then left Buck's hand hanging in the air as I unbuckled my holster. I hung the gun on a hook by the door. And then I had a drink.

By the time I'd downed my second whiskey, it was coming clear what had happened. Lill misunderstood. Lill thought I was leaving her behind, sweeping aside her dreams for my own, Omar abandoning India. What else was she to do but make the best of it? In her eyes I had forsaken her. Her dalliance with Buck, if it was that, was heartbreak camouflaged. And she *had* protested, I reminded myself, even if she did so with a trill in her voice.

I had to make her understand that I would never leave her behind. I would tell her, if she didn't come to Connecticut with

me, I simply would not go. I would give up every dream I had
to make her mine, for she was the biggest dream I had. As I
drank, I grew more and more assured that when I pledged my
troth—being *clear*, damn it, this time—the world would once
more take on the rosy light that held sway a mere hour ago.

Another two drinks, more toasts to the sure shot, and I wanted
the party *over*. I had my own piece to say, and if everyone would
just be quiet I could say it. But someone handed me more whiskey and sang false praises yet again. Heroism never felt so bad.
I could take no more. It was time for me to take charge, take
what I wanted, to demand Lill's hand. I stood, shouted, but my
voice was lost in the din of the room. I climbed onto a chair and
was yet ignored. So I threw my glass, and the sharp ring of breaking crystal finally silenced the crowd.

"*I want toast!*" I wobbled on my perch.

Buck took my elbow. "Ned, you want to make a toast?" I pulled
my arm away in great disdain and almost fell over. I righted myself, lifted my hand, but I had thrown my glass. Someone poured
quickly and handed me another drink. I thanked the man, though
he wormed and waggled so I could hardly target his offering. I
shouted, "Lill, where are you?"

Lill made her way through the crowd to stand in front of the
table. I lifted the glass. "Nightingale among sparrows! Beautiful
Lill!"

I bent and lifted her hand to my lips. What did I want to say?
I couldn't find the words I had labored so hard to arrange. Lill
gazed at me expectantly. The room's velocity increased. I sweated
profusely. This was my chance. It was imperative I say *something*.

Lill asked, "Ned?"

I wished I hadn't climbed onto the table; the floor was far, far away. Lill's face glowed in the kerosene light. *Speak, speak, speak,* I berated myself in a panic. I could hardly remember what I was doing. Who was I? Then I remembered. A young man named Ned.

I recited the limerick.

CHAPTER 7

Dear Lill,

It pains me to send the proposal to you I wrote on the day of the party, having planned to read it to you in person. Yet I hope you will read it and, in spite of what happened, give it consideration. What I did at the party is an error I would give my life to rescind, as well as being a complete riddle to me why my besotted tongue would have said it at all.

Ned

My dear Lill,

An angel like you can surely find it in yourself to take pity on a drunken fool.

Dearest India,

You are my life. The days devoid of your song are unendurable. Find it in your heart to allow me respite.

Lill,

Please forgive me!

Dear Ned,

I am perplexed and saddened that you so completely misread our relationship. I did love you as a brother, but that is all. I will now forgive you as a sister forgives a brother for an unkind taunt. I will not forget our time together, will treasure our sweet notes, but now is the time to let it go. I will see you at Avelina's wedding to give you my fond farewell and best wishes for your future

71

as a Yale scholar. Until that time, it is best that you desist from
contact.

Sincerely, Lill

Dear Mr. Bayard,
  My husband and I will not have you intrude on our daughter's
life any longer and will accept no further correspondence.

Mrs. Martine

Dear Brill,
  I am lost. My nerve, my spirit, my health have all failed. This
may be the last you hear of me. If ever you get the chance, tell my
mother what became of Edward Turrentine Bayard III.

I tossed and moaned, my head whirling and whingeing,
unable to hold anything down. My breath was short. I felt
feverish.

"Get a doctor!" I wheezed, when Avelina bent over the bed
to check on me.

"You don' *need* no doctor, yer jes' a little outta fix."

I moaned and she hissed.

"You ain't hot and anybody who put it away like you did is
going to be pukey."

"I need to be bled."

"*Pfft.* Bled. That's what'll kill you. If blood was bad for you,
skellytons would be dancin' around."

I poked myself in my chest. "I have been sick my *whole life.* I
know what it is and I *know* when I need a doctor."

72

"Well, well, Lord Turpentine. The doctor's *been* in, and it's his eddicated opinion that you caught pickled liver, so lay back and shut up. Soon as the whiskey's out of your system, you kin eat. Soon as you eat, you'll feel better."

"My chest, my asthma."

"Seems to me you got breath aplenty for complaining, and if you don't quit I'm putting you out, Ned—I can't take it no more."

She looked like she meant it, so I was quiet. The trouble was, with quiet came time to think, and when I thought, I was back in that room with the whiskey and the hushed crowd and the dreaded poem.

"There was a young man named Ned . . ."

I could clearly see Lill.

". . . and Lill he said he would wed . . ."

Her face growing pink, with pleasure perhaps.

". . . take her away . . . write poems every day . . ."

But as she'd heard the horrifying final line—"forget that she'd shot a man dead"—paling to white.

The room bursting into laughter. Lill disappearing even as my head and heart whirled, not with horror but absolute disbelief. I *hadn't* said that, had I? But why then was everyone laughing? Why did Buck pull me from the table and into a seat with that look of disgust? Where had Lill gone? What had I done?

"Avelina!" I yelled. She jerked aside my curtain. I put up a hand. "*Not* complaining. I want to know, have you seen Lill?"

She rolled her eyes. "That one's all right. Stuck to Buck like glue, I hear."

My heart sank, though I'd thought it was at rock bottom already. I stared at the ceiling, willing the tears forming at the

73

corners of my eyes not to run off into my ears. Avelina waited. I finally choked out, "You think they're in love?"

She sat down. "You don't know things like that from looking at someone. Love is when nobody's lookin', Ned. Those two . . . maybe just puttin' their pants together."

I ignored her vulgarity. "You think Lill might still be in love with me, when no one's looking?"

She sighed. "Ned. If she ever was . . . no more."

"You just *said* you couldn't know things like that from looking, and now you out and out proclaim she's not in love with me?" I couldn't keep the tears in any longer. In desperation I shouted, "Get out! Just leave me alone!"

Avelina slapped her knees in disgust and stood up. "Get dressed."

"What?"

"If you don't get out of bed now and get dressed, I'll throw you out nekkid."

"I'm *sick*. I feel terrible."

"Well, you won't feel worse outside, and it'll be a great relief to *me*. Go!"

"Avelina!"

She grabbed hold of me by one arm and my neck and lifted me like a flour sack and stood me on my feet. I stood in my underwear, incredulous.

"Get dressed."

"I pay *rent* on this squalid little corner."

Avelina's face went red; she dragged me to the front door and shoved me out into the yard and slammed the door behind me. I tried to get back in, but she had put the bar down. A moment later the bar was lifted, the door opened a crack, my clothes flew onto the dirt, and the bar slammed back in place.

"Avelina!" I pounded the door.

Tennessee came around the corner. "Well, looky there. Didn't know western heroes came in pink."

It was easily the worst week of my life. I wrote a despairing letter to Brill then ripped it up, not able to bear that he would feel not only that he'd been prescient in his worries but sorry for me on top of it. I had neither the spirit to look for Quillan's fossils nor to work for Tilfert. I barely choked down food. I wouldn't have gotten out of bed but for Avelina's strong-arm insistence. And then I moped around the fort until the livery master collared me.

"Do something about that overgrown horse a yours before I put a bullet in 'er. She makes a godawful noise, spooks up the other horses. I run her off, but she's right back agin."

At least Chin was glad of my company. I hitched her to the wagon and we wandered the prairie. "Go where you want, Chin. Lunch all day long for all I care." I let the reins loose and reclined in the wagon bed to watch clouds racing from one side of the huge blue bowl to the other—as if there were any means to escape.

My head in the hopeless sky and Chin in charge, of course we went to Martine's. I sat bolt upright, at hearing my name called, and saw Lill. I had a weird hopeful feeling that all that had happened before was a nightmare, or that it had been erased by a benevolent God and I was back where I was two months ago. A close look at Lill told me this was not the case. She looked beautiful but tired, subdued as I'd never seen her. She crossed her arms. "Why are you here?"

She did not look like a woman in love. Perhaps the entire Buck–Lill romance was a subterfuge or, banning that, a short-lived mistake. I looked around the compound, no one to be seen. "Are you alone?"

"Always." She shrugged. "I don't remember inviting you to call."

"We can't leave things like this between us."

"There's no leaving. It's the way they always were. You apparently didn't know it." She turned and spoke impatiently. "I *told* you no hard feelings. I *said* I forgave you. Respect me enough not to waste my time. I have other relationships to tender."

I wanted to be cool about it, but it spilled out. "So where is *Buck?*"

She smiled at me. "Buck left for New York this morning. I told you: He's starring in a Western drama."

I grinned back. "Forever?"

Lill frowned. "He'll be gone a couple of weeks, this time. Then, if it's a going concern, who knows?"

I shook my head. "I suppose you'll be going with him."

She turned away. I took this to be a hopeful sign. I jumped from the wagon and took her hand. "Come with me. I love you, Lill, I want you in my life. *I* could never go to New York without you. You are my life."

Lill smiled a pitying smile. "Ned. I am in love with Buck, and he did ask me to go with him to New York. He'd like me to perform with him."

I'd thought I'd bounced to the bottom of the well, but hearing her proclaim her love for Buck hove my poor heart deeper into black hopelessness. I, only by clenching my fists until my nails bit my palm, managed to stop from throwing myself at her feet and begging.

She looked to the horizon with a dreamy air. Did she imagine herself in a sequined dress and red boots? Gloves with mile-high fringe and an audience screaming her name as she shot glass balls from the air? That son of a bitch Mason waiting in the wings?

The wan look returned. "Of course I wouldn't *go.*" Then I understood. Lill Martine couldn't risk being revived as Lyllith Hayes. She'd been deluding herself with the India and Omar show. If she'd thought anyone would forget, or she'd be allowed to leave the past behind, thanks to me she now knew better. I mumbled miserably, "You couldn't."

"Nonsense," she snapped. "But I am a lady, ladies do not indulge in theatricals. I will wait for Buck's return."

"Are you . . . betrothed?"

"We have discussed it." She smiled coyly and would say no more.

She crossed her arms once again and asked if there was anything else. I invented a reason to leave, climbed back into the wagon, and departed, the weight of my lost happiness bowing my back.

Chin wandered back toward the fort, and at some point I became aware of more than my aching heart. I was terribly thirsty and hungry. I'd hardly eaten for days. A desperate need for sustenance assailed me. I couldn't think, couldn't plan, couldn't hatch possibilities between me and Lill until I had food. Did I have a fight in me? I was too hungry to know. I slapped the reins, hoping to encourage Chin to some speed.

Chin veered to the west. I pulled at her head. "No! To the fort!" Chin was the only horse I ever knew that could walk west while her head pointed south. It slowed her down only a little. "Chin! I have no patience left!"

I knew better than to pit myself against her, but I'd been through enough the last few days, both good and bad, that the steam of both went to my head. I got off the wagon and pushed at her, slapped her backside, tried to lead her in the right direction, but she would have none of it, ignoring me as completely as the rest of the world had. I was sick to death of it. She passed a plum thicket and I jumped out and grabbed a switch. When I caught up with the big horse, I struck her with it.

"Damn you, Chin! Can't anything go my way? Take me back to the fort, do you hear me, you stupid moronic horse! *I am the boss!*" She flinched at the bite and I hit her again. "That's right, back to the fort." She shied and whinnied. I hit her again and again. She reared and neighed, but I didn't stop whaling away until both Chin and I were trembling. I wiped my face and eyes then threw the stick like a javelin as far as I could make it go. I got into the wagon, and she plodded toward the fort.

The morning of Avelina's wedding, the sky was a soft blue and the temperature a limpid 85 degrees, even at an early hour. She pushed me out the door at dawn and closed her house to everyone. Not even the captain's wife would be allowed in to help the bride dress.

I imagined Avelina didn't want anyone to know she plucked hairs from her chin and ears. For such an unattractive woman she was astonishingly vain. I milled around outside with the other members of the fort community. The preacher had set up a box dais by which to officiate. Tilfert already stood beaming beside it, as happy a man as I'd ever seen and, as predicted by Avelina, dressed in his buffalo coat even in the August heat.

I had not seen Lill except from across the way, when she came to the fort to mail a stack of perfumed letters to Buck, and that took what little wind I had out of my sails. I knew those letters would smell of violets, could imagine the tender crackle of their paper.

If I had thought I might visit Lill again, my brutish conduct with Chin put that out of the question. Chin would not allow me to ride her, or even to harness her to the wagon. I knew the equine chastisement was just. I was relieved she would even keep company with me as I paced the prairie.

Lill arrived for the wedding with her parents, wearing a yellow and blue dress, fresh as a prairie flower. She took leave of her family and brushed her skirt free of creases; then, holding her head high, she walked across the packed dirt to where I stood. I shuddered at how smitten with her I still was.

She spoke gaily. "Are you yet deserting us for Connecticut?"

I smiled sadly at her. "I'd throw Connecticut over in an instant if you'd marry me." I motioned toward the box, hopeful. "We could have a double ceremony, you're dressed pretty as a bride. I'd find a jacket."

She laughed, though she didn't sound happy. "And what would I tell Buck?"

Avelina squeezed out the door of her house, looking less like an ornament for the top of a cake than a gigantic cake itself. Her heavily ruffled muslin dress pouffed from her body, making her look twice her usual estimable size. The veil she'd made from flour sacks by pulling every other thread from the weave struck from the top of her head like a haystack. She clasped a bouquet of lupine in one hand, and when she lifted her skirt to walk with the other, you could see her army-issue boots underneath.

There was a gasp of disbelief. Tilfert's mouth went slack. He moaned. "Wouldja look at her? She's a *beaut.*"

We all stood our places in a semicircle around the bride and groom. The minister intoned the ceremony, and everyone cheered when the lovers kissed. I tried not to envy their happiness, but if I could have yanked the adoration off Avelina's face, as she looked at Tilfert, and make Lill wear it looking at me, I would've cheated Tilfert in a second. Instead, Avelina threw her bouquet into the air, and Lill leapt, catching the nosegay as neatly as a cat playing with a mouse.

There were *oohs* and *ahs*.

Tennessee elbowed Lill. "You 'n Buck will throw another wedding before we know it."

Lill smiled coyly. I was sick.

Avelina and Tilfert danced a rollicking ground-shaking waltz. Anyone who played an instrument had been called on to join the wedding band, which therefore consisted of a fiddle, four mouth harps, bagpipe, washboard and two jugs, and a bugler who played reveille no matter what anyone else was playing. After the bride's dance, Tilfert threw off his buffalo coat and shouted, "Everyone shake yer sticks!" The men, taking turns with skirt duty, stomped square dances and waltzes for hours, which resembled shoving matches more than anything. The revelers ate the mountain of food that Avelina had taken a week to prepare and washed it down with barrels of yeast-clotted beer.

A good time was had by all—but for me. I slumped at the table, nursing my heartache with a mug of ale, and tried not to resent the happiness of others, especially Lill. She seemed in ex-traordinarily high spirits, dancing from one female-starved soldier to the next. She laughed loudly and often and even sang with the horrible band.

Finally she took pity and sat beside me, fanning herself with a slender hand. She tilted her head. "Oh, Neddy, cheer up." I nodded morosely. "You want me to be happy for Buck?" She took my hand. "Be glad for *me*. I love him." I looked away from her and she pressed my fingers. "You promised we'd always care for each other. I expect you to keep that promise." I said nothing. She pulled her hand away. "I still wish you wouldn't go. We'll all miss you terribly if you do." She paused. "*I'll* miss you terribly, Edward. I miss you now."

My heart leapt but I could find no words. She looked away— "Well"—and got up from the bench. "Mope if you must. I'd rather dance." She flung herself back into the melee, leaving my heart to twang and anguish.

Temperatures had peaked by this time, vests and shirts wilted across the backs of chairs as if they and not their owners had been exerting themselves. The last barrels were tapped, and hilarity tipped into vulgarity. Bottle-brave men played the ragtag instruments for the first time, replacing the fatigued musicians. Half a dozen good-natured fistfights resulted in a full dozen bloodied noses, lips and a possible broken bone. Tilfert had just thrown up behind the dais when the train sounded a sad wail and pulled up on the tracks. Tilfert demanded another drink, shouted to me, "Do we got some new customers debarking, Turp?"

But no dudes emerged from the train. Buck Mason took the first step off, not in his usual buckskin but dignified and dashing in a dark suit. Lill caught her breath beside me and, with an expectant glow on her face, took a step forward.

Buck offered his hand to a figure inside the train and helped a woman to the platform. She was tall, exotic, hair piled high on her head, olive complexion warm against a blue dress. The makeshift band stopped playing as Buck turned and, as if to answer all questions, kissed the woman on the mouth.

CHAPTER 8

Dear Mother,
   Why do I still write?
   How do you bear loneliness?

B uck had married her in New York, an actress by the name of Reta Valentine. Having finished a wildly successful vaudeville run on Broadway in which she played an Indian rani, riveted in sapphires and wound seaworthy into an azure sari, she was introduced to the romantically fringed and booted Mason. They swept each other off their feet and had posthaste written a play together in which they'd cast themselves in the romantic leads. It was to be produced instead of Buck's Western drama.

It was a terrible thing to see Lill's face, the pain and betrayal sweeping across like a hurricane, but she regained her composure in a tremor and stepped forward to put Valentine's Broadway success to shame. Lill enthusiastically hugged both Buck and Reta, singing congratulations. I took Lill's arm and asked her if she was all right.

Lill glared at me and shook free. "If you will excuse us, Ned. I so seldom have a woman of culture to speak with." She brought the new Mrs. Mason a drink and chatted about the East, the West, theater, and art, a nonstop storm of chatter that cleared only when Reta went in to lie down.

Lill looked more than a little desperate then. I walked across the dance plat to rescue her, but she'd taken hold of one of the newly arrived Norwegian farmers, Rhylander Osterlund, blond, blue-eyed, and stocky. His head went straight to shoulder, which barely tapered to ankles, so stiff he might have been carved from a block of birch. He stood in virtually the same place he had since morning, looking so awkward and uncomfortable I'd wondered why he didn't take pity on himself and just go home.

"Mr. Osterlund, would you do me the favor?" Lill gave him her hand.

Osterlund pinked up like he'd been boiled. He and Lill shuffled back and forth for the remainder of the song. It turned out to be a great concession on his part; Rhylander's religion did not allow for dancing. I suspect a great deal of praying went on to remove the blot from his card. Lill, however, keeping a firm grip on the farmer's calloused hands, nudged them toward the edge of the crowd during the ensuing dance and managed to bump into Buck. Lill spun around and laughed. "Oh, my. I am so sorry, Mr. Mason. Do you know Ry? Rhylander Osterlund. He owns the acreage out by the Little Wolf."

Ry extended his hand and Buck shook it. Lill immediately shooed Buck away. "Enough. I do not take kindly to sharing Ry with anyone. You two can talk some other time." Ry inclined his head, took Lill back into the yoke of his arms, and they shuffled away.

Lill camouflaged herself with Rhylander for the remainder of the party, chirping and fluttering with the stolid man like a bird flirting with a tree. She sent her parents home and stayed on, claiming she was having too fine a time to curtail. I remained on her periphery, listening to her one-sided conversations, worrying over what I should do to lessen her pain. Lill waved me off several times; then finally, as the afternoon lost its brilliance and she sent Ry to get the horses, she turned. "What *are* you doing? It's like having a hungry dog trailing me!"

"Lill?"

"I'm right as rain, Ned. You think my world was wrapped up in that man? I am more than right, I am relieved. I could have wasted years on that skunk, and now I've been set free with little more to mourn than an afternoon or two."

"I know better than that."

"Ned. Leave me be."

"Lill, you have me. I love you. *I* would never leave you. I have prospects, a job offer, my inheritance."

She lost the gay facade and choked out, "You have *nothing*. You are a boy who thinks the world was made for him. A prospect is nothing, an offer is nothing, and don't delude yourself: Your mother is lost, the money is *gone*. What you have is a rough road ahead of you, Mr. Bayard. And I am done with that kind of road. I don't want your love, and, believe me, you don't want to love me. Love is nothing *anyone* should wish for."

Rhylander stepped up, holding his horse and hers. Lill clasped her hands. "Thank you, Mr. Osterlund. I do appreciate your escorting me home. It is good to come across a real gentleman."

When Ry lifted her to her saddle, she sat both legs to one side as I'd never seen her ride before. "Goodbye, Ned. Please tell Avelina she made a beautiful bride."

I watched Lill and Ry diminish into the huge swath of grassland, wasting in the ocher field until they were no more than gnats. I again imagined shooting Buck but didn't have near the passion for it. Too quick an end, as well. I prayed he would suffer the way Lill was doing. Justice would turn Reta's head, her rani eyes would light on another romantic lead, and she would betray Buck the way Buck betrayed Lill. That was for later, however. It was wrong that he should be so happy now, while Lill endured. I watched Buck tossing back whiskeys and slapping backs, waiting for it to stir me to action, but it only made me unfathomably weary.

The door to the house was barred. Of course. I hadn't made plans where to sleep during Tilfert and Avelina's connubial extravaganza, but the dude tents were still up, the cots ready. I dragged one toward the tent flap, so that while I lay there I could see the stars and wonder why the intense spangle of night was so beautiful and close in the wilderness, indifferent in the city. I was drifting off to sleep when I heard someone approach and relieve himself in the bushes. I covered my ears against the rude splatter. Still, I could hear someone yell, "Buck! Where're you off to?"

He shouted from the bushes, "Takin' a leak. Be there in a minute."

He'd barely finished buttoning himself when I hit him broadside.

Buck spun about, swearing, and had me by the collar in a second. He swung back and punched me in the nose.

I came to on the cot, my face pulsating around my aching eyes. Buck held a cloth to my nose, which was streaming red.

"Damn it, Ned, what did you do that for? Lucky I didn't shoot you."

I grabbed the cloth from him and nursed my own nose. It crackled a bit when I dabbed at it. "Son of a bitch, you broke my nose!"

He put out his hands. "I didn't know it was you."

"You knew it was Lill."

"You don't know the whole story."

"I know enough."

He sighed and sat down beside me. "I'm sorry if I hurt her. I came back, at least. Let her know . . . how things stood."

I shook my head at him. He disgusted me.

He eyed me, then demanded, "How do you know she didn't break my heart first? Why are you so goddamn sure you know everything?"

"Did she?"

"It was coming." He strode to the tent flap. "I *asked* her to go with me, Ned. She could've done that."

"So you humiliated her?"

"What I feel for Reta is true. If I could've done it different, I would've. I care about Lill—I loved Lill—but it just wasn't going to work out. Believe me, it hurt me too."

I sneered at him, though it was dark. "You're an actor, all right."

"What are you, Lord Turpentine?"

I would have gone after him again, no matter my nose still bleeding like a stuck pig, but there was a terrible scream and the shriek of horses.

We ran out of the tent. The corrals had been opened and horses were stampeding through the revelers. A man on horseback tore past, the moonlight glinting off his bare legs.

Buck swore. "Raiders."

The commotion was over in a minute, the scream of horses silenced, dust rising bright in the moonlight, the fire showing tables tipped and broken, dishes lying in the dirt. Someone moaned; another called, "Goddamn cow stepped on my leg!"

At daybreak every man available who yet owned a horse mounted to search for the raiders and the livestock. Chin remained unfazed outside the stable, contentedly chewing grass, but she wouldn't let me or anyone else on her back. She would finally have met her demise at the business end of Captain Ellmore's pistol, after she pitched him into the dirt and shit on him for good measure, but I interceded and he took a private's horse instead.

I wanted to go with the men and begged Chin to take me, to allow me to do something useful instead of scuffling dirt, feeling weak and puny. She would not, and instead wandered a few steps toward the Martine homestead.

However ready and willing I was to meet warriors in battle, I quailed to face Lill, though I knew I should go to her. Her misery would only have bred in the night, and I couldn't bear to witness that pain.

About then, Avelina opened the door to the house and she and Tilfert strode out on the hour like the carved farmer and wife in a Swiss clock. Tilfert grinned as he surveyed the wreckage still strewn on the dirt. "Some party, huh? Where is everybody?"

I rolled my eyes. "Didn't you hear anything? Raiders stampeded and stole half the horses. It was bedlam."

Tilfert blushed. "We was kind of busy, Ned."

I didn't want to hear it.

* * *

After lunch I managed to marshal my dread. Chin was some ways up the trail to Martines' as if she were endorsing the direction. I trudged to her and stroked her muzzle. "Fine, I'll go. Are you taking me?" She stepped away. I put out my arms. "I saved you from the captain this morning. Doesn't that make us even?"

She waited for me to catch up and blew in my ear, but when I grabbed her mane to mount, she shied. All was not forgiven. If I wanted to see Lill, I'd have to hoof it. It was a long walk, but I didn't have anything else to do.

I commenced the journey, Chin alongside. It was a pretty day, a bunting cloud cover veiling the oppressive heat, and in spite of my miserable circumstances I felt my spirits rise. If I felt better, perhaps Lill did as well. She might have been telling the truth about being relieved to see Buck as the skunk he was. And she might have been lying when she called me a boy without prospects.

Surprisingly, it was almost faster walking to Martine's than riding Chin there—owing to the lack of side trips. My legs were strong, the day cool, and sometime before dinner I espied the Martine hold. As we approached I warned Chin. "Don't expect turnips for this."

Approaching Martines', my hopes rose further still. Conversation and laughter floated from inside the house, sounding more like a party than heartbreak. An unfamiliar wagon was tied in front. I eyed it curiously as I stepped onto the porch and knocked.

Mrs. Martine answered. "Why, Ned, come in, come in. You're just in time to help us celebrate!"

Lill ran to the door in the daffodil dress and put out her hand. Her face was strained, her color up. She looked overly excited, a little wild. I wondered if she wasn't feverish.

"Ned. Just whom I wished to see." When she kissed me on the cheek her lips were cold, her hands chill.

I walked with her hand still in mine to the dining room, where Mr. Martine greeted me. I was feeling both oddly concerned yet still hopeful when Ry Osterlund walked in from the kitchen.

"Ry, you met Ned last night?"

"*Ja.* How are you?"

I shook his hand. What was he doing here? The wagon in front must be his, but last night he had been on horseback. Lill put out her hand again. Again I took it. She shook me off this time, then held out her hand once more. "Ned, silly. *Look.*"

On her left hand was a thin gold band. I spoke slowly. "Pretty."

"Ned, Ry gave it to me."

"No."

"Yes." She walked over to Ry and leaned against him. The Ry who swallowed the canary.

"You are engaged?"

"Oh, no." She turned her hand one way and another to watch the light wink on the gold.

I felt a wash of relief that made my knees go weak and I sat down with a laugh.

Lill looked over the horizon of her hand at me. "We're married, Ned. We drove to North Platte this morning. I am now Mrs. Rhylander Osterlund."

CHAPTER 9

The sky, now darkened to charcoal and slate, was spitting rain by the time I slid off Chin's back at the fort. Tennessee came running out of the shack that served as mercantile and post office, waving a piece of paper.

"Turp! You got a letter from that greenhorn wag in Connecticut."

Chin walked sedately into the stables. I stared at the envelope in my hand. It was from Elias Montgomery, lawyer, buffalo mangler. I ripped open the flap and read the missive, praying for a change in fortune.

Dear Mr. Bayard,

Your artwork hangs in my office, a most felicitous memoir of my Wild Western Adventure, which receives constant compliment.

I wish I could offer as much to you.

I have been in contact with your grandmother's law office, Alan and Jamieson, a rather threadbare concern, I must say. They hastened to make clear that they were engaged by your grandmother, not by your mother or by you, and therefore have no responsibility to dispense information. I managed to persuade him to give me some vague sense of affairs.

Your mother is without means. At some point your grandmother borrowed money from a Mr. Cornelius Pierce, which necessitated the auction of your family's estate six months after her death and, I assume, after you had left for Nebraska.

91

Unfortunately, the proceeds were substantially less than the money owed the debtors, which included the law firm itself. Mr. Jamieson wished me to assure you that the firm not only forgave their portion of the debt but also worked diligently to ensure there would be no attachments against your future earnings. Be comforted that, though you are not wealthy, neither are you in arrears.

It seems that at some time after the settlement your mother journeyed to England with a pickle merchant. How Jamieson knew this he wouldn't say. The name of the merchant is not known.

I am sorry to send you such poor news. I hope that your mother has since contacted you and your mind is at rest.

Sincerely,

Montgomery Elias

P.S. The firm's clerk, a rather weasel-faced young man, caught me outside of the building and asked for your address. I, of course, would not give him the information. He gave me this slip of paper and said there was more. I hesitate to pass on the communication, as I did not trust the fellow as far as I could throw him.

I reeled. I was no closer to my mother than before, possibly more confused than ever, and now I didn't even have a home to return to thanks to the perfidy of Mr. Cornelius Pierce. He owned the estate to the east of us and was supposedly a friend. He and my grandmother would get together to tut-tut over the sad state of society with the focus and frequency with which drunkards enjoy gin.

It occurred to me that Cornelius Pierce had engineered the debt and auction in order to purge my mother and me from Connecticut society. He disapproved, to put it lightly, of mixed marriages such as my father had lowered himself to, he and Grandmother theorizing that my weak constitution was due to my mother's poisoning my father's elite blood with her base German heritage.

However, I couldn't imagine my grandmother borrowing money from anyone, much less enough to sink the estate. She was tight as new shoes. Furthermore, what about the shadowy man who waited on my mother in the parlor? Was he the pickle merchant? Why would he take my mother to England? I could feel the warmth drain from my face; my knees wobbled.

Tennessee took off his hat and fanned it toward the sky. "Gonna be a real goose drowner by the look of things." When I didn't respond, he stuck his hat back on his head and muttered, "Think I'll go check the damned horse."

I dazedly reread the letter as the paper shriveled around occasional drips of rain. Why hadn't my mother at least written? Ashamed, perhaps, of her plummet to picklemaker's wife? I could hardly blame her, for either the shame or her need. A woman without means, without relatives, would end up on the streets. The liaison was a desperate act: a small step, but still a step, above the abasement of homelessness.

I shook the envelope, looking for the scrap of paper the weasel clerk handed Elias. It was half the size of a dollar bill, charred and so smoke blackened I could hardly read it. Printed in what were once sizable blue letters were the letters ORIUM. In handwritten cursive, I read:

yard's health im
ungs cleared of phlegmat

Was it *Bayard's* health the note referred to? It was a stretch. The reference could be to anyone, about almost anything. I folded the letter carefully and slid it back into the envelope, tucked the burnt paper inside and placed it in my pocket. I trudged to Avelina's house.

Avelina sat in her rocker, asleep. A fire blazed on the hearth, making the room beastly hot. She snorted awake. "Ned. Lookit me, sleepin' in daylight. Feelin' better, aren't ya? A little fresh air'll lift a man."

I sat at the table and put my head on my arms.

"Ned?"

I spoke through the angle of my elbows. "Lill's married Rhylander Osterlund. My mother is in England with a pickle man. I've lost the house, the grounds. There is no inheritance. No goodbye."

Avelina sat beside me. "Aw, Ned. I know you were taken with Lill."

I waited, and when she didn't say anything else I raised my head and protested. "*Taken* with her? I love her and she's *lost*, along with my mother, my fortune, and my name."

Avelina made a rude sound with her lips. "It's not like Lill's dead, Ned. Your mother neither. She's in England. You can visit her, if it comes to that."

"Maybe we can even pound pickle barrels together *en famille*."

"That's the spirit."

I groaned again.

"Now, Ned. Don't forget that bone job. Drawin' all them pitchers you like to do. That's something." She got to her feet with a grave sigh, went to her bureau, pushed things from one side to another, and pulled out a gold disk on a ribbon. "Here. Take this. Sell it and make a start in Connecticut."

It was the medal she'd hung around Tilfert's neck for monumental buffalo killing. I took the disk and examined it closely, identifying what it really was: a medal for valorous conduct, engraved *Frank O'Hare Junior*.

She pointed. "My da."

"I thought he was in Portsmouth."

"He deserted me when I was twelve, thirteen. That's all I have of him."

I handed it back. "I couldn't take it."

She looked cross. "I tol' you, he deserted me." She pushed it back. "I want you to have it, Ned. Take this and your notebooks and that ticket money the bone man left you, and go back east." She collapsed back into the chair. "Make a life for yourself and forget Lill Martine. It don't matter how much you feel like you love her . . . you can only really love a body who loves you back."

I nodded, knowing Lill *did* love me; that was the pain of it. Avelina struck her hand like a gavel on the table. "Now get yourself somethin' to eat."

I felt in my pocket for the charred paper. "There was something else, kind of strange."

She waved me off. "Later, Turp. I'm not feelin' so perkish. I think all the wedding folderol took it out of me. Need a proper nap, I guess."

She did look tired, hands heavy in her lap, eyelids dark and low.

"Where's Tilfert?"

"Freightin' to Denver. Won't be back till a week from Sunday, and that's only if the weather holds." She shook her head sorrowfully. "Winter's comin' on already."

Certainly the rain had begun. Fat, then fatter drops slapped the wooden roof as the temperature dropped, making the fire welcome. Avelina got up, pulled the curtain around the bed, and called through it, "Keep the stove goin', would ya, Ned?"

She slept fitfully, mumbling and exclaiming between strangled snores, and so passed the last hours of afternoon and then into evening without even rising to make dinner. I didn't feel like eating anyway and chewed on a piece of bread as I thought my dismal thoughts. I took a walk in the rain, telling myself that Avelina was right, there was still the Peabody job and, though it seemed pale recompense, at least it gave me somewhere to go.

Avelina was still sleeping when I returned and went to my own bunk. I slept poorly myself, dreaming of a bright bird that I had allowed to fly from cat to cage when all it would have taken to save the beautiful thing was the offer of my hand.

In the morning, the fire was cold, no breakfast in sight. I went to Avelina's curtain and called through, but there was no answer. I called again and she spoke in a hoarse, breathless voice. "Let me sleep."

I peered through the curtain. I could see the mound that must be Avelina on the bed in the corner. I stepped in. "It's nine, are you sick?"

She was pasty gray in the face, shivering still in spite of having piled every cloth, quilt, and robe on top of her bed. She moaned when I came close. "Leave. I don't want comp'ny."

"You *are* sick."

"Enjoyin' a bit o' bad health's all. I'll sleep it off."

"You need anything?"

"Find out if Tilfert's on the way back, will you? And the fire, Ned. Witch's-tit in here."

I stoked the fire until the little house was again too warm for my comfort, even as rain poured from the skies and wind gusted.

Of course no one'd heard from Tilfert. By the time night came, Avelina was calling to him as if he were standing there and the day was high. "You bring in the kindlin' and I'll be making Mother's butter cake. I've got the butter from Snell, at a dear cost, that's sure. We should get our own cow. Maybe in the spring. The cow'll calve. If it would only be a heifer, that'd be a blessing."

She was no better by the next morning. I called Captain Ellmore's wife to sit with her, thinking she'd appreciate another woman, but Avelina found the strength to throw a pillow at the poor woman and tell her to get the *hell* out. She'd have no one but me.

"Ned, Neddy, have you heard from Tilfert?"

"He's still on the freight job, Avelina."

"Ask 'im to come home, would ya?" She took hold of my arm. Her grip was weak; her hands looked papery; her eyes, holes burnt in a blanket. "Tilfert should come home."

It hit me only then that Avelina might die. I honed my own malady for seventeen years before it promised the end. How could two days so diminish my titanic landlady?

I took the five dollars I'd earned on the portrait of Montgomery Elias and gave it to Tennessee. He pushed it back and said he was going that way anyhow, promising hell-for-leather until he reached Tilfert and called him home. However, by this time the rain was sheeting down and I worried Tennessee would not be able to traverse the rushing rivers and plains.

I tried to force broth into Avelina's dry mouth, but she wasn't having it. Shouting, "Out! Away! Leave me be! Arms and legs in the mud, they cut like kindlin'. Tell them to go. Just boys, ground up like meat!" I gave her water. I bathed her head with cool compresses. I kept the fire roaring.

Still, she worsened. She cried for Tilfert, she cried for Tommy, she cried for Da, her breathing ragged, face cadaverous, eyes unseeing.

"Avelina," I begged her, "hang on. Tilfert's coming. A day, maybe, and he'll be here."

Her face clouded. "A day?" She clutched at my hand, gasped, then looked at me, seeing me for the first time in hours. "Ned, you promise me. I don't want nothin' done to me if I die. Bury me as I am. No washing. No fancy dress. Promise, Ned. If I die, put me right into the ground *as I now lay*. As I am. *Don't let them touch me.*"

"You're not going to die, Avelina."

She growled at me and I stopped short. She spoke forcefully, "Your promise. As I lay now, I'll be buried."

"All right. If it comes to that, I'll make sure of it."

Two hours later, every breath a struggle, Avelina simply stopped. I waited for the breath that didn't come, the silence strange and loud like when a storm abates. I took Avelina's hand, I shook her, I called her back, but she would not return. There was only an awful vacancy, the whole room emptied out, myself as well. So hollowed, I couldn't get up, could not find my lost voice, my fugitive vigor, not a thought, not a tear.

It may have been an hour later, perhaps only ten minutes, when Tennessee came in, rivulets chasing from the brim of his hat, the corners of his mustache and from the hem of his coat. He took a look at Avelina, at me. He leaned over and shut her eyes, digging two pennies from his pocket and laying them on the lids. "Come on, Ned. You did what you could. Come on out here now."

"Tilfert?"

"I sent word. He'll be half a day behind, maybe more. There's some tricky fords, but he'll get here." He led me into the rain, and we walked to the captain's quarters. Tennessee knocked. The captain's wife answered, her spinster sister hovering over her shoulder. Tennessee took off his hat. "Ma'am, Avelina's passed."

Mrs. Ellmore nodded. "Sister and I will be right there."

Tennessee took my arm. "A drink'll pick you up, Ned. We'll drink to Avelina."

I started. "I can't leave her alone."

"She's gone, Ned. If you go in there, you're the one what'll be alone."

"Go get dry, Tennessee. I'll sit with her and wait for Tilfert."

I went back into the little house, put another log on the fire. When the women arrived, the first thing Mrs. Ellmore did when she came in was hug me. "I'm so sorry, Ned. Avelina thought the world of you."

The sister put a kettle of water on the fire and a stack of towels on the bed beside Avelina as Mrs. Ellmore shuffled through the dresses hanging on the cord along the wall. Mrs. Ellmore pulled out the muslin wedding dress. Holding it out at arm's length, she sighed and spoke to her sister. "They were so happy on their wedding day. As . . . unconventional . . . as they were, I don't think I've ever witnessed such elation, Nattie." She laid the dress on the bed. "One day I hope you find such happiness."

Nattie sighed—"God willing"—and poured heated water into a bowl.

I watched the two, as comfortable in Avelina's house as if it were their own, stirring Avelina's fire, going through Avelina's dresser, sifting Avelina's soap into the water. "What are you doing?"

Mrs. Ellmore touched my shoulder gently, her pale blue dress delicate as eggshell, yellow hair braided and coiled around her head. "Preparing Avelina for burial, Ned."

Mrs. Ellmore had a comfortingly pastel voice, but her sister's impassive list—"Wash her, put her in her dress . . ."—reminded me of my promise.

"Avelina's last request was to be buried as she was, no washing, no fuss."

Mrs. Ellmore pursed her lips. "I would no more think of laying her to rest without caring for her first than throw her into the snow for the wolves to eat." Her eyes filled with tears. "I knew her too, Ned."

Nattie concurred. "A woman knows what a woman wants."

I supposed that was right; she certainly seemed certain. Even now Nattie was combing the rag of Avelina's hair with hands so white and fine, Avelina looked all the more brutish.

Genetics were cruel. If anyone should have lived it should have been my giantess, and the candy women standing beside her melted away. I didn't want to see it and struggled to my feet and toward the door. Mrs. Ellmore stopped me. "Ned. We may need help turning her. She is such a *big* woman." She paused. "We will make it circumspect."

What could I do? I reseated myself against my sudden and unreasonable resentment of her prettiness. Nattie drew Avelina's curtain. I stared into the fire and wondered if I was shaken, how would Tilfert bear it?

I was staring at the door where rainwater seeped under the jamb when Mrs. Ellmore shrieked. There was quiet, then a sharp whispering between the two women. When Mrs. Ellmore spoke it was in a strangled sort of voice. "Ned. Come here, please."

I pushed aside the curtain. The two sisters had unbuttoned Avelina's blouse and shift, untied her corset. Mrs. Ellmore pointed. "Can you explain that?"

I had not actually seen a woman's chest before, but I had to admit it was not what I expected. Avelina's chest was hairy. I thought of Quillan proclaiming, "She's not a woman, she's an ape."

Nattie, her face turned away, grated, "Tell him. Tell him to check *down there*."

I was confused and terribly embarrassed. "I don't understand."

Mrs. Ellmore pointed. "Down. There. Look for *it*."

It took me a dense few minutes of staring *down there* to understand what I was to look for. When the sisters read the understanding on my face, they stepped away from the bed. Nattie drew the curtain with a sharp snap, leaving me alone with Avelina. I mumbled apology as I lifted her skirt, feeling a monster to dishonor my friend this way and wanting nothing more than to find *it* missing. Yet there it lay between her legs, woolly and unmistakable. I lowered Avelina's skirt and sat down heavily.

Mrs. Ellmore flung open the curtain. "I was right, wasn't I?"

I looked up at her. "Right?"

"She is a *he*."

She said this with such vindictiveness I was alarmed. "Mrs. Ellmore, please, let's keep this between us. No one need know."

"On the contrary, Mr. Bayard. She—*he*—will not be buried with the godfearing souls in our little cemetery. My lord, and they were *married*. A travesty before God. This is an *abomination*. That, that Tilfert"—she spat out his name like poison— "is an abomination."

I felt panic well. "Please, Mrs. Ellmore. Let me take care of this, keep it quiet."

The sisters glanced at each other. Nattie raised her chin and one eyebrow. "Mr. Bayard, *how* is it that you hadn't realized previously?"

"Like your sister, it hadn't occurred to me. There was no reason—"

"My sister wasn't living with these men. Is there perhaps another reason you would like this kept secret?"

A hundred thoughts filled the hollow places of ten minutes previous. Most concerning my own well-being. I knew what Mrs. Ellmore and her sister were intimating. Others would think the same. It seemed suddenly ludicrous that I hadn't seen what stood, wrestled, spit, grew hair, right in front of me for all these months. Had I known? What did this mean? How far would it go? I stood and paced the floor.

"Mr. Bayard?" Mrs. Ellmore pressed, her voice ominous. "Do you truly wish to keep silent?"

I was trapped. "No, ma'am. I don't."

"Then perhaps *you* will alert the men to the situation and do me the favor of explaining it to my husband."

CHAPTER 10

The storm was persistent, neither giving in nor stepping up throughout the night. The men waited until the small hours for the show that was to come, huddling and feeding fires, then finally putting their cold feet and icy revulsions to bed. They would not see Tilfert arrive, would not see his terror of too late, or the fresh horror of sorrow.

I'd sat at Avelina's table all night, getting up to add wood to the fire, though Avelina would never be warm again. Dawn had been trying to work through the heavy clouds for some time when Tilfert burst through the door like he'd been flung a far distance. He read Avelina's death on my face and stumbled against the door. The door slammed, the roar of the storm hushed. Tilfert's immense frame buckled. He grabbed at the jamb for support and stared for some time at the wood grain.

I gave him the only thing I could. "She went easy, Tilfert."

He turned. "Gone."

"The ague."

He gazed at the curtain. "She there?"

She was rigid. He could not pry open her fingers. He rested his forehead on hers and sobbed, shouted raw repudiations as he stroked her face. He had a moment. But that was all. I had to warn him.

"Tilfert. They know."

"Dead."

"They know Avelina's a man."

"Nobody knows nothin', Ned. *Nothin'*. My sweet Avelina. God damn, gone!"

He would not be distanced from his sorrow and sobbed for a good half hour before they arrived.

Private Anderson, new to Fort McPherson, was the first in the house. He was followed by four enlisted men: Boyer, Simmons, Ladd, and Cole, all tousle-haired and half buttoned like they'd come to Avelina's for pancake breakfast.

"Tilly!" Anderson leered. "You've been keepin' secrets, haven't you?"

Tilfert ignored them but for his silence.

"Ned tol' me and I couldn't believe it. I said, Naw, not Tilfert, he wouldn't do something as goddamn filthy as buggering a man, much less *bein'* buggered, but I looked, we *all* looked, and your Avelina's got a cock like a *mule*."

Boyer started singsonging, "He wound up a clock with the head of his cock and buggered his pal with the key. . . ."

Tilfert looked away from Avelina and glanced at me. I shook my head, imploring him to understand.

Anderson continued. "Well, a piece of meat like that don't lie, but I'm still not willing to believe you'd grind the glory hole, Tilly. Mebbe you're the bearded lady from the freak show, and you an' Avelina there just got mixed up. Fergot the cock wears the pants, the cunt wears the skirt. Is that what happened, Tilly?"

Tilfert remained silent, kneeling at Avelina's side. Boyer took a step forward and kicked Tilfert in the back. I shouted, "Hey!" but he ignored me and asked Tilfert, "What do you got in those pants?" Tilfert hardly moved but, white-knuckled, clutched Avelina's sleeve.

Anderson mock-whispered in Tilfert's ear. "We allus liked you, Tilfert. Really liked you. And if you are set up right, we'll all have a good time." He stood up. "And if you don't, there's gonna be trouble."

Boyer kicked him again. "Take 'em off. Let's see what's there."

Tilfert stood up with a roar. The men took a step back, their hands going to belts and pockets. What they hid in their pants would kill a man.

I yelled, "Get out! You've had your fun."

Anderson shook his head. "We've not had any fun for a long, long time, Neddy, boy. But we're gonna today, one way or another." Anderson nodded and the five jumped Tilfert and, with a stew of cursing and punching, pushed his face to the floor of the cabin, pinned and tied Tilfert's arms behind him.

I stepped forward and shouted again, my voice miserable and thin-sounding. "See here, that's enough!"

Anderson slapped me, and I fell back against the wall with a crash. "There's enough rope for two, Turpentine."

I should have taken my chances, launched myself into him, brought on the masculine punch against the insult of the open hand. But I was afraid of the transformation of these men. Dogs turned to wolves, and I fled into the rain to the captain's house, shouting for help. By the time Captain Ellmore answered the door, Tilfert was trussed in the back of his own wagon.

The captain called to Boyer over the hiss of rain, as if the men were going out to rodeo or race horses, "I expect no harm to come to that man."

Boyer saluted. The captain shut the door against me and returned to his bed.

The men drove into the waterlogged prairie, hooting and prodding Tilfert with names and boots. Tilfert, though not gagged, was silent.

As the wagon sloshed into the grass, the storm took a deeper breath into full fury, the wind shrieking, a curtain of rain blowing the dark morning to deep dusk. In the pall, Tennessee raced from the bunkhouse to the mess. I followed him in. "Help me! They're going to kill him!"

Tennessee looked uncomfortable. "Shit, they're not. Calm down." He pulled his hand through his wet hair. "Besides, he has it coming. Get his lesson taught to him, then he'll move on outta here." He put his hat on. "Maybe he won't be so quick to plug the rooster next time."

I threw my belated punch then, but Tennessee took hold of my arm. "Turpentine. You can't help Tilfert. He's fucked it all up himself, and if you try you'll fuck yourself too. Just keep quiet, keep your distance." He let go of my arm and walked away, turning as an afterthought. "And the *next* time you go after me, I'll give you what you're asking for."

I returned to the house and watched the puddle under the door creep in until the fire hissed with the moisture, thinking I should bank the door to keep the water out. Avelina would be aghast at her floor turning to wallow. So careful with a floor, why couldn't she anticipate what would happen? How could she have done this with Tilfert? How could she have done it to me? I watched water rise to the chair legs until I heard shouts rising over the wail of rain.

"Republican's over the banks! She's flooding!"

Avelina's house at the far perimeter of the fort was on the low point. I woke from my miserable reveries and pushed open the door against ankle-deep water, Avelina becalmed and oblivious to the deluge rising around her bedposts.

Every hand was at work, desperately filling feed sacks with sand, lugging the heavy wet bags to the stockade fence, and piling them into a dike to hold the river at bay. I saw Anderson hefting a bag to the fence, Cole, Boyer, and Simmons shoveling. I surveyed the area. Tilfert was not to be seen.

I confronted Anderson. "Where's Tilfert?"

Anderson grinned in spite of the bag leaking mud down his neck. "Walking the pourdown, pecker in hand, naked as a jaybird. By Jasus, he was hell fer fightin'! Gave Jonsson a month of recuperation, an' Bailey a broke nose."

"Naked, in *this*?"

"Son of a bitch's hairy as a bear. What a sight." He threw off the bag and headed back for another. "We left him his boots. By the time he gets his coat back on maybe he'll have learned something." He bent and hoisted another bag with a groan. "Joke's on me in the end, ain't it? Who's actually being punished here?" He laughed and shook his head. "That bastard Tilfert ain't the one toting wet sand, that's for sure."

The water continued to rise; we struggled to contain it. The rain poured down. Bags were filled from the high side, dragged to the low. Another hour, another foot of levee. The river could now be heard over the pour of rain, a menacing boom of boulders loosed from the grassland and knocking against one another in the river like giant marbles.

A shout went up; the east wall of the mess yawed. With a scream, it tipped into the race of water.

Mrs. Ellmore and her sister were routed from the captain's house to clamber through mud to safety, clutching heavy wool blankets like shawls that immediately peached with water, tripled in weight, and decanted over their yellow heads.

The river pulled at the sandbags, sucked them from the tenuous rim, and the entire company headed for the hill, choking. With water falling and blowing in sheets, little space remained for air, for light. Huddling in the rain, shrunk like wet cats, we waited.

A coyote swam by, twisting in the water; a silver chest rattled in the wake. Mice and rats washed onto the bank, only to be kicked back into the moiling river.

The captain's house torqued, its foundation foundering, and Mrs. Ellmore sagged and whimpered.

After what seemed a season, the storm shuddered and, finally, took a breath and did not exhale. Instead, she lifted her gray skirt and allowed some small light to dance across the poles and timbers tossing down the muddy river, disappearing into haze.

Tennessee blinked into mist. "She's letting go."

Another section of the mess hall surrendered to the muddy Republican. For though the rain hesitated, the river yet raged. A ridge beam, tossing in the flood, rammed Avelina's house. The house shuddered and lifted. Another log battered the tilting walls. The water chewed dirt until land loosed its hold, and the little cabin upended and bobbed with a creak of pegged beams, as if the cabin were a moored boat.

Tennessee shouted, "Man in the river!" A figure spun in the roiling water, banging against bank and flotsam, rushing through eddies and rapids, striking the cabin, partnering runaway logs.

The body was facedown, yet there was no mistaking the buffalo back, the curling hair streaming behind. Even in the wide torrent, he was a gigantic man, his big arms languid beside him as if he were transfixed with a world the rest of us couldn't appreciate. I plunged knee deep into the water but Tennessee grabbed hold of my hair and arm and hauled me back. "You ain't gonna drown for a dead man!"

Then Avelina's upended house pulled fully free, following Tilfert downriver, the front door pointing to the skies, a bucket, a tin plate, chunks of buffalo wood floating from a hole in the roof, the post of Avelina's bed and one ashen foot visible through the window.

CHAPTER 11

Dear Edward,

My life is complete. By the time you read this letter, if God is good, I will have my bride.

Brill

Dear Brill,

Congratulations. I will be in Pennsylvania on the fifteenth and wish to give you my best wishes in person.

Ned

Dear Professor Quillan,

I will arrive in New Haven Sunday after next.

Edward Bayard

Dear Mr. Montgomery,

I am returning east. I will avail you of my address once I arrive. If you see the clerk from Alan and Jamieson, tell him I want to know more.

Edward Turrentine Bayard III

Someone's joy is ever rising in spite of another's mortal wound.

Lill arrived to say goodbye. Who knows how she convinced Osterlund to drive her to the muddy tents and platforms that now made up the fort. Perhaps he knew, if he didn't give in, she would find a way to go herself. As he helped her from the wagon, he announced in his flat blond voice, "Ten minutes." I wondered if he was afraid she might get on the train with me. I wished it a possibility.

Lill and I sat in the mess tent. Nine in the morning and no one inside. Almost immediately, Lill began to cry. "You're really going?"

I nodded. "There's nothing here. Not for me."

She buried her face in her hands. "I can't stand it. Avelina and Tilfert, you, me . . . Everything is terrible."

I was unmoved by her tears, by her shaking hands. I didn't care that she was wearing, instead of satin and carmine, a rough brown dress, that her hair was caught in a tight bun, or that she was pale with ashen rings under her eyes. She had made this happen. Not fallen into it, not been victimized by circumstance. She'd run after trouble as if it were covered in diamonds, and by catching it she left me lonelier than I thought it was possible to be.

"Life was so bright at the beginning of the summer." She wiped her eyes, then took my hands. Her fingers were damp in my palm.

I wanted to pull back, but instead, even as I shouted, "Why did you do it?" I clutched at her fingers, pressed my palm against hers. I hungered to kiss the pulse at her wrist.

"I couldn't help it! Oh, Ned, don't be so angry with me."

"You could help it. You only did it to get back at Buck. For him you ruined yourself, and me, and maybe that farmer as well. At the end, it's Buck who's happy." I shook my head. "And at least Osterlund's got himself a cleaning woman out of the deal!"

She put her head into her arms and sobbed anew. "Ned, don't. You don't understand."

"Then make me understand!"

She looked up, hiccuping a little. "You hate me anyway, so I may as well explain. But please, Ned. Don't tell a soul." She glanced at the door. "I *had* to marry—someone." She stared into my face and repeated, "I *had* to."

Had to. She'd let her hand fall below her breast to her belly. Lill was expecting a child. I felt terribly betrayed. How was it possible that things kept getting worse? What I would give for her to be telling me this news, the child mine, our future sweet and rosy? But it wasn't mine. "My God. Buck's?"

She nodded. "I didn't have a choice, you see." She read the question in my face. "I didn't lie. I told Ry. He agreed to marry me in spite of it."

I was sorry for a minute, then angry all over again. "You know *I* would have married you, and I wouldn't have taken you on *in spite of it*. I would have married you because I loved you. I would have loved your baby."

"Shhhh!" She frowned at me. "You can't tell anyone, Ned. It would humiliate Ry."

I looked away. It pained me that she would protect the Norwegian. Lill put her hand on my arm. "Ned, I couldn't marry you. I had to marry . . . not a man . . . but a circumstance. I married a *house.* I married two hundred acres, a yoke of oxen, some seed corn, and a milk cow. *Please,* Ned."

"Please what? What can I give you now?"

"Please don't stop loving me. You haven't stopped loving me?"

She looked so transparent then, emptied of anything hopeful, she appeared almost blue. She was breaking my heart and still I wanted to hurt her. "No, Lill. I will never stop loving you, and because of this you've killed me."

"No, Ned!"

"My happiness is you, you know it, and now someone else has it."

She buried her face in her hands and murmured, "I have made such mistakes. And now I've lost all I've loved for cold mornings of prayer and porridge and everything that is brown and ugly and rough. No music, no dance, no color. Do you know Ry's religion frowns on poetry, Ned? It is *devil's work*." She laughed, a little hysterically, then took a breath and straightened her back. "But even now, I know it was the only thing to do." She looked up at me, took my hands again. "All I have left is patching mistakes with more mistakes. Doing what I did, Ned. . . ." She paused, looking stricken. "I attempted to free you from it. Please know that."

I softened. "Ah, God, Lill." I clutched at wild hope. "It's not too late. Come with me now, run away *now*."

"How I wish I'd never met Buck, that I didn't have this." She waved her hands at the seed growing in her. "I *would* go with you, Ned. I would shame myself as a runaway bride, I would shame my family, I would even shame *you* by doing it. I am a terrible selfish person. But somehow I cannot shame a child. I cannot doom him to a life that is cursed from conception. And with that one good intention, I am trapped."

"I won't let you be trapped, Lill. I will save you. I love you." I searched for a way out for us. "I will make good, I will be rich, a *giant*, and I will take you away from these base prisons." The train's whistle sounded and ended my pompous soliloquy. I took her hand again. "How can I go?"

"You have to go." She gave a wan smile, a shaft of light through clouds. "To become my colossus."

I saw Osterlund striding toward the tent. I squeezed Lill's hands. "I'll come back for you. I will not let you molder here."

"Don't promise anything but to love me, Ned. As long as I know that, I can keep on." She took her poetry ring from her pocket and a small photograph capturing her in a happier time. "Take these, Ned. And for God's sake, don't forget."

I put the photo in my pocket but placed the ring back on her finger. "I don't need a ring to keep a promise."

Osterlund walked in. Lill straightened and took her hand from my arm. He frowned. "It's time. The train."

Lill nodded at me. I stood slowly, powerless again. Lill chirped, "Please write, Ned. Ry and I will so look forward to your letters."

Ry hefted my bag. How could I leave her to the life she would have with him? I lifted Lill's hand to my lips. I whispered. "I'll come back for you."

Osterlund shouted from the stoop. "Mr. Bayard!" The whistle blasted. I left Lill, stiffly shook Ry's hand, and boarded the train.

I took a seat and threw my bag on another, then looked out the window. Osterlund helped Lill into his wagon. She looked once behind her before facing forward to her new life: a dusty homestead and future family. Tennessee stood awkwardly scuffing at the grass beside the tracks, trying to look like he had business there. I caught his eye as the train commenced to move, and we gave each other a nod.

Chin waited down the tracks, free again and unwanted. The best I managed to do for the big horse was beg no one shoot her. I gave the stable master what money I could to provide hay for her through the winter and told myself Chin had lived through lonely months before and would again. But it hurt to leave her. Though I felt silly I raised my hand in goodbye as the train groaned down the tracks. Chin pricked her ears forward then turned away as I passed.

Would trains always take me from one sorrow to another? With my first journey I was abandoned not only by my people but by my fortune and place. But that sorrow did not come close to the magnitude of this one. Leaving a circumstance was as shallow as marrying one.

I rifled through my bag, which contained what little had floated from Avelina's windows to be caught by plum briars in the flood. A pair of breeches, two shirts, my pistol, and Avelina's medal, which by dint of its weight had stayed close to the footprint of the absentee house, the long ribbon caught in a cleft of stone. I wore Tilfert's hat: wide-brimmed, deep-crowned, with a horsehair band to keep the shape in the rain.

Avelina and Tilfert. It was near to impossible to believe they were gone, easier to believe in the demise of thunder. I nursed resentment and anger, even disgust toward the two of them. But every time I tried to blame them, an image would rise of their kindness to me and to each other. I thought of the buffalo man spinning in the water. Had Tilfert fallen into the swollen Republican or met it purposely? His boots were found upright on the prairie, filled to their brims with water.

I hadn't paid attention. I hadn't surmised. I broke my promise to Avelina and let Mrs. Ellmore breach her petticoat defenses—all because I passively hoped it would come out all right, believed others must know better than I. It was easier than fighting.

I groaned in my seat. My negligence knew no bounds. Now I had left Lill to fend for herself, abandoned my horse to winter. But my back was against a wall. I swore I would make my name anew, rise in the ranks, then return to rescue Lill, wiping Osterlund and Mason from her memory with a joyous life. We would raise our children in a fine house, Chin pastured in clover. I would have money and power and no one would dare to take anything from me or hurt anyone I cared about.

"Ticket."

I handed the conductor the cash Quillan had left for my passage. The conductor took the money and handed me a slip. "End of the line."

"Excuse me?"

"You're takin' her all the way to the end of the line. We'll be tight as thieves in two days, son."

He winked but I looked away. I didn't need any more friends.

CHAPTER 12

Alan and Jamieson, Solicitors:

I demand information concerning my mother, her whereabouts, and the dealings she had with you. Further, I must have a full accounting of all sales and debts concerning my family's estate, especially that of the sale of the house. I am at this moment en route to Connecticut and I will no longer tolerate your silence. I will not be put off. I will be answered.

Edward Turrentine Bayard III

The Pittsburgh train depot was a beautiful station, marble friezes on the walls carved by great Italian stonemasons' grandsons. Ladies walked with fringed parasols lifted against whatever autumn sunshine wavered through the blanket of coal smoke. Gentlemen folded papers into shingles under their arms as short-pants paperboys hawked monkeynuts. Swaybacked carriage horses waited to transport travelers. A babushka'd woman, round and pink-cheeked as a nesting doll, sold tea from a wagon.

I had less than an hour before I resumed my journey and hoped that Brill would indeed meet me. Then I saw him standing with a young woman. He stood with impeccable posture, as always. I used to joke with him that he forever looked as if he were about to open someone's door, and he would reply with a clipped British accent, though he was born in Albany, New York, "One's standing can only *improve* one's standing."

I grinned and strode toward him, waving a hand. He looked at me, past me, left and right.

"Brill!" I called.

He drew his brows together and took the young woman's hand. "Yes?"

"Brill?"

Brill's frown upended into delight. "Good Lord, Ned, it *is* you!" He dropped the young woman's hand and shook mine with enthusiasm. He stepped away and put his hands on his hips. "*Look* at you! I tell you I would never have known you on the street." He turned to the young woman. "This dusty ruffian is the ailing Edward Turrentine Bayard the Third. Can you imagine the change?"

The young woman looked no more than sixteen or seventeen years. She wore a silk dress with ruching at the neck and pearl buttons down the bodice, an ornately decorated bonnet, and white kid gloves. Too young for marriage, too privileged for a tutor. I hazarded a guess. "Is this one of your students?"

Brill took her hand again. "My *best* student, Elizabeth. And now my wife."

I was stunned. The young woman spoke quietly. "Pleased to meet you, Mr. Bayard. Brill has told me so much about your friendship."

I looked closely at her. She looked strained, a trifle too pale, a trifle too thin, her expensive clothing not as well ironed as it could be. One of the pearl buttons at her wrist hung from a thread as she offered her hand.

I kissed it. "Brill, you have done exceedingly well." The young woman winced.

Brill cleared his throat and motioned toward the tea cart. "Shall we have tea?"

Elizabeth frowned. "Must it be here, Brill?"

Brill looked apologetic. "We have but three quarters of an hour, Elizabeth."

She smiled and put a hand to her throat. "I have not been feeling well, Mr. Bayard. I think I will return . . . home . . . to rest, if you will forgive me."

"Certainly. Brill, please, do not let me keep you."

Brill shook his head and searched his pockets, pulling out some change. "Take a cab, darling."

"It's not necessary. I can walk."

He pressed the money into her hand. "We're *fine*."

She inclined her head. "A pleasure to meet you, Mr. Bayard."

Brill sighed as he watched her glide across the floor and out the door. "She is the most remarkable woman. I am far luckier to have her than she is to have me."

"I'm sure *not*, Brill."

"I am well aware of it. She has stepped down to wed me, and everyone is being absolutely monstrous about it."

We ordered our tea and sat at a table. Brill spooned sugar into his cup. "Her family decries me a sharp, a schemer, married for the money." He looked abashed and admitted, "I suppose one cannot blame them, under the circumstances. Yet turn their backs on her entirely?" He fiddled with his napkin. "I've assured Elizabeth they will come around. I'm certain they will. But for now, her father has forbidden any contact. Her mother, her brothers, even her sisters have forsaken her. Elizabeth, a favored pampered child, is . . . *undone* by their conduct. I don't know what to do." He smiled briefly. "In any case, their true treasure is mine now. Thankfully, there's nothing they can do about that."

119

I sipped my tea, trying to keep the shock from my face, from my voice. "I guess you're out of work, as well."

He laughed. "Yes. I should be plying my bride with roses and rubies. Instead, she sold her granny's cameo for potatoes." He clenched his jaw. "*Damn* it all. If I had known, I would never have married her, no matter how desperately I love her."

I wondered at this. How could he not have known what would happen? An heiress and a tutor? My God.

As if he read my mind, Brill nodded. "Her family treated me like an equal—better perhaps. I was held up to their lunk-headed boys as an example of what one could do if they studied hard enough, worked hard enough. I ate at their table, I rode their horses. When I taught the girls Latin, they were as astounded as if I'd encouraged a cat into speech!"

"Ah, Brill."

He stared into space. "My vanity was at fault. I see it now. Only *I* believed myself to be an equal. Even the stupid boys knew better. I could talk and think better than they, but they are made of gold and I tin, to wind up and make my cymbals clang. No matter how clever my clockworks, still a toy."

"Elizabeth believes in you."

He looked stricken. "I know she did believe. If she yet does, I am certain she wonders if it is worth the price she pays."

"If their love for their daughter is so cheap to be discarded in such a manner—"

"Their love is anything but *cheap,* Edward. It is wrapped in gold leaf. Mine"—he crushed the paper napkin—"in pages of Shakespeare and botanica." He sighed mightily. "Which will yellow and crumple to dust."

I felt genuine pity for him and experienced a surge of righteous anger against Elizabeth's family, before recognizing I had no right. I was as black a pot as came.

My grandmother bought a cairn terrier for me when I turned sixteen. It was to sleep on my bed and provide companionship. Once it grew out of its sleepy puppyhood, however, it wanted to run the fields and sniff out rats in the barns. It fell to Brill to walk the animal, which he did punctiliously three times a day. Of course the dog loved him. Even when the dog reclined across *my* feet, his wet brown eyes followed Brill as if my tutor were a pork roast. When Brill left the room, the dog whined.

I had my mother get rid of the animal, told her to give it away. I could not bear that a retainer would have what I could not. A black pot indeed, and how far from Elizabeth's father?

We were silent for a moment, then Brill shook himself. "Forgive me my lachrymose thoughts. Tell me about you. How are Avelina and Tilfert"—he searched the ceiling for names—"the love of your life, Lill, and the scoundrel horse, Chin?"

"Dead, drowned, lost, and abandoned. Lachrymose indeed."

After I recounted the sad story, he sighed. "We are riders of stormy seas, friend. Yet what is one to do but buck the waves?"

I shrugged. "You haven't heard anything more about my mother? Nothing was amiss at the house after I left?"

Brill looked away. "I didn't go back after you left, Edward. Your mother handed me my packed bag at the station. Gave me my wages and sent me on my way." He checked his watch. "I need to get back to Elizabeth."

We stood to say our goodbyes, Brill promising when he got another position he would send his address to me in care of the

Peabody. He smiled. "*What* an opportunity, to work with Wallace Quillan. I am envious."

I nodded, feeling perfidious relief that, unlike Brill, at least I did have employment. Then I acknowledged, "I would have traded every museum in the world for Lill Martine if she would only have had me. You're a luckier man than I."

He walked me back to the train and shook my hand. "We'll be in touch."

I stared out the window or slept fitfully from Pennsylvania to Connecticut, waking with a start at the call, "New Haven!" I staggered from my cramped train compartment, bag in hand, and felt the impact of return like a hammer. With that first step off the train, the specter of my misplaced life thickened to meat.

When I'd visited New Haven six years ago, I was also on my way to the Peabody. Mother and I had taken the train from Cornwall, though Grandmother objected to my exposure to the unwashed public. A carriage with a matched team met us at the station and drove us to the museum. Though I was ill at the time, I was also moneyed; I was cosseted; I was Edward Turrentine Bayard III.

This time there was no one to meet me, to open my door. No Professor Quillan, and no one acting for him. Worst of all, there was really no Edward. Only Ned, and I most suddenly and certainly felt my ability to regrow my lost name and fortune was as likely as sprouting diamond teeth.

I waited some time, growing discomfited at the looks thrown up and down my dusty western garb. I'd looked fine in Nebraska, dressed like every other fellow in loose-legged California pants and a sack coat with a blanket liner over a gray shirt Avelina'd cut down for me. I straightened my vest, arranging my father's watch to peep from one of the pockets, removed Tilfert's hat and used it to swat my trousers free of dirt and ash, and shined my boots on the calves of my pants. The oak pegs that held the boot's soles to the uppers were working their way out, and I stamped hard to force them back in. Finally I reknotted the blue kerchief around my neck. Feeling a little more presentable, I asked one of the hansom drivers for directions to the Peabody Museum.

"Two bits a ride," he replied. I shook my head. The driver considered, decided I couldn't pay if I'd wanted to, and gave me directions. "Closed at this time of day, son."

I headed that way anyway, not knowing what else to do. I hoped there might be some clue at the museum to tell me what next. It wasn't far, a mile perhaps, before I came to the two-story building fashioned from great red-stone blocks, tarnished to black with the city's ubiquitous soot. I remembered my mother walking slowly up the flagstone walk beside me in a rustling gown, a wide hat with a stuffed bird on top, wings and bill open. I told her she looked like she was being attacked, and she laughed behind a hand. "Attacked by fashion, Edward. I am assured this is all the rage."

Was my mother still fashionable? What was the costume for a pickle merchant's wife?

I rattled the museum door and walked around the circumference of the stone building, hoping to see a lighted window or Professor Quillan walking along the well-kept lawns, raising his hand in greeting. However, after I'd taken three circumlocutions, reprimanding myself for not getting a personal address for the paleontologist, I gave up. The museum opened at 9 A.M. I would return in the morning.

I hefted my bag and journeyed past the rows of Georgian buildings that made up the Yale campus, their rows of equally spaced dormers, windows, shutters, and chimneys giving the buildings the look of a well-pressed army, soldiers intensely disciplined, eternally alert. They each had a name, Timothy Dwight, Pierson, Davenport, and Farnam. I stopped and stared at Connecticut Hall. Nathan Hale, Noah Webster, and Eli Whitney had all resided here. I had once thought that the only impediment to my sharing that residence as well was my poor health.

Several Elis strode by and gave me hostile looks. Another told me point-blank to move on.

Move on I did, walking onto the green: a nine-square lea, three churches at the perimeters staring one another down. To the east I could see Grove Cemetery with its curious Egyptian Gate. Looking north, elm-shaded streets reached toward the mansions of Orange Street and Whitney Avenue. I headed south to where smoke rose from factory stacks and lamps were being lit in the streets.

Wooster Square appeared the true city center. A bustling manufacturing area, the cramped neighborhood was bounded by Winchester Repeating Arms, Toledo Printing, and Harris Brothers Sailworks. Within their arms was a collection of congested tenement buildings and businesses that were run by grocers, butchers, barkeeps, chemists, fishmongers, bakers, stonecutters, milliners, cobblers, and weavers, who looked as diverse as the planet itself.

The briny smell of oysters rose from wooden carts pushed by ragtag vendors, making my stomach growl. I fingered the change in my pocket, worrying over my meager worth and my need of shelter. At least the weather was fine for September. Trees were arrayed in fiery raiment of crimson and orange, cheering me somewhat. I was sure to find a cheap room for the night and a light meal, and if Quillan had forgotten me or hired someone else—or perhaps, as people seemed to do these days, had died—there was no help in anticipating it now.

I happened on a lively block. The factories had just closed for the evening and workers teemed through the streets, stopping at saloons and eating roasted ears from the corn vendors on the street. Dance halls prepared to open and lines formed in anticipation. I eyed the would-be dancers curiously. They were my age but seemed so lighthearted as to make me feel an old man. Eager joes leaned on the walls of the nickel dump, calling to ladies, shouting invitations to dance even before the doors opened. Young women peeled off their work dusters to reveal dance dresses underneath. One man was already drunk, pressing his luck, picking a fight with someone twice his weight, while a girl begged him to lay off. Another practiced a jig while several girls giggled.

Every so often a bright dress made me think of Lill. How she would love to be in a gay line waiting for an evening of luminescent fun. But she was nailed into brown linsey-woolsey, growing distended and tired, swirling potatoes in a pan of buffalo tallow to feed the immotile Ry and his slack-faced brethren.

I bumped into a soft-looking girl with a pleasant round face and brown hair pulled back into a tail. I apologized and she smiled, her eyes trimmed to crescents. She wore a dirt-smudged duster unbuttoned to show a dress with blue flowers underneath. I walked on but turned back to look, for though she was rather nondescript, hardly standing out among other mouse-colored factory girls, she held a large cigar between two fingers. The cigar was unlit; I thought perhaps she held it for a gentleman friend.

She stared back at me as I stared at her and the cigar. She pointed the cigar and left her place in line. "You're not university." She grinned. "Are you a cowboy? You *look* like a cowboy."

I was flabbergasted as she, waiting for a response, bit off the tip of the cigar and spat the nose in the street, unsure if I wanted to draw the attention of such a girl.

"Why do you think I'm a cowboy?"

"Dressed like one. Brown as a Indian too." She walked around me. "I like it. Most boys bore me to *death*."

I looked down, reevaluating my canvas pants and scuffed leather boots. The newspaper I'd stuffed into Tilfert's hatband to keep it from sliding onto my ears was jabbing from the inside. I shifted the big hat, pushing the newspaper away from my temple, put down my valise, and rubbed the sweat from my hand.

She reached down and took my hand, smoothed my fingers open, and looked at my palm. She ran a finger across my hand. "I read palms. You want me to tell your future?"

I pulled my hand back. "I don't think I could handle it."

"Hand-le it. Ha! I'll have to use that one." She extended the cigar. "You got a match?"

I shook my head no.

She stuck the cigar in her mouth, extended her hand to me, palm out, and spoke out the side of her mouth. "Can you read *my* future?" I shook my head again. She wriggled her fingers. "Guess what I do." The tips of her fingers were stained sienna. She looked critically at her hand, then burnished her fingers on her duster and waggled the cigar again. "Tobacco." She pulled two cigars from her pocket. "You want to buy a couple, two bits a roll?"

"I don't smoke."

She looked at me impatiently. "If you buy them, we can go dancing. I'm Phaegin."

"Ned."

She was a pretty girl, even with the brown fingers, but I didn't know how to dance and told her so.

She puffed on the unlit cigar. "Where have you been that you don't know how to *dance*?"

"Fort McPherson, Nebraska." I drew up a little. "Buffalo hunting."

She looked appreciative. "What about the cigars?"

"I'm kind of hungry, actually." I shrugged and then, in spite of my dire financial situation, asked, "Would you like to join me for dinner?" As soon as I'd said it, I was sorry, overcome with a feeling of having done Lill wrong with the offer.

She handed me the cigar, removed the duster, and folded it, revealing the dress she must have been guarding all day. "Sorry. Just got off work. I have two hours"—she thumbed toward the dance hall—"to have some fun before I collapse."

I grinned in relief. She gave me a sharp look, put her hand out for the cigar, and I handed it back. "Maybe I'll see you again, cowboy."

She waved to two young ladies in muslin dresses who waited in the entry line, gave a mock curtsy goodbye, and then turned with advice. "If you're hungry, try Paddy's one street over. The food's not as bad as it is cheap."

"Do you know of a boardinghouse?"

"Men's rooms on Third and Fenton. All the cowboys bunk there."

* * *

As I walked I noticed two men, middle height, both with reddish-brown hair and caps pulled low over their brows, utilitarian jackets, and work boots, leaning against a lamppost some ways down the street. As I set out, they came to attention and began walking behind me. I looked behind twice. The first time, the two slowed and examined another lamppost. The second time, they were gone.

The house on Third and Fenton was a two-story clapboard dormitory with a muddy front yard bereft of shrubs, flowers, or anything green. An obese woman whose tiny features were in peril of being swallowed by her cheeks answered the bell. She blossomed from waist to shoulders with starched ruffles, waist down with a voluminous petticoated skirt, under which spit two tiny feet.

"Hello, hon," she chirruped, "I'm Mother Fenton." She bit the speckled apple in her girlish hand with white button teeth. She must at one time have been an extraordinarily petite girl. She swallowed. "What can we do you for?"

The first week's rent on a six-by-eight first-floor room took most of my remaining funds, and I was doubly relieved the girl at the nickel dump hadn't taken me up on my offer of dinner. Mother pointed to my room up the stairs and to the left. It was just big enough for a bed and boxy bureau, with a lamp set on top. I put my extra pants, shirt, and underwear in the drawer with my pistol, the medal, and my watch, set Lill's photograph on top, and hung my coat and Tilfert's hat on the hook on the door. I sat on the bed, the rope supports creaking, and gazed at the wallpaper.

Mother Fenton knocked and stuck her head in. "Evening meal's down and digesting, but I made you a sandwich." She put a plate and a glass of buttermilk on the little table beside the bed and tapped the wallpaper with a pointed finger. "Chinese newspaper. Mercantile got some dishware wrapped in the stuff. A real curiosity, isn't it?" She stared at it and shook her head. "I wonder and *wonder* what it says. I had a Chink over who cooked for one of the Orange Street families. He told me it was about a fella who made some new kind of writing machine and a piece on some theater hoo-rah. Of course I couldn't believe him. I've seen those people. Figured the fellow couldn't read at all, just put on like he did to save face. They're all about that."

She clapped her hands together. "No mind if it's Sunday, breakfast's at six. Porridge every day; if you don't like it, don't bother to say so. You want pancakes, go down the street where the university fellers lie abed till nine."

Mother Fenton's was an establishment for workingmen, and I came to understand there was no little animosity traveling back and forth between it and the gingerbreaded Beulah Inn, known at Mother Fenton's as the Boola Inn. Every year there was a game of bladder ball between the two houses, after which Mother Fenton tenderly cared for cuts, scrapes, and bruises and even paid to have a broken arm set one particularly contentious season. I decided I would not tell Mother the stratum to which I had been born and where I so fervently hoped to return.

"It's Sunday tomorrow?"

She nodded. "Every week, far as I know. It comes up right after Saturday, son."

After she left, I reclined on the straw-tick mattress and tried not to mind the feel of the ropes supporting the thin pad. I was suddenly stultifyingly tired, and after eating half of Mother

Fenton's lard and tomato sandwich, I wrapped the rest in my handkerchief and fell deeply to sleep.

In the morning I had Mother's porridge then wrote a long letter to Lill. I was careful to be careful. Lill had made it clear that both she and Ry would read our correspondence, and I couldn't risk raising his suspicions or his ire.

I took a nap after the letter, more tired than I'd thought. But when I woke, I felt more energetic than I had in weeks. Stepping out of the hodgepodge boardinghouse, I looked longingly down the street where the patrons ate pancakes and eggs every morning, sandwiches made with meat and cheese, where men had their own physicians on call, and the derision of the impoverished toward the rich was all but undetectable compared to the weight of each of their and their father's thumbs on the little men at Mother Fenton's. In my envious state, I wandered and was almost run over by a dappled gray. Chin, I thought, but the horse was small, blinkered, and braided and looked dull-witted to boot. I chuckled to think of Chin kicking her huge hooves here, but it made me sad and I swore not to think of her again.

Mother told me to head toward the green. The adjacent building of red stone, matching the red stone of the Peabody, was the Chittendon Library. I headed toward the esteemed depository and arrived within a quarter hour. I walked through the heavy double doors into a dim interior. The light through the stained-glass windows glowed deep burgundy, umber, and midnight blue, giving a somber cast to the place.

When my eyes adjusted to the conditions, I didn't look again at the lambent glass; there were more amazing things to see. A trove of hundreds, of thousands, of books, leather binding after leather binding, the titles written on the spines in gold and silver inks: books along the walls and books on heavy oaken shelving, marching in columns from one side of the large room to the other.

I walked from column to column, lifting a tome here and there and taking a taste of what was inside. Geography, the anatomy of the brain, commerce of sovereign nations, pomology of the tropics. Then I saw a familiar shape in the half shadows on the east side of the library. I watched the rotund figure for some time as it hummed and grunted and turned pages; once I was sure of its identity, I hurried over and cleared my throat. "Professor Quillan?"

He turned, slamming shut the book he was perusing with a loud crack. He hurriedly replaced it on the shelves before addressing me. "What do you want?"

I was taken aback at his vehemence. I stammered, "It's Ned."

"Ned?" He waved me off. "I know no Ned. Leave me be."

My heart sank. Had he forgotten? Changed his mind? What would I do? I put out my hand. When I touched him he stepped back and put up his fists, comically prepared to fight.

"Professor Quillan!" I squeaked. "Edward Turrentine Bayard from Nebraska. Fossils."

He loosed his fist into a hand and stuck it at me. "Ned! *That* Ned! Good to see you. I was wondering when you would get here."

I shook his hand with great relief, though the incident made me wonder if he was sane at all. He gave a little chuckle. "Have to say you gave me a start." He leaned closer. "When you work on the cutting edge of scientific inquiry, everyone looks to take what you've found, learn what you've learned, and if that doesn't

131

work"—he winked at me and watched me, one-eyed and nodding
—"if that doesn't work, they're not against taking you *out* of the
field altogether."

He motioned me toward a table, and we sat down. "Surprises
you, doesn't it, Ned? I expect so. The West, now there's a place
where men fight fair. Eye for an eye, bullet for a buffalo."

I couldn't figure out what he was talking about, but I nodded. He continued.

"Science is a corrupt business. Always watch your back. You
work for me, and you will be part of"—he waved his arms in a
circle—"the *whorl* of secrecy." Then he laughed shortly, as if he
were aware of his bizarre appearance.

"You were doing"—I inclined my head toward the stacks—
"some research?"

He looked uncomfortable. "I must go now, my wife will worry.
I will see you in the morning, Ned. Think about what I've told
you. Decide if you have the backbone for it." He eyed me closely
once more, took out a pad of paper, wrote with a flourish, then
handed it to me. "Get a haircut before you come. Give this to
the barber."

I read the note instructing the barber to give me a campaign
cut, noted the address on it, and nodded. After the double doors
closed behind the professor, I stuffed the paper in my pocket
and studied the books where Quillan had stood. In his hurry to
return the tome he was examining, he'd reshelved it upside down.
Coal Extraction in the Coastal Ranges. Why would Quillan be
reading that?

I flipped through the pages, scanning passages here and there;
finding no mention of paleontology, I shrugged and left the
annals of coal and mining and searched out books to my own

taste: Lamarck and the study by the upstart Darwin. By the time my stomach demanded I think of it and not my head, the librarians were lighting lamps. Outside in the shadows, two men stood smoking. I thought about the redheads who had followed me earlier and about what Quillan had said. But as I strode down the street, they did not follow.

CHAPTER 13

New Haven Barber and Shave
34 Branhurst
Mr. Sears—
    Remedy this young man's rat's nest. Give him a campaign cut.
                                          Professor Wallace Quillan

Montgomery Elias
Hartford, Connecticut
Dear Mr. Elias,
    I have lodging at Fenton's Boardinghouse. Please send any further information here. If you see the clerk from Alan and Jamieson, avail him of my address.

Dear Lill and Ry,
    I've made it to the East Coast. I'd almost forgotten what trees look like. The elms are colored like flame with the autumn chill.
    I have connected with Professor Quillan, a man of impressive intellect and stamina. I start work in the morning and am as eager as a child on Christmas Eve.
    It is fine to sleep on a real bed again, duvets and featherbeds instead of flour sacks and straw ticks. The housekeeper is a fine cook, I am, twenty-four hours in, already growing fat. I shall visit the barber and refurbish my wardrobe; there is a fine gentlemen's shop off the green. You will hardly recognize me at day's end. I shall, however, remain,

                                          Ever yours,
                            Edward Turrentine Bayard III

I arrived for my haircut as the barbershop opened. In response to my greeting, the barber merely narrowed his eyes at my shoddy appearance. I gave him the note, hoping the missive would warm his opinion. It did not. The barrel-chested man pointed to a hook where I should hang my jacket and pointed to the nickel chair where I should sit, then picked up his scissors. I had no idea what a campaign cut was and sat down with some trepidation. With the distaste of an earl shearing a sheep, the barber cropped my hair as short as shears would allow, then ran around the outskirts of the newly forested vale with a razor that left my neck pink and sensitive. He slapped a ripe-smelling tincture on the rash, making my eyes water with the sting, and demanded payment.

Itching with the detritus of my transformation, I waited at the Peabody for half an hour before an elderly man dressed in a doorman's jacket walked up the front steps and unlocked the heavy double doors. I asked after Quillan.

The doorman looked me up and down. "Round back. Ring th' bell on th' door."

Quillan opened the heavily paneled door to the lab and looked pointedly at his watch before motioning me inward. The room was filled with stones, ore, bones, and paper, floor to ceiling. It looked less like a laboratory than the interior of a cave, one in which every boulder, every pebble, every shard of bone had a number. Quillan folded his arms from the middle of the room. "What do you think?"

I examined a strange embossing on a rock. "Amazing." Quillan put out his hand and warned not to touch anything, an instruction I found amusing, looking at the array of stones, some still encrusted with western gumbo, that had been wrenched from the earth, pick and shovel. It was of no account. The specimens were as fine and fragile to Quillan as a porcelain vase.

He ran his fingertips over the embossed rock: "Smiledon jawbone." He drew me aside: "Megatherium." Pointed left: "Hadrosaurus, *Equus simplicidens*, Plesiosaur, Ceratops."

I was absolutely awed. Quillan was pleased, throwing out his chest and harrumphing happily. "It is but a drop, a *scattering* of dust, compared to the fossil record that waits to be discovered in the Permian era *alone*." He looked upward to where the fossilized bones of a strange bird flew on gossamer wires. "One day we will have it all, we will have a tome of history in which we can read our story within rifts and ghosts of stone, from the earliest tremor of life to where we now stand!"

He clapped his hands together. "There is work to be done." He pointed into his private office where a chair stood in the middle of the room. I sat.

Quillan opened a cupboard and withdrew a man's bald porcelain head, limned into sections like the ceramic cow at the butcher, as if the bust were a plan for cannibals. Instead of steak, tenderloin, and rump roast, each section was labeled with a number and a curious illustration.

Quillan murmured, "Relax, Ned. This will not take a moment."

My heart dropped. I had been right at the outset. The man was mad.

Quillan commenced to run his fingertips over my head. This must be why he'd wanted my hair so short. Alarmed, I stopped his hand. "Sir?"

Quillan harrumphed. "Phrenology is the only true science of the mind." He slapped my hand, and I dropped it into my lap.

136

He resumed pushing and prodding my skull, narrating as he went. "The brain is the organ of the mind, its different parts manifest distinct faculties, and the power of manifestation in regard to each is proportionate, *coeteris paribus,* to the size and activity of the organ." He referred to the porcelain head on his desk, murmuring, "Prominent frontal development; observant . . . width of the head at the temples bespeaks a resourceful man . . . full crown, stable, ambitious, a strong sense of moral obligation."

I peered at the porcelain head, smooth as a diviner's glass. The images drawn on it were unsettling: two glaring men lifting glasses of ale, a driver beating a horse, a boat capsizing in a quiet sea, a pair of women clutching at each other, a leering cherub.

Quillan's tone changed. "Not good."

"Not good?"

He whipped out a pair of wicked-looking calipers and measured from nape to nose, pricking me with the points. "A mastoid process behind the ear, bony protuberance. . . ."

He crossed his arms and looked sternly at me. "The seventh faculty: secrecy. At its best, a tendency to restrain, with the mind, involuntary thoughts and emotions, but *may* portend cunning duplicity, deceit, and lying." He tapped his nose. "We'll think the best, though it is something to be on guard over, certainly."

"Yes, sir."

Quillan slapped me on the back, the investigation apparently over. "You've a head of magnitude, Edward, well adapted to the life of letters, a bit of a philoprogenitive tendency, unfortunately"—he waggled his finger in chastisement— "affection toward the weak, a weakness in itself. Still, all in all, quite decent, quite decent."

He gazed at me, apparently pleased.

"I *will* take you on. Congratulations, my boy. You shall be instrumental in the grand effort."

He began pacing as if he'd started his engine and couldn't contain himself.

"When I saw your work in Nebraska, I *knew* it to be so. You, Edward, are my luck, my muse. Your draftsman's skills will make possible the next great forty-league stride in paleontology." He shook my hand in a congratulatory way and resumed pacing. "It's all come together, God's will. You see, I had gone to Nebraska, not only to search for fossils but also to clear my head, to find some way out of a dilemma."

"What dilemma, sir?"

He rubbed his thumbs and forefingers together.

I remembered his line. "If money and science could come together?"

"What strides might be made!" Quillan crowed. "Exactly! I am —science is—stymied, obstructed, *impeded* at every turn by want of capital. We two shall be alchemists, turning want into gold."

I nodded, not understanding at all. "How are we to do that?"

"By taking advantage of the passing of the whale."

"Sir?"

"Men are consumers of the dead, Edward. Eat of the dead, warm ourselves by the dead's flame. The whale has lit our way for centuries with its oily corpse. But no longer. The marine behemoth is reduced to lonely survivor. Gone are the great shoals; only sad flinders remain. Men must find other combustion for their dark nights, the remains of the *long* dead, the fossil fuels." He jabbed his finger toward me. "*Fossil* fuels." He nodded wisely.

I continued my clueless nodding.

Quillan took my arm and sat with me, crowding the single chair. "I must have your pledge to secrecy."

I nodded. "You have it."

"I have found . . . a marker, if you will. A means not only of identifying coal deposits but of ascertaining the richness of the veins. Do you know what this means, Edward?" He did not wait for my response but lowered his voice still further so I had to bend over the table to catch his words. "The coal companies can save millions, mining only the richest deposits and bypassing the poor imitators."

He sat back, smug as a toad.

I was still without a clue as to what this meant to paleontology, and certainly what I was to do about it. He slapped his knee. "All this requires full dedication. I trust you, Edward. In my gut, I knew you were the man I could rely on. Can you assure me that I am right?"

"Certainly, sir."

"I think I can." He inclined his head toward the corner of the office as if it were a far distance. "Come with me."

I was relieved to rise from our too-close seating and followed him across the room. Quillan drew out a box. From the box he took three items wrapped in newspaper. He indicated I should examine one.

I unwrapped it. A piece of coal.

"Do you know what this is?"

I leaned closer thinking it must be a trick, a test. I sniffed it. I looked at it from the side, then reported apologetically, "It looks like coal, Professor."

He clapped me on the back again. "Exactly! Common coal.

You can buy it out of a wagon on the lowliest street. A dollar a ton. Coal!"

Quillan laughed at my reaction, put up one finger, then sailed it slowly downward and landed it on the corner. "See here," he whispered. He handed me a magnifying glass. "Look closely."

I took the glass and examined the coal. Where Quillan had pointed was a tiny divot, the size of his fingertip as if he had impressed it in the black himself.

"*Platyceras parva.* An aquatic snail of the Permian."

"In coal?"

"Unexpected, I know. That is the beauty of it."

"Why?"

He whispered again. "I am not only finding fossils in coal, but rife in the material striping the richest anthracitic coal beds. Coal, the hard bed and anthracite in particular, is the future of mechanization, of great industry. If fossils mark coal beds, who will pay for the work of excavation? Hmmm? Yes! Coal is going to be our savior, Ned. No more begging and mewling after university funds, no longer competing against quacks and charlatans for money. The coal companies will be the Medicis of the fossil arts, paying us to search for fossils because of the ultimate advantage to them."

He pushed the handkerchief and coal lump to me. "I need you to draw this. Clean up the lines in the illustration. It is difficult for the layperson to identify a fossil for what it is."

I picked up the coal and studied the small mark. "Are you sure—"

"Of course I'm sure!" He went to the shelf, pulled a box out, and shuffled through the contents. He brought over a fossil embedded in limestone, crisp and clean. "You see? Another *Platyceras.*"

I nodded. "I can see this one."

"Use it for reference if you need to."

I picked up the glass again and peered from one fossil to the other. "I see it now. . . ." I murmured, though it was still no more than a sooty divot to me.

Quillan rifled through the box, pulling out another five coal lumps. "Each one of these also has a fossil. I've marked them." He pulled down another box filled with myriad smaller boxes; inside each, a different type of fossil. Quillan spread his hands proudly. "These are my teaching specimens. Study them, and you may as well have sat through an entire semester of paleontology. Allow these specimens to be your guides when drawing the fossils in the coal, which may be . . . a bit irresolute."

I nodded, as eager to open the stores as if the boxes were filled with pearls. Quillan tapped his pudgy fingers on the lab table's marble surface. "I must have the illustrations as soon as possible. Can you do it?"

"I will work day and night, sir."

He clapped me on the back. "You are going places, Ned. We are going places. The future looks bright indeed."

He put his hat on, and his coat. "I'll let you get to it. In the meantime, I have business to attend to, telegrams to send, contacts to make." He hesitated at the door, flicked the lock on behind him, and put a finger to his lips. "Secrecy, Edward . . . shhh," and the door latched behind him.

I was glad to have the odd professor leave me to my observations. He made me nervous: the inspection of my skull, the cloak-and-dagger mystery, in addition to the coal embedded with virtually imperceptible fossils. I spent only a moment peering at the black depressions. They were so rough as to be laughable.

Perhaps the professor, with his microscope and higher education, had means of ascertaining a fossil over a divot, but the coal held nothing but chips and hollows to my untutored eyes.

I pushed the coal aside and immersed myself in the other fossils. The beauty of the stones was not lost on me, and I was happy to turn the specimens over and over, celebrating the coils of shell, the beads of vertebrae so long preserved.

After a time I found the fossil of a small turtle, its head the size of a pea, its shell a pocket watch. What a change from the Nebraskan behemoth I'd drawn from western soil. It was so fine, a beak as fragile as the most diminutive wren's, hair lines rounding the fingernail scutes, morsel legs. How had it lived in a world of storms and wind and tossing oceans, of claw and craw and appetite? But it had, and if this one had lived, many others must have lived as well.

Truth be told, it gave me some relief. Remembering Lill pointing out that the Nebraska turtle's largeness might actually be a reflection of my own diminutive size, this turtle validated my *substantial* heft. If not gargantuan, I was at least middling. Quillan would not mind my study for a day or two. I would keep it near for a time, feel it between my fingers as I lay on my little bed with quiet and time. I slipped the fossil into my pocket. Within the week I would return the little turtle to its casket.

Quillan returned late afternoon and patted my head, as if I were a hound gifted with a pencil. "We have put the spin on the planet, Ned." He chuckled and retired to his office with barely a glance at my work.

When he finally emerged again, patting his round belly as if remembering its demands, it was after dark. "Good night, Ned."

I had been hungry for some hours, we had not broken for lunch, and I had now missed Mother Fenton's dinner hour. I jingled the few coins in my pocket, further diminished by the barber, and wondered how I would get by. I had no choice but to say something to Quillan, though it embarrassed me to do so. He motioned me out the open door. "Come, come. My wife has dinner waiting." I was hopeful this was an invitation, but Quillan continued. "I will see you tomorrow morning at *seven*, sharp."

I grabbed my coat off the back of the chair. "Professor, would it be possible for you to advance me some pay? I wouldn't ask, but I have nothing for food."

"I left money in Nebraska for you."

"Enough for the ticket only."

He looked a little bewildered. "No good, no good at all." He frowned and sighed. "All right, then, come to the house. I've got cash there."

Quillan lived in one of the fine turreted houses off Prospect with an expansive lawn and whitewashed fence. I waited outside on the porch while he went in. Almost immediately, Mrs. Quillan came out, a fine-boned woman with a mass of auburn hair piled high on her head that must have given her neck some exercise. She was dressed in gray silk; lace flumed from her neckline and sleeves. She was apologetic. "Leaving you on the porch: such manners." She put out her hand. "I am the professor's wife. You are Ned?"

I bowed. "Edward Turrentine Bayard the Third."

"Please come in. The professor mentioned he met you in Nebraska, on his buffalo hunt. What I got out of him sounded so exciting." She sighed and went in.

I walked into the foyer. A splendid hall tree graced the entry with dragon heads clutching coats in their jaws and a plush oriental rug protecting its feet from the marble floor.

"You have a beautiful home."

She smiled and twisted her ring. "It was my aunt's. She didn't have another heir. I suspect I will have to find a niece myself." She glanced upstairs. "I would *so* love to go west. Only four days by train now. Isn't it easy to go so far away?"

"Won't you go with your husband?"

She put her hand to her throat. "No. Professor Quillan goes to work and not to worry about me." She made a stern face. "'No place for a woman. So many dangers.'"

I thought of Lill, how happy she was for a time. "Marriage seems to be the greatest of them."

She laughed delightedly. "And I've already fallen into that trap." She leaned forward. "*Are* there women there?"

"More every day."

Quillan came down the stairs and into the parlor. He counted some bills, arrayed them into a fan. "Your first month's wages."

I took it without counting and thanked him profusely.

"No need to thank me. Wages, that's all there is to it." He turned to his wife. "Sylvia, what has happened to dinner?"

"It's been on the table for half an hour now, Wallace." Mrs. Quillan twisted her ring again. "Would you stay and eat with us, Mr. Bayard?"

Quillan shook his head. "Of course not, Mrs. Quillan. He's a young man, not prone to keeping company with us old folks." He chuckled, pleased with the observation.

Quillan and his wife exchanged glances, as if each was still, after ten years of marriage, wondering what the other was.

"Thank you, but I should take care of some business." I tipped my hat to Mrs. Quillan, who looked disappointed. "Professor, thank you."

He waved me off. "Seven sharp, sir. No more lying abed till eight."

CHAPTER 14

Dear Edward,

I am pleased to hear you are sailing ancient seas as captain of science, first rank. Continue to enthrall me with your exploits in academe and keep up the good and valued work, friend. One may easily add to ignorance, but it is blessed to advance knowledge.

As for myself, I have found more humble employment, serving as teacher for the town of Hammond, Indiana. Though the town is newly sprung and correspondingly rough, teaching here is gratifying work, if frustrating at times. So many of my students are in and out, threshing, planting, and milking being of greater importance than education. Still, if it were not for the little larnin' they get here, they would get none at all.

Elizabeth is not well. Ill-suited for rough edges and her family will not sneeze in her direction.

Brill

Dear Brill,

My illustrations of Semitherium equus *will accompany a paper the professor presents to the Geographic Society in April!*

Dear Lill and Ry,

It is blessed to advance knowledge. I spend my days in scholarly recourse, my education apportioned by the estimable Quillan. His home, at which I am a frequent visitor, is grandiloquent as to be near unbelievable, and is certainly the bar to which I endeavor. He insists on my seeing his tailor, but I care not to take advantage of the good man's generosity.

Quillan was a demanding taskmaster, and though I was discomfited by the ephemeral coal specimens, I was sidetracked by the education of image, the language of line, a semaphore of ink. A broken line reveals to a scientist certain meanings, as does the stippling of texture. One must not utilize a simple contour when a thick line is called for, just as one may not use a dit for a dot when speaking Morse code to the fellow on the other end of the line.

Further, though Quillan seemed uninterested in educating me in anything but the most prosaic craft of illustration, I fattened my understanding of the work by reading book after book in the Yale library, or borrowed from the lab, and read in the evenings at Mother's table or in my boardinghouse bed.

I had a strange sense of being carried upriver, going against the current of time, bereft of the present, steeped in the past. I woke before dawn, arriving at the museum in mist and gloom and did not leave until night had fallen. As I labored, the late fall rains gave way to early winter snow.

Quillan was thrilled with my drawings, though I constantly worried he would notice I drew not from the coal lumps but from the teaching specimens. I hesitated to reveal my neophyte vision, afraid that if he understood my inability to see the precious black fossils for anything more than scratchings in the soft surface I would be fired for my ignorance. The more he told me what good work I did, the more I wished to please him, and the longer my hours ran.

My correspondence with Brill, in which I masqueraded as scientific giant, finally pinched my scruples hard enough to force me to broach the subject of my actual failings to Quillan.

He was leafing through the pages of illustrations I had finished, nodding and murmuring. I cleared my throat. "I am pleased, Professor, that you are so . . . pleased. . . ."

"Good work, Ned, good work, yes."

"However."

Quillan's head snapped up. "What is it? I suppose you want a raise? Be patient, Ned, be patient. When our project is complete, you are assured of your piece of the pie. Can't help you until then."

"No, sir. I wasn't . . . it's the fossils. Truth be told, I have not been able to make heads or tails of them. They still look little more than abrasions to me."

The professor crossed his arms. "And yet your drawings are magnificent."

"I've actually been drawing from the teaching specimens, and I'm feeling much the imposter because of it, sir."

Quillan pushed away from the desk. "Have you heard further from your mother, Edward?"

"Nothing."

"Unbeknownst to you—I didn't want to get your hopes up—I've had feelers out." He wriggled his fingers as if he himself had tickled out the information. "Your mother is living in England, married to a maker of condiments, mustards, and the like."

He opened his desk drawer and pulled out a sheet of paper, looked at it, then handed it to me.

"My God, you've found Mother?" I murmured, as I took the form. The paper had my mother's name, my father's name, and my own. Below them, the name *Reggie Snook, Snook Mustard Works, Devon, England,* and the date of Mr. Snook's marriage to my mother, in New York City, one month after she had put me on the train to Nebraska.

Professor Quillan smoothed back his hair. "If you would like, I will put my man on finding an address so you may send a message."

I stared again at the paper, still trapped by *married* and *mustard*. Mr. Jamieson said the man was a purveyor of pickles and that my mother had not left for England until well after the auction, which did not occur until I had been in Nebraska for at least two months.

I shook the paper. "I have obviously been strung along, Professor. It is beyond bearing. It is corrupt and degenerate, and I must get to the bottom of this . . . this wanton deception!" Though tremendously flustered, I glanced at Quillan. He looked irate and had stiffened his backbone. I remembered my manners. "Professor Quillan, it is amazingly generous of you to have gone to this trouble, and I cannot tell you how I appreciate it."

Quillan relaxed. "Not at all, Ned. I want to help you. You see, I have not been blessed with children, and it seems, viewing Mrs. Quillan's fragile health, that is not likely to change."

Quillan sighed and looked so dysphoric, my heart wrenched. He supported his chin with one hand.

"I suppose it is not surprising that I have transferred what paternal feelings I would have for my own flesh and blood"—he straightened and smiled, inclining his head my way—"to you, Ned.

"I will help you find your mother and, further, take it on myself to give you the attention a young man needs. That attention, I may assure you, includes following your progress in the laboratory. Certainly, I can see that you *feel* you are not progressing at the speed at which you would like. You suffer from a lack of detailed and sensitive vision. Why do you think I gave you the teaching specimens? For the same reasons one stretches the net under the callow gymnast."

He stood to look out the window into cold daylight. "Given time, my boy, you will educate your eye and your mind, and your cloak of ignorance will be pushed aside. Until then, I want you to soldier on. Keep up your good work, my boy, make your mother proud, for soon you will be telling her of all your accomplishments. And *do not worry*. If I thought something was amiss, you can be assured I would intercede."

My head was spinning. Certain now I could not trust anything Alan and Jamieson had said, I was more than relieved to hear Quillan pledge his intent to find my mother and facilitate our communication. I felt my burden lightened and, further, I was touched. Quillan had good as called me *son*. He tracked down my mother to set my mind to rest. I thought he saw nothing but product, but on the contrary he cared about me and had faith I would overcome my shortcomings. I was not so naive as to believe that kindness was solely at the heart of his actions, but I did think I touched upon some paternal office in his ambitious soul, and—as one long deprived of anything paternal—it affected me deeply. "I will soldier on, sir."

"Good man." He sat back at his desk and waved me off. "Get to it, then."

I was a little unsettled by the change in tone. "My mother?"

"What about her?"

"I *would* like to send word to her, if I might."

"Certainly, of course. Write to your heart's content. You can send the good woman an entire trunk of letters, as soon as we get the address from my man." He laughed a little at his joke.

"Thank you, sir, thank you."

He looked off into space, frowning a little. "Never had much of a relationship with my own mother. Frankly, it is foreign to me that someone would want the complication of it, much less go scrambling after—"

He glanced at my surprised face.

"My want makes me all the more pleased to facilitate someone else's relationship, however. Even . . . grateful . . . in a way that I can ensure its ongoing . . . health. But enough of this sentimentality. We have work to do."

CHAPTER 15

Dear Mother,

I know nothing but the most spectral details of your where-abouts and your situation. I pray this soon remedied with the help of my mentor, the estimable Wallace Quillan. I am in the employ of the Peabody Museum and am in such fine health as you have never seen me. But there is so much more I want to tell you, if ever we are reunited.

Your son, Edward

The Christmas season arrived before I knew it. I mailed Lill a fine pen that cost me more than my week's room, imagining her opening the gift, shining and golden, while surrounded with the brown life of the prairie. What would Osterlund give her? A stewpot, perhaps, or a bolt of service-able cloth from which to shear diapers.

Professor Quillan, in a burst of Dickensian good feeling, invited me to his home for Christmas Eve dinner. Though he continued to call me *son*, he hardly treated me with more warmth than he gave the janitor. Therefore, I was greatly heartened by the invitation.

The first snows had melted, but on Christmas Eve it was finally cold enough, long enough, to keep the picturesque white shrouding on the streets and lawns. I rang the professor's bell at the appointed hour. Even as Mrs. Quillan opened the door, which was decorated with a pine wreath shining with glass balls, the professor shouted from inside, "Let the housekeeper get it, you forget your place!"

It hit me again what a beautiful woman Mrs. Quillan was, as pale and fine as Quillan was ruddy and stout. It was a pleasure to see something lovely again, especially as she seemed very pleased to see me. She showed no sign of hearing her husband's complaint but put out a hand as soft as petals. A smile lit her lovely face. "Ned!"

I bowed.

"Please come in."

The housekeeper took my coat and Mrs. Quillan led me into the parlor for a cordial before dinner. An enormous spruce was afire with candles set on aluminum reflectors. Hand-blown ornaments in the shapes of birds and snowmen, pinecones and peppermints shimmered with the light.

Mrs. Quillan patted the settee and handed me a ruby glass when I took the place beside her. "The professor is fussing with his cravat and will be down when the knot is to his satisfaction." She smiled. "So we may talk. I have been more than anxious to hear your stories. Tell me, Ned—anything and everything about wild Nebraska!"

I told her about Lill, about the homesteading families who arrived with wives and daughters. Her pale countenance took on color and she grew even more animated as I told her about the buffalo and the rolling plains. I made her laugh to the point of tears telling her about my travails with Chin.

Quillan came down the stairs and into the parlor. He took Mrs. Quillan's chin in his hand and looked at her critically. "Are you feverish? Your eyes are preternaturally bright."

Mrs. Quillan tossed her head. "Of course not, Professor."

Professor Quillan patted her hand. "Mrs. Quillan is my porcelain *vas*. See how fragile—her skin is so fine, almost transparent really. It is my second employment to keep her from harm's way."

"Professor, you do me an injustice." Mrs. Quillan smiled at me. "I am strong as a horse. If the professor would allow, I would lose this limpidity of mine and do some good in the world."

"My dear, you are like Hiram's marbles. It is enough good done for the world to allow us to gaze upon you. Few others can do so much."

Dinner was a masterpiece of yellow squash soup and crusty bread, prime rib, Yorkshire pudding, and Derby salad, followed by pumpkin, raisin, and pecan pies, topped with fresh cream. I barely spoke, being engaged with nothing but the tasting and eating of fine food. Mrs. Quillan laughed. "Professor, we must feed Ned more often. Look at the poor thing; he is virtually starving."

"Nonsense. A young man has better things to do. Eh, Ned?"

I swallowed, wondering if he wasn't aware that all my time was spent at the lab, or in some hours of sleep at the boardinghouse. "I would be most pleased to share the fine food and fine company of your household, Mrs. Quillan. I think this is the best meal I have ever eaten in my life."

Mrs. Quillan laughed. "You see, Professor?"

Professor Quillan harrumphed.

Mrs. Quillan rang a bell. The housekeeper came in and Mrs. Quillan directed her to bring the packages.

The professor frowned. "Packages, Mrs. Quillan?"

"*Small* things, Professor. Tiny celebrations." She handed a small box to me and a larger one to the professor. "You first, Ned."

Inside the box was a brass telescope small enough when compacted to fit inside my palm but extendable to eight inches. Thanking her profusely, I peered out the window and could see the family across the way at their dinner. The children around the table wore Christmas wrappings folded into party hats. The father laughed, his bald head topped with a bow.

Mrs. Quillan pressed the professor to open his gift. He carefully untied the ribbon, and the paper fell away. His face grew red. "What is this?"

Mrs. Quillan looked alarmed. "I was told it was the finest encyclopedia to date on fossils."

Incredibly, the professor threw it to the floor. "It is *not*, I assure you. The author is a scurrilous wag. I would as soon have a skunk in the house as that book."

"He seemed a very nice man." She rose from her seat, rushed over, and picked up the book, opening it to the frontispiece. "He wrote the most charming inscription."

"You *spoke* to him?"

"Yes." Mrs. Quillan squared her shoulders, and her quiet voice took on an edge. "I went to a great deal of trouble to find this gift, to *go* to his reading, and to get it signed for *you*, Professor."

"You went to a great deal of trouble to fund a cheat and a thief!" He took the book from his wife's hands and began flipping through it. "Wrong!" he shouted. "Wrong! And this, this is *mine!*" He pointed to another page. "Pure fiction." He turned and shouted to the housekeeper. "Mrs. Bryan!" He shoved the book into the housekeeper's arms. "Burn it!"

Mrs. Quillan's chin went up, her hands curled into fists, her lips tightened, yet she walked sedately to her chair. "Of course,

I couldn't know, *Professor*. If, perhaps, you would *speak* to me of your work. . . . Mrs. Bryan, if you please, after disposing of *that*"—she nodded at the book—"serve the coffee."

Professor Quillan tugged his waistcoat. "The men will have ours in the den."

Mrs. Quillan's face flushed. "I will bid you good night, then. Ned, please come by again. I did so enjoy your stories."

I thanked her again for the gift, my own face aflame for her, then followed Professor Quillan into his den, where we stood awkwardly until Mrs. Bryan left a tray.

The professor tossed a nugget of sugar into his mouth and slurped his coffee. "In the future, Ned, do *not* indulge Mrs. Quillan's thirst for adventure tales. It wears on her, as you can see. I will be up for hours tonight while she is in a generally overstimulated if not hysterical condition. I will consider myself lucky if it doesn't last for days." He popped another piece of sugar. "I will call our physician, a pity on a holiday, but he has been out to us on others. Holidays—magnifiers of emotions. I have oft thought to ban them in our household entirely." He hissed to himself. "Imagine *talking* to that man. A scurrilous imposter and she thought him charming?" Quillan put on a small smile. "My beautiful wife is a *particularly* gullible and sensitive woman among a clan markedly so. Our marriage has been one of keeping her on even keel."

"I'm sorry. I didn't know."

"How could you? Not to say she isn't well worth the trouble." His face softened momentarily. "*Well* worth the trouble." He popped the last nugget in his mouth and motioned toward the library door. I gulped my coffee and followed him out.

"Professor Quillan, I was wondering, have you yet heard anything from your contact? I have a letter I would like to send to my mother."

"Hmm. Perhaps, come to think of it, there *is* a missive at the lab I took to be nothing but a bill—no hurry in opening *that*, eh? However, it might indeed provide further information. Check with me the twenty-sixth, will you, Ned? Now, I'm sorry, but I have a . . . situation . . . to deal with."

I thought, from the foyer, I could hear crying, but it was only the cat, which ran in mewling when Quillan opened the door.

I went around the side on my way back to Mother's. Mrs. Bryan had tossed the book in the burning bin but had not lit the match. I opened the cover and read the inscription: *To my fellow sailor on the seas of the past, may your substantive wind fill your sails. Charles Laramore.* I turned a page. Judging from the credentials listed below his name, if Laramore was a cheat and a thief, he was an eminent one from Harvard. I flipped through thick text and hundreds of illustrations. Even reading briefly, I couldn't believe the paleontologist was the quack Quillan said he was. The writing was concise, that of a man experienced and insightful. He could be a thief, however. There were illustrations of specimens he claimed to have discovered that I'd seen, dated seven years before, in Quillan's lab.

Mrs. Quillan had claimed him as a charming man. Of course, there was no precluding a man from being both debased and charming; look at Buck Mason. I glanced back at the blank windows of the Quillan house and, seeing no one watching, pushed the book under my coat.

CHAPTER 16

Dear Lill and Ry,

I attended Christmas Eve festivities at the professor's mansion. This morning I recuperate from rich food and elevated conversation in deep featherbed laziness. I will soon arise to find what Christmas holds for me. I hope yours proves to be as jolly as my own.

Christmas Day was white and silent. I was intent on using much of it in the pursuit of indolence, enjoying the warmth under Mother's floursack quilts and, when awake enough, reading the book I'd saved from the burning bin. Until then, I ruminated on the strangeness of the evening before and, discomfited, stared at the Chinese characters on the wallpaper.

Mother Fenton claimed the Chinese cook was making up the stories of accomplishment on those pages, but she had only met orientals hobbled by our own culture. The Chinese had discovered gunpowder, porcelain, the printing press, had dynasties that lasted longer than the United States had been a country. And yet its citizens flocked to the States to be worked to death on the railroads, in our kitchens, washing laundry, and killing chickens. Why? A new land, a new West, the lure of the sun's path. Follow it, become rich, become strong, golden as light.

But gold doesn't often sit on the surface. It must be wrenched from its stone cradle through misery of one kind or another, bent, broken, detonated. Once acquired, keeping it has a cost. I thought once more of Peter the Great. How did it end for him? Was he wretched at the loss of his son? Did he find that being great was a bitter road, followed by an unendurable destination?

I got up from my bed and peered at the drawing of a Chinese sleeve dancer that could have come from a vase or a scroll. They say the Chinese drown their daughters, sell them into slavery, abandon them to mountains. I didn't believe it. I had never seen a Chinese woman, not in a kitchen, not on the railroad. The sleeve dancer had a beautiful coil of hair on her head, decorated with a pagoda of tiny bells, and a small smile on her rosebud lips. I imagined the Chinese revered their women, protected them; otherwise they would be sent to America instead of the men, less workers than work itself, a club to be swung until worn to nothing.

How was Lill faring in her days of unending toil? Oh, if she had only been born Chinese, she too would be sitting with a sable brush in hand, drawing black ink poetry onto lotus paper. I wondered if Lill had opened my present. Was she at this moment writing verse or a letter to me? It had been long since I'd heard from her.

Mother knocked on my door. "Are you ailing, Mr. Ned?"

I leapt back to the protection of the quilt and shouted from my bed. "Stay away! I am *trying* to sleep in."

She unlocked the door in spite of my protests. She was in flushed high humor. "Sleeping in's for toffs. Get yurrself up; we have Christmas porridge today and toddies to keep you warm. She grinned and chirruped. "If you sleep through your free day, you won't even know you had it."

Christmas porridge was everyday porridge with some hair-raising alcoholic beverage in it, the same that gave the toddies their punch. The men were, at half past eight in the morning, pickled in alcohol-induced high humor, which in turn effected outbreaks of wrestling, bursts of scatological japery, and much more loud slurred drinking. Yet, even with the song and laughter, the sight of those lonely men, drinking to forget that they had no one else but other lonely boarding men to celebrate Christmas with, was sad. Especially as I was one myself.

I tried to feign felicity, but after I was pinned to the floor by a trolley operator in an unsolicited grappling match, I pulled on my boots and went out.

The Boola Inn down the street was quiet, the Yale students having all gone home to warm houses, roast turkeys, and lavish gifts. I threw a snowball at the neat siding, then skidded along the sidewalk, pretending I was skating, with my beautiful Lill in scarlet hanging on my arm. After a bit, my head cleared enough to notice my stomach growling. I was terribly hungry, but the shops were closed. I doubted Mother was in any shape to lay food on the table. I'd left her spinning like a top to a raucous chorus of "See you at the bottom o' the barrel tonight," her hair having escaped its bun so the line between youth and age was visible in the gray and brown hair. Still, I was about to turn back and search her kitchen for bread when I saw Phaegin. She was gazing into a shop window at a display of rings and bracelets atop a cotton snowbank. I counseled myself to walk on, but my hunger was for more than food. I crossed the street. "Hello. Remember me?"

She jumped, then grinned. "Don't cowboys celebrate Christmas?"

I shrugged. "Looks like the same way you do."

"All cheapjack and woe." She laughed and stuck out her hand, shaking mine with a great deal of vigor. "I thought you'd gone back to Indian country. What've you been doing?"

"Working. Seven days a week."

She grinned. "Bastards." She chuckled at my shocked face, then linked her arm with mine. "*I* say we liven up a corked day. What do you want to do?"

My stomach pinched. "Eat."

Phaegin towed me along. "Don't tell me you're *still* looking for dinner! All this time without a bite? What can I expect? Not a buffalo or a rattlesnake for you to chew on in the whole state of Connecticut."

Phaegin took me to a hole-in-the-wall tavern in the basement of one of the tenement houses. Planks set up on carpenter's horses served as a bar and tables. A drunken group of elderly men sang Christmas carols in a thick brogue. Phaegin spoke to a fat man in the back, and he came out with a steaming plate of kedgeree. I tucked into the rice and fish, my upper lip sweating with the spice. Phaegin whistled.

I looked up apologetically. "I was so hungry, and this is excellent. I told my hostess dinner last night was the best meal I'd had. I think I'd have to hedge with this one."

Phaegin lit her cigar off the lamp. "Hostess? Are you courting?"

"Boss's wife." I told her about Professor and Mrs. Quillan and the strange evening. "I feel sorry for her," I confided.

Phaegin nodded. "Ah, yeah, the poor woman. Eating all them fine foods, living in that turrible state of shine and loveliness. She don't even get the thrill of figuring how she's gonna make it through tomorrow."

I eyed Phaegin and her soft curves. "You don't eat enough?"

She puffed the cigar. "For now, but I'd like to be a *truly* fat woman, and not potato fat neither." She looked at the cigar. "And this, while it's the best job I ever had, don't pay pork chops."

I nodded and finished off the kedgeree. "Still, he didn't even get her a Christmas present."

"For pity sake. Every day is Christmas for a woman like that." Phaegin blew smoke rings in the air. "Nine. I can do fifteen. Want to see?"

"Nine of them gave me the idea."

She extended the cigar to me. "You try."

"I'm not a smoker. My lungs are bad."

"Then you should smoke for your health. Kills the smut in your chest."

I took the cigar from her and took a small puff and coughed. I handed it back and took a drink. "I don't care for it."

Phaegin took it. "Of course you don't. You have to work at it. Pleasure is nasty until you've earned it."

I scoffed. "Pleasure is immediate."

She gave me a pained look. "Nah, comes with practice."

"What about cake? No one practices liking cake."

"Does a newborn babe want cake? No. A baby only wants milk. He has to learn to eat, and doesn't like it, I'll tell you."

I knew nothing about babies, so I would have to take her word for it. "Milk's a pleasure, then."

"No. A baby doesn't even want to be born, much less nurse. Wants to stay where it is. Doesn't want breathing, doesn't want smell or taste: no milk, no cake, no cigars." She took a long drag on the cigar and handed it to me. She motioned to take another drag. I pulled on the cigar, coughed again, my head spinning.

Phaegin looked critically at the cigar, stubbed it out, and wrapped it in her handkerchief for later.

"Come on, let's have a go with Christmas. Can you sing?"

In the corner of the tavern, a stick-thin man began sawing a fiddle like mad while another fellow beat a drum to another's guitar strumming. We stood with the trio of musicians amid a crowd of enthusiastic revelers to sing "Silent Night," "O Tannenbaum," "A Midnight Clear," and a host of carols I had never heard of. Nog was passed around, and more men and some women came through the door and joined us in the circle. The songs left Christmas and we sang "Danny Boy" and "Loch Lomond." More nog and the songs shifted into downright bawdy, "The Petticoat Left Behind" and Mother's "Bottom of the Barrel," while the rowdy congregation laughed and shouted more than they sang. I lost track of time as well as any sense of inadequacy after downing my third nog. By the fourth, I was reeling.

Phaegin showed me a few dance steps, characterized as far as I could see by haphazard and energetic stomping. I stomped away to the laughter of the others. No sylphen ballerina ever provided more pleasure to its audience than I did that night. Phaegin finally took pity on me and led me from the floor to a chair. "I don't know if you are truly so bad at dancin' or if it's the drink, but you'll hurt yourself if you keep on."

From my seat I watched the revelers, feeling warm and happy. Phaegin waved every time she came around the circle, stepping quick with her skirt in her hands. She switched it back and forth, laughing with her head back.

The trouble was, being part of the circle of dancers was great fun, but *watching* them was giving me vertigo. My head spun faster and I had trouble focusing. The crowd blurred into color and noise and disappeared into another place entirely. I wiped my forehead and stared at my feet.

The last time I'd danced was at Avelina's wedding, and the thought of her and Tilfert, their big leathery hands clasped as they waltzed, rose against my alcohol-weakened defenses and toppled them. I sat staring at the wrinkled leather of my boots, trying to stave off tears and loneliness and the mean teeth of guilt.

Phaegin put her hand on my shoulder. "Ned, are you well?"

I shook my head. "Not at all."

She sat down and took my hand. "What is it? I shouldn't have let you drink that way."

"It's not the whiskey." Her hand was small but strong. I turned it over and stared at her brown fingers. Avelina would approve. "Nothin' wrong with the mark of work, Ned," she'd told me. The memory seemed a sign, and so, with slurred address, I introduced Phaegin to Avelina and Tilfert. I told her everything about them, while keeping Lill to my heart's counsel.

Phaegin listened carefully, nodded, leaned on her hand, elbow on the table, and listened some more. When I was done, I moaned, "How could they? It's so wrong."

Phaegin took a minute. "I wouldn't say wrong, Ned. Avelina don't sound like she was wrong at all. Neither one. Maybe it was more . . . a *mistake.*"

"A *mistake?*" I snorted. "That's a pretty big mistake for either one of them to have made, and I believe they made it *over and over again.*"

"Not that. Not *their* mistake."

I didn't understand. "Whose?"

Phaegin looked upward, and I followed her gaze upward toward the offices on the second floor.

"Accountants?"

She slapped my arm. "Don't be daft! *God.* God's mistake."

I closed my eyes and shook my head. "Phaegin, Phaegin."

She sat back. "Don't go and tell me there are no mistakes, Ned Bayard. I've been to Barnum's. I seen the little baby with legs like a fish. The man with only one arm. My auntie's got a beard better than me da's. You wanta tell me my brother's brain wouldn't be in better service to a *squirrel* than it is to him?" She sat forward. "I talked to a black man once. He talked like the poshest posh you ever met. Had a book under his arm 'e wrote 'imself. If God put a white man in a black man's skin, why couldn't he have put a lady in a feller?"

I nodded. Perhaps she was right.

Phaegin was very pleased with herself. "And that Tilfert, he was the only one smart enough to see it. Saw with *piercin' vision* to what lay under all those layers to the pure heart beatin' underneath, the *fair lady* Avelina truly was."

She'd had me for a minute, but this was a bit much. I laughed. "Avelina mighta been a woman underneath it all, but she sure wasn't a *fair lady*." The thought of Avelina with a parasol tickled me, my sorrow broke, and I laughed until I almost fell off my chair.

I pulled myself together with yet another mug of drink and lurched away from the blurry chair to sweet Phaegin, toward whom I was feeling transcendentally warm. "Do you have a boyfriend, Phaegin? You must have them coming out of the woodwork."

She stood up and put her hands on my chest. "Not a one, and that's the way I'm keeping it, so no funny business. I'm an independent woman and ain't about to mess it up sellin' myself into marriage."

I took her hand in mine. "I wanna dance with you. You're the prettiest thing I've seen since Lill. And I haven't felt happy, not really really happy, since way back before. Now she won't even write to me, after all we've been through. But *you've* made me happy. So now I want to dance with *you*."

"Ned, you are drunk as a dog."

"Dogs drink?" As my knees sagged, she caught me around the waist.

"Come on, Neddy boy. You need to go home. Get outside, and the cold'll wake you up."

"You smell good."

She laughed. "Sweatin' like a dockworker and you think I smell good."

"And you're soft, and so pretty. Prettiest thing I've seen since Lill Martine."

"Yea, yea, I heard that."

She draped my coat around my shoulders, leaned me against the wall, and put her own coat on. Outside, the cold felt good. I rubbed my face.

"That's right, wake yourself up there, Ned. Where are you staying, Mother Fenton's?"

I nodded and gulped at the air. She took my arm and put it around her shoulders. I waved at the clear night stars. "Sky's so pretty. This has turned into my best Christmas ever."

"You *are* a miserable character then, aren't you?"

I nodded. Tears came to my eyes. "I was sick my whole life, then my mother married a pickle barrel, and now it's Christmas."

"That *is* sad. Well, glad I could cheer you up."

"When will I see you again, Phaegin, prettiest thing since—"

"Lill, I know, whoever." We stopped in front of Fenton's. I was sufficiently chilled to stand upright on my own. She gazed at me a minute before saying, "I have a week before I get busy again. I work at the cigar shop off the green. You want to go dancing, real dancing, we could go after work."

"Am I your boyfriend?"

She laughed. "Your ears ain't so sharp, are they? We can have some fun, but that's *it*. Bet you won't feel so good tomorrow, though."

She reached up and kissed me on the cheek, then patted her pockets and handed me two cigars. "Merry Christmas, Ned."

I was terribly touched at the gift. "Thank you, Phaegin." I patted my pockets. I pulled out the tiny turtle fossil. "This is for you."

She peered at it. "A *rock*." Slipped it into her pocket. "Why, *thank you*, Ned."

She knocked on the door. Mother answered, a rag tied around her head so that she looked like a corpulent pirate. She groaned, looking at me. "Between you, me, and the rest, this'll be a sorry house in the mornin'."

CHAPTER 17

Dear Ned,

I have had the child. So tiny no one thought she would live. I was not well myself. Had baby Lucy died, I would have followed. But she, though tiny, was strong and gave me courage to continue.

I expect great things of my beautiful girl, that she will excel where I have not.

Love, Lill

At dawn, Mother poured some vile concoction down my throat, waddled on to the next room, and dosed that occupant. "No sense in getting fired on top of being sick as dogs!" she squawked to the house. "This will teach you men to drink your days away. Work hard at your jobs, find yourselves a good woman, have at least five children to look after ye in your declining years, and *never pick up the bottle again.*"

The brew she dosed us with did no good at all. Judging by the reeling green reaction of myself and the rest of the boarders, she may have done it just to get us out the door in fear of a second go.

It does not rain but pour. As I escaped Mother's, I noticed a letter on the foyer table addressed in Lill's hand. Walking to the lab, I read it.

A baby. Though I had known it was coming, I felt a chill travel down my neck and down my back. I tried to imagine my bright Lill, distended and pale, an infant sucking at her breast, but could not. It didn't seem possible that she had a real child with hunger, weight, and a name. I entertained the evil wish the child had died. Lill, untethered, would have come to me. Certainly, I'd soon have means to provide her the life she deserved. Clouding my cruel fantasy was the knowledge that Lill, instead, was now doubly anchored to Osterlund.

I got to the lab and closed the door against the blinding light on the snow, put my head on the table, and waited for my organs to calm.

Quillan, emerging from his office, recoiled as though I were a snake. "Are you sick?" He put his sleeve to his face. "The flu is going around again."

I waved off the idea. "A little to drink yesterday."

He scowled and dropped his arm. "I do *not* expect a day off to result in two days off, Edward."

I sat up straight and tried to compose myself. "No, sir. And how is Mrs. Quillan?"

"She will be herself soon. Over the years she has bounced back from these episodes of hers ever more quickly. I am hopeful she will outgrow them altogether. They're a *damned nuisance*."

He was so irritated, I hesitated to ask him about the correspondence about my mother, so I worked through the hours, miserably.

The day was torture, and not only because of my head and stomach. The quiet of the lab had shifted from the muffled hallow of science and thought to out-and-out gloom: the clock ticking dutifully, dust of the long dead sifting through the impotent light of winter. Quillan, in his office, moved like a shade behind frosted windows, while I longed painfully for my mother's hand, wishing to pour out my heart to her. Though she had abandoned me, I yet believed in her love. I could not bear otherwise.

169

I stood to query Quillan for her address again, but the professor shouted and growled from inside his office, and I slumped back down.

The draw of my pen was thin. The paper was thin. I suddenly thought of Avelina looking at a drawing I'd done of an axle tree. "It's a beaut likeness, Ned. But why draw it when you kin look at the real thing?"

Why indeed? I put my head in my hands. Had my scientific spirit been exterminated in one night of merriment? Not exterminated, overshadowed. I was horribly lonely.

With that, I wondered what Phaegin must think of me and of all I told her. For a man who had hardly lived until a year ago, I carried a weight of skeletons on my back enough to belabor a workhorse.

I imagined Chin standing by the railroad track. It was bitterly cold in Nebraska now. "If the livery doesn't feed her, I'll kill them," I vowed, but this did little to assuage my conscience over the big horse, head down, drifted in. I groaned.

Quillan opened the door of his office, his arm shielding his face once more. "I am not convinced you are not contagious. There is quite a foreign population at that boardinghouse of yours. You may well have picked something up, and *I* don't have the time to get it. Go to bed, Ned. Don't come back until you've recuperated . . . but make it snappy."

I snatched at opportunity. "My mother's address, sir?"

He waved me off. "Not *now*. Out with you, out!"

Bells sounded as I entered the dim cigar shop, thick with spicy aromatic notes of tobacco leaves. Cubbyholes from floor to ceiling were filled with oily rolls of leaves. A glass case, dividing the room side to side, displayed stacked balsa wood boxes of cigars, in myriad sizes and prices. Even with the frigid outside temperatures I could feel leaking through its glass, the shop was hot and humid. Phaegin smiled when she saw me, her hair curled damply around her face. A sheen of warm moisture arose on my lip.

A somber man bowed formally to me. His rugose skin the same shade as the lightest tobacco; his handlebar mustache dyed a telltale blue-black; while his thick hair, on his scalp, in his ears, and beetling in a long stripe across his brow, was candescent silver. He asked, with a lilt to his voice, "Sir, may I help you?"

Phaegin shook her duster free of tobacco. "Mr. Cordassa, this is Ned. May I take leave, please?"

He pulled a silver watch from his waistcoat. "It is early, but a slow day." He bowed to her as well. "You may go, Miss Harte."

She curtsied back. "Thank you."

Phaegin grabbed her coat and bag. The old man watched her with a faint smile as one would watch a particularly winsome puppy. As Phaegin left, she pecked him on the cheek, and his faint smile grew, even as he waved her off with a flap of large hands and a "Shew, shew, Miss Harte."

"You like your boss," I observed, after the shop door rang shut.

Phaegin, holding her bag in her mouth as she threw on her coat, nodded. She spit out the clutch. "Very much. Came from Cuba, a *tremendously* rich man there. There was some revolt and he left with a knife at his back. Now he barely gets by, sends all he can back to what family he's got left, and he's a gentleman to everyone, and I mean everyone: me, the guttersnipe who delivers the oil paper, the rag lady. If I didn't have the future to think about and didn't hate brown fingers, I'd be happy."

I took her hand and looked at her fingertips. "Nothing wrong with work, and I suppose you'll be marrying before you know it."

She snorted as she pulled her hand back. "Men just can't bear to hear someone refusing to enter into the exalted state of marriage. My brothers foam at the mouth when I turn down one of their port-rat pals. Like I told you last night, I *won't* marry."

She spit on her fingertips, rubbed them on her coat, and held them up to show no effect. "I tried peroxide, lemon, bleach, pumice, arsenic powder. None of them work enough, and some of them took the skin off, but not enough to take the stain away. I figure I'm brown to the bone by this time."

"What's wrong with marriage?"

"You're either a bauble, like that Mrs. Quillan, or a slave. Actually, I might think about it if I could be a bauble, but as it stands the only opening for *my* sort is slave. So I'm going to open a shop when I get the money."

"Tobacco?"

"*No*. Men buy tobacco from men. Hats, I suspect. I'm too bunglesome for a dress shop. Tried one of them famdangle Singer's and sewed right through my finger."

"Shouldn't you be working in a hat shop now, then?"

"Lord, no. At the wages a feather trimmer makes, I'd *never* get liberated. Might as well work Chicopee cotton for a dollar a week."

She looked up from her fingers to appraise me. "I thought you'd be in worse shape."

I shook my head. "I'm *fine*, thinking about the dancing."

She grinned ruefully as we walked along. "I have had second thoughts over introducing you to a dance floor again. My poor bruised feet could hardly take my weight this morning."

"But you promised to teach me," I cajoled. "You plied me with drink. My clumsiness was your fault."

She grinned. "Maybe you will be the only man ever to be a better dancer sober." She threw her hands up. "All right. I'll give it a try. No more clogging, though. We'll go dancing for real, at the nickel dump."

The dance hall was a bleak-looking place, as nondescript as any other building on the muddy block. However, inside it opened into a bright bedlam of light and color. Noise thick as fog with a happy roll of rag piano and wail of gurdy, shouting, singing, shrieks of laughter.

I bought us each a tankard of ale and a boat of fried fish in a paper packet. After we'd eaten, Phaegin pulled me to my feet. "Come on, cowboy."

Even sober, and perhaps more so, I was a failure at the two-step. I was a failure at the waltz. Phaegin agreed I'd been lighter on my feet, and hers, the night before and insisted I have another beer.

I guaranteed I would get better. I counted careful: one and two, three and . . . then lost the thread. Phaegin finally lost her patience, and we sat down.

"I'm sure you can do other things, Ned. Though it's a sad thing not to dance." She fanned herself with a napkin. "By the way, who is this *Lill* you were going on about?"

I winced and gave her a shorthand account. Phaegin snorted.

"Men make mistake upon mistake to no bad end. A woman believes in a man, and the rest of her life is lost."

"Not Lill's," I avowed. "I won't let her life be wasted. That farmer is an ignorant lout, and she's washing his shirts!"

Phaegin raised an eyebrow. "Do you really want to be a help to her, Ned, or do you just want to feel like some fairy-tale knight righting the fair lady's wrongs?"

Quillan's admonition leapt to mind and I spoke without thought. "Philoprogenetive: affection for the weak."

"Exactly!"

I hastened to make amends. "*Lill's* not weak, though. She's magnificent, profound. . . ."

Phaegin shrugged. "No skin off my nose either way. But it's not like the world was sprung on her, it's been like that forever, and it's the way with every woman, not only your precious Lill."

Perhaps my dramatics had sounded fatuous, but her sarcasm was unnecessary. Phaegin, however, had been born into a different world from Lill and me, and it was not surprising she would see things with a coarser eye.

Phaegin gazed at me challengingly.

I changed the subject. "Tell me about your family."

"You could guess. Ma does piecework in the coat factory, Da works on the ships. My two brothers do the same, can't get work half the time, but drink a fortune anyhow. I don't see them much. Try not to. Like I said, they'd like me to marry a brother into the family, I suppose throw their dirty socks in to be washed with my new husband's. They don't like it much I won't kick on to their plan." Phaegin sighed and looked out to the dance floor again. When the music came up she smiled, looking more relieved than truly pleased. "Now's your chance. They're spieling. Even an ignorant cowboy like you can manage *that*." She stood on the dance floor, her arm out like a pump handle. I set my chin on her shoulder, she hers on mine.

"Hold my waist. Close. No, *really* close."

I complied, and she murmured instruction in my ear. "To spiel you make the tightest circle possible, go fast, hold on hard."

I clasped her waist in the vise of my arm and we began turning. Phaegin clutched the back of my neck. We revolved faster; my head spun. I had never been so close to a woman and my body was sensitized to immoderate awareness, like the sanded fingers of a thief. In spite of the layers of broadcloth and cotton, wire and whalebone, her hips, soft breasts, and the insistence of nipples were as vivid to me as if she were naked. Legs! Hidden under deep folds of fabric, it was easy to forget women had them at all, but Phaegin's two pushed against mine, *were* mine: knees, calves, thighs.

As we spun faster, I panted. Phaegin gasped into my ear. Sweat trailed down my back. We became the earth, revolving night and day, years on end, summers and winters passing, eons back and forward; dinosaurs walked our skins; the future coursed through our limbs; nothing else existed or mattered but that we held tight as one, the fractured world made whole.

When the music stopped, we wobbled like a slowing top and stood staring at each other. Phaegin's hair coiled in sweaty tendrils around her face; her face flushed to pink; her eyes dark and wet. For once she wasn't smiling or talking. I myself seemed to have lost my own ability to speak. I had no words to describe— or, worse, even to explain—what charged through me. I stood senseless and immobile. When the music for the next dance began, Phaegin stepped back, then close again, and kissed me.

Soft, she was so soft, her skin dewy and warm. I pressed my lips to hers, turned my face to feel her cheek against mine, kissed her ear, her neck. I put my hands on her cheeks and looked into her eyes again. Phaegin whispered, "Ah, Ned."

So beautiful. I pushed a tendril of hair behind her ear.

Someone bumped into us, a woman in a scarlet dress, the red skirt twirling like a giant poppy into the crowd. As if the color had broken the spell, Phaegin pulled back abruptly and began smoothing her dress and hair, glancing away. "You're looking a bit under the weather, Neddy. All that spinning. I should have thought better."

I nodded, thinking it was true. I didn't feel so well.

She spoke briskly. "You'll be all right, another night's rest. Speakin' of which, I have work in the morning, so I'll see you later." She reached up and kissed my cheek—"G'night"—and disappeared into the crowd. At the far end of the room, the door opened to black, then closed again.

I wandered the streets, cautioning myself. Hadn't Phaegin herself said she wanted nothing of me? Rightly so; we were worlds apart. Still, I desired nothing more than to follow her home and dance with her through the days, through every night. Also, I loved Lill, had pledged to come back for her and, having done so, possessed a gentleman's obligation toward her.

But now the baby sat pink-bowed between Lill and Osterlund, riveting the dystopian family together with its doughy hunger. Perhaps Phaegin was right. Was I playing the ridiculous, useless, and painfully unwanted part of the knight?

I turned the corner and almost ran into two men, both heavyset and thuggish-looking, with matching red hair. They looked familiar. One jabbed me in the shoulder. "Working for Peabody, Quillan's boy?"

I narrowed my eyes and tried to look larger. "What's it to you?"

He shoved me against the wall. "Keep your hands off what's not yours."

I shoved him back and the other grabbed my arm. Mother Fenton opened the door and called out, "Here now, what's goin' on?"

I straightened my coat as they backed off.

The one I pushed pointed at me and growled, "Nothin' *better* be goin' on. Remember that."

Mother watched the thugs depart. "What's this?"

"Something about Quillan."

"Well, that's not *all* the cark. Some suit man came by an hour ago, grim about you getting this."

I took the paper from her: my letter to Alan and Jamieson, demanding information, returned unopened. Mother crossed her arms. "Fella told me there'd be action if you didn't stop trimmin' whiskers off their egg."

I started to protest. Mother put up a tiny hand. "Don't want to know. Just ticker yourself, with *this* fellow and *that* professor. Men like them use men like you up. Grist for their mill, Ned. Grist for their mill."

Though I kept the suit man to myself, I mentioned the redheads to Quillan the next day.

He was apoplectic. "They mentioned my name? My God. Have you told anyone what I'm doing?"

I was a little miffed he didn't ask after my health but only questioned my circumspection. "No, sir, I don't talk to anyone."

"Good, good. Let's keep it that way."

That irritated me further still. He had a wife, colleagues. He suffered no solitude and yet demanded *my* continued isolation?

I frowned. "Sir, I *must* have my mother's address, or I'm afraid I'm going to have to go looking for her myself."

He pursed his lips. "Sit down, Ned."

Immediately, I feared the worst. "She's ill? Dead?"

"Not at all."

I sat down slowly. Quillan paced. "Your mother rather vociferously requested privacy, telling my agent she's left her past painful life behind, full of losses, her name, her husband, her mother, her home . . . and she wishes to be left to raise the ramparts of a new family, without the specters of the past"—Quillan fanned a hand my way—haunting her. She asked for your forgiveness and understanding that she has nothing to offer you but painful reminders of what was and is no longer."

He gripped my shoulder. "I have to admit—and apologize— I found this out a week ago. I could not bring myself to relay the message. It seemed cruel to make ruin of Christmas. But truth will tell in the end, and now you know."

I stammered, "How could she?"

Quillan sat on the edge of his desk and regarded me earnestly. "I don't know. I wish I could offer solace." He spread his hands. "All I can say, though in pale recompense: You have me. You have science and a future, and those are no small things."

I nodded. "Yes, sir. But please give me her address. You see, I absolutely *must* contact her, perhaps *go* to her. If we talk, I'm sure she will feel differently."

Now Quillan shook his head. "My agent, honorable to a fault perhaps, acquiesced to your mother's request and sent no address. He did provide her with yours. Perhaps, in time, she will change her mind. I recommend, until then, letting her rest with her decisions while you regain your family's standing."

I shook my head, going over what Quillan had reported. "But, sir, it does not sound like my mother: *ramparts* and *specters haunting.*"

"Don't be obtuse, Edward. I was paraphrasing."

"And that's the other thing. My mother is quite shy. To talk to a stranger rather than simply explaining to me? It's hard to believe she—"

Quillan had been patting his pockets. He interrupted. "Your mother obviously has had to learn to make her way in the world. The lower classes can not afford to be shy!" He pulled out an envelope from his coat and pushed it across the desk.

I opened it and found a letter stating Wallace Quillan's intent to sponsor Edward Turrentine Bayard III's application to Yale. It was a glowing letter attesting to my high intelligence, myriad abilities, and strong work ethic.

I was dumbfounded for a moment, two realms of information warring for attention, then said, "Thank you, Professor, thank you!" Professor Quillan took the letter back and folded it. "You've already made me proud, Ned. Your illustrations are excellent, your effort laudable, smart as a whip."

With great drama he wrote on the front of the envelope *Attention: President Dwight Woolsey* and clapped me on the back. "You are going places, Ned. *We* are going places. The future bright, the hounds are sounding. I have had a glimpse of the fox, he calls a meeting, and I will take not one of the hundreds of brilliant young Yale scholars whom I know, but *you,* Edward."

"A meeting?"

"With the vice president of American Coal Company. We *will* have our season." He took the letter of recommendation and tacked it to the wall behind his desk. "I'll walk this to the registrar myself when our little project is finished, so we must begin at once."

He tapped his temple. "Time to put emotion aside, all life's worries and questions, but for one: How finely to the bone do we cut? There is no room for waste, for folly, for indulgence. We work from dawn to dusk. After we have succeeded, we will turn again to personal matters."

Quillan lifted a bag from the floor filled with hunks of coal. "The draftsman turns to sculptural arts." He explained the coal bed fossils were far too fragile, too valuable to be shuffled from office to office by clumsy office boys. But the executives, lay-men all, must see, touch, be exhilarated by the anthracitic ar-chaeological remains.

And so I made replicas for days into weeks, I breathed coal dust, blew black snot into a handkerchief, shook black dust from my hair, ate coal on my bread, turned my very skin darker with its sheen. The professor, a wild taskmaster, practically hopped with impatience. We did indeed work dawn to dusk, seven days a week and then hours beyond.

My worries over my mother, my heartbreak over Lill, were blanketed by the choking labors. Mother Fenton clucked at my fagged condition and still I kept on, returning to the boarding-house hours after dinner, rising well before dawn, the sky yet blinkered by night, as if I'd not rested at all. The few times I walked in the midnight hours past the nickel dump and around the cigar shop, I did not espy Phaegin. My visions of her were relegated to irresponsible and undisciplined nights.

And after I dreamed of Phaegin, of her softness and the smell of her skin, I did not ask why it was not Lill who perfumed my reveries; I shrouded my dreams in the cadence of labor.

* * *

Finally, in early February, the wind blew from the southern vane. Quillan met me at the lab door and pumped my hand. "I've had word. We go." He paced, chortling. "Prepare the box of specimens, my files. The paper, of course, the paper for the scientific society." He looked at me. "Didn't I say to pack?"

"Now?"

"No, no, I need you at the house. I have a box."

I followed him to the mansion and waited when he went in, as instructed, on the porch. A few minutes later, I jumped as a window was flung open, then another, and another. Smoke wafted out. Mrs. Quillan shouted, "I can light a fire, for pity sake!"

Mr. Quillan answered, in furious condescension, "No, madam, obviously not."

"It burns perfectly, and if anyone had *told* me about the flue, I would have opened it."

"You don't need to know about flues or driving a chaise or any of the other foolishness you are getting up to. Are you mad?"

"I am *going* mad, yes. I cannot stand doing nothing any longer!"

"Then do something. Do you not have needles and linen?"

"I have sewn and picked enough stitches to put Penelope to shame. I can do no more."

"You will not start fires."

"I will burn this place *down* if I am not allowed some freedom!"

There was a long pause, Quillan obviously tendering the seriousness of the threat. He cleared his throat. "Talk to Dr. Parsons about this, my dear. I will abide by what he says is the best course of action."

"That charlatan and his ridiculous ideas of hysteria! His idea of action is inaction and you know it. Do me the favor of acknowledging I have some sense."

"I would happily do so if I saw any evidence to support it."

Mrs. Quillan began to shout. "This is *my* house, *my* life! I will light a fire if I choose. I will not be talked down to. It is absolutely insufferable that I am forced to answer to you, and I will not do it. I suffocate! I will not be treated so, I will not see that doctor, nor will I take his poisons!"

The professor shoved a box out the door and emerged, valise in hand, perspiring as if it were August, and slammed the door behind him. He pointed at the box. "Ned!"

I picked it up and followed the red-faced professor back to the lab. He had me stack another box on top of the first to demonstrate I could lift them both, gazing critically at the effort on my face. "Pack lightly, Ned."

I was beginning to understand why he wanted me on his journey.

"The train leaves at seven A.M. Be here by five, in case there are any difficulties." He brushed at his shirt, then patted his jacket pocket. "For the love of . . ." He sat down hard and threw up his hands. "Does nothing go right?"

"Sir?"

He brightened. "That's it, Ned. Go back to the house. Ask Mrs. Quillan for my wallet. I left it on the bureau upstairs. Bring it to me at Anthony's. I will be dining and staying at the club tonight."

"Sir?"

"I have too much to do to deal with Mrs. Quillan's histrionics tonight. This may well be the most important trip of my—

of our lives." He waved me off, then called me back. "Remember, Ned. Not a word to *anyone*. Everything depends on your circumspection. There are those who would do anything to thwart my progress."

I backtracked to the professor's house, following the fence around back, around the burning drum and the stacks of flowerpots and the pile of brush waiting for the gardener to clear off. It was there I heard the steps behind me. I thought it was perhaps the professor changing his mind, for the footfall was not at all surreptitious. I turned, smiling, only to see the thuggish duo who had accosted me previously. One of them grabbed me by the back of my jacket and pinned my arms behind my back while I yelped for help. The other clamped a hand smelling of sausages around my mouth. "We tol' ya, didn't we? And still you come. One more time: Don't get mixed up with what's not yours. This is to help you remember." He removed his hand and punched me in the nose.

A window flew up and I heard Mrs. Quillan shout, "What is going on here?" The fellow behind me dropped my arms, I staggered back into the brush pile, and the two men hightailed it.

Mrs. Quillan was by my side in seconds. "Ned, my God, what is going on?"

I put my hand to my nose. It was pouring blood. "I don't know."

She shouted to the housekeeper to bring a rag. "Do you know those men?"

I shook my head. "Not really." The housekeeper brought the rag. I gently stanched the blood from my tender nose, hoping the punch had at least bent it in the opposite direction of Buck Mason's blow. We went into the house.

Mrs. Quillan dabbed my nose clean. "I don't think it's broken." She smiled, looking amazingly happy, calm, and collected after her tirade only half an hour previous. "Though I'm sure it hurts."

I nodded.

"Now tell me about those men. Why did they do this?"

I remembered Quillan's admonishing me to say nothing to anyone, but certainly Mrs. Quillan should know there were nefarious characters hanging around. After all, they had attacked me at her house; perhaps they were waiting to kidnap her and I had merely stumbled into the situation. "Those roughs . . . approached me once before. I think they're trying to warn me off of helping the professor."

She laughed. "Why would they be doing that?"

I lowered my voice. "It's the work. I can't say much about it, but it's very important, big money."

She frowned. "Does this have to do with coal? The professor's shirts have been absolutely black."

I nodded.

She mused. "Something to do with his work, I suppose. Fossils, always fossils."

I nodded again. "The fossils."

"In coal?"

I put a finger to my lips. "You must be careful, Mrs. Quillan. They may have been lying in wait for you instead of me. They could be spies."

She smiled. "Pshaw."

"Please be careful."

She sighed. "Oh, Ned. All I ever am is careful."

I stood up and looked at the rag. My nose had stopped bleeding. "I think I should get going."

Mrs. Quillan nodded. "Keep the cloth." She pointed to her nose. "It may begin again on the way home."

I had my hand on the door before I remembered. "Er. The professor forgot his wallet."

Mrs. Quillan raised her eyebrows. "He needs it between now and dinner?"

I reddened. "He must need to buy the tickets to Pennsylvania."

"He's going to *Pennsylvania?*"

The professor must have forgotten to tell her in the commotion over the fire. "In the morning."

"The station stays open until nine. He'll have plenty of time."

I looked out the window. Why couldn't the professor get his own wallet? "He says he's staying at Anthony's tonight."

She tightened her lips but called the housekeeper and instructed her to retrieve the wallet. When Mrs. Bryan brought it, Mrs. Quillan opened the leather envelope, counted the bills, took out a good number, and handed the wallet to me. "I'm sure he'll understand I'll need some cash while he's away."

I nodded awkwardly and took my leave.

Packing took me all of two minutes, and I was faced with the first free time I'd had for weeks. I contemplated contacting Montgomery Elias again, but what I'd found out in the last month was complicated and confusing and I decided to put off writing the letter until I returned. I wrote a short halfhearted note to Lill. I stared at the Chinese characters on the wallpaper until they turned into pictures. I read another chapter in Laramore's book.

Finally, I gave up and gave in to the sunshine pouring in from the small window over my bed. We were having a false spring. Daffodils peeked from dark mud. They would almost certainly be frozen back for their intrepidity. I bought a cone of nuts from the vendor on the corner and wandered, looking in windows and trying to enjoy the pale sunshine.

I finally lit across from the cigar shop and watched patrons walking in, then out with boxes tucked under their arms. After some time, Phaegin emerged, walking slowly, her face pale under a dark scarf. I wondered if she'd been sick. She walked toward me and stepped into the street. I cautioned myself to steer clear, to head in the other direction, and instead awaited her approach. Having crossed the street, she recognized me with a start and hurried in the other direction.

I followed.

Phaegin crossed into an alley and up Third, while I took the short cut around. She came around the building's south side face-to-face with me. I spoke first. "Hello, Phaegin."

She put her hands on her hips. "Who do you think you are?"

"What do you mean?"

"I haven't seen you for a month."

"I had to work."

"So did most everyone else in the world. A kiss and you act like I've given you leprosy. Well, it was no more than I would give a brother, less even. And I'm sorry I gave you that. And if you're worried that I'm thinking anything of it, I'd sooner be seeing a *real* donkey."

She turned and walked away again. In spite of her not wanting to see me, or maybe because of it, I ran after her, remonstrating. "It was only work that kept me. Quillan has a big project." She was practically running and I strode behind her, my voice raised. "Phaegin!" I reached out and grabbed her sleeve. "I'm to start at Yale in September."

Phaegin stopped and put her hands to her neck. "Yale? But you're poor."

I shrugged. "Professor Quillan is sponsoring me."

She dropped her hands and stuck one out and shook mine. "That's wonderful, Ned. Congratulations."

I shrugged nonchalantly. "It's nothing."

She pointed toward the shop. "I've got to get back."

"You just left."

"I was out for some air."

"Let's have lunch. Come on, Phaegin. You're the only friend I have."

"What, did Lill throw her knight over?" She blushed. "Never mind. Tell you what, we'll have dinner tomorrow."

I stuck my hands in my pockets. "I can't. I'm leaving for Pennsylvania."

"Oh, so this was to be a 'So long, Sue' kind of lunch."

"I'm *coming* back."

She reached out and put her hand over mine. "I have to go. But it's been lovely to see you."

"What about dinner when I get back; dinner and dancing? It should be just a few days."

She gave my hand a squeeze and let go. "There can be nothing between us, Ned. I've been clear on that. I'm sorry."

I stammered. "We're friends, though, aren't we?"

She smiled. "Of course. But we won't go dancing again. The holidays are over, and I'm much busier." She glanced at my face and sighed. "You could come by the cigar shop sometime, just to let me know what you're up to." She gave a nod, walking away as she called, "Congratulations again, Ned. I'm very happy for you."

It was for the best. I trudged back to Mother's, passing the Boola Inn. I had so longed for that better place. But now, though it finally seemed within grasp, even the scent of the roast wafting from the window didn't cheer me up.

CHAPTER 18

Dear Ned,

I have tried. My hands are red and cracked so I cry to wash dishes. Must everything in my life be harsh? Ash for dishes, lye for clothes, cold water and splinters, even the rooster draws blood.

Dear Ned,

Will winter ever end? I wake up to ice on dark windows and it never brightens.

Dear Ned,

The baby has colic. Breaks my heart to hear her cry, then I want to put her in a snowbank. Heaven help both of us.

Dear Ned,

What happened to beauty? Certainly once my life was brilliant.

Dear Ned,

Why live if the balance of pain and pleasure is weighted so poorly?

Dear Brill,

I have finally heard again from Lill. My heart sings, "She is unhappy!" even as I die to hear of her misery.

The train trip to Pennsylvania was uneventful. We boarded the train in near silence. I imagined the professor was deep in his thoughts of science, while I ruminated over the sad letters from Lill and my sadder response to them. Both overwrought by our mentation, the professor and I fell quickly asleep to the susurrant *chock* of the train wheels and didn't wake up until we were almost there.

Scranton was a city of gloom, the coal furnaces breathing into continuous darkness. The children of this place could not fathom a blue sky. It was also colder than New Haven, without the tempering effect of ocean breezes. We took a hansom to the American Coal offices, a limestone building with ornate carvings above every door and window, each cloaked in soot. I carted the boxes up the stairs and was told to wait in the lobby while the professor went into an office with a gold placard hung on it that said CORNELIUS PLACET. When the professor finally emerged, hours later, he was grinning like a dog, shaking hands with a dark-suited man wearing diamond cuff links, with a cigarette tipped rakishly in his lips. Quillan walked out of the lobby, reached the street, and called a cab. It was only when he stood with his foot on the cab step that he seemed to remember me. "Ned. Keep up, will you?"

The professor told me nothing of the proceedings. When we got to the inn where we'd spend the night, he went straight to his room while I took a cot behind the laundry.

At dawn we juddered across washboard roads for miles before arriving at American Coal's unfortunately named Widowmaker Mine in the late morning. Wilson Dunlaw, vice president in charge of Widowmaker, met us at the control house. I found him to be an amazingly obsequious man, as rotund as Quillan and as hard to take.

"We at American Coal are exhilarated to receive a man of science as eminent as Professor Quillan to our humble concern."

Quillan puffed. "We are pleased to be here."

I was pretty sure Quillan was using the royal *we*, but I nodded in agreement.

Dunlaw inclined his head. "I am to understand that time is of the utmost importance and therefore"—he handed us each a steel hat and demonstrated wearing it by slowly lowering it onto his skull—"we shall commence our subterranean journey."

He explained with a surplusage of words that a shaft mine was struck to provide the greatest profit, but only if the deep veins were rich. The extensive costs of digging, hoisting, and pumping proved disastrous if the bed provided less coal than expected and initial costs were never recovered.

Dunlaw's voice dropped to a whisper. "I understand the great man has discovered a means of ascertaining the emplacement and generosity of the coal bed, thereby conserving our tremendous industrial complex's fortune."

We approached the elevator. I was hesitant to descend into the mines. Standing at the mouth of the shaft, I could feel the rush of air escaping, as if even the wind knew better than to tarry below.

Dunlaw warned us of the fluctuating temperatures. We would first experience cold, farther down the air would be warm, then heat great enough at the lowest seams to melt candles. Dunlaw waved an arm, knocked on his steel skull, and shouted gaily, "Let the entertainment commence!"

The steel caps each had a sconce attached in which balanced a candlestick behind a mesh enclosure. We lit our candles and descended into the mines on an open platform called a cage, supported by a wrist-thick steel cable—a thin security. Descending slowly, a tortured creaking and groaning emanating from the ropes, Dunlaw grinned as if the noise was melody itself.

We dropped ten men's height, then twenty, then thirty. Soon we'd not have climbed out if our fellows were a hundred strong and willing to stand on one another's shoulders. Sunlight was lost. The candles flickered and tossed weedy shadows on the black walls.

Dunlaw's good humor only slipped when the basket that served as counterweight to the platform almost collided with us in "a wedding." Dunlaw lost the grin and swore, "*Goddamn it!*" but when the basket rose out of sight he laughed. "Miss is as good as a mile, men."

By the time we reached the mine's floor, my heart was pounding, my stomach moiled, and my skin was clammy at the 50 degrees on the floor of the first seam. The eye of the shaft in which we had descended winked, a sad and singular star in a night of coal. The air smelled of sulfur and ordure. Our nervous candles sporadically illuminated low overhead beams, sagging across the ceiling of the mine.

The hole in the earth was initially as wide as the Philadelphia train station, narrowing as its many legs slithered back and away into perpetual black. The idea that the thin steel carapace on my skull could do anything to protect me from a hundred million tons of coal and earth over my head now seemed more than ridiculous, as were the supports for the earth above us. Twelve-by-twelve-inch timbers, propped up with other twelve-by-twelve timbers, tatted a lacy construction of wood against rock. One would better expect toothpicks to support a Clydesdale.

Coal cars appeared and disappeared in the wavering light, and the black smudged faces of miners, eyes ghostly aglow in the lamplight, presented a spectral pickax minstrel show as they worked. Coal glistened on the walls as if wet, yet it was dry as dust.

From this ghastly blackness came the dissonance of picks and shovels, ringing like mad wind chimes in the stagnant air. Trips rumbled by, pulled by mules, their dark bodies virtually invisible but for the insides of their ears, the thin circlet of white around their brown eyes, and the surprise of teeth when the animals brayed.

I could barely hold back my terror. I calmed myself by feigning scientific interest in the dark walls, by anticipating recounting the experience to Phaegin, by composing a letter to Lill detailing hell, and so trudged along, barely attending the reports of production and richness, veins, strikes, and future direction, as I dodged swells of panic.

Dunlaw turned at a hacking cough at his elbow. Jim McNulty, the foreman for the Lucky Lady shaft, warned, "There's been a cave-in at the south tunnel, won't be opened till day's end."

The term *cave-in* yielded a new wave of dizziness, but then my attention was drawn by a small scream and a wail.

McNulty's owl eyes saw what I could not. He shouted with exasperation, "Put 'im on the wagon if he can't handle the pick." A boy who looked no older than seven trudged by, examining his hand and wrapping his dirty handkerchief around it. My first thought was that it seemed ludicrous to have the nicety of a handkerchief in this filthy hole. I leaned over to McNulty. "How *old* is that boy?"

"Eleven years old, he is. Danny Rate. Good worker mostly, but puny for the pick. His family's longtime coal people."

I noticed other children working the mine, some few on picks, more loading carts pulled by stunted black donkeys. One child, a girl, hefted a knob of cannel the size of her head. The pile of coal they loaded was a week of my heat at Mother's. If charged to excavate it myself, I'd prefer to freeze.

As I shuddered, Quillan basked, as animated as if he'd discovered mermaids. He hummed indecently amid the misery, took notes, bent almost nose to notebook to discern the marks of his pencil squeaking over black-dusted paper. He tapped the walls, scraped at the ceiling, which had seemingly descended on us as we walked as was now within our reach.

"Ned." He handed me a surveyor's pick, speaking as if he wished me to answer the door. "Get that, will you?"

I took the tool and began to chip away at a section of coal that Quillan inferred had a fossil embedded in it. It seemed the force that I had to work the rock coal in order to chip the specimen out would certainly bring down the walls, and I shivered, thinking of the muscular swings the real miners were making.

As we descended farther, the atmosphere went south, becoming as hot and damp as a New Orleans summer. The timbers were lanate with the yellow-white filaments of a particular mine fungus. Moths fluttered around this subterranean vegetation as if famished for any life at all.

I wished I had better company in this perilous place. Depending on Quillan and Dunlaw was like trailing carnival balloons into a firestorm. I could have depended on Tilfert and Avelina to get me out posthaste, but that was beyond conjecture now. Buck Mason, though good with a gun, had proved himself to be too interested in his own skin to be reliable. Osterlund came to mind. Stalwart and no-nonsense, the solid Norwegian might well thrust his neckless shoulders against a failing beam. I acknowledged some wisdom in Lill's choice.

I jumped at the worrisome sensation of something passing over my feet and stared intently at the floor: rats. Meandering along the floor as if they were carting coal themselves.

Quillan noticed as well. "Good Christ, rats!"

Dunlaw laughed. "The damned vermin eat the men's lunches, the oats the mules drop, even chew meat from the animals' forelocks. We put out poison, the men shovel a ton or so of dead rats out every month, and still they proliferate."

How long we trudged the dark rooms and galleys of the mine I am not sure. The dark began to tell on me, even as the feather of rats across my feet failed to worry. A sharp crackling over our heads was the rock "working," we were told. Dunlaw seemed complacent, though the noise finally gave Quillan pause. His voice lost its gustatory tone. "I think we are finished here, Mr. Dunlaw. You may escort us back."

Dunlaw, however, motioned us on. "It would be a shame to miss the pump as long as you're here. Won't be another ten minutes."

The floor pitched downward at a ten-degree slope. Ahead of us a vast pool glimmered like oil in lamplight. Next to it rumbled, roared, and chugged a gigantic machine. "For every ton of coal we pull out of the earth, ten *tons* of water must be extracted." Dunlaw pointed proudly. "A Watt's engine."

Quillan had obviously caught my fear and now tried to hurry the man along. He squeaked, "Impressive, but I have no time!"

For my part, the hammer of my chest had metamorphosed into a curiously weak sensation. My legs were going numb, my head was light. I stammered, "I am not feeling well."

"Happens to folks new to the mines," Dunlaw shouted from ahead. "Takes a strong man to handle it."

I ignored his blustering as another two curiosities made themselves apparent. The rats, hitherto meandering through the tunnels, now coursed en masse out of the black grotto from the tunnels beyond.

Quillan lifted his feet, one after the other, and said, "Lord."

I asked, "Do you smell violets?"

At the bellow of "White damp!" men and children dropped their tools with a clatter and raced with the teeming vermin toward the main shaft. The percussion of tools gave way to shuffling feet, the huff of lungs, the shriek of rats.

All raced toward the cage. Rats coursed up its ropes, biting, scratching, and falling like ripe fruit on the heads of the dozen or so miners already clapped to the tiny platform like limpets. Dunlaw pushed ahead of the waiting men, dragging us with him by the arms of our coats. One of the miners on the floor shouted, "Brush the roof!" and men tore the shirts from their chests and began manically waving them overhead to fan the gas away.

Dunlaw shoved two miners from the elevator, who gave their space without struggle, and we got on. One of the miners picked up a boy of perhaps eight and shoved him forward. "Please! Take the boy." The platform rose. Dunlaw shouted, as he fiercely shoved the child back into his father's arms, "Enough, we can't all perish for stupidity!"

The miner continued to hold the child beseechingly as we ascended. There was more than enough time for me to have put out my hands; I could have taken the child. I could have traded my space for the boy. Instead I sighted overhead, praying for the distant eye of God to fix yet another omnipotent error. I stared upward to will day to rise. When I looked back down, when I finally called out, "We can't leave him there!" my chance had safely gone.

As it was, all the miners made it out alive, men and children, though twelve of the mules succumbed to the sweet-smelling gas that had alerted us to its presence. White damp, a mixture of gases sometimes created after routine blasting, was deadly even in small quantities. We had been more than lucky. Dunlaw clapped me on the shoulder, called me "sweet canary," and stuck a Havana cigar in my pocket, avowing I'd saved the lives of all of them with that nose of mine. I was a hero. Again.

The image of the terrified eyes of the miniature laborer, and the hopeless sneer on the face of the man holding the child before him, bore mute testimony. I was no more a hero of the mines than I was of the plains.

Can you be a despicable coward once and go on to be a decent human being or does it foul your soul forever? Perhaps my soul was already dark and heavy, and until now there had been no way of knowing.

More likely it is sin that is white, colorless, and weightless, and we must fill our days, our mind, with the weight of what we don't want to face. Mine our own selves, turn away from the easy impulse of pale natures. Dishonored and stunned, I walked away from the place, past the mule-drawn trips and black holes in the earth. It was only midmorning, and the men who had cheated death descended into accessorial holes to cheat it again.

Quillan and I returned to our rooms and Dunlaw to his office to sit and shake loose his close call in a large leather chair.

As pickaxes rang and Quillan schemed, I slept away the after-noon, the night, and most of the next morning. When my wak-ing overcame my sleeping and I was forced to keep company with what I had done, I cast about for means of relief. Redemption is expensive. A moral stance requires stock. It is seldom that even a twelve-by-twelve timber can be righted against the world's great injustices without a trust and an inheritance. What did *I* have to buy a clean conscience? I'd upped my cigar stash to three and had two dollars in my pocket, five in Connecticut. Not much of a launder would be done with that.

I went outside and stared up at the eternal gray, at the cinder-covered world around the mine, and felt as hopeless as the drained landscape, hungry—in fact starved—for blue and red and yellow. And if *I* was hungry after a day, what hungers did the miners feel? If I could conjure color, I would give the miners a brilliance of geese, a glow of new grass, a flourish of buttercups. Only roots would be privy to underground. For men are no more made to be subterranean than birds and blooms.

CHAPTER 19

SAINT PATRICK'S HOME FOR CHILDREN

BLENNING, PENNSYLVANIA

Transfer to Widowmaker Mine, Scranton

Period of indenture: seven years

Name: Patrick O'Grady

While the professor napped, I returned to the mine wearing his jacket.

Dunlaw was in his office, handing a stack of papers and filing to his secretary. I straightened my lapels and spoke with authority.

"I'm here for the boy."

He looked puzzled. "Which boy?"

"The first push out of the gas, a boy was left behind."

"Tut. They all came out in good time, not a casualty among them."

He was acting as if he didn't know what I was talking about. Perhaps he didn't, but I would press my case. "What was the child's name, sir?"

"I *tell* you, there were several hundred miners in that vein alone, many of them boys. I couldn't possibly know all their names."

"Do you know who would know who he was?" I was getting impatient. "I have employment for that boy. Professor Quillan expressly asked for *that* child. There will be trouble if I return without him."

The secretary, still standing with the armful of papers, broke in. "O'Grady. They call him Curly." The woman had a slight accent, modulating the brogue from her voice. She turned and began pushing papers into drawers. "I heard of the incident yesterday."

The VP looked vexed.

I pressed her. "Do you know where to find him?"

She continued filing as she spoke offhand. "A boy from the orphanage. Staying with the Hennesys. House twenty-one." She finished her filing and slammed the drawer shut. "That's all I know."

I said thank you, but she had already disappeared into the back office.

The VP looked flabbergasted. "What do you mean, employment?"

He was not so much set against the idea as disbelieving.

"The professor has several more boxes to transport back to the museum." I pulled out the two cigars Phaegin had given me at Christmas, offered Dunlaw one, and stuck the other in my mouth. "Dr. Quillan was certain you would be of assistance."

Dunlaw hemmed. "If he's an orphan boy, he has company debt to pay."

"Certainly he could be discharged into my care, pay his debt working for us." I lowered my voice. "After all, we work for the same *tremendous machine,* eh? A little grease from you, we give a little grease back."

He looked dubious but rubbed his chin and walked to the file cabinets. Shuffled through and called his secretary again. She appeared as if she'd been standing just outside the door. "Patricia, get me the boy's indenture." She withdrew it as if the paper were magnetic.

Dunlaw tapped the paper. "O'Grady. He's got two years to work off." He looked over his glasses at me. "They come in with seven." He slapped the paper down on the desk, initialed the bottom with a flourish, and handed it over.

I nodded. "The professor will be most pleased. Expect a letter of commendation."

The VP put up a hand. "Let's keep the specifics between us. A good general word, however, would be most gratifying."

The houses leaned slightly one direction and another as if they'd all had a little to drink: mean shanties with only one window, holes in the roofs repaired with pieces of steel, tarred paper, awkwardly nailed sheets of wood, and even a tattered quilt. The Hennesys' house had a large 21 chalked over its door. I knocked.

A woman, Mrs. Hennesy I presumed, yelled, "Wot!" She was a stocky woman, bent over a washtub scrubbing canvas pants in black water. A small girl scooted into the shadows under the table.

Mrs. Hennesy looked me over. I bowed. "Mrs. Hennesy? I am here for Curly."

She frowned. "Wot's he done now? He ain't nowhat my business. Boards, but he's nown a mine."

I looked around the room. Two little girls peered out from behind a curtain hung as a partition. "How many of your family work in the mine?"

"Three. Not counting the boy." She repeated, "He's nowt mine." I nodded, acknowledging the lack of relation between them. She flung the pants over a chair with a slap and crossed her arms. "I'm a fremit bearer, but I broke my ankle and canna take the weight."

"Fremit bearer?"

"The hewer hacks the coal off'n the seam. Wimmin and gurls take it out in baskets."

I nodded. "Is Curly here?"

"Has he trouble?"

"No, no, not at all. I'm going to take him with me."

"Why?"

"Employment."

"An' you take *Curly*?"

I nodded and repeated. "Is he here?"

"I'm owed 'is board. You take 'im, I still don' have the quarter."

I looked around the tiny room, the filthy wasted faces peering at me from under the table, behind the curtain. I felt the two dollars in my pocket. I handed both to Mrs. Hennesy whose tired face twisted into a jack-o'-lantern grin. She reached under the table and drew a squirming girl out. "Go get yer Curly."

The little girl, with a panicked look at me, went racing out. The woman invited me to sit on a crate at the sawbuck table and went on with her washing. In ten minutes the little girl came back, towing a red-headed boy behind her. Though still filthy, he looked as though he'd had some washing and looked less like the skeletal waif with burning eyes whose face had haunted me through the night. The boy, maybe closer to ten years than the eight I had thought, stood breathless from his run—bandy legs in short pants and socks darned at the ankles into lumps, hands in his pockets—and studied me with his head tilted to the side, a raggedy cap under which sprouted curly hair kinked every which way, almost hiding his protuberant ears. He squinted one eye shut. I said hello and he stuck his hand out manfully. "Oy."

I shook his hand. "Are you Curly?"

"I yam."

"I saw you, yesterday—"

"On the lift."

"Well, Curly, I need some help, back in New Haven. I wondered if you'd come and work off your time with me."

He grinned and his other eye squinted up as well. His two front teeth were not grown back in. "Sure'n I would."

Mrs. Hennesy snorted. "Sure'n he *would*. Good luck."

Curly wrapped his arms around her and gave her a big kiss. "You been like a ma to me, you 'ave. I'll send you chocolate on Christmas." She pursed her lips.

The little girls shot out from behind the curtain. "Will you send *us* chocolate, Curly?"

He scooped them up. Small as he was, they were half his size. "Nah, I'm sending you peppermint piggies. That's what you'll get. Each with a penny in 'is snout." He kissed each one, then crossed his arms. "Ready, sir."

"Don't you need to pack?"

He slapped his chest. "All I own's on me."

CHAPTER 20

I told Quillan that Curly'd been provided by the VP to help with the boxes of samples the professor had collected in the mines. Quillan looked Curly over and shook his head. "You'd think they could've found someone a little older. What's your age, boy? Nine, ten?"

Curly drew himself up. "Fourteen, mister."

"Fourteen?!" I was incredulous. "You're not four feet tall."

"Try livin' offa potatoes peppered with coal dust and see how tall *you* get."

I supposed that was right, but I felt somewhat disappointed in not having rescued a waif but an adolescent. I pointed to my mouth. "So the teeth . . . ?"

He laughed. "Lost the first two when I's three, hit with a ax handle. Lost the second two in a fight, not two weeks after they grew in. I take it my mouth don't like them teeth in front."

I was floored. Curly, however, was oblivious to my incredulity. He cheerfully carried the boxes to the train, strong as a horse despite his small size, climbed on top of the seats to stow the boxes in the overhead, and plopped himself down on the horsehair cushion.

Quillan frowned. "Here now. Get off there. You sit in the aisle."

Curly looked at me. I nodded. He dragged hangdog off the seat and posited himself outside the door of the compartment, so we could see the kinked flame of his hair bobbing with the train's movement. After some minutes, a woman in a brown dress walked by, then gave a little scream as she passed. Quillan and I looked at each other, puzzled. When it happened a second time I opened the door and asked Curly what that had been about. Curly shrugged. "Maybe a sharp in the rug."

I saw no such thing in the aisle, but did see one of the cabin attendants hurrying down. Curly shrunk up and put his face in his knees.

The attendant looked apologetic. "Do you know this boy?"

"I do."

"A lady has complained." The attendant took off his hat and leaned toward me. "She says he grabbed her ankle."

Curly looked up, his blue eyes swimming with tears. "I didn't. She stepped on my hand. Didn't even look at me. Didn't want to trouble her, but the heel hurt so, I pushed her foot away, that's all." He sniffed. A fat tear rolled down his cheek.

The attendant nodded. "No need for tears. Just keep yourself from underfoot."

Curly nodded soulfully, and the attendant departed. As soon as the man was beyond hearing range, Curly shook his head. "Cow. Smiled at me at the time. That's who you have to watch for, the ones who like it." He wiggled his fingers at his stomach. "Guilt starts eating on 'em."

I grabbed his collar, dragged him inside, and sat him on the floor there. Quillan frowned.

"Rules about keeping the aisle clear," I explained.

When we got back to New Haven, Quillan hired a cab for himself and the boxes, instructing us to make it back alone. Curly swaggered around the station. "Nice place." He walked over to the tea woman and purchased two pastries and some tea. I took the proffered treats. "Where did you get money for this?"

"I got me money saved. Few pennies in my sock." He winked.

I shook my head. "Well, don't spend it on me. Though this is very kind. Thank you."

Curly tipped his cap, stuffed the entire pastry into his mouth, sucked tea into the balloon of his cheeks, and swallowed. "Let's go, eh?"

When Curly stepped outside he moaned rapturously. "Would you *look* at it. Purty blue sky an' white clouds jus' like a pitcher book."

I grinned at his pleasure. "Come on, this way." As we turned the corner of the building, the thug brothers stepped back into the shadows. I pulled Curly close, but though I looked behind me repeatedly, there was no sign of the men following us. After I was certain there was to be no attack, I engaged my new charge in conversation. "So, Curly, you're an orphan?"

"Nah. My mam couldna take care of me. Put me in the orphanage so's I could eat."

"Did you know her?"

"Oh, yeah, I know 'er. She's *beautiful*. Works in a fancy office for a rich man. Sleeps with a piller, fancy shoes, and lace on 'er knickers. Cakes ever' day for tea and sometimes saves one for me."

I felt sorry for him. If he had a living mother at all, she most likely worked as a prostitute.

He continued. "Someday she's goin' ta take me back. We'll live in a nice house and have chickens in the back, eggs ever' day."

"Sounds nice. Will she know what happened to you, you coming with me?"

"Oh, sure. She knows ever'thin'."

* * *

Mother Fenton had apparently seen us coming, for when we arrived at the house she was standing on the stoop, her arms crossed and her face stormy. "Yer not bringin' *that one* in this house! I seen the like of 'im, I had one meself, and I won't have that brand a trouble again, and lice to boot."

"He's a *child*. I'm sort of . . . adopting him."

"Well, you undopt him if you know what's good for you."

Curly hung his head and wiped at his nose disconsolately. I told her Curly's story. Mother rolled her eyes and stared at the sky for a minute before sighing, then shook a finger at me. "You scrub him up, Ned. If he passes muster, we'll talk about it, but I won't have vermin in my establishment." She shook her head. "So close to dinner. No help for it."

We followed her into the bath and she pulled the hip tub out of the closet. "He'll have it cold. Can't cook and heat water at the same time." She handed me a big bar of soap and a ferocious-looking brush. "If he don't come clean, Ned, I won't hear any more. Behooves you to do it right." She turned to Curly. "Unlessen you want to be back in that pit, you keep your mouth shut. No howlin' no cryin'; you jus' take it till you're the right color for livin' with civilized people."

Curly looked at Mother in awe and nodded. When she left he shook his head. "Cor' she's a giant one, ain' she?" He licked his lips. "Like to put 'er on a spit and *roast* 'er."

Under all the grime, Curly had very white skin, his hair practically glowed flame. He was terribly thin and, worse, scarred from one end of his body to the other. He pointed out the scars, like someone showing artifacts of his travels. "Knacker horse kicked

207

me. Priest at the orphanage with a stick. Skritchin' under a fence. Burn movin' water. Rat bite got all stinky. Fell outta a tree."

I was relieved to hear some usual childhood activity. "You like to climb trees?"

"Nah. Pinched a loaf a bread and thought they couldna see me up there." He peered at the jagged scar on his calf. "Dog could *smell* me well enough, though."

Mother took a slit-eyed look at Curly when presented to her, at his shiny face, fingernails pared free of coal, my other set of clothes rolled up around his wrists and ankles. She tipped her head to one side as Curly grinned widely at her, then drew back and slapped him hard enough to knock him to the floor.

Curly jumped to his feet, his fists balled and his skinny lips twisted. "Wot's fer?"

Mother pointed a tiny finger at him. "Don't look *me* straight in the face. Not me, an' not anybody who 'as more'n you. *Got it?*"

"Me ma said I was good as anybody. Good 'nuff *for* anybody. Good 'nuff wot look 'em in the eye."

"That may or may not be so, but keep yer good opinion of yerself *to* yerself if yer goin' to bed here. I won't have you draggin' trouble to my house!"

Curly glared. I didn't relish being between these two in a scrap and I elbowed him sharply. He dropped his gaze to his feet.

Mother nodded. "He can sleep on your floor, quarter a day, Ned. But if I catch 'im on the bed, you're both out."

I drew her aside. "Professor Quillan owes me two weeks' pay. Can I give you the money later?"

Mother frowned. "I've aready done my charity in this life, Ned Bayard. You don't pay, I lose my house, I don't eat, and I don't *like* not eating."

"He's strong as a horse," I promised. "He'll do chores."

She glared, her arms crossed, then sighed and patted her belly. "Lucky for you, I got some reserves. And a jam of work. You have a week to make good." She wagged her finger. "And no more. I don' care if you've brought baby Jesus home."

Curly ate his dinner with relish, chewing huge bites with his mouth wide open, murmuring and humming and gulping with pleasure.

Mother seemed to soften toward him and his appetite, providing nonstop helpings as if he were a baby bird. Curly took a long drink of buttermilk and looked up at Mother, delighted. "Wondered why you was so fat." He shook his head wonderingly and took another huge bite. "Here *I* come!"

That night, on a blanket on the floor beside my bed, my coat for a pillow, Curly sighed happily. "Ain' this nice?" In less than a minute he was snoring like an old man.

The next day I left Curly to do Mother's bidding and headed in to work. I expected Quillan would be in the same ebullient mood he had left Pittsburgh in. But when I came into the lab, he was sitting in his office at his desk, head in his hands.

I called through the open door, "Professor, are you all right?"

He looked up. His eyes were red, his face puffy. He shook his head, then nodded, finally mumbled, "Problem at home. Soon straightened out, I'm sure."

I thought of the thugs. "Is Mrs. Quillan all right?"

He looked stricken, tottered from his desk, and shut his door.

Quillan paced behind his frosted door throughout the day. Sometimes I discerned the sound of crying. I kept quiet, taking it on myself to clean the lab. I carefully reboxed the samples we had been working with, dusted and wiped the shelves, the tables, the tops of dozens and dozens of boxes, and still the professor did not emerge. I swept the floors, I mopped. I had begun to wash windows when a telegram came. I signed for it and knocked on the office door. "Professor, a telegram for you."

He bolted from the room, took the telegram with a shaking hand. He stared at the front of it with terrible disappointment. "It's not from *her*." He dropped it on the table.

I picked it up. "It's from American Coal, sir. Shouldn't you read it?"

"I don't care, not a *whit*, not anymore." He stared at the paper in my hand, looking as formless and lethargic as a landed jellyfish. After a moment he put out his hand, halfheartedly ripped open the envelope. When he read the contents he groaned, then staggered to the chair and sat down. "No, no, no. It can't be. How can this be?"

"What is it?"

"Pulling the funding. Someone . . . has said . . . something." He seemed to regrow bones, straightened, and glared at me. "Did you tell anyone, *anyone* about our project?"

"No sir. No one. I don't even *know* anyone to tell."

"The men who struck you, did you break? Tell them under duress?"

"No! Mrs. Quillan came out after the one punched me in the nose. I told her to be careful, that they were working for the other side, and I got your wallet, dropped it off, and went straight to the boardinghouse. I saw no one else."

He looked at me, incredulous. "You talked to Mrs. Quillan?"

"Yes. It happened right outside her window, and I thought maybe they were waiting for her, that she might be attacked."

He seemed to be struggling with mighty currents of emotion. His face washed from anger to sorrow to disbelief and back to anger. He choked out, "What did you tell her?"

"Nothing. I only said you were working on an important project, that they were trying to stop you, so she must be careful."

"Did you say anything about coal?"

"She knew. Your blackened shirts."

He worked his mouth. "Did you let on about Pennsylvania?"

"I said you needed the wallet to buy tickets."

The professor's face had gone to purple. "Fool! Traitor!" He stood up, his fists at his side. Was he going to hit me? I took a step back just as there was a knock on the outside door. I jogged to the entry, glad of the interruption.

Phaegin stood on the other side with her arms akimbo. "*What* are you doing?"

I stepped outside. "Excuse me?"

"That *guttersnipe*. What are you doing with him?"

"Are you talking about Curly?" I stepped out and shut the door behind us. "Listen, I've got a situation here. . . . How did you know about Curly?"

She sighed. "My brothers saw you at the train station."

I narrowed my eyes. "Are those two thugs—"

"My brothers."

"Your brothers? Why have they been following me?"

She shrugged. "They thought you were makin' moves on me."

"I thought they were spies. You know one of them almost broke my nose?"

Phaegin shook her head and waved her hands as if to fan the question away. "The *guttersnipe,* Ned. What are you doing with him? My brothers say he's trouble, and if they think he's trouble, I can't imagine. You want to do yourself out of your Yale education? Don't be stupid."

Quillan flung open the door. Phaegin's eyes went round as saucers at the florid man. Quillan jabbed his finger in her direction. "Who is *this*?"

"A friend," I stammered. "Phaegin Harte, Professor Quillan."

Phaegin curtsied but Quillan ignored her to shout at me. "You said you didn't know anyone."

I shrugged. "Except for Phaegin."

He looked at her. "What *kind* of friend is she? What have you been telling her?"

Phaegin frowned. "Whaddaya mean, *what kind of friend*?"

He stared at her a minute, then pointed at the chain around her neck. "What the deuce is that?" He grabbed it and jerked while Phaegin shrieked and slapped at him.

The professor stared at his palm. "*Where did you get this?*"

Phaegin looked at me. I looked at what lay on the professor's palm. It was the tiny turtle fossil I had given Phaegin on Christmas, hung on a chain.

My heart sank. "I am so sorry, Professor. This is my fault. My mistake."

"Your *mistake*? No. My trust in you is the mistake. This is robbery! Get out. *Get out!* Leave now, before I call the police!"

He backed into the lab, banged the door shut, the lock grating into place.

CHAPTER 21

I pounded on the door. I yelled, "Please, Professor, let me explain! Please!" I went around and shouted under the high window of his office until Phaegin stopped me.

"This is doing no good at all. You'll just convince him he was right if you act panicked."

I shook my head. "I *am* panicked. My life is in there. My future. My Yale education, my career, my patron." I paced. "My notebook is in there." I threw up my hands. "My jacket is in there and Tilfert's *hat*."

Phaegin took hold of my arm and shook it. "Calm down. He's not opening the door, is he? If you don't stop he'll call someone to make you. Is that going to be an improvement?"

My knees shook. It was worse than the mine, because there wasn't any tiny bright star to crawl out to. How had this happened?

Phaegin led me away. "Come on, let's go get something to eat, and—"

"Eat? With what? My last pennies are in my *jacket*!"

Phaegin glared at me. "*I'll* buy you a blasted roll. You'll sit down, tell me what this is about, and we'll figure what's what."

"I don't know what it's about!"

She put her hand on my chest. "There. It's gonna be fine. Ready?" She waited a minute as I panted, wild-eyed. "You *gotta* be ready, Ned. No coat, you'll catch your death out here with all

213

the dramatics, and none of us got the haves for a doctor. Now, let's go." She strode off.

I took a steadying breath and followed her.

Phaegin brought two mugs of tea to the table at the Royal Finch, and I filled her in on what had happened in the three days since the professor and I had left for Pittsburgh.

She dunked a fried doughnut in her tea. "It's the kid. You've brought on bad luck with that one."

I scoffed. "You haven't even met him."

"My brother said he saw him pinch a lady's wallet and pick a pocket in five minutes."

I frowned, thinking of Curly and the pastries he'd paid for at the station, then snapped at Phaegin. "Why have your brothers been dogging me?"

"Because they're stupid." She shrugged. "They thought you and I . . . don't worry. I straightened them out. You're safe."

"Safe? I'm *wrecked*. Why did you have to wear the stupid fossil like that?"

Phaegin stiffened. "Why did you have to give me stolen goods as a gift?"

"Why did you have to get me drunk?"

"'Cause I never saw anybody get drunk on *half a beer* before."

We glared at each other. Phaegin put her chin in her hand. "It couldna been just the fossil, Ned. He was mad before he saw it."

I nodded. "It's something about his wife, and then the money the coal company was giving him was canceled or something in that telegraph. I told him I warned Mrs. Quillan about your brothers and told her we were going to Pittsburgh, and he called me a fool and a traitor."

"Whoo. Can you make heads or tails of it?"

I shook my head. "He never told me anything except how big it was and how I had to keep quiet about it all."

Phaegin finished off her drink. "Well, now you can lose the kid."

I was aghast. "You're kidding."

"You shouldna taken him on in the first place. If he wanted out of that mine, he's got two legs to walk."

"He was indentured."

"Now he's free. Give him his paper and off with him."

"You're softhearted."

"But not softheaded."

"Just meet him. He's not bad."

But Curly wasn't at Mother's. Mother waved at a pile of kindling. "I gave him a job to do, and he did it all right, but that one wasn't hangin' round for the next instruction. I haven't seen him since lunch."

Phaegin nodded. "Well, there's a problem that took care of itself."

But Curly walked in, his hands behind his back. "Ned, I been lookin' for ya!" He stared at me accusingly. "You said you'd be at the Peabody."

"Oh, God, you didn't go there, did you?"

He grinned. "Did. They said you worked downstairs. The outside door was locked, so I nipped through the museum." Curly shook his head. "That Quillan fella's worse today than he was yestiday. Said *you* was fired and called *me* a thief and a sneak." He brought his arms forward and offered my jacket and Tilfert's hat. "Got these back for ya."

I groaned. Curly looked dejected. I took the jacket and hat then had another look at him. "You're dressed different." He'd lost the short pants, newsboy cap, and scuffed shoes. He had dungarees on, a woolen vest, and boots. I fingered the cloth he'd tied around his neck: a dishrag.

Curly stuck his thumbs in his lapels. "Wanted to look like a cowboy. Like you. But I couldn't find a hat."

"Where did you get the money?"

Curly pulled a sly face. "Folks *gave* me these clothes. They're jus' throw-ways."

Mother clicked her tongue.

Phaegin snorted loudly and Curly took a good look at her. He whistled. "Hey, sweet *potato!*"

Phaegin smacked him on the cheek and Curly laughed like he'd been tickled. Phaegin pointed at him. "Cut your line before he drags you in."

Curly looked astonished. "He's the one two-handin' that professor's wife's hooty-toot. Least I got morals about married wimmin."

"What are you talking about?"

He looked sorry. "I don't fault you, Ned. Can't make a mare drink an' all."

I wanted to strangle him. "What about the professor's wife?"

He grinned. "They're all bombilatin' 'bout it, museum-wise. Honey's gone off with some dinosaur fella from Boston."

Mother clucked again. "Oh, dear. You've been stirred in the stew."

Phaegin nodded. "You weren't the fool and traitor, Ned. He was calling himself a fool, and his *wife* is the traitor!"

Curly nodded. "An' the fella found out about Professor Q
turnin' the sheets inside out and sellin' 'em new." He poked the
air. "Makin' 'is own fossils, Quillan was. Carvin' 'em out of coal.
And that other fella breaks wind about it to American Coal and
all bets is off!"

I felt my knees wobble. How could this be happening? At
breakfast I was a man of prospects. It wasn't even lunchtime yet.
I grabbed Curly's shoulder. "How could you know this?"

He looked proud. "Hid in the teeny elevator. Had to wait
the longest time for the room to clear out; they was *all* in a chatter. Then the box went down—somebody pullin' the rope. I
thought I was a goner fer sure—and when the door opened,
Quillan was lookin' at me like he seen a ghost. But when he got
his hoo-hah back—*ohhh*, boy! Tried to trim my hair with his
shovel. I grabbed those"—he waved at the coat and hat—"on
my way *out*."

I sank down, my back against the wall. "This just gets worse."

Mother shook her finger at me. "I tol' you to watch that fellow. Anybody works a man like he worked you is going to have
no good in him, and *now* look at the state of Molly. Shit always
drops, Ned."

"What am I going to do?" One week ago I was practically
Edward Turrentine Bayard III again; now, Mother and Phaegin
were looking at me with pity. And they didn't know the half of
it. No one would hire me as a scientist, now that I had inadvert-
ently aided Quillan with his scheme. They'd mark me an idiot,
and they'd be right.

Curly looked absolutely nonplussed. "Ah, it always works out."
He fussed with the dishcloth around his neck.

Mother cleared her throat. "Hurts to say it, Neddy, but you have to go. Between you and that one"—she nodded toward Curly—"there's upset all over you, and I can't have it here."

I nodded. "I'll get my things."

I put my change of clothing, the pistol, my father's watch, Avelina's gold medal, and the photograph of Lill in my leather bag. I'd come with all those things, plus my notebook and hope. I'd acquired nothing but Curly, lost the notebook, and all hope had evaporated. Mother hugged me as I left and pressed a few dollars into my palm. "Of course you take it, Ned. I'd keep you if I could, but I got a past that won't take trouble, and this looks like it all over again."

I nodded. "Thanks."

She whispered, "Keep in touch, if you can."

Phaegin clapped her hat on her head. "I'm late. No good for me to lose *my* job. Hurry up, and I'll drop you at Sean and Pete's."

"Your brothers'? I don't think so."

"I told you it was a misunderstanding. You've got nowhere to go, no money to speak of. They'll let you stay until you've figured something out." She looked grim. "I'll make 'em."

She led us to a basement room close to the saloon where we had first sung Christmas carols. She rapped on the door and opened it without waiting. "Get awake, will you? It's two in the afternoon, for pity's sake!"

Her brothers sat up groggily from a pile of filthy blankets on the floor. Phaegin motioned toward Curly and me. "They're stayin' for a time." She pulled one red head toward her by the hair and whispered in his ear. He frowned and looked at us. She whispered again, jerking his head for punctuation, and he shouted, "All right, all right, will ya?"

Phaegin nodded. "See you later."

I followed her toward the door. "Are you coming here after work?"

She shook her head. "I can't. I have to work till late. I'll be goin' straight to bed after. But I'll see you tomorrow. Don't worry about *them*." She inclined her head toward her glowering brothers. "I've taken care of it."

I felt Phaegin had left us in a lion's den, but Curly was perfectly happy. He patted his vest pocket and pulled out a deck of cards. "Three-hand draw?" Sean and Pete grinned and pulled some change from their pockets. Curly whispered, "See me a quarter?"

I shook my head. "We're homeless and practically penniless. I'm not throwing money away on games."

Curly glared at me and whispered again. "It's not throwin', it's investin'. Come on, Ned. Trust me."

I handed him a nickel. I had to have quiet to think. Curly looked at it and sighed. "Better'n nothin', I guess."

In three hours I'd come up with no plan at all. The more I thought about my situation, the more hopeless it seemed. Curly, however, had amassed the princely sum of two dollars. He piled the coins into towers on the table, swept them with a clatter into his palm, and poured them dramatically into his pocket. Pete and Sean looked to be on the edge of violence. Curly grinned, jumped up and down jangling his winnings to torture them, then addressed me. "Let's cut outta here and let these fishes come to terms with their failures." He giggled and gave me an aside. "Or we're gonna have to defend ourselves." I followed him to the door, regarded the brothers' resentful demeanor, and grabbed my valise to take with me.

Curly whistled. Night was gathering and the chill deepened. "Warmer than Widowmaker, but still. . . ." He shivered. "Where should we go?"

"I don't know, Curly."

He patted my back. "Cheer up, Ned. It's gonna be all right. No matter what that Phaegin says, I'm lucky."

I exploded. "How do you figure that? You're covered with scars, stunted from lack of nutrition, stuck in an orphanage, and then indentured for seven years—"

He shook his orange head. "Most woulda been killed by what I took. Got lucky. Bein' short lets you slip by unnoticed-like. No one 'spects *nothin'* from you. That's lucky. If I wasn't in the orphanage, wouldna ate; not indentured, wouldna met you. Only had to work five of the seven I owed. Lucky, lucky." He jingled again. "Luck is Curly's middle name."

I nodded. He rubbed his arms briskly. "Lucky but cold." He pointed to the nickel dump down the street. "Warm and lively." He sniffed. "I smell eats. Let's go."

"Costs to get in."

"On me."

Curly bought us battered cod and ale. Watching him quaff his drink was like seeing a puppy bring down an elephant. Then he scrabbled around on the floor until he had a fist full of cigarette butts.

"Don't *tell* me you're smoking those."

"OK." He lit one and offered another to me. When I refused, he sat back and puffed the stubs with great relish. "Hey, there's that harridan of yourn."

I looked across the dance floor. Phaegin was coming through the door alongside a fellow with a straw boater and shiny patent oxfords.

"*She* got a strike!"

"She'll be looking for us."

"She's lookin' for somewhat else, mate." He glanced at me and shook his head. "She ain't lookin' for *us*."

I put my hand up but Curly grabbed my arm. "Don' go embarrassin' yourself."

It was quickly evident that Phaegin wasn't looking for us at all. She had eyes for no one but the man she was leaning on. She laughed and smiled and preened at every single thing he said.

Curly grinned. "He must be a conversin' hero over there, she's so . . ." He drew his shoulders up and twinked his face into a girlish simulation of adoration.

"Shut up."

He looked surprised. "I thought there wasn't nothing between—"

"There's not."

He smoked another butt. Phaegin and the fellow sat down; she had her hand on his arm. She wore white kid gloves.

Curly stood up. "Another round."

We drank two more ales. Now Phaegin was talking and the man laughed uproariously, his head back and his mouth open like a hippo's.

Curly slurped. "Lotsa dames in the world. That one, *she's* not so great."

"Never said she was."

"Not even very pretty. Got a lot of eyebrow, only get worse."

Curly smoked another butt then threw it on the sanded floor. "This ain't *half* the fun I thought it was going to be!"

I ignored him.

He sighed. "Those salt-and-pepper shakers are probably out for the night by now. Let's go back and get some shuteye."

The man stood and offered his arm to Phaegin. I didn't want to see them dance. If I had thought I felt as emptied as I could get before, I'd been wrong. Further, the empty was filling quickly with something hard and sour.

I grabbed Tilfert's hat, pulled it on, and kicked over my chair. "Yep. We've got a whole load of *nothing* to do tomorrow, Curly. We'd better rest up."

As we rounded the corner outside, we almost ran into Phaegin's brothers crouching by a window. They straightened. "What the hell do you want?"

Curly nodded. "This is a better crap hole than I thought if they won't let you two in."

Pete sneered, "We could get in all right if we wanted to."

I narrowed my eyes. "You're dogging Phaegin. Why?"

"She's got a taste for posh types, and we don't *like* it."

Sean concurred. "She wants a fella, she can have one from her own people."

Pete poked me in the chest. "Not one a *you*."

I laughed. "I'm broke, no job, no family, I'm sleeping on your floor. How low do I have to fall to be good enough for your sister?"

Curly laughed like a coot. He pulled me along behind him. "Come on, Ned. You got better things ahead a you than this lot."

CHAPTER 22

Dear Lill,

Hold on. Our lives have seasons we can't predict. When it rains it feels forever, but we must believe that the sun will shine again.

"I look out for you, find you a place to stay, and this is the thanks I get?" Phaegin laughed in a way that showed she was *not* amused.

"You said you were *working* last night."

"I was. Kind of."

Now Curly guffawed and Phaegin grabbed a bottle from the table, walked over to where Curly lay with a blanket over him, and sloshed what was left of the beer on his orange curls.

Curly sat up and shouted *"Hey!"*

She pointed. "You'll get more'n that if you don't shut up."

I glared at her. "Don't take it out on Curly. You lied to me."

"It wasn't a lie, it was none of your business."

"You said Yale boys bored you to tears."

She crossed her arms. "If being bored is the only thing I cry about in my life, I am going to be a very happy woman indeed."

"You said you wouldn't marry. Obviously *I* wasn't good enough for you."

"You never *asked.*"

This stopped me for a moment with the sweet specter of connubial bliss. Then bitterness crept in. "So, you would have had me, maybe if I actually had gotten into Yale, maybe if my inheritance materialized?"

"No, Ned, that's not it."

I shook my head in disgust. "You're going to marry some biscuit because he's rich."

"I'm not marrying anybody. And if I was, so what? At least I wasn't falsifying anything or stealing."

"Right. All of that cooing and giggling and lip pursing and nose crinkling came right from the heart." I snorted. "Not falsifying anything."

Curly laughed. Phaegin shouted at him, "Get out!"

Curly, still laughing, struggled up from the blanket. "I'm going, I'm going." He paused when he walked by her, farted loudly, laughed uproariously, and went out.

Phaegin sat down. "*Did* you tell me he *wasn't* bad?"

I shrugged.

Phaegin patted the table. "Sit with me, Ned."

We sat in silence for quite a while. I refused to look at her. Finally Phaegin slapped her hand to her forehead. "You are such a mug. I wasn't courting Chester, not like that." She sighed. "He's investing in my hat shop."

I snorted. "What's the interest on the loan that swine is offering?"

"Nothing I wouldn't be *happy* to give, all right? I'm sorry if you're hurt, but it's silly. You've got Lill on your mind, I have old age on mine." She took my hand. "Chester's got a funny lip. Makes it so that no one else wants anything to do with him, but it makes him sweeter than most, too. He likes to laugh, he don't mind who I am or where I came from. He thinks I'm smart." She squeezed my hand. "Don't you be a pig. You said we were friends. I told you that's all we could be. After all you said, are you gonna tell me it isn't enough? Are you just the kind of man you seem to think Chester is?"

I gritted my teeth. Her cajoling was way off the mark. I was supposed to feel better because we had a pure friendship while she sold herself for a boatload of feathers and ribbon?

I pulled my hand from hers. "Go ahead, ruin your life. Take money from that man and you might as well *be* married, all the joy *that* will provide. And you're wrong if you think a borrowed milliner's life is going to make you happy."

She leaned across the table. "Who expects happiness, Ned?"

Who, indeed? I put my head on the table. At one time, I'd thought if I could just breathe, expand my chest fully in deep draws, I would be happy. Now, I hardly noticed the miracle of my clear lungs.

Phaegin recaptured my hands in hers. "Ned, please."

I stared at her soft earnest face, good brown hair, good brown eyes, and sweet but sad mouth and felt my antagonism melting. Why shouldn't she believe in better? Maybe that was happiness, just thinking it was coming.

I nodded. "Sure. Do what you want. We'll be friends. Just . . . don't lie to me. Friends don't lie to each other."

She spit on her palm and held it to her heart. "Honesty forever."

Curly burst in the door. "Shit! I'm *not* here!" He dove under the blankets.

There was shouting from outside. "He went in *there!*"

Phaegin jumped into my lap, stuck my hand on her backside, pulled the pin from her hair, and planted her lips on mine.

The door banged open. Two policemen stood in the opening. Phaegin panted. "'Ere, now, can't a woman have a private moment?" The policemen looked at her mussed hair, my hand, our flushed faces, and closed the door.

Phaegin whispered, her lips against mine, "Just until they're truly gone. For safety." The shouting faded outside, but I couldn't tell if it was because the men had actually left or if it was merely masked by the wash of my heart, camouflaged by the softness on my palms.

I didn't know how long the kiss lasted. It seemed both forever and hardly a moment before Curly broke the spell. "*Enough* already. Gone a mile down the road by now."

I stepped back and Curly giggled.

"Ned's got a handle, don't he now!"

Phaegin walked over and grabbed Curly by the ear and stuck a hand down his shirt. She pulled out a cheese, half a salami, and seven sticks of horehound candy, put them on the table, and flung Curly back onto the blanket. Curly howled and clapped a hand to his ear.

Phaegin *tsk-tsk*ed. "You'll have us ruined for *this*?"

We stared at the meager plunder.

Phaegin rubbed her hands together and announced, "Let's get rid of the evidence."

For a week I lectured Curly on ending his thievery. I told him morality tales, narrated what would happen if he was caught, threatened to turn him in, leave him, send him back to the mine. He always looked sorry, not really about the stealing itself but sorry at bothering me so much with it. He told me over and over that he'd try to stop; then he'd bring in a ham or show up in a new hat, or I'd find him examining a flowered vase he'd taken off a windowsill.

"You said you'd stop!" I shouted.

"Nah, I said I'd try, and I *really* did."

I was terribly afraid that Curly would be caught. Though he was rough, he was also childlike and seemed to adore me like no one ever had; I was good and softened by it. I would catch him studying me, practicing a small mannerism of mine. He liked to walk beside me, and I found his company sunny and droll. But then he would disappear and I dreaded the sound of the police whistle.

I was afraid Curly felt he had to steal to keep us, and though I tried to disavow him of that notion, I didn't have much of a leg to stand on. We ate Sean and Pete's leavings, we ate Curly's pilfered goods, or we ate nothing. Phaegin stopped by every so often, leaving a basket of bread and a salami, but she was working overtime for her hat concern, both at the cigar shop and with Chester.

Pete and Sean were furious with her.

"What are you so mad about?" I asked. "Knowing her, she'll make a go of it, and things might be easier for you."

Sean snorted. "Easier, nuthin'. She'll be too falutin' for real people. She won't have the time of day for her ol' family, too damn good for us."

Pete reddened with the thought. "Too damn good. She's a piece o' work, all right, with her business and rubbin' elbows with ladies and their furs."

"Won't want us on the sidewalk, much less embarrassin' her inside," Sean shouted.

"Drivin' away the business!" Pete roared.

Curly grinned. "That's right. She tol' me she was gonna have you arrested for loiterin'. Lost four lady customers las' week on account of you dogs lollin' in the hat window, tryin' on the lids."

"I knew it!" Sean knocked over the table in his fury.

I jumped back from the crash. "Call your brains back, Sean, are you running on cornmeal? She doesn't even *have* the shop yet."

Sean pulled himself together and kicked the giggling Curly in the pants. "Just thinkin' the way things are gonna go."

I shook my head. "It could go well for you too. Put a good hat on your head, you might get a job."

Curly sneered. "Dress a dog in pinstripes, you got a striped dog. Think of what it'd do to these two."

Sean shook his head. "You laugh, but Ned should know, usta *be* a gennleman."

There it was again, the past tense. At this rate I *would have been* more things before I was twenty than most people are in an entire lifetime. I protested, "I'm *still* a gentleman."

Curly shook his head sadly. "Easier to fall down than get up."

I tried to see Quillan again and again, at the lab and even at his house, but the housekeeper told me he had gone on vacation for an unlimited time.

My attempt to find work went no better. The city was filled with hordes of unemployed. All I could do was hang on until Quillan returned, calmer, I hoped, out of hot water himself and ready to listen to reason. I told myself he'd be fine. If I knew Quillan, he wouldn't let anything stand between him and his fossils. He'd pick up and pick me up too.

* * *

Friday morning I woke up, headed out to use the water closet, and tripped on a bare leg. Comely, not the ape shank of a twin or one of Curly's scarred bandy legs. A naked woman lay in the tangle of blanket. She opened one eye and slowly drew her leg out of the way. Curly snuggled in her arms, his orange head buttressed by large breasts.

The paint on her lips and cheeks if not her nudity told me what she was. And the sight of little Curly in her arms was more than shocking. I asked stupidly, "What are you doing here?"

The woman was haggard; her suety hair hadn't seen a brush in a year. She put a finger to her lips and rasped, "Doll's just gone to sleep."

"Doll?" I reached over and shook Curly. "Get *up!*"

He sat up, naked as she was, rubbing his fists in his eyes. He leaned back on his arms and smiled. "You meet Sapphire?"

Sapphire put out her hand. "Charmed."

I pulled the clothes from the back of the chair and threw them at her. "Out. Now."

She stood up, not at all abashed at her nakedness, though I glowed like a lantern. Sapphire put her hands on her hips and waggled them and her head, flesh jiggling like aspic. "S'cuse *me,* Mr. Toity." She threw a raggedy dance dress over her head, sat down, and began lacing her shoes. "I kin see what yer problem is." She slid her legs open. "Come on, you'll like it. Make the first time real special."

Curly watched her happily. "Go 'head, she's just the prettiest thing!"

She smiled at him. "You are sweet." She kissed the top of his head, then gazed at me. "Well?"

"Get out."

She shrugged and held out her hand. Curly reached under the pillow and gave her the bill he drew out.

"Five dollars?" I was incredulous.

Sapphire tucked it into her bodice and hurried from the room, as if she could tell I was contemplating wresting it from her grip.

I pointed at the closed door. "We're broke and you gave *her* five dollars?"

Curly nodded sleepily and lay back down. "Shoulda tried her. She's so nice. Warm and softish. Wish I had a fiver every day." He sighed. "I'd give it to her just to fall asleep on her bosoms."

"Is that all? You just slept?"

He grinned, his eyes closed. "Whatta waste *that* woulda been."

I was in over my head. If we judged by experience, Curly should have adopted *me*. Even the prostitute could see it. I shook my head. The act notwithstanding, how had Curly got hold of five dollars? Did I want to know? The tide just kept pouring in, and I couldn't take a breath. I grabbed my coat. Curly sat upright. "Wait, I'll go with ya."

"I don't want you with me."

He began putting his pants on nonetheless. "What're we doin' today, Ned?"

"*We're* not doing anything. Go back to sleep."

"I'm not really tired."

I slammed the door behind me. He yelled, "Wait up!" He opened the door, one boot on, one in hand, his shirt in his teeth. I took off at a jog. Curly shrieked, "Ned!"

I stopped. Curly caught up, one foot still bare and muddy. He dropped the boot and stuck his arms in his shirt, panting. "Hol' on, left my coat, gotta go back, jus' wait, 'kay, Ned? Jus' wait?"

I put out my hand to steady him while he put his other boot on. "Curly, I don't *want* you with me. Stay here, go somewhere else, I don't care. Just don't follow me."

"Well, sure, if you want. Maybe we can meet somewhere." He brightened. "I know where I can get a pie. I'll bring a pie."

"How are you going to get a pie? You spent five dollars on the whore. Do you have more money, Curly?"

"Nah, not right now."

"I don't want a stolen pie, Curly. I don't want a stolen dollar."

Curly shrugged. "We gotta *eat*, Ned. Mother won't notice one less pie."

"You would steal from Mother?"

"*Look* at 'er, Ned," Curly protested. "It's a service to keep her *from* it!"

I couldn't help myself and laughed at his reasoning, then sobered. "If she found out you stole a pie it would hurt her, Curly."

"Nah, nah, wouldn't."

"It *would*."

Curly looked suddenly worried and perhaps even sorry. I took pity on him.

"You can meet me later, *without the pie*, on the green, at—" I felt my pocket, then another. "Where's my watch, Curly?"

He looked uneasy. "It's safe, Ned. Don' worry."

I grabbed his shoulders. "Where's my watch?"

He smiled at me. "I borrowed it, but I kin get it back."

I shook him. "I'm asking you one more time. *Where's my watch?*"

"Pawned it for the five dollars. I'll get it back, Ned. Easy. That's what pawning is."

"That's my *father's* watch. It's all I have, you little guttersnipe!"
I spun away and balled my fists. The last tie I had with Edward
Turrentine Bayard, the only proof of who I was, the only picture I had to look at to get back to him, gone. The filament
snapped. I was well and truly hopelessly adrift. I snatched off
Tilfert's hat and shouted into the sky, "God damn you! Phaegin
was right. All I've had is bad luck since I met you." I wanted to
smack him, flatten him. Instead I walked away.

He followed. "I promise I'll get it back. Somebody's got some
work for me, said *big* pay. I shoulda done it afore, but I can get
it yet, maybe tomorrow or the day after. I promise."

He put out his hand and touched my jacket. I spun and took
hold of the front of his shirt, which hung unbuttoned on his
skinny white chest. I spoke close to his snub nose and worried
grin. "Get—away—from—me. We are no longer associates." I
shoved him, he fell into the street, and except for a small "Ned?,"
he did nothing but watch me leave.

CHAPTER 23

Curly didn't show at Pete and Sean's that night. He wasn't in his nest of blankets the next morning. By afternoon I was swinging from furious to terrified.

Pete shrugged. "He probably found that whore again. Paid her enough for a solid *week*."

I walked around downtown and didn't see him. Asked around the nickel dump, searched for both Sapphire and Curly. Curly was nowhere to be seen, but I found Sapphire by the train station.

She sashayed over. "Little fella tell you what you was missing, cowboy?"

"*He's* missing. Have you seen him?"

She looked worried. "No, hope he's all right, though. That night I was with him, he jus' curled up like a little kitten after he finished. Usually I won't stay over, but he was just so cuddlesome I wanted to play house with that one."

I went to Mother's and asked if a pie went missing. She said not, tut-tutted over Curly, gave me a sandwich, and told me it was for the best, that boy going his own bad way. She patted my arm and smiled. "I know what'll cheer you. Another letter arrived from that girl in Nebraska, *and* a feller stopped by with a paper for you." She waddled out and returned with a letter from Lill that I put in my pocket to read later. The paper was pale brown and crackling, as if it had been toasted over a flame. I opened it and found an accounting of the auction of our house

233

in Cornwall. It brought $32,650, less $800 paid to Cornelius Pierce.

I sat down. I turned the paper over. It was blank. Where did the money go? Why was the house auctioned at all? Certainly not for an eight-hundred-dollar debt. "Who gave you this?"

"Youngish man, like you. Wanted to know if Edward Turrentine Bayard the Third was stayin' here. Took me aback a minit, but then I remembered it were you." She chuckled. "Turrentine, hoo-la-da!" Mother Fenton noticed I wasn't in the mood for humor and continued. "Anyhow, fella looked a little mouse-'n-corner, but earnest-like, so I said you'd be by." She nodded at the paper. "He gave me that and said he were mailing more. *Expect a packet tomorrow,* he said."

"Was the fellow weasel-faced?"

Mother Fenton nodded.

It must be the clerk Montgomery Elias had mentioned. Oh, I'd trusted too much and waited too long to take matters into my own hands. That was going to change. I would make a personal visit to Alan and Jamieson immediately and demand a full accounting of my affairs. I'd *walk* all the way to Danbury if need be.

I took a deep breath, attempting to stem my impatience. I would wait one more day. I'd be better informed once the packet arrived. Besides, right now I had to find Curly—if I *could* find him. I had looked almost everywhere. The only places left were terrible possibilities.

I went to the neighborhood precinct and asked the police captain if they'd picked up a boy. Then, perspiring with dread, I went to the hospital and asked there. They checked both the patient list and the morgue.

Relieved of some worry, I then figured maybe Curly'd gone back to Scranton. Maybe he'd decided his old hell was better than mine. I hated to think of him in the mines again. The image of him abandoned, eyes aglow as I rose to safety, made me shudder.

I waited outside the cigar shop for Phaegin. When she saw me she squealed and ran over. "I was going to come by. Look!" She waved a card in her hand. "Chester's loaning me the money. We sign the papers this afternoon!"

I nodded. "Congratulations. Have you seen Curly?"

"Congratulations? That's *it?*"

"Phaegin, Curly's been gone for two days."

"Well, congratulations to *you,* is all I can say."

I put my hands to my head then waved her off. "Fine. Hope you'll be very happy in the hat business."

She stamped her foot. "I'm sorry the stinking ash cat's gone. But you know he's up to no good somewhere. Find trouble and you'll find him. Or worse, vice versa."

"I *have* to find him."

She pointed at me. "You have a problem with wanting to save people who shouldn't be saved. First that Lill girl, now the guttersnipe."

"Yeah, well, I tried to talk you out of prostituting yourself too."

"I'm *not* . . . don't *do* this, Ned."

I glared at her a minute, but she looked so hopeful, so happy, I gave in. "Fine. I'm sorry. But help me find Curly. I've received some very important information and I've got to get to Danbury right away. I can't go without knowing Curly's all right."

She glanced at the card and smiled before looking up. "All right. I'll look for *one hour.* I don't care if he's being boiled alive after that. I have to get ready for the bank and nothing's going to stop me from being on time."

As evening came on we searched downtown in a tightening circle. We asked everyone who would look at us if they had seen a skinny red-headed boy wearing a dishcloth around his neck. No one had.

Phaegin asked me for the time. I shook my head. "I lost my watch."

"*No*. Your father's?"

I looked away.

"It was Curly, wasn't it? I can't *believe* you're looking for him after he stole your father's watch." She shook her head. "I can't be late." She grabbed my hand and towed me over to where a crowd had gathered around a fellow giving a speech from the top of a pile of crates. A policeman paced, his billy in hand. Phaegin asked him for the time then told me she had to go.

"Ten more minutes," I pleaded. "Phaegin, please."

She pursed her lips. "It won't make a difference. He's gone, Ned. An' if he's in this crowd—" her voice dropped to a whisper "—he's picking pockets."

The green was fair bursting with people. Men carried signs that exhorted workers to unite while others leaned against lampposts or stood, hands in pockets, listening to the speechmaking. About a quarter of the onlookers looked like workers; the rest were business people, investor types, in pressed suits of good fabric and shining shoes. The ranks of police swelled as we searched. The officers looked tense and irate, more interested in breaking up than uniting anything.

A wagon was pushed into place facing the crate dais. It was draped in bunting with an American flag fluttering from a make-shift pole. A man in a black suit was helped onto the bed and he took off his jacket and began shouting down the other fellows. Several boys handed out flyers. I wished Curly had found such wholesome employment, but Curly was not among them.

The action picked up. The orators shouted more and more vehemently, a shoving match broke out in the crowd. I couldn't make out what anyone was saying in the din. I nudged Phaegin. "What's going on here, anyway?"

Phaegin glanced up then back at the banker's card again. "Gun factory works. Owners trying to break a start-up union. Gotta eat the little people all up, deny 'em a decent wage." Phaegin shouted through the cup of her hands. "Rich pigs!"

Someone behind us shouted, "Eight-hour days!"

The man with the bunting shouted something about the threat of socialism, rusting our good society from within. A roar of agreement. A tumult of booing.

"You're going to be one of the rich pigs, Phaegin," I pointed out. "Soon enough you'll work poor little Irish girls to the bone for pennies, sewing ribbon on hats."

She snorted, then grabbed my arm. "There's your boy."

I searched the crowd. "Where?"

"There. Got somethin' in 'is hand. Stole it, I'll bet anythin'."

Phaegin pushed her way through the tight knots of people. By the time I got there, she had a hold of his ear and Curly was hissing venom, attempting to hide a curious grapefruit-sized orb under his vest, then holding it at arm's length from Phaegin's reach. "Let go of me, you bloody whore!"

She shook him. "You're not going nowhere. What are you up to?"

He looked up and saw me. His eyes got huge. "Ned, get outta here. Take Phaegin, *quick*. You gotta run, hurry!" He gave Phaegin a mighty kick in the shin. She screamed and all eyes turned our way. She spat "Filthy rotter!" at him as he twisted free. Curly danced away with the orb, screamed, "Run, Ned! Now or never!"

I shook my head, confused.

Curly moaned and considered the ball, which was welded from zinc or maybe tin, a bolt protruding from one side to the other, with a length of what looked like candlewick protruding from a hole in the seam. He shook his head, tucked the ball gingerly back into his vest, and shouted, "Forget them, let's git!"

By this time we had attracted a great deal of attention. Two policemen were heading our way with some dispatch when I saw, in the gloaming, a little tail of fire quivering overhead. I thought for a split second someone had thrown a cigar, but then heard a hissing sound and figured it for a firecracker or squib tossed by a prankish boy.

I followed Curly and Phaegin with some haste, hoping the squib might prove a distraction in our favor. When I glanced back to gauge the law's proximity, a vivid column of fire erupted six to eight feet above the crowd and rained down upon them. As if a thick dark sheet was then thrown over the world, nothing was visible for a blink. Then an entire wave of people shrank to the ground, followed by a deafening roar and a screech of breaching wood. I was hit by what felt like a giant's fist, lofted backward some fifteen feet into the people behind me.

The horrible din was shadowed by uncanny silence. I could see a wheel in the air. The wagon from which the suited man had been shouting dispersed as if made of paper. All around, flitting through gauzy smoke, hovered bits and pieces of wood and brick and what else I could not think about.

I dumbly surveyed the scene confused by the silence, all those mouths open with no voice, rubble falling quiet as feathers, animals flailing with no scuff or breath. I cupped my ears, and like an oncoming train the sound returned: a hum rising to terrible volume. There came the horrendous shriek of horses, screams of terror, agonized moans. A chimney collapsed amid shouts of warning, followed by the clatter and thud of masonry on slate and sod.

I looked at my hands. They were covered with blood. I found it was not mine, but the gentleman's on whom I'd fallen. A piece of debris had been shot through his neck, leaving a hole the size of a silver dollar. I could see the carotid artery pulse, and I hastened to stanch his wound with my jacket, but his eyes were already dull and unseeing.

In horror, I began shouting for Phaegin, for Curly, but doubted they would hear me as the riot of screaming and crying was considerable. I searched through the haze, terrified I would recognize them among the terribly wounded and dead. One man sat staring at his foot, still in a shiny patent wingtip, which hung by a mere shred of skin to his ankle. Another was crawling along the ground, shouting for help. A woman cradled her sobbing husband in her arms. The closer to the wagons, the less the victims resembled humans than ghastly meat, and I turned from the sight. An old man pulled out a Bible and began reading from it. Policemen whistled for help.

With relief that made my eyes run and stomach clench I saw Phaegin pulling Curly to his feet. Their faces were dark with smoke and dust, Phaegin's lip was split, and Curly had a bleeding scrape across his cheek, but they were otherwise unscathed. We clutched each other for a moment, but Curly whispered, "We need hightail it outta here."

A man whose dusty gray suit had been ripped by a piece of flying debris stood unsteadily staring at us, mouth agape. He pulled his jacket aside to stare at a six-inch piece of shingle that protruded from his side, then considered us once again. I went to him at once, shouting, "Help! This man needs help!" Phaegin took his elbow. The policeman who'd given Phaegin the time came running.

The injured man did not take his eyes off Curly. When the policeman was near, the man gasped, "I am Cyrus Wright, president of Wright Steelworks." He lifted a shaking arm to point at Curly. "*He* did it, officer, I saw it. He did it. Had a bomb and some woman"—he looked right and left at Phaegin and me— "it was her." He struggled free of us and shouted again, "Those three! Anarchists!"

The officer turned toward Phaegin as she shook her head. "No."

The man looked at the piece of bloody wood in his side and the red stain that grew down his white shirt and darkened his trousers. He hissed, "Murderers! They've killed me!" and fell over.

Curly took advantage of the collapse, ducking into the crowd while shouting, "Ned, save yer skin!"

The policeman immediately grabbed Phaegin. She was still shaking her head, protesting, "No, not me! Not me!"

I took hold of her waist. "Let her go, she didn't do anything!"

Phaegin was struggling hard now. The policeman pulled out his gun and pointed it at my head. "Haul up, or I'll shoot you both."

Phaegin and I froze.

There was a bloodcurdling scream, louder than any of the others. Curly launched himself at the policeman in a whirlwind of arms, legs, and wild orange hair, knocking the gun from the man's grasp. The policeman swore, swung the billy from his belt, and struck Curly across the skull. Curly fell, picked himself up, kicked the officer in the groin, and when the man doubled over the three of us fled through the smoke and the fallen.

CHAPTER 24

We returned to Pete and Sean's. Curly placed the tin orb on the table. Phaegin sobbed in the corner. I went to her, but when I put my hand on her shoulder she swung around and almost bloodied my nose.

Pete and Sean looked alarmed, shuffling their big feet back and forth on the wood floor. "Wot's she goin' on about? Did that Chester give her the heave? Wot's wrong?" Pete picked up the tin ball and tossed it idly into the air.

Curly yelped, "Mother Mary Magdalene!" and threw himself into the corner. Pete started and the ball dropped with a thud. Pete bent to pick it up, but Phaegin screamed, "Don't touch it!"

Pete snorted and picked it up. "Why not? Just an empty float."

Curly stood up and put his hands on his hips. "Huh?"

Pete rolled the nut off the bolt and peered inside. "Done as a bottle."

Curly started laughing crazily. He peered in the orb himself. "What nobs. Empty as Sunday, kin you believe?"

Phaegin shoved him into a chair and wiped her eyes with the back of her hands. "Who are you talkin' about? Cud it out now, Curly, or I'll have Sean squeeze it from you."

Curly stared at his feet. "Some dupes, I don't know nowhat else about 'em, tol' me I'd be a hero fer the workers if I lit an' threw that"—he indicated the tin orb on the floor—"into the crowd of swanks. And they'd pay me five dollars for the trouble." He leaned over, picked up the float, and rolled it back and forth on the table. "It was supposed to pop like a squib, jus' to get folks' scare up." He looked disturbed; his lip trembled. "Made a muddle of it, they did. One working naught, the other too good." He flung the orb back to the floor and put his head in his arms on the table. His shoulders shook. Phaegin looked away.

Suddenly Curly jumped and slapped his thigh. "On top of trouble, I can't get the watch. They were gonna pay me after." He shook his head at me. I could see the track of tears through the ash on his face. "If I charred the fuse, Ned, mebbe I could still collect. That it didn't pop is their mistake."

Phaegin wilted to the floor. "There was no mistake, you nit. They wouldn't trust *you* to throw the real bomb. You did everything they wanted perfectly. Showed up at the rally with your bush of red hair, made yourself conspicuous shoutin' and wavin' that fake bomb around. Whoever lit the real fuse is drinkin' grenadine right now while you're good as broiled for everything that happened." She gave me a tragic look. "And us along with him."

Curly sniffed. "I woulda been secret as a . . . as a . . . secret"— he pointed at Phaegin—"if you had not took hold of my ear thatta way."

I stared at him incredulously. He grinned apologetically at me. "Don't worry, Ned, I'll get that watch back somehow. *I will.*"

"Forget the watch, Curly! My God, that is nothing compared to the mess we're in now."

Curly apparently took that as forgiveness and, looking somewhat relieved, took a piece of folded paper and began to clean his nails, humming tonelessly.

Phaegin shouted hysterically. "Put a cork in it!" She gave an anguished sob, drew her hands through her hair, and rubbed her streaked face. "Pete, Sean. Listen to me. You have to go some-where else, out of town. Don't talk to anyone or let anyone see you. Stop only at Ma and Da's. Tell them not to worry, I'll make out. Then get out of New Haven and don't come back."

"Ever?"

"I don't know. Maybe. You're going to have to use your own sense. I'm not going to be here."

"Where are you going?"

"You don't need to know anything more. Just leave." She kissed them both. "Go now."

They shuffled out. Phaegin commenced to cry again as she went through the room, putting a few things in a bag. "This'll have to do, can't risk goin' back to my place." She snuffled. "Get your bag, let's go."

I shook my head. "Where?"

"We have to get *out* of here."

"No, we have to go to the police." I trailed along behind her as she threw a knife, a hunk of bread, a towel into her bag. "We did nothing wrong." I kicked Curly's boot. "And *he* was hoodwinked."

"Don't be so bloody *stupid*," Phaegin growled. "We're leaving."

I grabbed my bag, protesting, and followed her to the door, Curly trailing me.

Phaegin swung around and shoved Curly so that he stumbled back to the wall. "Not you. *You* can hang for all I care."

"No one's going to hang!" I shouted. "We have to explain!"

Phaegin turned on me. "Idiot! We were *seen* there, no matter if we *did* anything or not. There were hurt, dead, rich people involved. Even if *he* owns up, though that's a fat chance, we'd be *in it*. If we don't leave now, and lose that piece of pig seed, we're gonna die."

Curly whimpered.

I said, "Curly didn't mean it, Phaegin. He didn't know what was going to happen."

Phaegin wrenched open the door. "Not him."

I put out my hands. "I can't leave him to hang."

She grit her teeth. "There is *no time.*"

"Please, Phaegin."

I slapped the back of Curly's head. He mumbled, "I'm sorry, Phaegin."

Phaegin clenched her hands and shut her eyes. She kicked the door so it bounced on its hinges. I stopped it from slamming. She looked at Curly staring at the floor, then at me, then out the door, where an aureole of yellow light showed faint over the buildings. It was a long minute she considered, until she spat, "All right!" She pointed at me. "*Everything that follows, Edward Turrentine Bayard the Third . . .*" She didn't finish, only squared her shoulders. "Just keep your tongue between your teeth, both of you, and follow me."

We slunk downtown, skirting the green where flares still burned, illuminating the bodies of dead horses and the devastated buildings, until we came to the cigar shop.

"Wait here." Phaegin dumped her bag beside me and stepped toward the door.

I grabbed her skirt. "Are you crazy?" From this distance I could still hear the shouts of reporters and police.

She pulled her hem from my grasp and repeated, "Stay here!"

Phaegin dashed across the street. In the lamplight I could see her lifting the rocks in the border in front of the shop. She must have found the key, for she looked right and left, then opened the door. In a minute, she was back, two cigar boxes in her hands. "Let's go."

"What's that?"

"Cigars."

"You risk our lives for cigars?"

Curly whispered. "They're *good* cigars."

She rounded on him. "If you ever touch these cigars, sniff them, or look at them, I'll cut your eyes out." She glanced at me. "I had wages coming. I get what's owed me."

She wouldn't have taken the risk of breaking into the shop for cigars; it must be she'd cleaned Mr. Cordassa out. We would now face bona fide larceny charges along with the spurious claims of murder and anarchy. There was no time to deal with it now, however.

We fled, weaving in and out of the streets, keeping close to shrubbery and as far from the light as we could. At the edge of town loomed a blocky factory, reeking of bitter vinegar. A sign over the door read SNOOK MUSTARD WORKS. I stopped dumbfounded until Curly charged into me and Phaegin, stumbling into him, ordered us to get our sticks moving.

We continued without speaking for hours, following the train tracks, slipping on the graveled banks. The crescent moon cast so little light, it was almost worse than no light at all as we lurched through the high grass and eventually through the tangled wood, tripping over hickory roots, slapped by vines and creepers festooning branches of black walnut and elms. Clumps of willows impeded our paths, and the humidity rising from the waste of vegetation was oppressive if not poisonous.

All the while I repeated to myself that this couldn't be happening. It was a mistake. We shouldn't be running. If we had stayed in New Haven, the misunderstanding would be cleared up, but now there would be hell to pay in bringing things to rights. I told myself to stop running; the sooner I commenced explanation, the better. Still, I couldn't make myself turn around, for even though I told myself that justice was as sharp and right as steel, I knew that justice had been a stranger to me for some time.

When dawn came, we collapsed within a small copse of trees. Curly fell to sleep in an instant, his arms raised above his head as if he were surrendering in his dreams.

Phaegin curled up a few feet away, using her bag for a pillow. I stretched out below an oak tree. No matter that I was exhausted to the point of pain, I could not sleep. Beyond the horror of the last hours came the realization I would not be picking up the papers to be delivered at Mother Fenton's tomorrow. My mother, my past, my identity continued to shuffle beyond my reach, even though I raced to reach them, my heart bursting from the strain.

After some time I heard Phaegin, crying again, this time muffling it with her jacket. I inched over and put my arm around her. She turned and buried her face in my chest. The paper she clutched in her hand crackled.

"Chester was such a nice man, Ned. He believed in me, no matter that I was a shopgirl. Said I was smart. He lent me money to get a dress to look right for the bank. Now they'll make such fun of him. It is so unfair. They'll tell him he was just a cover for my *secret anarchist's life,* a harelipped dupe. He'll be sure I never really appreciated him, even liked him. And I can never tell him now . . . that I did."

She smoothed the paper. "I wrote a poem for him, paid a feller to write it down for me, but he won't get it." She began crying again. My chest grew damp and hot under her cheek, my arm numbed under her weight, but finally she slept.

The sun climbed and warmed. The perfume of wildflowers rose in the heat. Trees wove early twigs into irregular lace. I lay back and looked at the blue sky all in pieces through the limbs. A haze of green. In another week, there would be no seeing the sky at all for the leaves. Who would have thought that country was so close to the city trumpet we'd left behind? Humans, less imaginative than other animals, cannot believe in a blizzard when the summer reigns. We could have had picnics here. There was a hill across the way, a giant sleeping a long grassy sleep. Just last month we could have sledded. Happiness had been sighing in our faces all along.

I listened intently for the sound of dogs, the jangle of horses, the shout of policemen, but it was as if we had dreamed trouble and were merely on an excursion, birds and crickets singing around us.

The crumpled paper tumbled from Phaegin's relaxed palm and rocked in the breeze. What poem had she written? I slipped carefully from her embrace and read:

> Constant's grace, imperfect form,
> perfect fruit kept from harm,
> a song of sweet
> life and long
> will always keep
> a heart so strong.

I closed my eyes. And when the wash of shame and sorrow had diminished, I folded the paper and placed it again within the clutch of Phaegin's hand.

It occurred to me I had a letter of my own that Mother Fenton had given me, what seemed like years before. I pulled Lill's missive from my pocket.

Dear Ned,

Come to me now. The skies here are cold and hard as I become. I have not the courage to live as I have had to live any longer. I sold your gold pen and, with the proceeds, Lucy and I fled Rhylander and his brown life. I must tell you, I am expecting another baby. I fear I will not survive the labor, either before or after the birth.

I imagine you in Yale robes, wandering the halls of the Peabody, thinking deep thoughts, cementing your stakes in that civilized world. You have achieved what you promised there, and now I must ask you to remember your promise to me. I will wait as long as it takes here in Omaha. Or until I am forced to leave. Heaven help me. You are a success and of true heart and soul. Perhaps the many allies you have made, the connections you have forged, can somehow save me from myself.

I will keep you safe with my hopes and dreams.

Love, ever,

Lill

I crushed the letter into a ball. Pregnant again? He must have been on her the hour of the baby's birth. I was furious with Lill, with her miseries, with her complaints, all of her own doing. She did not know what it meant to need heaven's intervention. What

I would give to be in a warm little house, nothing to worry about but the effort of putting meals on the table, scrubbing diapers, figuring what to name my next child and whether a stupid lovelorn boy could rescue me from my own foolishness.

She had made a terrific error now. How *could* she be certain of me, how *dare* she presume, how *could* she stake her future on *me*?

I felt sick. My anger gave way to shame. She staked her future on my stupid, fatuous promises, on my arrogance and deceptions. I couldn't dream of helping her now. *I* was lost. And while I felt I had but a gossamer tie to her before, I now saw that filament was stronger than I'd thought, and, further, it was around her neck and would drag her to the depths.

As for my mother, it occurred to me now that perhaps it was she who had kept the money and taken her leave. Well, she would have what she wanted. Now I would ever be dead to her as she would be to me.

The thought was indeed black, and I immediately regretted my lack of faith. Part of the horror was that I would now never know, would never receive the packet the clerk was to send on, would never face Alan and Jamieson, would never enjoy a home and family. I tossed the balled paper into the weeds. I had damn well killed us all. Lill, Phaegin, my mother, Avelina, Tilfert, my horse, and even Curly. Had I left him in the mines, he would be serving a mere two years of indenture instead of facing the hangman's noose.

It was an ice-thin sheet we danced on, breaking apart as spring finally arrived. Setting fools adrift, never to return. Our circumstances dangerous as a loaded gun. *All* of my past was gone. Edward Turrentine Bayard III was dead.

I closed my eyes. The blue sky went orange against my lids, then gray, then black.

I was on the ocean. A white sand beach ahead, waves breaking like lace along the shore. Through the shimmering heat, an elephant decorated in sapphire and ruby thundered through palm trees. I yearned. I stretched out my hands. It was all so far away.

Then I found, having sent my hands, sent my heart over that water, I could not get them back—and that was the true horror, the failure of desire, which had delivered only the vague chill of absence. The only thing to do was to pursue my errant shares, to be whole once again.

I rose to gloaming and shook the others awake.

Phaegin clutched her bag and nodded. Curly rubbed his eyes and shivered, then grinned like Christmas when I told him we were going west.

CHAPTER 25

We took a snaking path up the coast, away from the nexus of the bomb and its aftermath. How many steps to outrun a bomb? How many miles to leave the bodies behind? How many days would we stumble through the trees of the coastal forests before we were safe from another's insanity?

On the first day Curly talked a mile a minute about what he was going to do when he got to Indian country. "I'm takin' a scalp a week. I'll be Dan'l Boone or Bill Hickok, scourge of the country!"

Phaegin was yet sandbagged, taking step after step without seeing anything but the place her foot would next fall.

And I fought despair, attempting to shove it aside by ruminating that with this second trip to the wilds, I supposed I was having the true American experience of western expansion: flight. From the time of Plymouth Colony, the country *sluiced* with the shadowed, persecution looming at each labored step. Supposedly running *to* something—to riches, to a new life—in fact they ran away. An escape from poverty, from poor decisions, away from trouble and hopelessness, away from the war, away from the law.

On the second day, Curly exchanged his wild anticipation over adventures to be had for complaints: "We gonna eat?"; "We gonna eat other than tack bread?"; "So hungry my throat's suckin' on my tongue, Ned"; "How many days till Indians?"; "Couldn't we get a horse? We cain't show up without a horse"; "I need a western peg, Prairie Prince, Snake-eye maybe, been thinkin' and thinkin' and I cain't come up with anythin' real good." I finally told him we'd turn around and head to Florida if he didn't shut up.

On the third day we arrived outside a little town, stopping on a hill overlooking the scattering of buildings and the gray-green conifer forest beyond. Curly narrowed his eyes and set his hat. "Where the hell're we at?"

I shrugged, but I could see railroad tracks. "We'll catch the train here."

Curly nodded and pointed toward town. "Tavern?"

"You'd be spotted in a second."

"Me? I'd blend in."

Phaegin sneered at him. "Redheaded guttersnipe tot playacting Deadwood Dick? Sore thumb."

"Better a sore thumb than stickin' my little brown finger out fer tea, playactin' Missus Vanderbilt," Curly growled back.

I smacked Curly on the back of the head. "Stop. I'm going in and I'll get us something to eat."

Phaegin sat down on a rock. "Maybe we should go awhile longer. Somebody nabs you now, we all swing."

Three days tearing through underbrush with little more to eat than crackers. We were briar-whipped, filthy, and ravenously hungry and had to stop. Further, not only did I desire to fill our bellies, my hope was that in town I would find the bombing ascribed to those who deserved the blame, so we could return to New Haven, pick up our lives, and forget these miserable hours ever happened.

"It'll be fine." I whacked my hat on my leg a couple of times to clear it of debris, dusted my jeans, and rubbed my shoes on my calves to give them a little shine.

Phaegin motioned me over, spit on her handkerchief, and rubbed smut from my face. "Take this." She handed me a ten-dollar bill.

"Where did you get it?" I thought of the cigar boxes.

She shrugged. "Goin'-to-the-bank dress. Never did buy it."

It seemed a lifetime ago, and the girl pirouetting in the square, anticipating her future, seemed a much younger version of the grimly exhausted woman with me now. "Ah, Phaegin."

"Go on. We can't eat money."

In town I found a marker. I was in Mercator, a quiet little place that would not have survived its lonely post if it weren't for the railroad passing through. I walked into the ten-by-ten timber-framed commissary, a lean-to addendum on the gabled living quarters alongside.

"Can I help you?" An old woman with every other tooth missing or awry, hair neatly combed into a thin bun, and wearing a patched apron, sat in a rocker amid barrels and boxes.

"Do you have dried apples?"

"Nope. Wintered out. Dry grapes, though. A little moldy, so I give a good price."

"Bread?"

"Oh, yeah." She leaned from her chair to a shelf, patted a hard brown loaf proudly. "Make it myself. Where are you from?"

"Georgia. My ma's waiting in Boston."

She nodded. "Getting close now. You on the train?"

I shook my head. "Nah, hoofing it, picking up rides when I get lucky."

"Train's frightful expensive. You want coffee?"

"No. Salt pork? Pickles?"

"Sure. Good cheese, too. My boy raises the goats." She stood from the rocker with a groan and commenced placing goods in a slat box.

I nodded. "Been on the road a while, wondering what the world's doing. You got a paper in this town?"

She pointed. "Yestiday's *Boston Globe*. Gotta read it in here, though. Town shares it, and not everbody's been in."

I took the paper, nonchalantly. "Anything interesting happening?"

"Always is."

I scanned the front page: nothing, but when I turned to the second my heart sank. A story on the bombing, and an artist's rendition of the three responsible. Two cowboys, one like a dwarf, the big one with dark beetling brows and a long nose. The woman was depicted in a low-cut gown with ostrich feathers stuck in her curly hair.

"Ain't that something? See that one?" The old woman pointed at the one I supposed was me.

"Built his bomb in a rooming house. Snookered the coal company and a Yale professor to boot." She cackled.

"With a bomb?"

"Carved coal lumps. Duped the educated fool who took 'im in. The scoundrel almos' ruint the fellow; lucky he weren't killed. The thief held up the professor with his fancy silver pistol, stole a important rock. They say he may've killed the professor's wife. She's missing."

I managed to wrestle the impulse to shout innocence, decry the reporters, Quillan, and the cops as miserable liars. I swallowed my panicked anger and, still disbelieving, I read on. Sure enough, Quillan blamed Mrs. Quillan's disappearance and the entire coal fiasco on me. Said I had stolen a priceless fossil. A chemist found lead and traces of antimony, iron and tin in the bomb casing and Quillan verified one of his pewter candlesticks had gone missing as well as the spyglass Mrs. Quillan had given me. The police figured I had melted down stolen goods to cast the sphere. Two of the boarders to whom I had proudly shown my gun reported that I was armed and dangerous and described my pistol in detail. The pawnshop turned in my watch, and the police had found my real name inside and were now calling me the blueblood bandit, Phaegin my harlot, and Curly our bastard child.

"My God." I put the paper down.

The old woman *tsk*ed. "Evil, ain't it? Anarchists, foreigners. The ringleader, he looks Italian to me, or Oriental even." She turned the paper, found her place, and pointed to a number. "You keep yer eyes peeled, out there on the road. Come across the three of 'em and you can make some money. First class in red velvet with *that* reward."

A thousand-dollar bounty on our heads.

"'Course, you might get killed sooner than you get the cash. They's carrying dynamite, pistols, rifles. Bad news."

I cracked a weak smile. "I just want to get home."

"You're a good boy, then. Grocery's three dollar 'n two bits."

* * *

I didn't share the particulars with Phaegin and Curly, at least not the harlot/bastard characterization, but gave them the general dismal scope of things. Phaegin took a moment from pushing bread and cheese into her mouth and dug her fists into her eyes. I thought she might start crying all over again, but she looked up. "The pictures don't look like us?"

"No." I gestured toward Curly. "They drew him like a miniature deformed cowboy and I look like evil incarnate."

She raised her eyebrow. "You said they *didn't* capture a likeness."

Curly didn't flinch, but smiled. "I look like a cowboy?" He stuck his thumbs in his vest.

I glared at him. "Thing is, there's a reward. People are going to be looking for anything close to those pictures. We have to make sure we don't resemble our descriptions at all. Disguise ourselves."

Curly sat up. "I'll get chaps."

Phaegin shook her head at him. "You are a deformed elf with a tiny deformed brain."

Curly turned to me. "Did the pitcher show me with chaps, Ned? No. So it's a disguise."

I took Tilfert's hat and stuffed it in my bag. "Keep your mouth closed, Curly. It'll hide the gap in your teeth. Take off your vest, boots too."

"Won't!"

I turned to Phaegin. "You got those scissors?"

She pulled them out of her bag and handed them to me. I motioned to a downed tree. "Have a seat."

"Why?"

"Scarlet fever. You've been sick, barely over it. All your hair fell out."

"You're not cutting *my* hair!"

"Phaegin. In your picture you looked . . . very healthy."

She crossed her arms, worked her mouth back and forth, then flounced over and sat on the log. "I had scarlet fever two months ago at least, Ned. Don't cut it too short."

Curly sank to the ground and, sitting cross-legged, watched me snip Phaegin's hair, groaning as the long locks dropped to the ground. His eyes welled. A few more snips and tears coursed down his grimy cheeks. When I moved to cut the front, he commenced sobbing.

Phaegin snapped, "What's *wrong* with you?"

He hiccuped. Snot dripped from his nose. "I'm sorry, Phaegin. I'm so, so sorry."

She pivoted and looked at me. "Do I look *that* bad, Ned?"

"No." And in fact she did not. Her hair, released from its long weight, waved about her face, giving her a girlish demeanor.

Phaegin wagged her finger at Curly. "Stop it. You're making me feel bad."

Curly hid his face in his hands. His shoulders shook. I cut the last lock of Phaegin's hair. Phaegin brushed industriously at her skirt, strode over to Curly, and nudged him with her toe. "What's this about, then?"

Curly looked up, streaked, slimy, and abject. "You had the purtiest hair I ever *ever* seen."

Phaegin crossed her arms and looked away. "Well, it'll grow back." He sniveled loudly and she wheeled on him. "I said, *Stop!*"

Curly jumped to his feet, peeled off his hat, his vest, struggled to extricate his feet from the still-damp boots. "Here! You kin have 'em, Phaegin. I don' deserve to be a cowboy. I'll walk to Kansas in my socks."

Phaegin looked at me, rolling her brown eyes, and stuffed Curly's gear into my bag. "You can wear 'em when we get to the wild, Curly. By then, my hair'll be longer. Now, enough caterwaulin'."

Curly took her hand. "I'm sorry, really, Phaegin."

She sighed loudly and deeply. "All right. Fine. You're sorry." She glanced at me again and jerked her hand from his. "Just . . . let off."

My disguise was to keep a smile on my face and try not to look dangerous. Phaegin suggested I grow a beard. I laughed. "In a week I'd have seventeen really long hairs."

"I think you've got the making of a good beard, here." She took my face in her hands, looked at my chin critically, petted my upper lip. "You'll definitely have a mustache in no time. Get yourself a different hat, a bowler, say, and you'll be transformed."

I patted the change remaining from the ten in my pocket. "This is getting awful thin to buy tickets, shoes for Curly, and a hat for me."

Curly grinned. "I can pinch the shoes."

"A thief and a menace," Phaegin snarled. "Paying for that one's shoes is like buying the devil a stick. We should drown him." She shook her head and counted on her fingers. "Shoes for him, a jacket and hat for you, and a kerchief for my head. What's left we can only pray will buy three train tickets to—God knows where we'll be safe. Do you have any idea where that could be?"

I was a-sail on a friendless sea, with no safe harbors in sight. The only place to go was the big nowhere. Every soul I counted an ally was dead or missing—but one. "Brill!" With great relief

I answered Phaegin's look. "My old tutor—he'll help—the smartest man I know. We'll take the train to Hammond, Indiana. I'll send a telegram in the morning. He'll meet us and we'll straighten all this out." The train was dear, the telegraph cash-hungry as well. "But six dollars isn't going to cover it."

Phaegin gave me an incredulous look. "A tutor. Straighten all this out? Uh-huh." She turned her back and went through her bag. When she turned back, she handed me ten dollars.

I eyed the money. Twenty dollars in two days, a preposterous sum for a shopgirl. "How much were you going to spend on that dress?"

"You'll wish it was more before we're done."

I walked to her bag and peered in. "What's really in those cigar boxes?"

She shoved me back. "Cigars. I told you."

"Twenty bucks out of thin air."

"I had a little saved."

"Let's see."

"What?"

I grabbed for the bag. "The boxes."

She slapped at me. "Get off!"

Her lack of trust infuriated me. "So high and mighty with Curly, and yet you cleaned Mr. Cordassa out." I threw my hands in the air. "Now, even if the bombing gets cleared up we'll be jailed for burglary. How much are we in for, petty theft or grand larceny?"

"I didn't steal anything. I'm no *thief*."

I stared at her. Phaegin tightened her lips to white. Gave an exasperated "Oh!" and upended her bag at my feet. "Matches, knife, my ma's picture, scissors, blanket, stocking, another stocking—"

I put out a hand. "The boxes."

She opened one with a flourish. Inside, a dozen beautifully wrapped umber cigars. I poked through them, sniffed them, knocked on the bottom of the box.

I nodded. "The other."

Phaegin opened the other box practically on my nose. Another dozen cigars, redolent of Cordassa's shop. "You want to go through my *pockets* now, Ned?"

"I'm sorry. You keep pulling out money."

"Don't worry, it won't happen again!"

I looked away. Curly was euphorically slashing the bushes with a stick, making leaves fly as if he were on a camping excursion. "I really am sorry. I'm so good at being wrong, I don't know why I would believe my stomach growling. And you've been right. Especially about him." Curly stooped and used the stick to draw in the dirt. Puffy face intent, tongue stuck out from his pink lips. "Trouble and just can't help it."

"Too bad you didn't listen first bloom. Now we're good and stuck."

"Keep your money." I held up the pistol. "I'll sell this, pawn it maybe."

"Are you crazy? It's been described in the paper. Besides—" she smiled for the first time in three days—"you're going to need it in Nebraska. All those buffalo needing killing."

"I never actually killed a buffalo," I admitted. "I was a skinner, and not a very good one."

She shook her head. "Can you even *shoot* that thing?"

I smiled back at her. "I have saved lives with my pistol. Though I never shot a buffalo, I *am* a true western hero."

"Then, for God's sake, Ned, don't pawn it. That gun might be our only hope."

CHAPTER 26

At first light I made my second foray into Mercator and, as if by divine intervention, found a pile of clothing inviting its own theft, drying over a chair on the porch of a house, the result, perhaps, of a child's foray into a pond. I transferred the blouse, breeches, and shoes under a bush to be retrieved later and continued into town to purchase a kerchief and hat from the same merchant who'd lent me the newspaper.

She seemed glad to see me and, after taking my money, sent me off with a card for my waiting mother imprinted with roses and the Lord's Prayer. "You're a good boy, wish't that *my* boy could come home. He's a sailor. Ever' storm, I'm on my knees, even though I know if it's blowin' here, *he's* likely lodged in sunshine."

From there I headed to the train station, a sleepy place. From twenty yards away I could see the bright white of a new poster tacked to the door. I looked around, but no one seemed to be giving me any untoward looks, yet I still approached obliquely, trying to read the notice as if I were hardly interested.

It gave me the shivers to see our odd simulacra gazing boldly from the paper. Names, descriptions of our crimes, the immense thousand-dollar reward printed in lurid red.

I ducked into the station house: another poster on the cage. It would be madness to buy passage for three now, tipping the station agent for sure. I rubbed my chin, checking my camouflage, mastered my breathing, plastered a big friendly grin on my face, and purchased one ticket. Phaegin would ride as Delores Reed, scarlet fever victim, journeying to recuperate with her sister in Chicago. Curly and I would have to hobo.

After I pocketed the ticket I sojourned to the telegraph office. I sent Brill a simple message: ARRIVE MAY 15, 10 A.M. IMPERATIVE TO MEET. I prayed he would get it.

That afternoon, Phaegin boarded the train.

Curly and I waited on the outskirts of Mercator, listening for the train's whistle, the hiss of brakes, the dim shout of the engineer. After a time the locomotive pulled out, chugged carefully into its next leg. As it turned the corner into our sight, Curly and I crouched like sprinters, waited until the engine passed, the passenger cars huffed by, saw Phaegin's strained face in the train window. When the freight cars came alongside, Curly and I commenced running. I overtook one of the rear cars in a hundred yards. Curly raced behind me.

Had he been six feet tall, Curly would easily have been the fastest man I ever had or would meet. He barreled along the tracks with the power of a train himself, pumping his arms, his legs chugging into a blur, face constricted, teeth clenched.

But he hardly made four feet six inches, and Curly powered along on his stubby gams for a hundred yards, barely making headway. I lay on my belly on the rough freight platform, reaching for him, shouting encouragement. I became convinced he would burst before he managed to catch up with the freight car. The blood already congesting in his head colored his face from red to purple.

Phaegin was ensconced in the passenger car. If I were forced to jump off and join him, how would we let her know we hadn't made it? How would we ever catch up with her again?

"Come on, Curly!" I screamed. "Run! Run! You're gaining!"

Curly's eyes were bugged and wild. His mouth yawed for breath. His white fists pummeled the air. I stretched my hands toward him. "Almost there, almost there! Come *on!*"

Just as I thought Curly might actually make it, his outstretched fingers nearing my own, not six inches between them, the train picked up an iota of speed or Curly slowed.

The train and he fell into a horribly long moment of stasis, and then the six inches between us grew to eight, then a foot.

We were lost. I dropped my head in defeat, grabbed my valise. I would have to jump before there was any more speed on or I'd break my neck.

Curly squawked, "*Corner!*"

We'd come to a bend. Curly cut across the inside curve, leaping over berms, flying over the stuttered grasses, to meet the car on the other side, three feet to spare. He grabbed my hand, I took hold of the back of his shirt. He kicked, I wrested him up, imagining his feet catching in the iron wheels, dragged him slowly along the threshold, and finally lifted him into the car.

Curly lay gasping like a landed fish. He put a hand to his throat and glared at me. "You . . . almos'. . . hung me . . . on my own collar."

I leaned, panting, against a crate and grinned at him.

For hours, for a day, all went well. The train rolled west, stopping and starting in half a dozen stations with nothing amiss. At each stop, Phaegin, Curly, and I would step out and stretch our legs, give each other a cursory nod of all's well before re-boarding. Curly and I napped on the hard boards, relieved our-selves out the door—a particular pleasure for Curly, who claimed he had a half mile bladder. The knot had begun to loosen in my belly as the eastern forests and knots of habitation eased into open spaces. The stops became often nothing more than a platform and a stationmaster's house. There was no way to get provisions, so Curly and I chewed stale bread and more than a few moldy raisins.

Curly grimaced. "I ain't eatin' any more *rot*." He turned to me with a tortured expression on his face. "Ned, I gotta have some real food. I gotta have some taters, or maybe some meat, or"—his face grew dreamy—"a blueberry pie like Mother Fenton made. She did it real nice."

The train whistled a stop and began groaning slow.

"I'll betcha Phaegin's havin' chicken 'n biscuits in the dining car." He pulled at his hair. "I cain't stand it. I gotta have some-thing good to eat."

I laughed at his theatrics. "Calm down, Curly. You're not starving." He gave me such a pleading look I relented. "All right, we'll meander down when the train stops and see if we can get something from Phaegin."

We jumped from the platform and wandered nonchalantly down the line toward the passenger seating. About the time Phaegin stepped out, however, a man in a dark suit exited one of the further cars and gave Curly and me, then Phaegin, a searching look. I pushed Curly back toward the cars. The man tipped his hat to Phaegin, who inclined her head. And then the man came our way.

I didn't know if he was just stretching his legs, but something about him seemed worrisome. As soon as we had rounded the bend I shoved open a freight car door and gave Curly a boost in. I followed and closed the door.

Curly yelped, "Cor, it's winter in here!"

"Hush! Not a sound!" I hissed into the black cold.

I imagined Curly was puffing vapor rings, but though I could hear his whooshing breaths, I couldn't see him in the aphotic car. All was quiet, no shouts or police whistles, only the shriek of the steam siren and the call of the conductor to board. When my eyes grew accustomed to the dim, I discerned hulking forms swinging from the ceiling. Curly backed up against me. "Wot is it? Who are they?"

The train jerked to a start. "Damn it!" I pushed Curly aside as he gazed at the figures. "We can't stay here, we'll freeze to death."

I pulled on the door. It was jammed. "Curly, help me!"

Curly tugged alongside me, but we could not open the door from the inside. I slumped against the wall, then straightened away from the chill of the wet boards. The train picked up speed. We were stuck.

"What are they?" Curly's voice shook.

My eyes adjusted to the dark. "Pigs, Curly. Butchered pigs. We're in a cold car."

"I know it's *cold*, how do they do it that way?"

I walked to a chest from which issued an ongoing fog. "Ice."

Curly peered in and shivered. "Don't like it. All them pigs look so sad."

Indeed they did. Hung snout down, the skinned hogs seemed to be reaching their trotters yearningly toward solid earth; dark eyes unseeing, tusks protruding, mouths in a state of perpetual howl, they swayed like synchronized dancers to the train's movement.

I laughed to cover up my own discomfort. "You said you wanted meat, Curly, now you've got it."

"Hit's not meat if it's got a *face* on it." He crouched down and addressed the animal's snout. "Hope the end were quick, brother."

We huddled together for hours, torpor growing like hoarfrost. My knees ached from the chill, my arms ricked, but worst of all was the worry that we, trapped in twilight winter, would miss the stop.

I could do little about it. My only recourse was shouting and we could not risk discovery by a false champion. We could only hope that we would be released by some hobo-friendly platform workers before it was too late. I drew the warm nugget of Curly in my arms, and fell into such a sound cold-induced sleep that had the knock not repeated, I might have missed it all together.

I shook Curly from my grasp and knocked hesitantly back. Phaegin hissed from the other side of the door. "Ned?"

"Get us out! The door won't open from the inside!"

There was a click and I threw my arm over my face as light poured into the refrigerator car. Phaegin demanded, "What *are* you doing in there?"

"Freezing to death," Curly moaned.

She looked behind her. "Get out and quick. Jig's up."

I could barely unhinge my knees and, along with Curly, more fell than stepped out of the car, and hobbled as quickly as we could manage behind the fleeing Phaegin.

We hid in the bushes, until the train pulled out of sight. Phaegin sat heavily on her bag, looking morose. She gave a half-hearted wave. "The suited man you saw last stop? Law. Plied me with questions. Didn't know at first if he was flirting or figuring. Some other fella came up and called 'im *sir*, got a ball-kickin' look for it too." She shook her head miserably. "I think he's Pinkerton."

"A Pinkerton agent?" I tried to sound incredulous. "Looking for *us?*"

She glared at me. "Yeah. Lookin' for us: the cowboy, the harlot, and their bastard son!"

Curly looked pleased once again, but parsing it out he lost the smile. "Did somebody call me a bastard?" He put his fists up. "I've charged teeth for that, I'll do it again."

Phaegin closed her eyes.

I looked across the top of the bushes to where the station was planted, a derelict sign painted HAMMOND over the door. There was no one around. "Did you see Brill?"

Phaegin didn't open her eyes. "How would I know?"

"You two stay here. I'll take a look and come back for you."

Phaegin nodded. Curly was spread-eagled in a pool of sunshine. "Feel like a snake, jes' soakin' up the sun."

I wandered to the station and peered in the dusty window. Brill sat on a bench inside, staring at the crumpled hat in his hands. His clothes hung on him. If I didn't know him I'd think he was a hobo himself, for his pants were dusty and ill-kempt, his shirt stained. I opened the door and whispered, "Brill." I was aghast at how pale he was, the disarray of his hair.

He rose from the bench and made his way outside as if he was made not of flesh but of some inorganic weight. He put out his hand, and I shook it.

"Brill, are you poorly?"

He worked his jaw, his lips twitched, but he seemed unable to speak. I took his arm. He jerked away. "Elizabeth. She's dead."

"What? My God, how?"

"Hanged herself. A week ago."

I didn't know what to do. What to say. "I'm so—so sorry, Brill. I am so terribly sorry."

He nodded. We stared at each other. Brill nodded again. "I got your telegram."

"I see. Brill, are you all right?"

He glowered. "Of course not."

"No, idiotic thing to say." I wished desperately to offer some aid, but I had nothing but sympathy, so I repeated, "I'm sorry. This is unbelievable—"

Brill cut in, speaking in a monotone. "Truly, she was murdered."

"I don't understand."

Brill drew his brows. He looked less like my friend and more as if something monstrous was in his skin, eating up what was left of his insides. I guessed at what he was feeling, having married a beloved daughter, delivered her into penury, and watched her wither and die. "Brill, don't blame yourself. You loved Elizabeth, idolized her. You did your best by her."

He smiled shortly. "The best was not enough, not even close. But I don't count myself among her murderers, Edward. Her parents killed her, as well as her sisters, her peers, neighbors, the class of rich young men she was supposed to marry into, the rich young men's rich powerful fathers." He lifted his gaze from his shoes to look me in the face. "Men like you, Edward, supposedly good, generous, intelligent men. You've all killed my sweet Elizabeth."

"You're not well, Brill. This has been a terrible shock."

"It is a shock. I am *not* well. But truth does not rely on health." He continued his mad regard of me. I had to look away, and when I did he laughed. "You believe yourself innocent. Takes not a bit of effort. The privileged don't have to delude themselves because the poor do even that work for them, building facades for the wealthy."

"Brill, it's terrible to see you like this. What can I do?"

He laughed hysterically. "How sad. I feel touched, even comforted, perhaps honored you would ask. Just as I was honored by what little kindness you showed me in the past. It must be said, Edward, you *are* the kindest of the cruel."

"I never wished to be cruel."

"No holidays, no raises. I scarpered when you rang your bell, ate your leftovers whilst smacking my lips, emptied your bedpan with pride. I walked your dog and, when your dog made me happy, you had it shot. You had a physician on call twenty-four hours a day, but when I sprained *my* arm, the liveryman bound it. With barely a day's notice, I was turned out to beg employment."

I was horrified. "My mother was to *give* the dog away, not shoot it."

He leered at me. I shouted, "So why did you even come today, if you find me so reprehensible?"

"To learn if the bomb was indeed your doing."

The news had come this far. I shook my head. "Good God, of course not!"

He clapped his hat on his head. "Then the next time we meet will be in hell, Edward Turrentine Bayard the Third." Brill took his leave, treading like an old man down the road.

I sat on the steps to collect myself until I noticed the stationmaster peering out the window at me. I dusted my pants and disguised my upset with a thready whistling. I had no time or energy to spend on dark motives or truth; I had to pull myself together and get my compatriots and myself out of a dire predicament. How, I hoped, would make itself clear as we went. When I got to Phaegin and Curly I clapped my hands and tried to speak cheerfully. "All right, let's start walking."

Phaegin sat up. "What happened to your friend?"

"Can't help us, has his own troubles. Chicago's not far, though. We can get there in no time."

"And what do we do there?"

"I'm going to have to pawn the pistol."

Phaegin's eyes widened. "We'll be rowlocked, Ned. That fella on the train, by now he's put it all together. They'll be watching for that gun, staking out pawnshops."

I searched through my bag. "I've also got the medal, but I don't know if it's worth anything." I dug it out and gazed at the golden disk. What would Avelina say, the gift she'd given me to make a new start, pawned to flee a murder charge?

Curly peered at it. "Wot's on it?"

I read the inscription aloud. *"Medal of honor: Frank O'Hare Junior. Valorous conduct in the face of battle.* Chicago *Fifth Battalion."*

Phaegin looked over my shoulder. "Who's Frank O'Hare Junior?"

"Avelina's father. She gave it to me before she died."

"Is he still alive? Maybe he's at home."

I shrugged. Avelina didn't say her dad died, only that he'd deserted her. "No reason to think he'd still be there if he was."

"Maybe he'd give you a reward or something."

"Something like a kick in the pants. I'm guessing there wasn't much love lost between them." I wondered, Did Avelina's father know his son's secret?

Phaegin sat back. "I think you should try. If he's a hero, he'll sure enough want the proof of it back. Besides, even if it didn't go sugar between them, folks still want to hear of their boys."

Curly looked somber. "Sure'n they do. My ma would. I'll send her a letter when I learn to write."

There was no other option. If we could find him, I would see Avelina's father, refer to her as his *son,* and hope all went well.

In less than a week we made the city. Right away we decided on a meeting place if we lost each other, for we had a terrible time finding our way through the labyrinthine streets. Chicago was split by rail yards, factories, and the Chicago River, all of these providing a hedge against our attempts to transect the city. We skirted the most impoverished sections but were forced to dive into the filthy tenements, where men, women, and children alike were sick, starving, and soused on the street. The faces were foreign; Italians, Russians, Poles, Chinese, Greeks, Czechs, and Swedes answered in their native tongues when we asked directions.

Fagged women with garish faces leaned against timber-framed shanties.

Curly grinned appreciatively. "Sapphire tol' me she's goin' to Chicago. More whores here 'n anywheres else."

Phaegin shuddered. "An' I thought New Haven was bad."

The smell was not just bad, it was hideous. Smoke clouded the sky as if the city itself were burning. Black fumes poured from thousands of rusty-necked pipes, jutting out of patched wooden roofs, and from the wide mouths of barrels dotting the roadways, where small groups burned trash for warmth rather than any desire to clean the streets.

Kitchen waste rotted in the gutters, and ordure reeked from outhouses, the only sewage depositories most of the tenement buildings had. The housing was so cramped on the lots it was near impossible to see any distance down road or any decent piece of sky.

No gentleman would walk through these streets. Every so often a carriage passed, occupants holding hankies to noses, windows shaded from the sights and smells of the rank slum.

Street by street, the living improved, scented with trees and soup cooking, the walkways passably clean, plump children played on rope swings. After much wandering we finally broke onto the shores of the commercial center of the city, where if the light was diminished it was by the height and splendor of the buildings or the competing shine of gold leaf and gold watches and the gleaming silks of the rich. It had an eternal air, a scent of omnipotence about it, but just beyond rose the blackened spires from a four mile sea of rubble, remnants of the great fire, reminder all can be lost with a snap of spark. The city was already rebuilding, however, closing the wound with brick and stone. And from the satisfied demeanors of the well-appointed pedestrians we passed, one would never know such horrific tragedy had ever occured. We found Frank O'Hare's address in the social register at the library. His offices were on Gilmore Street.

Gilmore Street was a swank avenue, stone buildings flanked with topiary, studded with heavy oak doors on which brass plates announced the business within. Frank O'Hare's secretary pursed her lips when I told her my name was John Smith, eyed my worn clothes, ready to have me put out, but when I told her I knew Mr. O'Hare's son, she slipped into the inner office. When she came out, she announced Mr. O'Hare would see me.

The office was as plush as the facade would have me believe: oak desk, oak shelves, brocade draperies, and a wide wool-tufted carpet. However, Mr. O'Hare, a huge man with a lantern jaw, looked like he'd be more at home on the waterfront.

He stood and stared at me distrustfully. "You say you know my son?"

I pulled the medal from my pocket. Mr. O'Hare's face lost all expression. Slowly he took the medal from me and sat down. "Gone, is he?"

I nodded. "Ague took him."

Mr. O'Hare, in his leather chair, gazed at the gold disk. "Hell. Bloody hell."

I waited. When he looked up he asked, "You were his friend?"

I nodded. "He showed me the ropes, out in Nebraska."

He perked up a little. "Went to Nebraska, did he? Had grit. Always had grit." He half smiled. "What was he doing out there?"

"Buffalo hunting."

Now he grinned widely, very pleased. "*Was* he?"

"He and Til—guided."

Frank narrowed his eyes. "Till?"

"They married. I was his best man."

Now the man out-and-out laughed, a great booming laugh, slapping the desktop in delight. "Married, did he? Well, *hell*, good for him. Married!" He sobered. "Damn it, and now he's gone. Isn't that the way?"

He leaned forward. "Maybe he said, and in any case you've likely deduced, my boy and I had been out of contact. Little Frank had a rocky youth, his . . . not the usual course." He looked not at me but past me. "Glad to hear he straightened out. Thought he would, if I could bear doing what was needed."

"*Little* Frank?"

He punched himself in the chest. "Big Frank. We called *him* Little." He glanced at me, tapped the medal. "Takes real bravery to get one of these. He signed up, a man at only sixteen years old."

"*He* was in the army?"

"You don't get a Medal of Honor peelin' potatoes. Heroic conduct." He shook his head. "The war was going to be the making of him. Give him backbone. Teach him what control, what restraint, what discipline is." Mr. O'Hare smiled scornfully. "A *friend* followed him in. You remind me of that boy, something in the face. You read Whitman?"

"Sir?"

Mr. O'Hare offered me a cigarette, took one himself, and lit it. "The blame is on that boy for the sorrow my son and I suffered. A scheming, unnatural, sick child who turned into an unnatural sick man. Hung around Frankie from the time they were small."

Mr. O'Hare tapped the medal on his desk. "Frankie marched into heavy fire, carried out six soldiers two at a time, one of them—that friend." He nodded with some satisfaction, then shrugged. "Shot in the back. Shook Frankie up."

O'Hare smiled. "To say I was glad Frank was finally free of him is an understatement. Frank didn't care for me speaking out. We fought." Mr. O'Hare puffed three times in quick succession, then stubbed the smoke out. "I sent him away that night, and it was the last I saw of him. Chewed from the toes up all these years, wondering about Frank, waiting for word."

His eyes were moist, and he drew his brows together in an effort of control. "Now you've set me free, John. It was like dying slow, what I had to do, but it made *him* stronger." He picked up the medal again. "And what life he had left, he made it a good one?"

Mr. O'Hare looked at me, the medal in hand, ribbon swinging like a noose. "His bride, Tilly, what of her?"

"Died two days after—Little Frank."

Mr. O'Hare stared at the gold disk again, then pressed it to his lips. "Did he ask you to bring this to me?"

I nodded. What was the harm in solace?

Mr. O'Hare frowned as if in pain. His tone changed. "Where have you come from, John?"

"I've been in Connecticut, wandering, odd jobs."

"You met Frank in Nebraska?"

"Yes, sir."

He puffed on his cigarette. "Your manners, boy, polished for a wanderer. . . . Got a mind on you as well." He stared at me so long I grew uncomfortable in his gaze. The clock ticked as if it were his brain working. I shifted and O'Hare nodded. "Let's say you and me have dinner, talk things over."

"That's generous of you, sir, but I have friends waiting."

He nodded. "Friends." He pointed at my sooted clothes with a big finger. "Looks like wandering has taken its toll. How are you for money?"

I shrugged. "Tight."

He pulled out his wallet. "I appreciate your coming by, John. This is to make your journey a little more comfortable." He handed me a fan of dollar bills.

I didn't hesitate to take them. "Thank you, sir."

He penned an address on a piece of paper and slid it across the desk to me. "Go to the Abbot Mercantile on Fifth Street, get some provisions. I'll let them know to put it on my tab. Least I can do."

"Thank you, sir. I appreciate it."

He nodded, put out his hand. As I shook it he smiled. "You have put my mind to rest, John. Thank you."

I left the office feeling lonelier than going in. O'Hare's relief smacked of better-a-dead-Little-Frankie-than-a-live-Avelina, and that, though he'd thanked me, gave me a chill. I shrugged off my worry. It was time to get on with saving ourselves. Stock up at the mercantile and put more time and miles between us and trouble.

Phaegin and I lodged Curly in the branches of an elm behind the mercantile with instructions to remain on watch until we came out. Phaegin and I entered through the back. The shop was empty. The clerk seemed startled at our appearance and nervously wiped the counter with a red cloth as he asked, "Mr. Smith?"

I nodded. The clerk nodded back. "I'm to put your purchases on Mr. O'Hare's tab."

Phaegin took my arm. I handed the clerk the list and he began to fill it, making more of a mess of flour and coffee than I would have thought any clerk could make and still keep his job. While he worked I discerned a tapping. I caught Phaegin's eye and we wandered nonchalantly to dry goods from where, behind bolts of cloth, came the noise. I shoved aside a calico to see Curly by the side window.

"Curly!" I looked behind me. We were hidden from the clerk's view by a forest of calico bolts. "Can't you ever do what you're told?"

He was agitated, could hardly get the words out. "Things is *pickin' up*. A fella's shown up with a *gun* on the roof and two 'cross the street."

Phaegin went white. "We've been gulled."

I put my finger to my lips. "Don't let on we know." The clerk was craning his neck, trying to get a look at us through the fabrics. I cleared the window of the heavy bolts. "Phaegin, out quick. Head back to the livery stable we passed coming in. I'll keep the clerk busy."

Phaegin shook her head. "I can't *fit* through that little window."

"Sure you can," Curly whispered. "Mebbe a little squeeze through the backside, but it's squashy."

Phaegin glared and pushed his face back from the opening with the flat of her hand, crawled onto the table, and slipped her head and arms through the window. With only a short burst of pushing and pulling, she tumbled out while I kept up a faux conversation. "I don't care, red *or* blue. They're both nice."

I picked my way back to the front, complaining to the clerk, "We'll be here all day while *she* reckons between one pattern and another."

The clerk stared at me gobble-eyed. I scratched my head and thumbed to where Phaegin supposedly was. "Fashion sense of a fish. You got pickles?" The clerk pointed to a barrel as he craned his neck for a peek of Phaegin.

I tipped the barrel. "You're almost out here. How do you expect me to reach—" I feigned a slip and the barrel washed vinegar over the floor.

The clerk looked stricken, glancing from the front window, to where he'd last seen Phaegin, then back at me and the pickle juice running along the floor.

I put my hands out. "Got a mop?"

The clerk glanced out the front window again, then sprinted to the broom closet for the mop. When he turned, I had my gun at his belly. I put a finger to my lips, then whispered, "Hand over the apron and cap." The clerk shot his glasses across the floor in his haste to pull the apron off. I backed him into the closet. Before I closed the door I warned, "Don't make a peep. I don't care if there's a door and eight barrels between us, try anything and I'll make your hide leak like a rotten bucket." I locked the door, put the apron and cap on, returned to the front counter, and waited.

I peered out the front window trying to discern what the clerk had been looking at, but could see nothing. I waited another couple of minutes, polishing the counter with the same cloth the clerk had used, then pulled the ornate atlas out from the glass case. I ripped out the pages covering Chicago to Wyoming Territory, then several southern states and Texas in case they used the vandalism as a clue. A pocket knife was in the case, a compass, and a hat pin. I took them along with a small journal to replace the one I'd lost and was fingering a blue-enameled fountain pen when five cops burst in through the front door. "Where did they go?"

I didn't have to feign terror. I pointed toward the back and stammered, "They ran out!"

The cop picked up a red neckerchief. "You were supposed to *wave* this when the three of them were in or if anybody made a break, you dumb *shit!*" They piled out the back, then returned. "How long?"

I slumped on the counter. "Not five minutes. I thought I was going to have a heart attack. They are some *hard*-looking folks."

One cop pulled out a notebook. "Let's get a description."

My ears ached with the effort of listening for the clerk in the closet. How long until he began to yell? "One was a dwarf."

"The woman?"

I looked baffled. "No woman, a fella dressed up like one. Oriental. Just the dwarf and the Oriental."

"He was *Oriental?*"

"Oh, yeah. Spoke Chinese, maybe Italian."

There was a thump: the clerk? The policeman looked toward the closet. I moaned. "He was going to kill me, the Italian. Another ten minutes, and you woulda been visiting my ma with the news." I put a hand to my stomach. "I think I'm going to be *sick.*" I covered my mouth, burped, retched.

The cop stepped back, disgusted, and I beat it, bent at the waist and moaning, bumping into the door and counter in my haste, then out the front door. I rounded the corner, sped through a length of alley, tossed the apron and cap into a garbage bin, and meandered through shops, across streets, losing myself easily within the noisome crowds of the Chicago slums. Once there, I was in greater danger of dying from typhoid than being found in the teeming streets. By dusk I'd hit the outskirts of town. I headed north until, near our predetermined meeting point, I picked up the thready whistle of Curly's curlew. I drubbed the bushes until Phaegin poked her head from the brush and waved me over. When I got to her, she threw her arms around me. She was shaking.

"You took so long, my God, I thought you bagged."

"We're fine, but we'd be wise to go *now*."

Curly was hopping up and down from one leg to the other, looking more like a kid heading for a birthday party than someone fleeing for his life. "Now where? What's next?"

I pulled the folded atlas pages from my pocket, turned them to catch the rising moonlight. After some studying, I pointed at the trace of blue line. "To the Mississippi."

Curly looked around. "*I* don't see no river."

I pulled the compass from my pocket, pointed, and spoke as if I were as savvy in the wilderness as they believed. "The Big Drink, this way."

We followed the compass heading, losing ourselves in deep greenery of the hickory and oak forests surrounding the big waters of the Great Lakes. At one point I thought I heard dogs baying and my heart dropped, but then it was gone.

To hide any scent, we waded some ways through a creek, torrential with spring runoff, holding hands to keep Curly from being carried away.

"Don't let go," he moaned. "I swim like a cannonball."

I squeezed his palm even harder and yelled, over the rushing water, "I didn't let go on the train, did I?"

He nodded and attempted a smile that wrung my heart. No matter all this, he was still a boy.

* * *

Curly caught a cold right off, sneezing with the intensity of an elephant. We couldn't chance a fire, though we were cold and miserable in wet boots and legs. We huddled together, shivering. Phaegin was wan, slumped. Even Curly seemed downhearted. I clapped him on the back. "Curly, you saved us back there."

Curly looked pleased. "Did, didn't I?"

Phaegin pulled the blanket closer. "What happened, Ned, how'd they know?"

I shook my head. "Big Frank told the cops, I guess."

"How did he know it was us? You were going to make up a name."

"I did. John Smith."

She groaned. "Might as well have told him your name was *William Criminal*."

"There *are* John Smiths in the world."

"What else?"

"I told him I knew his son. I gave him the medal and didn't even ask for money; he offered it. Then he wanted to take me for dinner, but I had to meet a couple of friends."

Phaegin groaned again.

"He said I'd set his mind at ease, and I could pick up supplies at the mercantile."

Curly sneezed twice more. "It was in the paper you'd been to Nebraska."

I winced. "I told him I'd been to Connecticut."

Phaegin shook her head. "You practically put two and two together for the gorilla."

"I can't believe he'd turn me in. He was in tears over the medal."

283

"A thousand dollars is a thousand dollars."

But that wasn't it. I thought I knew what was. He figured I was a friend like the other fellow was a friend, like Tilfert had been a friend.

Phaegin nudged me. "You look so sad."

"I was thinking about Avelina."

Phaegin shifted closer. She rested her head on my shoulder. "You thought enough for today, Neddy-boy. No more. Close your eyes." She hummed a melody from the nickel dump. I closed my eyes and within minutes left the hard ground for the dance floor, and nothing existed but the smell of her hair and the pressure of her soft body against mine.

CHAPTER 27

By midafternoon, seven days out of Chicago, the grip of hickory and oak had loosed and, instead, spreading in an undulating mantle, thick grass made bright with spring. "Hit's the perrairy!" Curly was ecstatic.

Phaegin also had a look of wonder on her face and I remembered, even as sick as I had been, what glory the open space held upon my first sighting. It was at once immense and then diminished by the even more astonishing immensity of sky overhead. A wondrous grassy ocean, islands of trees dotting the horizon.

The prairie turned our luck. Gone was the chill, gone were wet legs and wet shoes, gone were the shadows. We walked through open air, feeling a false safety because, in the long views, nothing could creep up on us. In fact, when a horse and cart clattered up the rutted road we trod, we had an indecisive half hour to decide what peril it might or might not hold for us, before we decided to chance a meeting.

When we saw the driver of the cart was a weary-looking farmer rather than a Pinkerton, Curly ran down the road and asked the driver with a disarming grin, "How 'bout a ride, mister?"

"No room." The farmer nodded behind him where, stacked two deep in the cart, were stick crates, each with a substantial-looking piglet inside who commenced squealing as if in answer to the human voices. "Takin' weaners t' home."

Curly announced, his fingers poking into one of the cages, "I *love* pigs. These 're good 'uns, too."

The farmer nodded but did not waver from his path.

Curly trotted alongside the wagon, grunting softly to the pigs. He picked up a stick, scratched one of their backs. The pig leaned into it, grunting with pleasure. The farmer, in spite of himself, loosed a small smile. Curly took his advantage, jogging toward the front and pointing to the seat beside the farmer. "Could the lady sit there, mister?"

The farmer nodded. "Help yerself."

Phaegin glanced at me, looking relieved and not a little touched by Curly's gesture. "Might as well get on with a load off." She climbed on. The farmer looked neither right nor left.

We kept along for some time with our taciturn guide, Curly jogging along on short legs to keep up. After half an hour, Curly panted, "Cain't keep it up." He shook his head then called to the farmer, "We could sit on the cages."

"Nyope. They break."

Phaegin looked at Curly. "You sit awhile, I'll walk."

She and Curly exchanged places. But she was almost as short-legged as he was, and in ten minutes she was panting, face pink. In fifteen she was bright red.

I was alarmed. "Curly, give over."

"I hardly got a rest!"

I shouted, "Curly!"

I boosted Phaegin onto the bench seat. She arranged her skirt and, when she'd regained her breath, asked the driver, "If we buy a pig, can we take its spot?" The driver shrugged. Phaegin asked, "How much did you pay for them?"

"Dollar each."

Phaegin looked at me, tipped her head toward the farmer. I nodded, figured Curly and I, sitting cross-legged, could squeeze into two pigs' worth of space, and produced two dollars.

The farmer shook his head. "When done, they'll be *two-'n-a-half*-dollar pigs."

Phaegin tipped her head again and I mouthed, *No.*

Phaegin glared, mouthed back, *Pay him.*

I fingered the cash Mr. O'Hare had given me. "How far are you going?"

The farmer nodded toward the horizon. "Two days, this pace."

It was as good a disguise as we were going to get, I figured, looking like a family on the way back to the family farm. I handed him five dollars. "Two pigs."

He took the bills, pulled his horse to a stop.

Phaegin grinned. "We might as well introduce ourselves. I'm Alice."

The farmer shook his head. "Don't care to know. I like things quiet."

Curly and I lifted out two crates, the smallest two pigs. We opened the first door and one of the pigs ran lightheartedly into the grass, disappearing in the green curtain. The farmer looked sorrowful. "Coyotes will have a meal tonight."

Curly gasped. He slammed the door shut on the second cage as the pig was preparing to make its getaway. "No!"

"You can't leave him in there, Curly, he'll starve to death."

"Don't care. Won't have a stinking coyote chewin the hams offa him."

The farmer made a *chk* noise and the horse began to plod away.

Phaegin yelled, *"Get in!"*

Curly looked at me pleadingly. "He's a baby. I cain't leave him to coyotes. I'll hold him on my lap."

I knew that arrangement wouldn't last long. I shrugged. "It's your lap."

He somehow made it into the wagon bed with the struggling animal. I got into my corner, piled some hay into a backrest, and within minutes fell sound asleep.

When I woke, Curly was still in possession of the pig. He'd shoved it into a burlap sack, a hole cut into the fabric that just let the pig's head stick out. The pig seemed more than happy, leaning against Curly's side like a cat, head up, while Curly scratched under its chin, around the moon of its leathery ears. I glanced at Phaegin. She watched the pair looking disgusted. "He's one of them accidents, a pig in a human body."

We journeyed with the farmer for two days and one night and never knew the man's name. He had a brief spate of loquaciousness around the campfire and told us he'd been cheated by the railroad and God. "Sunk my entire life savings on four hunnert acres and seed to cover it. Green an' pretty, grass to my armpits. Planted wheat and God took the rain away. Got half a crop of horseradish in the kitchen garden and the locusts came even for that. Now there's nothin' but three hunnert acres of desert and a hunnert of rock. Only pigs can find enough to eat. I sup on pork mornin', noon, 'n night no matter the sabbath or holy day." He sighed. "Wife left after the boy died. This country makes for one plague after another. Keep lookin' for Moses to come over the hill and rescue me."

He turned his back to the fire, pulled the blanket over his head, and said nothing further. The next morning he poured a dish of water for each piglet and threw a dessicated cob of corn into each cage, harnessed the horse and, once we were all in, plodded toward his ill-fated farm.

We rode in silence, as if his troubles had sucked the words from the air. Even Curly's pig, better fed on Curly's breakfast than Curly, slept mildly in his burlap purse.

We reached the banks of the Mississippi before noon and paid the ferryman to take us across on a crude flatboat knocked together from green oak and powered by a swayback horse on the other side. It seemed a dear price—a nickel a pig and a dollar for the wagon and human passengers—for such a rickety craft, but the conveyance swam true as a swan; in five minutes we were on the far shore.

Our good crossing seemed to me to indicate our fortunes were changing. The breeze over the water blew cool as I reclined in the straw among the softly grunting piglets.

By midafternoon, however, the sun blazed. The farmer climbed down from the cart, pulled a tarp over the pigs, poured another measure of water. He handed me the half-filled canvas that served as canteen and stood staring at us.

I looked out over the country, which did indeed look as if it had been abandoned by moisture, if not God himself. "Guess it's time to leave."

Phaegin shouldered her bag. Curly grabbed the burlap sack, the pig pitching and squealing with his trotters off solid footing.

"Good luck." I shook the farmer's hand.

"There's none here, only bad." He hesitated, then added, "Consider it well to get no luck at all."

He got back in the cart and drove away without a backward glance.

I checked our bearings. Phaegin looked over my shoulder. "Where exactly are we going, Ned?"

I pointed to a dot on the map. "Omaha." I drew my hand across the country between us into Nebraska, where Lill waited for help she wouldn't get. All I could give her was the truth about what I was and what I'd done. And when she had it, I was sure, her life would seem sweet in comparison.

"Why?"

I shrugged. "It's empty, and there's stops along the way to get provisions. We'll ghost the train without getting on. That way we'll be safe from the law but won't get lost."

The first small town we'd hit, according to the map, was Philip, Iowa. We'd have a careful time of water and food between here and there but would be all right if we kept up a pace.

I warned Curly, watching him trudging along half bent over with the weight of the pig, riding like a spotted pasha, on his back, "If that pig is a problem, that's the end of him."

"He won't be. He's a good pig, hardly weighs anything." The pig lifted its snout and squealed assent.

"I'm not talking about his character, Curly. I'm warning you that we have only so much water, only so much food, only so much energy. If there's misery to go round, he's getting it first."

With the skies overcast, the cloud cover gave us respite from the torrid temperatures. I thought of the farmer: Was God going to provide rain after all? But it did not even spit, bad news for the farmer though I was relieved we would not be slogging through mud again on this leg of our trip. We made good time in the cool air, passed an easy and uneventful night, and the next day we did indeed approach the small burg of Philip.

I eyed the settlement, astonished that it would have earned a place on any map, much less a fancy one in an atlas. Surely there was a lot of empty space to fill, once past the Mississippi. They were desperate for anything to indicate settlement on the wide spaces.

As before, Phaegin and Curly remained back. I took our canvas and filled it at the PHILIP WELL in front of the shack demarcated PHILIP COMMISSARY, which was next door to an outhouse labeled PHILIP CRAPPER. I leaned the wet bag against the porch post, knocked on the commissary door, and walked in. The tiny building was filled with enough goods to stock a warehouse. Provisions leaned from every wall, hung from the ceiling, were stacked on the floor.

The proprietor looked startled at my arrival, looking around me toward the tracks as if the train had crept in unbeknownst. "Howdy, there, I'm Philip. How'd *you* get here?"

"Walked."

He grinned. "Goddamn. Are you crazy, man?"

"Broke."

He grew instantly serious. "This ain't a charity. If I had ha'penny for every down-and-outer's story I've been forced to listen to, I might just make some money for once."

"I'm not looking for a handout."

He regained his good humor. "You going northwest for the gold?"

"Gold?"

"Black Hills. It's Callyfornia all over again. Nuggets the size of horse turds." He motioned from floor to ceiling. "This is *my* gold mine: picks, coffee, pans. Folks stop and they clear me out."

I nodded. "Yep. Strike it rich, won't be walking anymore."

"Run into the goddamn Injuns, you won't be walkin' neither." He laughed uproariously.

I pointed to salt pork, tack, jerked venison, and dried apples. "Whatever three dollars'll get me."

He shook his head. "Won't get you all *that*."

"What?"

"Inflation." He took a canteen from the wall. "A year ago I'd be hard pressed to sell this child for two bits. It's a ten-dollar piece of equipment today."

"Ten *dollars?*"

"Like I said, *this* is the *real* gold mine, son."

I pulled the last two bills from Avelina's father out of my pocket and counted out change. Omaha was suddenly much farther away.

Philip, noting my lack of funds, again lost his smile, seeming to become someone else entirely than the genial shopkeep of a moment ago.

He tossed off his hat. "Fuck. I knew it. Every *goddamned* time." He slapped the zinc countertop. "Give me your damned money."

I laid it on the table. With disdain and great drama, Philip swept the cash into a drawer, violently pulled apples, tack, and coffee off the shelves, and wrapped them in a sheet of brown paper that he shoved across the counter. "Go. Get the hell out before anybody sees I'm goddamn *giving* my crap away."

"Thank you."

"Don't goddamn thank me, get the hell out of my establishment!"

I walked to the door before I remembered. "Do you, by any chance, have a newspaper?"

"To give a man with no goddamn money? Well, looky here, I sure enough goddamn *do!*" He reached under the counter, pulled out a slim paper, balled it, and threw it at me. I ducked the missile, but it still hit me in the head. He laughed, his voice breaking. "Now, you want to fuck my wife for free? She's still in bed, ain't *that* handy?" He started unbuttoning his shirt. "You'll be wanting this, I'm sure. And my pants! Got a couple of balls in there that, apparently, *I'm not using!*"

I grabbed the crumpled paper from the floor, the waterbag from the porch, and lit out as he shouted, "Wait, hold on there, you son of a bitch, I haven't deeded over the whole goddamn business to you yet! You'll want to be renaming the fucking town before the train comes in!"

We hightailed it out of there, and when Philip's ranting had faded into the distance I uncrumpled the ball of paper. We were still in the news, farther back in the reporting, though the charges against me had mounted. My reputation had not only grown but flowered and fruited. I was now recognized as the ringleader for an entire anarchists confederation, and there was speculation that a bombing in Maryland and one in South Carolina might well be my doing, as well as the Connecticut explosion that I had at least been present for. I was being charged with three murders by dynamite and with the murder of Mrs. Quillan, who had yet to be found and, according to her spouse, would never have left of her own volition.

The goods Mr. O'Hare had promised to pay for at the mercantile were being charged to me as armed robbery, plus the robbery at the cigar shop. Further, Mr. Cordassa claimed I must have kidnapped Phaegin, like I had Mrs. Quillan, for Phaegin was a good girl, like his own daughter.

Phaegin grinned when I read her the paper. She whispered, "Isn't that sweet? Mr. Cordassa's *such* a nice man. I hope Chester reads that. It'll make him feel better."

I gawked at her. "It's not sweet. I'm getting blamed for everything. *I'm* the most innocent of us all, and they paint *me* as a murderer, kidnapper, burglar, and anarchist."

We departed from the train tracks and headed southwest for a time. It would cut days off our journey, and we'd reunite with the railway on the quieter leg of rail between Sioux City and Omaha.

That night, however, with Phaegin snoring lightly beside me and Curly spooned around the bagged pig, who was growing at a pace I wouldn't have believed possible on a diet of grass and crackers, I thought over the situation.

It was a good thing for Phaegin that the crimes and her absence were all being blamed on me. After all, Mrs. Quillan was benefiting from the situation, Professor Quillan as well. The real anarchists benefited. There was no reason why Phaegin should not receive the much-deserved relief of my being charged with the whole burden. Maybe she could pick up where she left off, return to the East Coast armed with a story, hardly the worse for wear.

Though I knew sending her back was the right thing, I wavered because of the desolation I felt at the thought of her leaving us. I am ashamed to recount how close I came to remaining silent, for the prospect of losing Phaegin seemed to ensure an absolute erosion. I might survive without her, but not for long. The dikes would surely fail.

The night was a long one as I shored myself up and made plans for Phaegin's departure. Tomorrow we could make it to the station in Grundy. Phaegin would use the last dimes we had to push back east on the train. When she was far enough away for our safety and hers, she would spill the beans of her identity and her capture, how she was treated as a human shield, a possible hostage. They would certainly return her to New Haven, where she would emerge a heroine, a model of pluck. She'd be in all the papers: her tortured indenture to the devilish murderer, her clever escape.

I worked out the details, one by one. She would be safe. Though I would be alone again.

As we ate our wretched breakfast, Curly feeding half of his to the pig, I presented my plan to Phaegin.

Curly stopped stuffing the pig, who squealed in alarm as Curly howled, "You *cain't* leave. You're part of the gang."

I smacked the squealing pig on the snout while shouting at Curly. "Shut up! She has a chance to go home, make hats, be *free*. You want to take that from her?"

He glowered as he'd done when I'd tried to take his vest and boots, then turned his attention to Phaegin. He reached over and took her hand, looking pleadingly orphan-like. Phaegin, incredibly, looked at him sweetly, as if he were a pet and not a menace.

I threw my hands in the air. "Whatever Curly wants, Curly takes, no matter what happens to anyone else? You're the one who went and ruined her life. Now you're going to insist it stays ruined so you can have her company?" I shook my head in disgust. "You're a shoddy, manipulative hoodlum." I pointed at Phaegin. "And you're a fool if you fall for it."

Curly launched himself at me. "Take it back. I ain't no shoddy hoodlum."

I put up my hands to protect my face and he bruised my ribs. Phaegin grabbed his ear and pulled him off me. "You two. Don't be so stupid!"

She let go of Curly. He rubbed his ear. I felt my ribs, glaring at Curly. Phaegin picked up my bag and handed it to me. She picked up her own. "And you call me a fool? Let's go."

She strode off. Curly and I followed. Curly ran up to her and took her hand. "You're not going, are ya, Phaegin?"

"Of course I'm not going," she snapped, then turned on me. "Do you *really* think I could go back and pick up where I left off? The *only* chance I had was to slip in unnoticed. Is anyone going to lend me money now with all this hoo-rah, much less buy a goddamn *hat* from me? Might as well be a burlesque girl and try to marry the president. It's over, Ned. I don't want to talk about it again. Ever."

As we trudged along, summer came on with vengeance. It was hot for June. It would have been hot for August. The dreary landscape, with nothing but the skeletal arms of sagebrush, emaciated prickly pear, and the short curly buffalo and grama grass clothing its naked desolation, went on and on. We took the smallest sips of water we could bear as our water supply dropped to dangerously low levels.

I assured Phaegin and Curly, with a certainty I did not feel, that our water would last us until we hit the train tracks and a station. There we'd fill our canteens to last us to the Missouri River. By early evening on the morrow, however, we were yet in the middle of a vast pool of hardpan and heat. We pressed into the shimmer of baked earth. The next day, it was 90 degrees by midmorning. The water barely sloshed in the canvas skin. The pig screed pitifully in thirst from his bag on Curly's back. Curly looked ready to keel over.

I dumped the pig out of the bag, and Curly didn't even protest. For his part, the pig had enough sense to know running off would be certain death, and the animal wobbled close beside Curly. I poured a jigger of water. "Don't give this to the pig, Curly. He's doing better than he sounds. Down low, it's cooler."

Curly frowned. "He don't look cooler." He tossed his jigger back, then dribbled a couple of drops into his hand, and the pig licked his palm with vengeance.

"Poor pig," he murmured, then took up his own whine. "Never could take the heat. Cold don' bother me, I could sleep without a blanket all winter, but the heat? Kin I have one more drink, Ned, one more?"

Curly complained as much as Phaegin deserved to. She was swaddled in layers of petticoats, a high-necked blouse, and who knows what mysteries of underclothes. Though we'd cut her hair, it was still thick as a pelt around her face. She was sunburned, the kerchief she wore provided no protection for her face and neck whatsoever, and she wore woolen stockings and leather shoes.

Phaegin fanned herself, walking with feet dragging the hard dirt. I took her bag to relieve her of the weight.

Phaegin came to attention, jerked on the strap. "Give it back." "I'll carry it."

She tugged again. I put up my hands. "Fine. It's not me that looks like a bratwurst."

She grimaced, receiving the bag. "You can take some of it." She handed me a blanket and Curly his western costume. "You might as well carry 'em."

I shrugged. "Might as well wear 'em, at this point."

The duds were a tonic. Curly leapt to his feet, pulled on his vest with relish, and clapped the hat on his head. When he tried to pull his boots on, however, he tugged and jerked and pulled and swore. "Damn things won' go!"

"Then wear your shoes, we got to get going." I looked west, where I willed the river to rise from the dun landscape.

Curly continued his struggle, avowing, "I'm not wearin' shoes ever again." He groaned and huffed and stood teetering on the heels until his own weight forced his feet into the boot. He grinned, licked his thumbs and ran them over the brim of his hat, and struck a pose. "How do I look, Ned?"

"Like a real cowboy."

A thirsty cowboy. His lips were white and cracked, and he was dusted from head to toe with a fine silt. I sloshed the waterbag.

Phaegin pointed to the almost weightless bag on my shoulder. "What are we going to do?"

"River's *got* to be right over there."

"And if it isn't?"

"I got lots of tricks. Cactus is full of juice." She didn't look convinced. No one mentioned we hadn't seen a prickly pear for half a day. "You can slash your mules' ears and drink the blood."

She shuddered and hoisted her bag. "*We're* the mules, Ned."

I scanned the horizon. "Well, we're headed into buffalo territory. They carry extra water around, like a camel but in their gut. We'll just kill one. I got my pistol."

"You're going to kill your first buffalo with that little gun?"

I patted the bag. "This child here could kill an elephant in *my* capable hands."

Phaegin rolled her eyes. "Impressive. I wish it could read a compass."

We slogged along, sun almost whining with heat, dirt baked so hard not even dust rose.

By the time the sun had reached its zenith, Curly had fallen back. I walked backward, shouting through cupped hands, "Curly, keep up."

"These boots are killin' me. What did you *do* to 'em?" He attempted a short run, grimacing with the effort, but got within talking range. After another half hour or so, however, he had fallen back again, limping, and soon he stopped altogether and sat down in the dirt. "I can't take it no more!" He tried to pull his boots off, pulling, yanking, and shouting. "They're tight as pussy." He sounded panicked. "Whaddid you *do* to my boots?"

I wondered if he was getting sunstroke. But there was nothing to do but get to some water, find some shade. I turned and kept walking, shouting behind me, "Nobody did anything to your boots, Curly. Get up, we have to keep on."

Phaegin said, "Wait, Ned. Look at him."

For the third time I saw Curly in tears. He angrily wiped his face. "I *cain't* go no further, I'm telling you. I tried, but I cain't. They were fine before, now they's too small.

Phaegin put her hands on her hips, looking worried. "They fit two weeks ago. You couldna raised up *that* fast, Curly."

Curly glowered. "Maybe I'm finally gettin' my grow on, I don' know. I just know they wanta squeeze me to death now."

I remembered putting his boots in my bag, still damp from fording the streams. "You got them wet in the creek, Curly. The leather shrunk. Just put your shoes on instead and let's get going."

"Cain't." He mumbled and lay back in the dirt, looking at the sky. "Threw 'em away."

"You threw them away? Damn, Curly." I looked behind us as if I could see them. "How far ago?"

"Far."

"Then you're going to have to put up with tight boots."

Curly nodded, struggled to his feet, and took a few steps, looking sick and pinched.

Phaegin shook her head. "He's really hurtin'. I'll give him my socks."

"Putting more socks on isn't going to make his boots bigger."

Curly collapsed back onto the dirt. The pig sat in the shade he cast. I sighed loudly, put my hands on my hips, and, nothing else to be done, directed, "Let's get 'em off, take a look. Maybe we can cut the toes open or something."

Phaegin held him in a lock around his chest, and I tugged on the incredibly stuck boots while Curly groaned and howled. The pig bit fiercely at my pant legs like a dog until Curly stopped yelling when the boots came off. Under the cowboy boots, Curly's socks were crusted and black. Phaegin *tsk*ed. "When's the last time you washed these?"

"*Never* washed 'em. They's my lucky socks. Ned gave 'em to me in Pennsylvania."

Phaegin peeled the socks slowly from Curly's feet. Curly bit his lip while tears rolled down his cheeks.

"Ah, poor Curly."

Curly wiped his face and squinted at his feet. "I really rubbed the skin off 'em." He had blisters on each toe and along the spine of his heels that had burst and bled. His feet festered in the vile crud left by the socks.

Phaegin spoke cheerfully. "Finally, an excuse to get rid of these petticoats." But behind the smile I could see worry.

We ripped Phaegin's petticoats into pieces. Damping one, we attempted to clean Curly's wounds and then bandaged his feet with the remaining strips. There was no possibility Curly would squeeze into his boots now. I prayed the oozing sores would not become further infected. We were in a mess. We sat on the heat-baked earth. I sloshed the canteen again. Barely a trickle.

"Exactly where did you throw the shoes away?"

"Somewheres after I put the boots on."

Three hours of walking, but it had been slow walking. Alone, I'd make better time. If we pushed ahead, I'd be forced to carry Curly, and who knows how long it would take us to reach water. "I'm going to go back and look."

Phaegin said, "You'll never ever find a pair of shoes, Ned. You can't even hit a *river*. Leave, and we'll never see you again."

I grit my teeth against the diatribe.

She attempted to soften her criticism. "The dirt's too hard to leave a track; not even Daniel Boone could retrace our steps." I said nothing. Phaegin continued. "He threw them away *miles* back. You veer ten yards to one side, and you might as well be a thousand miles off."

"I can find them."

"Ned, you can't."

I took hold of her arm. "He can't walk without shoes. He may not be able to walk with them. I *can't* carry him across the country, especially without water, and we don't have any water. We don't have any mules, and we don't have any buffalo. All we can hope for is shoes to get us out of here. I'm leaving you what water

301

we have left. I'll be gone three hours at most, and we can get on with it."

She looked out across the wavering scrub like she was hoping to see a waterlogged buffalo on the horizon. "What if you lose us?"

I checked the howling wilderness around us, the grisly hills, the sky so hot and clear as to be almost colorless. "If I'm not back by sundown . . ." I took my pistol from the bag ". . . shoot once. I'll hear it and know where you are." I handed her the pistol and she took it hesitantly. I asked, "Do you know how to shoot it?"

"Oh, sure, I'm the star of the nickel dump rifle club."

I showed her how to work it, told Curly to work his boots—bend them, chew them, soften them up any way he could—because if I couldn't find the shoes, he was going to be wearing them, on his knees or hands or feet: his choice—and I took off.

I picked my way through the scrub, losing sight of Phaegin and Curly with alarming rapidity, following what I was pretty sure was our path by looking for the broken stems of brush. I was thankful for Curly's predisposition for swordplay. He had crushed bush after bush in his imaginings of himself as pirate or Viking. But the bushes were few and far between in this nude and grim landscape. After some time, he must have taken a rest, for I found no mark of his destruction. I backed some distance, searched again for a footprint: a snapped twig, a crushed spline, or a bruised blade of grass. I checked the compass and hesitantly went forward, scanning from north to south for the brown leather shoes.

I checked the sky, wishing I had my father's watch. I had gone far enough, at least an hour out, maybe an hour and a half. Phaegin was right: I might be a dozen yards off, I might be five,

I might be a hundred; it might as well be a mile. I sat down and fought the panic that was billowing. We were going to die of thirst. And that would be a far worse death than hanging in New Haven would have been. The sky dimmed. I should head back. Phaegin would worry and, worse, use one of our precious bullets. I struggled to my feet and scanned the ground once again, willing myself to find the shoes.

A blur of dust rose from the east. A fire? A dust devil? But I felt no wind. After some minutes, the blur closer, I heard lowing. A minute more, a wagon pulled by a yoke of oxen rose from the swell of prairie, a strangely printed canvas cover stretched over its bows. Two people sat on the forward jockey box and another peered out the box to the rear. I waved my arms and shouted like a banshee.

CHAPTER 28

It was a Conestoga, painted like a gypsy's with a yellow box and blue wheels. Incredibly, its white canvas was painted with fossils I well recognized—a slothlike Megatherium, a curvilinear nautilus, the hulking club of a megalosaurus femur —and on the back, clinging to the wooden ribs of the frame like an orangutan, a paintbrush-armed man was dabbing black paint on the canvas.

Even more incredibly, on the seat of the Conestoga, wearing a wide-brimmed hat decorated with a spray of chokecherry leaves, was Mrs. Quillan.

She leaned forward, beaming with amazement, and clapped her hands together as she ascertained it was I. "Ned Bayard! Am I dreaming?"

I felt dizzy, almost certain that Mrs. Quillan and the strange wagon were a product of heat and my burgeoning despair. "Mrs. Quillan?"

She laughed. "My lord, what are you doing out *here*?" She looked around. "It's like you sprouted from the sand. Did you fly?"

"Walked. Partway." I motioned. "I have friends over there. Where are we?"

As Mrs. Quillan laughed, the driver of the wagon, a vigorous-looking man with a Montana peaked hat, canvas mining pants, and scuffed work boots, pushed the brim of his hat up, his eyes blue as the sky. Mrs. Quillan took his hand. "A friend found, what are the chances?"

He kissed her hand and shrugged. "The country is vast, but roads and rivers *are* few." He looked at me. "Des Moines is about three days directly east."

I blanched. We must have been walking parallel to the Missouri. If we'd maintained our trajectory, we would not have survived to hit the great river.

Mrs. Quillan made introductions. "This is Charles Laramore. Charles, this is Edward Turrentine Bayard the Third."

He said "Pleased" and stuck his hand out.

I shook it. "The other paleontologist?"

Charles Laramore laughed. "The other paleontologist. Do you hear that, Sylvia? The *other* paleontologist."

Mrs. Quillan turned and motioned toward the simian man in the back. "And this is Mr. Dawbs. We are giving him a lift. It is certainly our week for finding wandering souls on the prairie."

The man in back, as dusty and derelict-looking as I supposed I was, clenched his brush between his teeth, leaned down from his perch to shake my hand, and grated, "Just Dawbs," sounding as if his throat was as dusty on the inside as it was on the out.

"Do you know," I asked Mrs. Quillan, "about what's going on in New Haven?"

"Not a clue," she said gaily. "And I don't *care*."

"Were you the one who spilled the beans? About the fossils?"

"The coal scam? I certainly did. I took the train to Pittsburgh all by myself. Walked into the offices, all by myself. I revealed Professor Quillan as the charlatan he is, all by myself. And then, I went to Boston and bumped into Charles. All by myself." Her eyes sparked. "Professor Quillan labored under the sad misapprehension that I was weak. I trust he thinks otherwise now."

"What he *thinks*, what the entire world seems to think, is that I've murdered you and that the coal scam is of *my* doing."

Laramore disembarked from the wagon, went around, and helped Mrs. Quillan from her seat as if he escorted her to the opera. For her part, she beamed at him as if he'd given her a diamond, then dragged her attention back to me. "What are you talking about?"

I told her the entire story, from the time I went to Pennsylvania with Quillan and adopted Curly: about being fired, the bombing, and our subsequent flight. I pulled the folded and tattered newspaper articles from my pocket and handed them to her. "You see? I am being blamed for your disappearance!"

"That man!" She shook the papers at Laramore. "He says I can't possibly have left him, and so I must have been kidnapped and murdered. He still has no *idea* of what I am capable of."

I said, "Mrs. Quillan, the professor underestimating you is a small matter compared to my situation, don't you think?"

She waved me off. "Pshaw. You are free. You are a man in a wild country. No one can touch you."

"Mrs. Quillan, they *can* touch me—with the noosed end of a rope. They *can* and they mean to, and they've come awful close already!"

She looked sad. She put out her hand and drew me near her. She spoke quietly. "I know it must seem a difficult situation, Ned, but only because you are *in* it. Put yourself in my place, and you will feel so much better."

"What are you talking about?"

She sighed. "I cannot go back. Ever. I was a cat's whisker *away* from . . ." She looked into the sky and clasped her hands tightly in her lap. "Ned, the bump behind my ear and the swale of my neck have damned me."

I was visited by the image of the professor, his porcelain phrenologist's skull at his side, palpating Mrs. Quillan's head just as he had done mine.

She touched her temple. "Have you ever seen the inside of a mental institution? If you are rational going in, you do not remain so long. I took a three-day 'cure.' *Three days*, and it almost undid me. It was a year before I could sit in a room with a closed window or door. If I were to return to the professor, if I were in any way to make myself known, they would come after me and I would not see the light of day again—nor, I fear, the light of my sanity."

I began to protest and she put her hand to my lips. "No. You do *not* know. You do not *know*. Do know I will never go back. Not for anything." She glanced at Laramore. "Not for anyone. Never."

Her face was set. There was no more glittering anger or hilarity, only a concrete fixedness I would not break.

I pleaded. "Then Dr. Laramore. He can tell the authorities about you, about my innocence."

"I must ever be a secret, I fear. Besides"—she smiled at me, as though her thought were a pleasing one—"if they would hang you for the bombing, it doesn't really matter if they believe you've done me in as well. In fact, it is rather a silver lining, don't you think? A sort of inadvertent good deed you may take to heaven."

I pounded my fist into my palm. "I don't want to take anything to heaven. You have to *tell* them, explain everything about the bombing, about Quillan. You have to tell them it wasn't me who was trying to cheat the coal company. Please!"

307

Laramore took a bag of tobacco from his jacket. "Certainly I can make an attempt. I will tell the authorities some safe version of your story when I return to Boston in September."

"September! My neck will be stretched by then!"

Charles Laramore filled his pipe. As he tamped the tobacco with his thumb he grinned awkwardly. "Sorry about that, but nothing I can do. We've—" he gestured with the bowl of the pipe toward Mrs. Quillan "—got to wait on some cooling of rather warm situations ourselves."

Mrs. Quillan glanced at Dawbs, who was putting the finishing touches on a trilobite. She leaned forward and whispered to me. "Yet another unfortunate marriage. It promises to be a very sticky situation, drama, recriminations, threats of terminations, and that's just Harvard. His wife is sure to be livid as well. He left rather abruptly. The world wants a facade, Ned. Chip away at it, and you are in peril."

"You're talking about peril to *me*?"

"I know you understand. Allow a few months for the passions to cool, and Charles will return with his new discoveries. Harvard will ignore the old excitement for the new. And then—" she gazed at him with adoration "—Charles, you will do what you can?"

Laramore lit his pipe and puffed and nodded. From the distance came the sound of a pistol shot.

"That's Phaegin, she'll be worried." I remembered the shoes, my friends' thirst. The situation was hopeless. All I could do was keep one step away from utter failure.

Phaegin almost collapsed with relief when she saw me in the wagon. Curly crawled forward with the pig squealing beside him,

"Give poor pig somethin' to drink, he don't care if it's water or booze or piss, as long's it's wet."

Laramore handed Curly one canteen. I traded Phaegin the pistol for the other. Curly watered the piglet before gulping his own water. When they'd finished drinking, I made introductions but forestalled Phaegin's questions. "They can't help us with the police. We're going to have to go on without."

Mrs. Quillan patted a meal bag. "We are happy to share our water and supplies, however."

I nodded. "We need shoes."

Curly lifted his crusty feet for perusal and Mrs. Quillan made a face.

Laramore shook his head and handed a bag of beans and a bag of flour to Phaegin. "No shoes, sorry."

Dawbs looked at Curly's swollen oozing toes with interest. "Gangrene."

Curly paled. "Nah."

Dawbs asked Laramore, "What do you have?"

Laramore went to the back, shuffled through the supplies, and returned with a vial of iodine.

Dawbs sneered and pushed it away. "To my wagon."

Laramore was amused. "Dawbs is a man of few words. Practically prehistoric himself."

Dawbs shut one eye. "You could keep a windmill goin'."

Laramore laughed self-consciously. "Fair enough, fair enough. Let's get on then; we'll drive you."

Dawbs pointed across a rocky draw. "Walk. Too long around."

Phaegin put her hands on her hips. "Walk? Have you forgotten the state of his feet?"

Dawbs didn't say a word, just hunkered down for Curly to take hold around his neck. Dawbs headed west with Curly hanging behind, the slaked pig trotting along. Phaegin picked up her bag and skirts, and followed, yelling, "Ned, let's go!"

Laramore lost his grin, calling, "Hey, there, my canteen!" Mrs. Quillan put her hand on his arm and he added, "Ah, well, we've another. Good luck to you."

He shook my hand cheerfully and pointed toward the diminishing trio. "You'd better catch up, son."

I didn't like this man's cheer. I might have understood him, even admired him under different circumstances. But this was not the time to feel anything but scorn for abstract ideals. The quest for knowledge, the vision of the past, science and truth: These are great gleaming treasures in better times, but at knife's blade, in baking heat, they are thinner than water.

I narrowed my eyes and stood straight. I was easily Laramore's height, so I leaned toward him as I repeated, "We are in need of shoes."

"Sorry, son. *As I said,* I can't help you there."

I strode to the back of the wagon and began to rifle the stores.

Laramore shouted. "First the canteen and now this? Give an inch. . . ." He took hold of my shoulder and swung me around. I shoved him off and he came back and punched me on the side of my skull, knocking me to the ground.

I had the pistol out in a second. He put his hands in the air at once. Mrs. Quillan ran to his side. I struggled to my feet, my ear buzzing. "Take off your boots."

"Excuse me?"

I waved my pistol toward his feet. "I want your boots."

Laramore placed his hands on his hips and smiled. "You're not taking my boots, son."

Without hesitation and certainly without remorse, I shot. Laramore howled and jumped about on one leg.

"Charles!" Mrs. Quillan screamed. "*Give him the boots!*"

He fell to the ground and began unlacing. He threw one boot, then the other to me. The right boot had a small hole in the leather; Laramore's right toe was bleeding where the bullet had torn a pebble of flesh from the tip. I gathered the footwear and tied the laces together.

"You'll be fine, Laramore. You're a man in *wild country,* after all." I backed slowly away. "Better put some iodine on that, and if you're thinking of retaliating, alerting the authorities as to our whereabouts instead of as to our innocence, let me warn you, I wouldn't think twice about paring a nice little silver lining into an institution for the lady."

Strangely enough, Mrs. Quillan smiled at that, and as I retreated she called, real friendly, "Ned, I think your mother is in Connecticut. I saw a woman of such resemblance to you a week before I left, it was breathtaking."

That did throw me for a loop, wondering what effect she hoped the news would have on me and if I could trust her on it. She put up a hand, however, and waved so sadly that she reminded me of my mother, long ago now, on the station platform in Connecticut. I smiled back in spite of myself. "Take care, Sylvia."

I followed Dawbs, Curly, and Phaegin toward the draw. Dawbs turned, stared at the departing wagon, and grinned. Curly, in spite of his discomfort, whistled wolfishly, and Phaegin pursed her lips and shook her head.

I turned to see what the fuss was about. It was the canvas covering on the wagon. At a distance the Megatherium, the nautilus, and the long thick bone of the megalosaurus merged together to become a reclining, buxom, and naked woman.

Dawbs was not only a skilled illusionist, he was a powerful man. He climbed across rocks, jumped dry gulches, and clambered up silty hummocks as if he didn't have Curly on his back. We were at odds to keep up with him. After about two hours of nonstop clambering, we found Dawbs's handcart at the mouth of the little canyon. Though a handcart, it was of decent size, its wheels set wide enough to fit in a Conestoga's ruts.

If we had thought Laramore's wagon had been well painted, Dawbs's cart was an absolute circus of erotica. There were enough sylphs, mermaids, madonnas, Venuses, Eves, and sirens cavorting in abandon across the wooden planks to keep a cow town busy for a month.

Dawbs dumped Curly into the shadow that the wagon cast and then ran his hands over the reliefs like he was seeing a lost friend.

Phaegin rolled her eyes.

Curly had his nose practically on the wood, forgetting about his infected feet. "Hit's nice," he breathed.

Dawbs pulled back the tarp from the back, drew out a keg of turpentine, an empty bucket, and a jug of what he called "tarantula juice." He offered the jug to Curly. "Take a belt. In fact, take two or three."

Curly sniffed, grinned, and poured back a glug of liquid, grimaced, shuddered, and shouted, "Whooooo-*hoo*! Tha's *leg stretcher*, all right!"

After Curly'd downed his moonshine, Dawbs poured turpentine from the keg into the bucket, pointed at the bucket. "Put cher walkin' pegs in."

Curly lowered his feet into the liquid, screamed, and jerked his knees up around his chin, his entire face screwed tight. "Jeeesus, you're killin' me!" Pig commenced squealing.

Dawbs watched Curly, unmoved. "Beats having no feet at all." He nodded as Curly whimpered and set his feet in the tincture once again. "Won't hurt so in a minute. A poultice of gunpowder and lint, you'll be right as rain."

As Dawbs doctored Curly, Phaegin and I gathered scrub for a fire. Dawbs stirred up cornmeal and jerked venison and baked it in a cast-iron pot covered with coals. He prepared our rough food with peculiar nicety, trimming a piece of sage into slivers for flavoring and scooping the yellow lumps into a careful mound on the tin plate before offering it to Phaegin.

Dawbs passed his jug around. The liquor kicked like a mule, dissolving weeks into a blurry memory so I had the first evening of relaxation in ages. The fire crackled, the stars like lamps. Fireflies waxed and waned like the edge of imagination.

Curly sat happily munching his food, Laramore's boots huge on his feet, allowing for both the poultice and the strips of petticoat binding to fit in as well. He admired his footwear. "Not good as cowboy boots, but they're *big*. Look a man in these, I *sure* do." He gazed at Dawbs. "How'd you know about feet? You a doctor?"

Dawbs spoke with that dry growl that seemed inherent rather than a product of thirst. "Artist."

Curly nodded. "You sure are. An' a good 'n. You should make people pay to take a gander at your wagon."

313

"Thank you."

Phaegin still had not said a word about the bevy of carven females. She said nothing now. I asked, "What's an artist doing out here? Kind of empty to find an audience, isn't it?"

"Audience?" Dawbs snorted. "*My* audience calls me an animal and my art filth. I am the black sheep even to my family, and all because of what I find beautiful. Why? I don't know. The Greeks, the Romans, the ancient Egyptians—we worship the relics of their lives, we applaud the Venus, classical nudes, kore, black-ground vases. But not my work."

Phaegin finally spoke. "*Come on.* If you wanted to make art, you'd have made 'em with their arms missing, or draped with chains like that Greek slave. That makes the difference, and you know it. You are crude little boys who want to stare at dirty pictures and so call it art to make it permissible You're not making art, you're . . . *playin'* with yerselves."

Dawbs bellowed, "That *isn't* art?" We men all laughed boisterously and passed the jug.

Phaegin took a drink and grinned through the guffaws. "If a person practices anything enough, I'm sure it seems like art to 'im." She arched her brow. "You lot do, I'm *sure*."

Dawbs leaned his elbows on his knees. "You know there's three kinds of love?"

Phaegin pursed her lips.

Dawbs stuck his thumb in the air. "Moral love." He nodded until Phaegin gave a short nod in agreement.

Dawbs stuck his forefinger in company with the thumb. "Physical love."

Phaegin narrowed her eyes. "Uh-huh."

Now Dawbs slowly raised his other three fingers. "And then

314

there's manual." He made a yanking motion that sent us men into another fit of laughter.

Phaegin sat with her arms crossed. "Now I wonder why they call that *man*-ual. If any one of you was worth a woman, you wouldn't have to resort to it, would you?"

Curly lost his grin and nodded mournfully. "'S'truth. If Sapphire was my girl, I'd never jerk off again."

The next morning, perhaps taking pity on our hungover miseries, Dawbs offered us a partnership. "White harvest. Make yourself a stake. Stay under cover while things cool down."

Curly gave me a pleased look, imagining, I supposed, being hauled across the plains in the erotically charged cart. But Dawbs's offer gave me pause: I had a pledge to keep. The pause was short, for though Lill waited in Omaha, she did not wait for what I had become: more trouble. I was useless to her until my flaming life had cooled considerably. And so, when Phaegin whispered, "Beats dyin' a thirst," I took Dawbs's meaty hand and shook it. "We'd be grateful to keep your company."

Curly hooted with pleasure. "What do we do?"

Dawbs mimed the proceedings, scooping energetically with his simian arms. "Pick up bones. Put them in the cart. Dump the cart at the tracks. Train comes through, they pay us."

Curly looked puzzled. "Why would anybody want buffalo *bones?*"

"Grind 'em to fertilizer."

"They really pay?"

"Last year I worked into January, until the bad storms hit. Left the pushcart here in the canyon, walked to the railroad tracks, flagged down the train, and rode into Kansas City *first class* on my proceeds. Handsomest man in the world for two weeks. I owned a fine Arabian horse for about an hour, before I lost it again in a poker game. A great bed to myself, unless I chose otherwise." He considered. "Then I shared a room with a fella, then with two fellas, then I was sleepin' like a dog in a pack on a pile of blankets, sweepin' floors and cleanin' spittoons until I worked off what I owed. Riches to rags. Had some time gettin' back to the wagon as a poor man. Long time walkin'."

Curly snorted. "Don't I know it."

We finally forded the elusive Missouri. The plains drying more with each step west made me more than nervous to leave the big water and risk the desert thirst again. But Dawbs seemed to know the area inside out. He'd crisscrossed the dry earth so many times he'd lost his fear of it. After some days we began picking up bones.

Four decades of wholesale buffalo slaughter was recorded on the plains, though the bones of the dead beasts were so ubiquitous they barely registered, as common as the twisted stems of sage or the heat fissures in the gumbo soil. Coyotes and wolves had dragged the bones hither and yon, so there was no sense of any individual animal, more the feeling that a giant hand had sown the skeletal pieces as carefully and evenly as a farmer broadcasting seed. Some of the bones were bleached and hollow, others chewed by calcium-hungry rodents, cracked by powerful jaws, made porous by minuscule animals beyond our sight. Others still evinced their origin with a leathery sinew, a flag of hide, a certain weight that the fauna and the weather had not yet dissipated.

In our work, the pelvis was a find, as was the femur, the humerus. The hulking skull was best of all, weighty, broad between the eyes, the fore skull two inches thick, and—though the shiny brown horn had long fallen away—the horn stem yet protruded powerfully, a fine handle. The commas of broken ribs were likely as not to be woven over with seasons of grass and not worth the effort to extricate. Tarsus, metatarsus, and the smaller vertebrae of the tail all required too much time and effort to make use of.

It was mindless but physically demanding work, the sun an inescapable sweltering blanket from nine in the morning until the gloaming breezes picked up. It seemed we walked more miles back and forth from the wagon than we had in our escape from Connecticut. Our only respite was when Dawbs would take the handcart across the prairie to the tracks to dump another load on our growing mountain of bones.

The first days were the worst for Phaegin and me. Our shoulders and elbows ached terribly. Phaegin could hardly turn her neck by the end of the second day.

Curly, however, had been suckled on hefting and dragging heavy loads. That in itself was no problem for him. Of course, his feet gave him trouble. He was still limping, and the overlarge shoes did not make the going any easier, but mostly Curly resented the fact he had come west and was not doing cowboy work.

"Pick up, put in cart, dump cart. This is too much like coal work. Cowboys don't do this. I thought I was gonna get to be a cowboy. What I need is a horse."

I pointed at his shoes. "You can't even wear boots, and you're going to get a horse?"

He drew himself up. "I'll be wearin' my boots soon's my feet heal up altogether. Dawbs tol' me: soak the leather—it'll get all soft—then put 'em on and don' take 'em off till they're cracker.

They'll be exactly your size when they dry." He nodded and threw a femur into the wagon. "Gauchos strip the leather off a horse's legs, put 'em on still wet with blood. Best boots ever made."

"If they're so good why doesn't everyone have 'em?"

"'Cause you gotta be willin' to kill a horse, that's why. Who would kill a horse but a filthy Argentine?"

As our travels took us deeper west, it was easy to sidestep human contact. Every so often we would see the dust of wagon trains moving through to greener pastures: to California gold and oranges, to Dakota land, to the Mormon Salt Lake.

My shoulders grew stronger, and Phaegin's neck healed. The days passed like the rails in the train track, each one virtually the same, and a whole lot of them before you might even think to get where you're going.

Curly never let up on his complaints, his jaw exercised more than his legs. As we dogged back and forth with armloads he continued to whine. "This ain't no good at all. I'm goin' to Wyomin' Territory when this is over. I'm gonna have a spread with a hunnert thousand cattle, longhorns from the south. I'll pick out a different horse from my string ever' single day and spend the whole day on its back. I'm gonna have a black one, a palomino, and a roan. I'm gonna have one of ever' kind there is. I'll be the fastest rider too, and a great bronc buster. There's not a horse in the world that'll unseat me. Why do we hafta *do* this, Ned?"

"Money, Curly, laying low. Don't worry, we'll be going before too long."

I sympathized with Curly's itchy feet, however. I also was impatient with the slow work, with biding time. Though we put miles and miles on our shoes, it was trod east to west to east to west, to and fro across the plains in passages of five miles one way, five miles back, so that in all the time we worked we had hardly penetrated Nebraska.

Still, as days and then weeks passed with no further excitement, I began to believe we had achieved some safety. Not only were we cloaked in this dense emptiness but the memory of men was weak, the character of the nation even weaker. There would certainly soon be another crime and another hunt to eclipse *our* drama. Then, perhaps, we could find names in places that would pay us no heed for the rest of our tranquil lives.

Before that sweet disappearance could happen, I reminded myself, I had many responsibilities to answer.

By this time Lill would have heard of my troubles. I hoped so, for I could hardly bear to think of her waiting for me, whiling her days and growing further and further embittered at my hard heart. Would she finally have fled Omaha? Would she have returned to Osterlund—and to what account? I must find her. If Lill's candle had burned low, even a wanted man might answer a need. If so, having given Lill my promise, I would stand by it.

Further, my mother haunted me. I wondered if Mrs. Quillan was right that I should not give up on her. I wondered if my mother had given up on me. Did she hope one day to be forgiven and to hold me in her gaze? For my part, I prayed someone had provided my mother a decent life and that she would not hear of what actually had come to *me*.

At night I counted my other debts instead of counting sleep. Not only had I made assurances to Lill, I also owed Curly. I certainly owed Phaegin whatever I could to make sure her life was in some way whole and as safe as ever it could be. By taking the partnership with Dawbs, I became indebted to him. It was a long list and with little hope, to be sure. My successes were few, my failures many. Avelina, Tilfert, Lill, Chin, Phaegin, and Curly were all certainly much worse off than before they had met me. To a lesser degree but no less certain, so were Mother Fenton, Mr. Cordassa, Phaegin's brothers, even Chester. If I could ever clear my dishonored plate, I swore I would never promise anything to anyone again.

The pig forsook Curly and lay against me. I scratched his bristly hide. "I want you to know, Pig, you're nothing but future bacon to me, so don't take this as anything more than a moment of consolation."

We continued our zigzagging for weeks. When Curly's boils had healed, he soaked his beloved boots in a little creek then pulled on the sodden footgear. Just as Dawbs had promised, the leather stretched and dried to a perfect fit on Curly's now calloused feet.

The morning after that, Phaegin looked out across the flat prairie. Shading her eyes against the early sun, she called, "Look, a soddy."

Dawbs squinted across the prairie to the eyebrow hump that shimmered in the heat. "Swing station, I s'pose. Wagon stop, overpriced booze, food, maybe whores."

Curly was immediately rejuvenated from seconds before, when he'd said he couldn't take another step. "Let's take a gander, whaddaya say, Ned, you think?"

I kept working. "We'd be crazy to chance it."

Curly was hopping up and down beside me. "Been so long, Ned. Nowhere and no way's anybody gonna know us from Adam, clear out here."

I picked up a scythic rib and pointed it at him. "We've no money and you know it."

Dawbs stared toward the soddy and stated, "I'm in need."

Phaegin huffed. "Of *what?*"

Dawbs hitched up his pants and set off. "Too numerous to count. Good thing is, being so necessitous I'll likely find something to scratch *one* of my itches."

Curly was already at Dawbs's heels, Pig at Curly's. I wouldn't keep them back now. I shrugged at Phaegin, who had her fists on her hips, then followed my eager friends. Phaegin shouted behind us, "For the love of Pete!" but caught up at a trot.

Soon the station came into clearer view. It was built against a short cliff and the three walls supporting the sod roof were of rough timbers from which one tiny window was cut. A plank door stood warped and permanently open. A three-legged table leaned against the outside wall, littered with open cans, partially filled bottles, and a black haze of flies that, even from a distance, sounded like a swarm of bees. The crude sign jutting from the ragged grass in the yard proclaimed LIQOR, MEALS 75¢, AMMO-DUDS-DRUGS, and GOODS.

As we came around the swale, we could see a coach parked along the north side of the shanty. Apart from the flies, there was not a sound to be heard. Not a voice, not a horse's whinny, not a whistle or snore.

We approached slowly, something wrong feeling heavier and heavier in the air, though nothing but silence gave hint of it. Then I tripped, falling headlong into the grass. At my nose: a human head and, where the ear should have been, a bloody hole. I scrabbled, huffing panic, into a stand, then tripped over the dead man's legs.

As I stumbled away, Dawbs hissed, "Lord Jesus, mother of God!"

Phaegin covered her mouth, while Curly hunkered down by the man, who stared up into the sky with fly-covered eyes, the ears, lopped from his head, neatly on his chest, his hair missing in a stripe across his bloodied skull. "Cor, he caught it all right."

Dawbs looked north and south and walked closer. Another three bodies lay camouflaged on burnt grass, charred almost beyond recognition as human.

In the wagon another body, a corpulent man, bloating still larger in the heat, had a horrified look on his face but no marks to indicate he'd died in any way but out of terror. Behind the wagon, two women, stripped of clothing, facedown. Dawbs rolled one over. Her bodice was ripped asunder, the breasts severed from her chest.

Phaegin screamed. Pig took it as chastisement and tore into the scrub around the station. I pulled Phaegin away from the wagon, back to the soddy.

"Who would do this, why would they do this? It's evil, it's horrible! Oh, Ned, I want to go home, I just want to go home!"

I clutched her to me. What could I say? I wanted to go home too, but there was no home for us. I was sick of bombs and death and ugliness, of flies and heat and terror, but I couldn't for the life of me find a way past them. All I could do was murmur it would be all right. And in the midst of my useless assurances, there came a voice.

"Help me."

Phaegin pulled away. "My God, someone's in there."

I peered into the dark soddy. "Hello?"

"Hello?" came the cracked reply.

I told Phaegin to remain where she was and crept inside. It was filthy, smelling of offal. More cans and bottles littered the floor. A rat jumped from my path. In the corner, nested on a litter of rags, was a man. In the dark I could tell no more. "Are you all right?"

He made a bitter noise. "I am a long journey from right." He coughed. "It would be a blessing if you would provide me with water."

I stepped back out of the soddy and shouted, "Dawbs, bring the water! We have a survivor!"

When we'd pulled the man into the light, however, I wasn't sure *survivor* was the right word. His eyes put out, blood crusted down his face as if he'd wept red tears. His hands had been severed across the palm, leaving his thumbs intact; his feet were removed at the arch.

Phaegin trembled like a leaf but pulled herself together to sit at the man's side. "You poor man. Poor, poor man."

Curly walked around him. "'E's more 'n poor. He's a calamity."

The man took a long drink from the canteen. "That's about it."

Phaegin made him a pillow from a coat and placed it under his head. Dawbs demanded, "What happened here?"

The man turned his head toward Dawbs as if he were yet sighted. "Injuns." He moved his hand, the thumb weirdly animate on the stump. "Rode in like the apocalypse. Burned a coupl'a fellows alive, tortured th' others." He rocked his head in agony. "Them poor wimmin, and my pard. My fault. All of it." Incredibly, real tears leaked down his cheeks. "*My* goddamn fault."

Phaegin put her hand on his chest. "It can't be. Don't torment yourself with the thought."

He asked for more water. Dawbs trickled some into his mouth. When the man had swallowed he commenced his story.

"I'm Jim Harrier. I worked this swing station with my partner, did you see him? Set him on fire and poor Hitch danced like pain itself."

He worked his mouth for some time, then began again. "There's been trouble with the Injuns roun' here: scalpings, horse theft. Escalating trouble. Folks, homesteaders, get tired of working ever' hour of ever' day to see it go up in smoke 'cause some Injuns want to get somethin' for free. The army half the time don't do nothin' about it. So we set up a committee of sorts, biblical, you might say. Eye for an eye.

"Ole Severin, upriver there twenty mile, he loses twenty good head of horses, and the Mexican man who works his livery gets his head smashed in. We head out for justice. Sure 'nuff, there's the horses way out the hell in Washoe. Sioux Indians got 'em. Sons o' bitches are out marauding someplace else, we s'pose, but the squaws are there.

"We take what's ourn, the horses and such, and those squaws are like the goddamn furies. They put a knife in Peterson's leg. Little Injun boy shoots Tender's horse with an arrow.

"Some of the men, they're liquored up, het up, and they start shootin' and gettin' a little wild. These are good men, who maybe aren't doin' the best, on account of hard times. It ain't right, only unnerstan'able.

"Well, during all the screamin' I see this woman. Still as a statue, arms raised up. She's an Injun, so I don' know why, but

I jes' see somethin' . . . right . . . in her. At the same time ol' Bill Packard, he sees somethin' in her too, and he's off his horse and got her down on the ground."

He shook his head slowly. "Had the last words I figure I'll ever have with Bill, and it's a shame 'cause he's been a friend to me. I take the woman. I picked up some of the lingo over time but even without it I could tell she don' wanta go. She's screamin' her babies are dead, to kill her too. An' I tell her I'll take care of her. Not to worry. She's safe."

Harrier opened his mouth like a baby bird. Dawbs dribbled a stream of water into his maw.

"I bring her back here and I do take care of her. Still, she never speaks a word, sometimes keens so long and lasting I regret taking her for the noise. She tries to kill herself time after time, with a knife, a cutting piece of stone, a wire she hones to sharp. She gets to havin' scars up and down her arms. I tie her hands and her feet.

"I feed her, sometimes I gotta force it down 'er. She almost dies, jes for wantin' t'die. But I stick with her, don' let her go. After months, she kinda snaps out of it. Not friendly like, still don't talk, but she eats. She gets hold of a knife and she don't try to cut herself, jes takes off her hair, like they do in mournin'.

"Enough time an' she's purty again. Fine, dark-eyed, skin the color of a new fawn. We come to an unnerstandin', not warm but companionable, know what I mean? I'm thinkin' it was a good thing, what I did.

"Someway, though, they *know,* the Injuns know she's here. And while we're thinkin' we learned 'em a lesson, it don't turn out that way. Hell, mebbe she was hootin' like an owl out back or some such thing, because they come down and they exacted their revenge, by God."

He was crying again. "I watch it all. And when every one of the poor sons o' bitches was dead she finally talked to me. First time. She *knows* English. She tol' me she would never walk with her children again. She would never feel their skin on her fingers. She would never see their faces."

He worked his face; the struggle to continue fought in the muscles of his mouth. "Because of this, they took my *feet*. They took my *hands*. They took my *eyes*, and they left me alive." The man gulped and sobbed. He rubbed what was left of his palms across his scarred face. "I made a mistake. I made a mistake!"

Phaegin looked hopelessly up at me from beside me. What could you say to a man who suffered the knowledge of terrible sin?

"I made a mistake!" he cried again. He took several long breaths. "I was *wrong*. There *warn't* any good in her after all. I shoulda left her to Bill Packard."

Phaegin stopped patting his shoulder. She rose from her knees and stumbled into the grass even as Jim Harrier ranted.

"But that squaw made her own mistake, leavin' me alive, for I will forsake all but retaliation! She and her kind will pay!" He kicked and flailed in his madness. "*She* made a mistake too. *She* made a mistake *too*!"

We put the bodies within the wagon, arranging the timbers and the tumble-down railings that were once the corral around it. By the time we'd finished, Jim Harrier had spent his final breaths on his vow to exact payment, and we posited him in the wheeled casket as well. We took the soddy door and carved the names of the dead on its warped surface and staked it in the grass for any who passed and cared to know. Had it been spring or winter, we would have lit a flame and dispatched the dead respectfully with fire, but under the circumstances, a wildfire was the last thing we needed as traveling companion. We walked away, the dead watching from the windows of the black lacquered stagecoach.

Though it was only a few hours since we'd sojourned across to the swing station, it seemed we'd crossed some far boundary. We rolled the handcart, Pig keeping a fair distance from Phaegin, until the soddy was long past view. Phaegin stopped. "I can't be out here anymore."

She was solemn and spoke firmly, as if by saying it she would be transported away.

I shook my head. "We're putting some distance between it and us."

She waved toward the bones in the cart. "I mean, I'm not doing this anymore. I don't want bones. I don't want bombs. I don't want the dead or the dying, the killed or killers." She nodded like a toy. "It's too much. I want dancing and smoking and drinking and laughing. I want it *now*."

Curly took her hand. "You want to dance?"

Phaegin withdrew her hand. "I don't want to dance. I want *dancing*. I want dancing! Do you hear me? I want *laughing!*"

Curly looked flummoxed. Dawbs, however, crooked his arm and threaded her hand through it. "We'll walk some, and we'll head thataway. It's time to find comfort."

She nodded stiffly. "Yes. There is none here, and while I think I am a strong enough person, I want you to know that . . . this is the end. I must be going now. I can't be here any longer." She gestured in front of her. "There is a line I have not seen before and now I can, and it is close, and I am afraid to cross."

She shook her head and Dawbs squeezed her arm. "There's no reason to cross. We'll be away soon."

Curly and I took over pulling the cart while Dawbs and Phaegin walked ahead, Phaegin explaining herself. "I thought it was bad being poor. But at least the rich are hostile in my own language. I don't know why it's better—maybe it should be worse—but if the worst happens and I'm strung up, at least I can have my say. Even if most don't listen, *someone* might, or at least I'd think so. Here, I can't tell the good from the bad. I can't tell one Indian from another. I don't know their story. I can't remember the names of their families or tribes or who hates who. And *they* won't know that me and Jim Harrier and Bill Packard ain't practically the same thing!"

I thought of our walk through Chicago, and all the poor and sick who spoke in what seemed a hundred languages. Our nation spoke, but who understood?

Phaegin stopped again, breathing close to panic, then turned and walked stiffly to me. Dawbs took over my station, and I swung Phaegin into my arms. She buried her face in my shoulder as I trudged on. She hardly weighed anything, had left all plump good humor behind.

CHAPTER 29

We went with Dawbs to the railroad tracks and waited there until the train came through. Phaegin, Curly, and I lay low while Dawbs flagged down the engine. The men in charge of loading and paying for bones knew Dawbs well. "Big goddamn pile this time, now mebbe you can afford a shave an' a haircut. You look like a goddamn dog with a squirrel in its mouth!"

When the laden train pulled away, Dawbs divided the money, then pulled me aside and took a folded piece of paper from his pocket. Another poster of Curly, Phaegin, and me, this one with the additional drawing of a severe-looking gentleman with a goatee and a well-waxed mustache. Dawbs shook the paper. "Conductor had a mess of these."

I peered at the now-familiar images, then at the severe man. "Who's that?"

"Coy Hayes. Pinkerton and a rattlesnake. Rumor is, he never fails to bring in his man."

"How do you know?"

"You can read about him for a dime if you got it: *Coy Hayes, Defender of Peace.* He wasn't always a big shot." Dawbs thumbed toward the cart. "*I* had a run-in with him in New York years ago. Jailed for nine months: pornographic, indecent, lubricious, *and* salacious conduct."

Dawbs looked out over the grassland. We'd spent a good part of the summer together and he'd already said that the cold nights told him to leave before the real chill set in. He nodded at the southern horizon. "It's time for us to part ways, friend. I'm givin' you the cart and all the supplies save one bedroll and a canteen. You best head north. Right out there." He pointed behind him to some distant hills, then gestured beyond. "You'll meet up with some wagon train, Mormons or California-bound folks, with better to do than follow others' business. Peg on with 'em. Get yourself swallowed up." He nodded toward Phaegin, who still had a dazed look on her face. "Do her good."

"And you?"

He smiled. "The women in this country say, 'I loved him, but then I married him.' In the *islands* they say, 'I don't know if I love him, I haven't slept with him yet.' I'm on my way to where the blood runs warmer, Ned: Mexico, South America maybe. If I'm lucky, I'll light on an island where there's nothing but loincloths, fruit, and bodily love. This is a *mean* goddamn country, and I'm . . . a *gentle* man."

He lifted his hat. "Luck to you." Shook Curly's hand.

He hesitated, then approached Phaegin. "That line you were talkin' about. If you can see it, it's yet a considerable distance."

Phaegin smiled wanly. "I'm gonna miss you, Dawbs. Good luck finding paradise."

Dawbs nodded and walked away whistling. Pig squealed and followed until Curly called him back.

We spent the day nailing planks, pilfered from the train, over Dawbs's carvings on the cart. Curly protested loudly. "The only thin' keeps me goin' is that cart." He pointed to each figure. "Mary, Kerry, Sally, Leodora . . ."

Phaegin showed some sign of life, slapping his finger away. "We'll not be welcomed by decent folks with a wagon fulla smut." Curly scoffed. "Then they ain't so *decent*, is they? This is art." He nodded and confabbed with Pig. "When I'm a cowboy, I'm gonna have art round me at all times."

When the cart was made presentable, I made show of checking the compass. Picked up the cart handles and shouted with great confidence, "Let's head out. This way!"

Though Phaegin had not lost the hunted look, she followed my lead, taking her place behind the now-heavier wagon, pushing as I pulled. Curly called Pig, who trotted sensibly in the shadows we cast.

We headed for the junction of the trail with no disasters but the inexorable diminishing of the supplies Dawbs got us from his friends on the train. After some days we were forced to such short rations that when I spied a small herd of four pronghorn antelope, my mouth actually watered.

Curly pounded me on the back. "Now's yer chance to show us what a sure shot you are, Ned!"

I laughed. "The bullet couldn't make it that far, Curly."

Phaegin sat on the cart. "Can't you sneak up on them?"

"On an antelope? They've got eyes like opera glasses." Curly and Phaegin looked so disappointed, however, not to mention ravenous, I agreed to try.

Antelope, as well as having the best eyesight of any animal I'd ever seen, also suffered from an insatiable curiosity. Young pronghorns would pronk around a rattlesnake, sensing the thing was bad news yet compelled to figure it out. Older antelope retained this inquisitive disposition. I'd heard of Indians getting easy meat as antelope scrutinized windblown tethers on tepees. I hoped the stories were true.

Curly lent me his red kerchief. I tied it to a stick then crept through a shallow gully until I had halved the distance between myself and the herd. I hacked a sagebrush free of the ground. Holding that and the stick in my forward hand, my pistol in the other, I began creeping forward.

The animals raised their heads, the white rump hair bristling in alarm at the approaching brush. I dropped to my belly and waited. I despaired as three of the pronghorns bounced away. The big male, with an impressive pair of black cleft horns, held his ground. After minutes when the male did nothing more than stare, I crawled forward on my belly.

Not only did this maneuver require much more of me athletically than I'd anticipated, it was very painful on my knees and elbows. I desperately wished I'd thought to create makeshift pads instead of scraping over the rocky ground. I stopped and caught my breath, feeling like the sun had just increased twenty degrees in temperature over the last ten minutes.

The antelope was intrigued with my odd movements and took a few hesitant steps closer. I willed my heart to calm, moved forward another yard or two, stopped again, and fluttered the red kerchief.

The antelope extended his neck in seeming amazement. I waited, willing him to come closer. Praying he would, not only because we needed the meat but because I was in misery. My muscles cramped. Sweat ran into my eyes and into the cuts and scrapes I had incurred in my crawl forward, stinging mightily. Biting flies tortured me and, finding me a passive victim, fed to their hearts' content and seemingly called their brothers to sup as well.

I crawled on, the smell of dust and sage filling my nose. I struggled not to sneeze, but lost the battle. I held my nose with my pistol hand and popped my ears with the ferocity of the blow.

The antelope jumped but did not run. Nor did he come closer. I remained statue still for a few agonized minutes, the tension suffocating. When I commenced my wriggle forward, I right off jammed my elbow into a cactus. I moaned.

I figured that was the end of the hunt. However, the sound seemed to further captivate my prey; he took several steps toward me. I wiggled the kerchief and moaned again.

As the antelope circled, I cocked my pistol. At this point I could see his liquid black eyes, intent on the scarf, his ears pricked so far forward it was as if the buck were pointing at what provoked his curiosity. His wonder seemed so human, so endearing, I hated to do it. But I had responsibilities. I pulled the trigger.

For three days we ate well. The day we finished the last scrap of pronghorn steak we arrived at the trail. We kept watch for more game, though I hoped I wouldn't have to make another stalk. I was still plucking spines from my hide. As it turned out there was little reason to worry. We saw no sign of life, but for the far flight of birds and an occasional coyote. I mentioned that the soldiers called them wolf mutton, but Phaegin proclaimed she wasn't that desperate. Yet.

After three days of no wagon train and no game, Phaegin began calling Pig "chitlin." She cajoled, "Here, pork chop." When she recited a recipe for pork roast with rosemary, Curly howled in fury.

Phaegin threw up her hands, "It's only a joke, for crying out loud!"

Curly pointed at her. "You'd eat 'im in a minute if I weren't here."

"Now how could I catch him, Curly?" she groused. "I'd have a better chance of running down another of them antelope."

I tried to distract Curly by calling his attention to the grooves worn in the granite trail. "Huge numbers of brave pilgrims have made their way down this trail. The ruts give testament to the great days of the American West, the wide-open country, the danger, the great civilizing of the wilderness." I clapped him on the back. "And you are a part of it."

Phaegin gave a bitter laugh. "Bravery and civilizing? I hardly think so."

Curly scratched the vault of Pig's back with a stick. "*I* been brave. An' when you see me a cowboy, you'll not scoff."

Pig threw up his head and started squealing. Curly looked surprised. "Doncha like that? Sorry. How 'bout here?" He scratched behind the ears, but still Pig cried.

Phaegin stiffened beside me and pointed a shaking finger. Three Indians approached, riding over the swell that formed the surrounding basin.

Phaegin grabbed my arm. She trembled as she whispered, "We're done for, Ned. You think they're the soddy Indians?"

I shook my head while searching for signs of blood thirst, a demeanor of violence. The men were impassive, their faces arranged in no expression at all. They wore no paint save for vermilion dusted into the parting of their hair, which formed into two braids. One wore several feathers in his braid, another a necklace of blue beads and a scarlet blanket. The one with the feathers had tattered flannel shirting and canvas pantaloons made into leggings.

I squeezed Phaegin's hand. "Just be calm. Curly, don't do *anything.*" I stood, put my hand up in greeting.

The Indians looked us over, then spoke in their language.

I shook my head, smiling. "No parley."

The Indians made motions of eating. One of them was missing two fingers on the left hand.

Phaegin riffled through the food box, finding some moldy pilot bread. I handed it over with a quarter bag of beans.

The Indian looped the bean bag on his mount, sniffed the bread and said "Phaw!," throwing it down, and said, "Whiskey."

I shook my head.

"Sugar."

I again made a mournful gesture.

The Indian tried once more, making a sign with his crooked index finger at his lips to describe a pipe, waving an open hand from his mouth indicating smoke.

I looked at Phaegin. "The cigars. Give them the cigars."

She blanched. "No."

The Indians waited. They each held a rifle, and though I had assured Phaegin it would be all right and these were not the same Indians that had perpetrated the torture at Jim Harrier's soddy, to tell the truth I didn't know any such thing and I was terrified. I smiled and pretended smoking. The Indians nodded. I eyed my bag. I could pull out my pistol rather than the cigars, but if the Indians' rifles were loaded, we'd all be dead in an instant. Even if they weren't, the knives at their waists would do enough damage that I wouldn't risk it if I didn't have to. I hissed at Phaegin, who was clutching at my arm. "I'm getting the cigars."

"They can't *have* my cigars."

I pushed past her and went for her bag; she followed, clutching at my arm. "No, Ned. You can't take them! Please!"

I pushed her off and grabbed one of the boxes of cigars and, while Phaegin yelled, "Goddamn, Ned!" I returned to the Indians. Phaegin went silent. I held up the box. One took it, opened it, murmured in a pleased way, took a cigar, and handed the box to the others. They each took two cigars and laughed, apparently making a joke by play-acting white people, gesturing widely and pompously in the air. One of the Indians said, "Fire."

I pulled a match from my pocket and lit the cigar.

Phaegin moaned. The first Indian leaned from his pony and puffed. He straightened and made a strange face. He puffed again, grimaced, and coughed spasmodically, spitting and hawking. Once the spasm passed, he threw the lit cigar at me. As I brushed the cigar away, he kicked me in the chest, shouting something to his friends, and I went sprawling into the dirt and away from my gun. The others disposed of their cigars and raised their rifles.

The coughing Indian jumped from his horse and grabbed Phaegin, jerking her head back so the whites of her eyes showed, her nostrils flaring in terror. I shouted, "No!"

The Indian pointed his knife at me and shouted back.

Curly, who until now had obeyed me perfectly, shouted, "Pig!"

The pig had wisely retired to the shade under the wagon when the Indians approached. He seemed to know the company would mean no good end for him, for as Curly dove under the wagon and pulled him out, he wriggled and squealed like a banshee. Curly clutched Pig in his arms, an admirable feat as the animal was now the size of Curly's torso and seemingly made of nothing but muscle and sinew.

Curly said, " Mmmmmm! Good!" He pinched the fat hocks and hams. "Yummy." He pantomimed taking a bite of the succulent neck. The Indian watched him, released Phaegin, and held out his hands for the animal. Curly looked at Pig and whispered, "Sorry," kissed his snout, and lifted him up.

Pig twisted and squealed. Curly got an awful agonized look on his face and pulled back as if he'd changed his mind. Curly and the Indian engaged in a short tug-of-war as Pig protested; then the Indian jerked Pig out of Curly's hands. The Indian dropped his knee onto Pig's back and drew his knife across Pig's throat. After a minute of gurgling struggle, the animal went still as stone. The Indian, throwing an irritated look at Curly, slung the carcass over the horse, and the three horsemen departed.

Curly didn't move, but Phaegin rushed to the still smoldering cigar, tamped it out furiously, collected the others from where they had been thrown in the grass, and quick as a snake returned them to her bag. I watched her curious behavior but had to deal with Curly, who had yet to move a muscle.

"Curly?"

He spoke with difficulty. "Yeah, Ned?"

"You OK?"

"Sure."

"Are you sure?"

"Sure."

"That was a hard thing . . ."

Curly stared at the wet dirt where Pig had bled. He shuddered. "I been real hungry, that knothead Pig eatin' like he did." He rubbed his hair then, down his neck, and covered his mouth for a moment, speaking through his fingers. "Tonight, I'm gonna get a whole meal fer once."

Phaegin approached. She didn't say anything but put her arms around Curly. His face in her bosom, she stroked his hair and kissed his forehead.

Curly snuffled. "I'm not feelin' bad 'bout your hair *no more*."

"OK." Phaegin waited a minute. "I take it back about you not being brave, Curly."

"Wait till you see when I'm a cowboy."

She kissed him again. "You'll be the best there is."

Later that evening, I insisted that Phaegin show me the cigars.

She frowned. "You've seen 'em before."

"I want to see them again."

She took out a handful. I examined the smokes carefully. Nothing untoward about them. "Let's see the burnt one."

"I think I threw it away."

I went to her bag and searched through it until I found the burnt cigar.

I examined the blackened end, pinched it. Nothing but cigar.

Phaegin crossed her arms. "Happy now?"

I frowned at her and the cigars. "Happy that you would risk our lives for a box of cigars? I don't think so, and I don't believe it." I looked at the ash end again. I scraped the black away, peeled the wrap back: a glimpse of green and a white powdery substance. I rubbed the white powder between my fingers and sniffed it; it smelled medicinal, chemical. I peeled some more and saw that the cigars were fashioned not from tobacco but from coiled ten-dollar bills dusted with what I thought must be some kind of insecticide. I felt sick. Betrayed. "You lied to me."

"I did *not.*"

"You did, and you promised you never would."

"I did not lie."

"You said you didn't steal from Mr. Cordassa."

"I didn't."

I didn't want to think of what it meant if she hadn't stolen the money. How had she gotten so many ten-dollar bills? What was it in payment for? I thought of her, dancing at the nickel dump night after night, and felt furious. I held out the cigar. "Are they all like this?"

"I didn't steal the money. I earned it."

"Earned it doing what?"

She slapped me. I grabbed her wrist. She tried to hit me with her other hand, and I grabbed her arm and held it behind her. Her nose was inches from mine. Her breath was warm as she panted, "Damn you, Ned Bayard, I hate you more than I can say. I wish I had never met you."

I could feel her chest rise against me, her hips against mine. If I were to close my eyes I could imagine we were back in New Haven, dancing.

I closed my eyes.

I pressed my lips against hers. She was slightly salty, soft, and sweet. I wanted to forget everything else about my life and live in Phaegin's embrace forever. I relinquished her arm, clasped her neck. She threw her arms around me and kissed me back. I held her tight, as I had in New Haven, and wished the moment never end.

But one cannot live in a moment. I could not stop myself from wondering: Where *had* the money come from? If it was hers, why was it hidden in the cigars? And had she been involved in something I didn't want to know about? I stepped back with a groan. "Where did the money come from, Phaegin?"

"You son of a bitch." She turned away. I waited. She finally spoke. "I earned it rolling cigars, Ned. For every twenty I earned, I put ten away. I didn't want my brothers or my da to drink it up, so Mr. Cordassa told me what to do. Each cigar: thirty dollars. Six years of savings, Ned. A dozen cigars is everything I got. Are you happy?"

I imagined the kind Mr. Cordassa showing her how to hide her money; surely he'd done the same to flee his own country. Of course, it all made sense.

"I'm sorry." I was more than sorry, I was ashamed to have thought she'd prostituted herself. I was glad I had not actually voiced my suspicions, hoped she might let what I had intimated pass. I put out my hand but Phaegin pushed it away, dashing my hopes on that course.

"It's better to know what you think of me. Remember, Ned. I never lied to you. I kept my promise."

"Why didn't you tell me everything right off?"

"Why men think it's a woman's job to report to them, I don't know. Do I ask you what's in your bag? Do I demand to know what *you're* worth, what good or bad things you may have done?

340

If I had earned that money in a way you didn't approve of, would you have taken it from me? You probably will anyway."

"I'm *not* taking your money. I was just . . . curious."

"Curious is a funny word for it."

I glared at her. "Don't get too high and mighty. You put our *lives* on the line for that money. More than once."

"No. Not purposefully, anyway."

"Just now?"

"They thought you were *poisoning* them, Ned. *That's* what almost got us killed."

"Chicago."

"I didn't think it was going to go that way."

"Just retrieving it in New Haven was a terrible risk."

"We had to have some stock." She glared at me. "I'm done explaining myself. Soon as we can go our own ways, we will. I'll find respectable work and start over, and you can go to hell as far as I'm concerned. In the meantime, keep your distance. A wagon train's bound to come through. I'm just hoping it isn't Mormons." She smiled at me, meanly. "But if it is, even cannibals and pluralists are better than a false friend."

We waited a day more at Emigration Road in virtual silence, Curly looking wan and sad and Phaegin perpetually furious, which, though not pleasant, was preferable to her shattered expression of before. Two days passed. We finished off the rejected bread then ate flour mixed with water and sage leaves thickened to glop over the fire. I used another of our precious bullets and shot a rabbit that proved more fur than meat. We shared the meager meal one day and the broth we boiled the bones in on the next. Starvation threatened. We had little energy for anything but dark thoughts.

When the sun was going down late the next afternoon, Curly showed sudden energy, leaping up and jiggering his hands like a fast-draw artist. I watched him languidly. "What's going on?"

He shook his head, still staring across the grass. After another minute, he shouted, "Heyho, there!" and did a little jig. "We's a gonna eat, gonna eat!"

I roused myself. A filmy line of dust on the horizon lifted like a mare's tail into the pale blue sky; giving rise to that earthen smoke, a fantastical procession of white elephants. One could discern their lumbering gait, their mammoth size, could imagine trunks clutching tails, could almost believe we'd transported to the savannahs of Africa.

Phaegin took my arm, then remembered our fight, releasing me to watch, alone, the wide backs of the tremendous beasts transmogrify into canvas straining over the keel and ribs of willow rods bent across the beds of wagons, the lumbering gait into nothing more than the pitching of the road.

Underneath each wagon bed, a bucket swung and rang against the grasses, so that a thin song emanated from the line, along with the deep shout of the rippers snapping their whips, the bellowing of oxen, and the creaking of the wooden ships. Tailing the wagons were six or seven handcarts pushed by human beasts in what must have been a stifling flume of dust. Men on horses patrolled up and down the lines.

Curly shaded his eyes, watching their approach, then broke into laughter. "*Somebody* cain't ride worth beans! Over there! A horse jes' walkin' along, saddle upside down under him."

I was too busy counting the carts—and sizing up the men on the horses who seemed to be in charge—to pay attention.

Phaegin said, "That *is* odd. A big ol' horse with a saddle between his legs and nobody doing a thing about it."

I quit sizing up the men in the lead of the train and sighted where Phaegin was pointing. A huge horse, grazing, the saddle slipped underneath, girth over its back, stirrups flipped to the side like wilted leaves. I laughed, then stopped agog when the animal raised its head. "It's Chin!"

CHAPTER 30

Though it had been only a year since Chin and I had parted, it seemed a hundred lifetimes ago. Any question of whether or not she would recognize me disappeared as soon as she heard me shout her name. She raced across the prairie, raising dust and divots of hard-packed earth, and stopped short in front of me, Curly and Phaegin diving for cover behind the cart.

She whickered into my ear; I threw my arms around her enormous neck as if I embraced redemption itself. "Chin, Chin! How are you doing, girl? Aw, it's good to see you, it's good to see you!"

Curly crept out, awe on his face. "You got a *horse*, Ned? By gor, it's a *big* un!"

"Phaegin! It's Chin!"

She stepped forward. "The horse from the fort?"

I nodded and Phaegin offered her hand, stroked Chin's nose.

Curly whooped, climbed onto the cart, and tried to mount Chin from that platform.

Chin neighed loudly and kicked, with Curly holding tight to her mane. The saddle shifted, the stirrups hit her in the backside, and Chin began bucking. Phaegin screamed; Curly finally let go and curled into a ball in the dirt.

"Chin!" I yelled. Chin calmed, whickered again, and nosed me in the back, as if nothing had happened.

Curly looked up, mournful. "Why won' she let me ride 'er?"

I shrugged. "She's got opinions."

Phaegin helped Curly up. "You call yourself a cowboy? Hollerin' like a catamount and throwin' yourself at her? No wonder. You gotta get to know her."

By then one of the horsemen from the wagon train had arrived. He was a heavy-bodied blondin, with yellow hair and yellow beard, white eyelashes, and a veil of freckles under a peeling sunburn. He was dressed in buckskin, a large dragoon pistol on the right side of his wide leather belt, an ivory-handled Bowie on the other.

I took off my hat, shook the man's hand, and said, "Howdy. I'm Cal Morton, my wife Alice, and our son, Ben."

The horseman nodded. "You folks are taking a chance, out here alone. You know about the Indians?"

Curly was still circling Chin but called out, "Do we? You bet."

I nodded. "Swing station to the south, every man and woman dead. We are not a little nervous: hoping to join up with some good people for safety." I rolled the brim of Tilfert's hat. "Would you be agreeable to our joining on with you folks for a while?"

The man on horseback took his time looking us over. I glanced at Phaegin and Curly. Phaegin stared demurely at her feet.

The man gestured to the horse. "Your horse?"

I nodded slowly. "Left her to board in Nebraska a year past. Don't know how she got here."

"We found her ganted up alongside the train line in St. Joseph. Fed her, tried to put her to use. Got a saddle on her two weeks ago." He narrowed his eyes at Chin. "Get it off, or we'll shoot her to save it."

I nodded. The man waited, apparently meaning to get it off *now*.

I murmured to Chin, "Take it easy, girl. Just hold on."

Chin stood stalwart as a soldier as I unbuckled the straps. The saddle fell to the dirt; she stepped delicately over it. I hefted it to the horseman, who held it to one side, turning his horse to leave.

I felt the edge of panic. "*Could* we join you, sir?"

He stopped his horse, seemingly thinking about it. "I am Captain Lowe of the Latter-Day Saints. We welcome any and all, providing you are willing to abide by our beliefs."

Curly grinned. "We'd be willing to—"

Phaegin shot him a look, and I filled in. "We'd be willing to abide with you good people most happily."

Far from my expectations, and excepting the six handcarts at the back of the procession, the Mormons were well fed and well appointed. They drove Conestoga wagons or green and red Concord coaches pulled by spans of stout oxen and mules. Though the wagons were weatherbeaten, they boasted leather cushions on the drivers' seats and white awnings of twilled cotton or Osnaburg canvas. Drivers wore huge green goggles to protect their eyes from the sun, and the women walking sedately beside their wagons to conserve their animals had donned sunbonnets, a long veil flagging behind like a cape or shawl.

As the procession passed, riders and hoofers alike stared as if we were the progeny of Satan. Where Curly seemed to be not at all aware, poor Phaegin was blushing through the dirt and deep freckling of her face.

After the Conestogas and Concords passed, the handcarts brought up the rear, and they *were* a sorry lot. The thought that they, in fact, were likely better kempt than we was shocking. These travelers had willowed cheeks, filthy hair, their apparel ripped, patched, raveled, and scuffed.

We took the last place in line, and the fellow ahead of us grinned, his teeth white as a minstrel in his silt-crusted face. "Nothin' makes a body happier than no longer bein' the last in line. Almost like movin' up in the world. Almost. Wish't I didn't know better, but do." He dropped the handles of his cart, ran over quick-like, and hurriedly shook each of our hands. "Will Smith, Will Smith, Will Smith," he murmured, and returned to his cart, catching up to the one in front with a quick step. "If you don't look like something the cat dragged in, I don't know what does," he called back to us. "Don't worry. We'll be stopping in another hour or so. We take care of each other here. You'll be fed."

Sure enough, the captain called a halt after a few jarring miles, and with military precision the wagons relaxed into a chattering, bustling campground. Severity seemed to drop with the stilling of the wheels. A few men dropped back to make our acquaintance, and women came back to say hello to Phaegin and deliver a morsel of bacon, a cup of meal, a strip of dried beef. By the time we'd got the pot to boil, we had enough to make three stews.

Will Smith sidled over. "Hold some back," he cautioned. "Feast and famine, y'know. Wimmin get tight in a heartbeat."

Phaegin glared at him. She whispered to me, "I don't *like* that man. Even if this is the last we get, that don't mean they're tight. Generosity is generosity. Those women are lovely."

I shrugged, glad that Phaegin was at all happy. I was a little on tenterhooks myself, waiting for some kind of instruction, some ritual of union that we would be expected to go through. I'd heard plenty about the Mormons: practicing cannibals and plural marriages. Would I be expected to marry not one but three of these women? I entertained myself by picking out three I would not be averse to. Would we also be forced to take oaths, let blood, commit some trial? It seemed not. The night passed uneventfully. We woke at dawn to finish off last night's dinner, pulled back into line, and the journey toward the Great Salt Lake commenced once more.

Predictably, Chin would not make herself useful but followed along like a dog and I was happy with that. She was a marker to me that my life was not altogether blowing up and being remade but that some small part could indeed survive one phase to surface in another. Further, I appreciated the horse's obvious pleasure to see me. She seldom strayed from my side, blowing air down my neck and whickering companionably in a show of affection toward a man starved for tenderness. Phaegin, though we identified ourselves as man and wife, hardly spoke to me at all.

Will took it on himself to educate us as to what was acceptable and what was not, hanging back and allowing some space to fall between him and the cart ahead. "Don't worry, you won't be the final feather for too long, not if you behave. Some other poor sod will be demoted. Likely it'll be me." He nodded. "I'll warn you: Don't swear, don't gamble, don't even think about tobacco."

I eyed Phaegin meaningfully and she looked away.

"Don't drink ardent spirits, except for medicinal purposes. Even that is frowned on " He nodded up the line. "Dose yerself to the point of hilarity, no matter what the reason, and there's trouble." He gave a glance to my journal, bouncing in the bed of the cart. "Men, not books. Deeds, not words."

I raised my eyebrows.

"One of the few rules I have no trouble with, my interlect bein' uncorrupted by larnin'."

"What *do* you have trouble with, Will?" Phaegin snapped. "Why *are* you back here?"

Will looked pitiful. "I am a poor man and tempted by all manner of sin, but pained particularly by a certain proclivity for the Lord's most fine handiwork without the means to support it."

Curly nodded. "Wimmin."

Will threw his head back. "Oh, the temptations of the flesh! Lord, save me from myself, and if you can't deliver me from desire, make me rich enough to support a hundred wives!"

Curly was desperate to make good with Chin and spent every moment with her, stroking her back, scratching her ears. At night he slept fearlessly at her feet.

Phaegin and I, in our ruse as husband and wife, slept back to back in the blankets. The invisible yet steely barrier between us softened only in her sleeping hours.

That and not the chill was true torture. With the sighing regularity of sleeping breath, she nudged her backside against mine or spooned into my embrace, and me with no choice but to thrill and suffer, respond with no response, hope and despair. I prayed the nightly intimacies reflected her deep though unfathomed feeling for me. If so, in the daylit hours, I was unable to mine even a dusting of admiration from that abyss in which she apparently kept her regard. I woke each morning to find Phaegin cold and unrelenting, and the distance between us widened every day.

She made friends without me, abandoning me in order to hen with the other women of the company while Curly dogged Chin.

I pulled the cart alone and without much conversation, but for Will. The other men of the train seemed not only wary of me but absolutely condescending. We sat at a lonely dinner one night and Will told me not to take it "personal."

"Until you's one of 'em, they won' trust."

"But Phaegin—"

"They kin see she's none too happy with you," he observed bluntly. "They're figurin' she might well be a sister one o' these days." He thought it over for a minute. "Don' do you any good neither, talkin' wif me. Collapsed so many times, I hardly have knees left. Makes you suspicious-like, hangin' 'round with the low end of the stick."

"But you're Mormon."

"Barely." He sighed. "I owe 'em. Thirty year ago I was low down. Dad a damn drunk, Marm dead, wagon broke down, and me with the diaree. Shoulda died but they took me into Nauvoo. Never did make enough of m'self to be decent, but I was baptized and did my mission. Came this close to a marriage before I fell. Been risin' and fallin' like sourdough ever since." He stirred the fire and leaned in. "Don't recommend it to ever'one. There's some who will profit and those who will pay."

"What do you mean?"

"What *do* you mean, Will?" Hiram Ansel stood over us, Phaegin on his arm.

Will spoke amiably. "That there's some who may hear the voice of the Lord, and they will be rewarded. Others are false, and to them will be borne a mighty and uncomfortable debt."

Hiram nodded to me. "Escorting your wife home." He gave her a small bow. "My wife welcomes your company." He looked around. "Where is your son?"

I pointed into the moonlit prairie. "Wooing my horse."

Phaegin smiled tightly. "Husband, call him in and say goodbye to your *friend*. It is time for sleep."

Back-to-back that evening, the steely four inches again between us, I whispered over her silence, "Will told me something you need to know."

"What?"

"A fellow just a month ago was found shot. He was a new-comer and they didn't like him."

"That's foolishness. He and his partner were newcomers. And his partner killed him and ran off."

"That's what they say, I suppose. Are you going to believe them? Will says he was sniffing around some other man's wife."

"More like Will was sniffing around some other man's wife. He's crazy, Ned. They've put up with his craziness since he was a child."

"I don't think he's the nut."

"Think what you want."

"I think Mr. Ansel has designs on you, that's what I think. *My wife welcomes your company?*"

"Yes, Mr. Ansel's wife and I like each other very well. She is a wonderful woman."

"Which wife?"

"The *only* wife."

"Come off it, he's got four more in Salt Lake."

"Who told you that, the trustworthy Will?" She snorted. "You better put air between you and him."

"Why, they going to hang me for bein' friendly?"

"Not if you'd be friendly to the right people."

351

"Like Hiram Ansel?"

"Like anyone *worth* being friendly to."

"I *like* Will."

Phaegin flipped over and jabbed me in the chest. "Yeah, an' you like Curly and Avelina, Professor Coal, and that Little Miss trouble, Lill Martine, too. Ned, cain't you like anybody who won't get you in trouble, who's worth more'n a plugged *nickel*?"

"I liked *you*, Phaegin."

I regretted the tense as soon as I'd said it. But I said nothing as she rolled away from me again.

As if to prove her right, Curly lodged himself neck deep in upset the following evening. I was under a juniper tree taking forty winks before supper. Phaegin was cooking with Mrs. Ansel.

The captain rang the bell to assemble the company, an unusual occurrence at that hour. When I arrived at the gathering point, the wagon train's command was grouped around our cart. The side piece was pried off, and Dawbs's women cavorted uninhibitedly along the plank. Brother Helms gripped a struggling Curly by the arm. As I approached, the captain intoned, "You have agreed to abide by our beliefs. Section thirty-eight: *If any person import, print, publish, sell, or distribute any obscene prints, pictures, or descriptions manifestly tending to corrupt the morals of youth, he shall be punished by fine not exceeding four hundred dollars.*"

"Four hundred dollars?" I was not really so worried. Unless Phaegin came clean about the cigars, they might as well squeeze water from a stone. Still, I could see they were fully stirred by the wagon and I stepped forward. "We came by this cart already in this condition and did our best to hide the obscenities on it."

The captain spoke flatly. "He removed the planking."

Curly looked miserable.

I shrugged. "Boys . . . will be curious. I'll . . . punish him."

The captain gave a small smile. "If it had been a small matter of prurient interest by an unschooled child, then a father's punishment would be enough. However—"

I glanced again at Curly, then at Phaegin, who, across the way, standing at Sister Ansel's side, looked terrified.

The captain continued. "We can not allow the commerce of pornography to be so lightly admonished."

Curly had not, as he had told me, been soliciting Chin's regard for the past week. Instead he'd busied himself spiriting Mormon boys who were game (and, judging by the jangle in his pocket, there were plenty) to the cart for a nickel's peek at Dawbs's handiwork.

"What's going to happen to him?"

Captain Lowe motioned to Brother Helms, and Curly was led away. "He will be kept watch over until we decide on punishment. The cart will be burned."

This was a blow. As heavy as the cart was, it was easier to push than to carry our bags and supplies. It meant the loss of the possessions we couldn't carry, like the water barrel, the tool kit, and Dawbs's straw-tick pad that I'd grown awfully fond of over hard ground. It meant the loss of some little protection from rain or even attack. It meant we were without any value whatsoever. Still, the fear of losing the wagon was nothing compared to my mounting fear for Curly. I couldn't help but think of the man Will had told me about. If he'd been killed for a roving eye, what would they do to Curly for tempting others? Phaegin told me the story was erroneous; could I chance it?

"May I have a word with my son?"

Captain Lowe didn't deign to spare me a glance. "No."

After Curly had been led away, Phaegin found me. "*What* did I tell you?" She pulled at her hair. "Why couldn't you have watched him?"

"Me? *You're* the boy's mother."

Phaegin shoved me. "This isn't *funny*. Curly's big trouble means we're in trouble *with* him. As far out into the middle of nowhere as we were a week ago, we're worse off now. If they decide to dump us—"

"Dump us? We won't give them that chance."

Phaegin nodded.

"We're leaving tonight."

Phaegin sat down. "*What*? No! Curly's got to apologize. He's got to make amends, take what's coming to him. You've got to take the oath, show you're serious."

"Take the oath? Are you kidding?"

"I'm not asking you to rip your heart out. Don't you believe in God?"

"A boatload of misery ago."

"Damn it, Ned, don't do this to me. I don't want to be . . . out there. I told you, I can't."

"We can't *stay*. Even if we manage to squeak through this, you know it won't be long until Curly does something else."

She was silent for too long. Then she drew her hands over her mouth. "Go. You and Curly, go. We were going to part ways anyhow. This is the time."

"Go? Without you? What are you going to tell them? We're married!"

"We weren't married in the church so we're not married in *their* eyes, Ned."

"Oh, that's handy. You're up for grabs!"

"Yes, I am! What else is new?"

I paced before her.

She put out her hand and stopped me. "You've done enough, Ned. Four months ago, I was happy, heading for easy street. Now look at me. Are you going to ruin my chances at finding any sort of comfort at all?"

"What comfort?"

"In Salt Lake City, there is no crime. It is clean and pretty, and every man, woman, and baby has plenty to eat. Each brother helps his brother, each sister helps her sister."

"They're fanatics, Phaegin!"

"They are fanatics who don't drink, swear, or carouse. I wish to hell my da had been Mormon."

"Are you going to be happy being the fifth wife, happy when five more come after?"

"Yes. I'll have a tenth of a husband, ten entire sisters!"

I groaned. "Ah, Phaegin, no. No. Please." I paced again. "What about me?"

"What about Lill Martine? I shouldn't of, but I read that letter."

I said nothing and she turned away. "You are the *almost* in my life, Ned. I can't bear feeling you brush by again and again. It will kill me."

She dug through her bag and handed me a cigar. "Good luck."

"I don't want your money."

She let the cigar fall back into her bag. "Don't tell me when you're leaving. Just go."

* * *

I waited for the moon to rise. Curly was sitting outside the captain's wagon, tethered by a thin cord. I whistled. When he looked up, I inclined my head, indicating away. All he had to do was untie the knot. The cart waited for us just over the hill, Chin grazing on a small pile of oats. No attempt to stop us. They'd known exactly what we would do and wanted us to do it.

Yet how could I leave Phaegin? How could I not?

Curly was pleased as all get out with the adventure, the brilliant escape. "Where's Phaegin meeting us?"

I shushed him.

He kept looking behind and asked again, after another half mile, "Where's Phaegin? She's gonna get lost."

I turned on him. "We're on our own. She's staying with *them.*"

Curly turned back, shouting, "She ain't, she b'longs with us!" But after a few steps he looked around perplexed. "Which way is it?"

"This way, Curly."

We walked a couple of miles, then Curly shouted, "I want Phaegin!"

"*Shut up,* Curly!" I was on the verge of tears. "We've done enough to Phaegin, don't you think? Maybe she can be happy now." I didn't see how, though, nor could I see my own way to happiness. Phaegin had disappeared like everyone else I'd loved, and I was feeling her absence like an endless winter.

I released the cart with a shudder in order to take a look at the little compass I'd stolen in Chicago. Chin was leading the way and it seemed she was taking us back toward our stamping grounds around Fort McPherson. She turned and whickered. I shrugged and began pulling the cart again. Why not? There was as much emptiness to disappear into there as anywhere. Besides, if I was ever to find a place of respite, it would hold no solace for me until I'd learned what had happened to Lill Martine.

CHAPTER 31

Like a gigantic horsefly, Curly lit on Chin's back time and time again, only to be shrugged off, tossed off, kicked off. She gave him a grapefruit-sized bite on his skinny arm, kicked him full in the chest, and swung her heavy tail in his face with such power he had welts across his cheek. Curly picked himself up from the dirt, shouting invective after her for miles, even while wiping tears of disappointment and frustration from his filthy face. Still, he did not give up. Chin's demeanor slipped from balky to out-and-out difficult, and any hope I'd had that she would eventually be of use in pulling the cart evaporated, leaving me resentful to furious, depending on how difficult the going was. With effort, I had been able to pull the cart over the tracks left by the wagons, but now in the grass and stone-hummocked prairie it was close to impossible.

We had managed without a trail before because Phaegin had stood behind me, pushing the cart from behind, every step of the way. I had not realized how much aid she'd provided. With every step, I knew now. And I could do nothing but think of her. Think of what was missing in this leg of our journey. I missed not only her help but her conversation. I missed looking back and seeing her. I missed being able to confer with her; I missed having a reason to go on. It seemed our journey was nothing now but wandering and worrying. Wandering aimlessly and worrying Chin. I told myself we were not aimless; I had a plan. Though it felt to me now less the golden opportunity I had once envisioned than a plain gray responsibility too long on my brow.

We were less than a day now from Fort McPherson. Obviously we would have to steer well clear of the fort, but it meant we were also close to Osterlund's place. I would finally ascertain what I had done to Lill and what I needed to do as recompense. It could be dangerous. Osterlund was a strapping brute. If he was sore enough—and of course he would be—he could take me. I, however, had the pistol and four remaining shells.

I would wait until dark, waylay Osterlund in his sleep, hold the gun to his head, and make him tell me where Lill was. I only hoped he had some inkling. Then I'd hightail it out of there, casting our trajectory from whatever information I'd extracted.

Chin neighed, Curly screamed. He was lying on the ground kicking his legs and flailing his arms, a child in full throes of a tantrum. Chin, for her part, stood looking at him with a satisfied long-toothed smile.

"What now?"

Curly stood up and held his arms out wide. "She shit on me, *shit* on me, *shit on me!*"

"Help me with the cart, goddamn it!" I snapped.

"I need a bath!"

"You've needed a bath since before we left Connecticut. Chin's shit likely makes you smell *better!*"

"You sure are bad-tempered since Phaegin left."

"Since I've had to pull this thing on my own." I put the handles down. "I mean it, Curly, I can't keep on. Get thee behind me, Satan, and put your back into it."

Curly made a face and positioned himself against the cart, but it seemed I was dragging him rather than getting any aid whatsoever. I groaned. "Gobawful, ain't it?" Curly chirruped from behind.

I agreed but said nothing. The country had begun to look familiar. The sun was high. This would be an evening of reckoning.

Late afternoon I left Curly napping under the cart, parked in a copse of cottonwoods. "Don't go anywhere, don't do anything, just sleep, *please*," I begged him.

He stretched in his shady nook. "Fine by me. What are you doing?"

"Getting the lay of the land. Maybe I'll find something to eat."

"You'll bring some back? You *are* comin' back, aren'tcha?"

"Curly. If I didn't leave you before, why would I now?"

"Woren down. Like my ma. Dint wanta, but she was jus' woren down."

I nodded. "I got some ways to go yet, Curly."

He smiled, curled into a ball, and closed his eyes.

In the year I'd been gone, it seemed a road a month had been built across the previously barren prairie. I traversed one rutted avenue after another and in an hour came to the Osterlund homestead. It had not suffered any. A bramble rose coiled up the porch railing and along the eave. The yard was dirt but clean, and a verdant kitchen garden graced the side yard. Had Osterlund found another woman to manage his needs? I hunkered down behind a bush to wait until nightfall. If Osterlund had another woman, my plan was in jeopardy. Though I felt no qualms at holding Ry hostage, I hadn't the heart to terrify an innocent woman.

From the house came the shriek of a child. A child as well? Another complication. Perhaps I should just go. If Osterlund had a new wife, a different family, why would he keep track of Lill? I might well know more about her whereabouts than he did.

I took notice of a chicken coop with hens pecking amiably about. Perhaps I would relieve Osterlund of a chicken dinner as soon as it was dusk. I settled down for a wait. Maybe two hens, one to eat, one to save. My stomach growled. Perhaps a quick foray into the garden. I stared into the green rectangle. The corn was finished, but bright orbs of tomatoes glistened on waist-high bushes. Squash leaves, twice as big as Chin's hooves, would certainly be hiding pumpkins and zucchini.

Another shriek. The screen door banged open and a child tipped out onto the porch then crawled furiously to the step, backed down, and toddled across the swept dirt of the yard.

"Lucy!" A familiar voice. A woman swept through the door herself, laughing. "You escape artist!"

I gawped. It was Lill Martine.

Dressed in drab brown, her hair caught in a braid down her back, she lifted the child into the air, her belly a swollen sphere, then nose-to-nose scolded the baby. "What am I to do with this little rabbit!" She looked not just well but happy.

Osterlund materialized at the door, leaned languidly against the jamb, and regarded the pair with pleasure.

I wish I could say it wasn't so, but my first reaction was anger. My face heating, my hands shaking, I had too long thought of Osterlund as the enemy. But then Lill grimaced, and Osterlund strode from the porch and took the baby from her, putting a hand on her arm as Lill waved him off, one hand on her back. "It's nothing."

He led her back to the porch, pulled a chair from the shadows, and helped her sit, before turning the little girl upside down to make her laugh.

What does one do, realizing his shining armor is pure imagination? I was as naked as the emperor, and my future, my reason, my past as spectral as any flight of fancy. Can one blame the catalyst of desire for the fan of action that follows?

I couldn't. As I watched the little family on the cozy porch, my heat slowly dissipated into the cool evening and was replaced by longing. Not for Lill, but for what it seemed she had. The three spent a quiet hour in small talk and baby games as the sun played its colorful set. I watched, a hungry man witnessing the feast, until they went inside at dark, Ry holding the door for Lill, the child half asleep now in his arms.

I turned away, desperate to escape the abandoned yard, leave them to their chickens, their tomatoes, their happiness. She had done well without me. I hoped the same for my mother. And, though it pained horribly, I knew deep down I wished the same for Phaegin.

Curly was bitterly disappointed when I returned with nothing edible. He scowled. "No fault a yers you cain't forrige, I s'pose." He shook his head. "*I* shoulda gone. *I* woulda brought somethin' back, that's fer sure. Wouldna been eatin' porridge fer supper. If I never see another pot of cornmeal it'll be too soon; never eat another bean, OK with me. I want some meat, some potato, and *brown gravy.*"

I didn't have the energy to deal with him. "Fine. Next time you go. I'm sure we'll be eating like kings."

Halfway through the next morning we heard lowing and bawling, so we pulled the cart to the slow rise of a hill and looked over. A couple hundred red and black cattle skirted a line of cottonwoods that themselves skirted a dry creek. Half a dozen men rode along, drifting up and down and keeping the herd in a shifting bunch. Farther downcountry beyond the herd was the remuda and, in a little flat on the creek bottom, the roundup wagon and camp of the outfit.

Curly hunkered down with a hungry look on his face and watched, imagining himself one of them and accompanying the silent actions of the cowboys with dime-novel dialogue. "You's the cow boss? I'm looking to fill in on yer spread. I broke ever' horse thrown me, but fer two that broke their necks while I was in the middle of 'em. Won' give me a post? I'll show you punkin' rollers what fer. Take a look at the busy end of my gun, gonna comb yer hair with my forty-five, knock yer jaw so far back you'll scratch the back o' yer neck with yer front teeth. I ain't never *drunk* milk, much less pumped a cow. Seein' things different, are ye? Sure. Gimme that cayuse right there, make a shine cow pony, bunch them dogies." He sighed and glanced at me. "Look at 'em. *That's* the life."

"It's work, Curly. Give it a week for the glow to wear off, and you'd be complaining about that too." I inclined my head, indicating *Go*.

"Wouldn't complain." He looked at me pleadingly. "Let's join up with 'em."

I shook my head. I didn't want to tell him real cowboys would be as likely to want Curly along on their trail as they would desire a hippopotamus to nursemaid. "They're going the wrong way, Curly, likely heading for Leavenworth. Besides, it's too risky. They might figure out who we are."

"You stopped with the dirty Mormons!"

"That didn't turn out so well, did it?"

I felt kind of bad, the desire on his face so raw I relented and let him watch for another half hour as the cattle headed northeast and out of our way. When the cattle and the men were distant enough, I prodded him. "Let's go."

"Don't want to."

"Curly." I trudged forward with the cart. When I was some distance away and beginning to worry he might just trade me in for the wranglers, creating yet another fiasco, he caught up. Though I was relieved not to have to fight to make him come with me, my relief was short-lived. The cowboy bug had given Curly a new head of steam in trying to ride Chin.

Chin wasn't about to let Curly near. I tried not to resent the energy the two consumed as they zigzagged, trading off to pursue or elude, trotting in front and behind the cart I strained against. I gritted my teeth and told myself that at least it was keeping Curly moving at a decent clip.

He hollered, "Here, Chin, come on now, gimme a little ride, you'll like it, you know you will." He whined. He yelled invectives. He wheedled.

Finally Curly picked up a dirt clod and threw it at Chin. "Stump-sucking, shad-bellied, pot-gutted, hog-backed piece of crow bait! You're no horse. Pig was a better horse'n you! You're a pile of pig *crap!*" Curly picked up a juniper stem and with a whistling thwack laid a stripe across her haunch. Chin neighed and bucked. I grabbed Curly's arm and shook him. "She doesn't want to be ridden, she doesn't like you, and, believe me, beating her isn't going to make her warm up!"

Curly shook free and glared at me. "Leave it to you to have a no-good horse."

I laughed. "Leave it to me to have a no-good Curly!"

"Fuck you, Ned. I don' blame Phaegin for not comin' with us. You cain't be nice to anybody."

The comment on Phaegin smarted and I gave up to my temper, rounding on Curly. "I was nice enough to you to get myself on a wanted poster, you damned hoodlum."

"I ain't no damned hoodlum!" He balled his fists and advanced on me.

"You're worse than a hoodlum. You're a petty thief and about as far from a cowboy as a snot-nosed tiddler can get." I balled my own fists. Chin shook her head at the commotion, blowing and stamping.

"If you'd get a decent horse I'd be a cowboy for sure, but you cain't get nothin', not a horse, not a girl, not even anythin' good to eat."

Chin, Curly, and I circled one another.

"You want a horse, Curly, do some work for one. Couldn't even stir yourself to pick up a few bones. For Pete's sake, you can't even manage to put your back into your own escape."

"I done more work in my lifetime than you ever have, and you know it."

I did know it, but I didn't care. "You ruin my life, and you have the gall to complain about me?"

"You *ruint* mine. I shoulda stayed where I was. My mother woulda come to get me by now."

"Your mother couldn't care less."

He dropped his fists. I dropped mine. His lip quivered but his eyes narrowed. "Sure enough my ma *could* care less, Ned. She could care about me like your mam cared 'bout *you*."

The three of us stood our ground, ten feet between each of us and no means to draw closer, so we merely faced the sun and went on, in an unforgiving triangle of grass, for miles of misery.

At day's end we built a fire. It was cold now in the evenings; our blankets did not do the weather justice. Curly and I ate our wormy cornmeal and glared at each other across the flames. The only pleasure in the night, hating each other for our own misfortunes.

I woke in the morning to a skin of hoarfrost on my blanket. The longer hair along Chin's back was white as well. I laughed and went to shake Curly awake to see Chin looking like a skunk, but he was gone. I figured he'd gone to take a pee, but I couldn't see him anywhere. I waited for some time, playing one possibility in my head out and then another. His bedroll was slept in and still here. If he was leaving for good, he would've taken that. Nobody could've abducted him. First of all, who would want to; second of all, I was a light sleeper and I would have heard. Could he have fallen, knocked himself out rolling down an embankment? I circled the camp in wider and wider passes, calling Curly's name, finding nothing. Chin acted peculiarly, trotting off a few paces then back. Not finding him after an hour of searching, I gave in.

"You think you know where he is? Fine. Show me."

I followed Chin at a jog. She took me toward where Curly had lain on his stomach and watched the cowboys. He must have walked half the night to reach the new camp.

"Of course." I hunkered down and watched the men, hoping to catch sight of Curly and get a sense of what was waiting for me. I discerned a strangeness to the cowboys' movements. Some of them drifted along the lines of cattle as before, but a crew of four or five were scouring the grass near where the remuda had been picketed. There was no sign of Curly. I'd have to go down and figure out what was going on. To do that I needed to ride Chin. Men in this country did not treat horses like pets.

I patted the big horse. "Girl. Let's go." Chin bobbed her head and stood patiently while I grabbed her mane, took a leap, and swung my leg over her back.

Riding like the farmer I hoped they'd take me for, I rode down to where the cowboys were traversing a square of grass.

"Hey, there," I called from some distance. If they were going to be unfriendly, I wanted some head start. But they nodded. A slight youth took off a hat and waved it.

When I got within twenty feet I asked, "What are you doing?"

An old cowboy, hunched and puckered like his strings had pulled too tight, spit and snarled, "May as well look for a hair on a frog."

The freckle-faced kid, already bowlegged and squint-eyed though he looked barely sixteen, grinned. "We had a *horse thief* last night. Meaner'n a basket of snakes!"

My pulse picked up. It couldn't be, I told myself. The old cowboy straightened as much as he could, which seemed to make his legs bow wider in recompense, snapped, "Who're you?"

I pointed east. "I homestead out that way. Wheat farmer. Heard your dogies bawlin', thought I'd check it out."

The old man guffawed. "Wheat. You people don't learn nothin'." He went back to kicking the grass, moving slowly forward.

"So. What happened with this horse thief you saw?"

"Saw nothing!" The young one beamed. "We *got* him! He was trying to take one of the cow ponies and they put up a fuss. Fred over there was first on the scene, and there was this little shrimp cussing like a sailor with the foreman's horse in hand. Fred said, 'Reach for the sky, pardner!'"

The cowboy with the full beard spat and shook his head. "Danny, you're so full of shit. Fred didn't say no fool thing like *reach for the sky*. He prob'ly said, *Let go the horse* if he said anything."

Danny shrugged. "So the thief pulls his gun, but he's got a case of slow and Fred fires back and lets sunshine through him like he was a pane of glass!"

I relaxed my jaw enough to try to effect a nonchalant, "Yeah, he hit 'im?" and willed my stomach to keep in place.

"You bet. Nailed him in the arm. But he got fight enough left, we wore him out. Time his horns was clipped. He's so skinned up, looked like the U.S. flag! We tied him up—"

"I ain't never seen a horse thief before." I cut him off. "You mind if I take a look?"

The bearded cowboy looked up. "Fred took him in to Ogallala. We was gonna hang him ourselves, but he was no bigger 'n a badger."

"Mean as one too, cross as a snappin' turtle, crooked as a snake in a cactus patch, could swaller nails and spit out corkscrews. A redhead loco!"

The old cowboy swore and shouted at the young fellow. "Would you put a *plug* in your talk box?"

I turned Chin and headed back toward the handcart. After a couple of steps I called out, "What are you fellas looking for?"

The young cowboy didn't reply, looking hot and embarrassed. The bearded cowboy grunted. "When Fred shot the little bastard, the kid threw his pistol somewheres."

When I got back to camp I looked through my bag. Sure enough, my pistol was gone and all the ammunition. They hadn't known who Curly was in the cattle outfit, but when the law got ahold of him in Ogallala, they'd figure it out in a minute. "God damn stupid, stupid, stupid!" I kicked Curly's bedroll. "What the *hell* am I supposed to do now?"

I sat down. Chin stuck her muzzle on the top of my head, denting my hat. I reached up and stroked her pie-plate cheek. "They shot him, Chin. He's a boy, and they shot him. And now they'll hang him." They'd hang him twice if they could.

"And we can't do anything about it!" I put my head on my knees and let misery wash over me. Misery and guilt, panic, and no little amount of pure pity for myself. After some time Chin pushed at me. I pushed back. She shoved hard enough I was pitched onto my side.

"Fine. I suppose we should go take a look." It wouldn't be any good for me to be caught as well, so I trimmed my beard as neatly as I could with a knife and no mirror, dug my long coat from my bag, then ripped a piece of cloth from Curly's blanket into a collar, hoping that would give me the look of a preacher. Once we commenced on our journey, I was glad of the coat. The weather had suddenly turned cold. Seventy degrees the week before, and now a chill wind blew the temperatures down enough I was wishing for gloves and glad of Chin's warmth underneath me.

Ogallala was not much more than a row of thrown-together pine boards, masquerading as mercantiles, bars, and a boxlike structure that served as jailhouse. I rode sedately in, circled the buildings and tents, and headed back to the jail. As I neared I saw a familiar face I couldn't place. He was leaned against the door, frowning and stroking his goatee and mustache as he talked to the sheriff. The sheriff wore a circular pin on which was stamped a star. I glanced at the other man several times, trying to figure where I had seen him before: the fort, the train? Then it hit me. On the poster Dawbs had shown me. The man leaning against the door was Coy Hayes. The bounty hunter, mean as a snake, who always got his man.

I kept going. When I rounded the corner by the saloon, I stopped, got off Chin, and told her to stay put. I wandered back toward the jail. The two men had left. I walked around the jail, looking for anyone who might be keeping a lookout on the premises. Nothing. I went round back. There was a small barred window up high. I pushed a rain barrel from the corner, stood on it, and looked in.

Curly was sitting on a narrow slat bed, his left arm wrapped in bandages, his head down.

"Curly!"

His head shot up. His face was streaked with dirt, he looked like he had a black eye, and blood crusted from his nose to his chin. Still, he smiled. "Ah, Ned, you came."

"Of course I came, Curly. Are you all right?"

Curly shrugged and lifted his arm. "Lost a little meat's all. Worse 'n that is the pants rats I caught sitting in here."

I laughed, then shook my head. "Curly, what the hell have you done?"

He clouded. "I'm in *big* trouble, Ned. Huge trouble. That fella Dawbs tol' us about says he's gonna hang me. I don't wanna be hanged, Ned. I don' mind bein' shot, but they say dyin' on the rope goes *real* slow. Feels like hours, all the time being strangulated, and yer eyes pop out. I wouldn't mind if they shot me. . . ." He tightened his lips and looked away. "You gotta get outta here, Ned, they're lookin' for you too. Tryin' to help me's like barkin' at a knot. I just gotta tell you one thing, ask you one favor."

"No, you don't. We'll get you out of this, Curly."

He shook his head. "You know that snooker you saw in the coal mine? It warn't me."

I frowned. "It wasn't?"

"Nah, the lady in that office, she just gave you my name to get *me* out of the mine. I was playin' poker in the mule barn when it happened."

"Why would she do that?"

His eyes filled. "She's my mam."

I thought back to that day in the office. The secretary fluttering along the edges, pretty woman, red curly hair pulled back in a bun. So she was the woman who worked for the rich man, who saved Curly cakes from tea when she could. I'd thought it all yarn.

Curly nodded. "She put me in the orphanage when I's born. She weren't married and all, but she always kep' track. She and I were gonna get chickens." He paused. "Would you tell her, Ned, that . . . I don't know. If I say I'm OK she'll wonder why I don' come for her. Tell her I was some kinda hero, tell her I did something good, I can't even think what but you're good with words, come up with somethin'. Tell her I bit it while I was doin' the good thing. That'd be best."

Someone pulled at the back of my jacket. "What's going on here?"

I jumped off the barrel and faced a thin man with an entirely bald head. I put out my hand. "Preacher Owens. I hear this man is on trial for horse thievery."

"Thievery ain't the half of it." The man ran his hand over his slick scalp. "He's an anarchist. Getting the rope tomorrow. Coy Hayes hisself is in town." He rubbed his head again. "Say, you got a dime for a drink?"

I drew myself up. "God does not want you to salve your sins with drink. Go to Him and feel the rapture of the soul."

He waved me off. "Faw! Go t'hell."

Coy Hayes came around the corner. I put up my hand and shouted after the bald man. "Seek Him and He will provide the solace the bottle promises and never truly offers."

Coy Hayes eyed me.

I stuck out my hand and shook his. "Preacher Owens. From outpost to outpost of Satan's constabulary, I preach to the wicked, the lost, and those waiting to be saved. Sixty-eight jailhouses in this year alone."

Coy rubbed his chin. "Get out of here. He needs savin' like a steer needs a saddle blanket."

"All God's creatures—"

"I said get the hell out."

I shrugged and walked away, Coy Hayes's formidable stare burning into my back. Halfway down the street, Coy seemed to think better of my proscription. He yelled, "Hold up there, *preacher!*" And the way he said it made me think there was no good in letting on I heard his call. Though he shouted again, I held myself to a walk for a few more steps, turned the corner, and then I ran. I zigzagged through the alleys of tents and squatters' huts and headed for the livery. Once there, I dove into the hay. Five minutes later three men came in, looked around, and called, "He's not here!"

Another whistled through hard breathing. "Can you believe it, come to town public as a zebra. Still, he made it this far."

"Luck's runnin' muddy now. Let's go. You can rest when we got the reward."

I waited there for a good two hours, sucking in dust motes and straw, more terrified than I'd ever been before. Seeing Curly locked into that miserable box seemed to mark a destination that I was foolish ever to think I could sidestep. There was to be no say, there was to be no law or justice or any kind of truth. We'd been pushed into a river, and though we had swum mightily, we would assuredly drown.

A couple of men came in and left their mounts. I was almost stepped on by a recalcitrant horse. I told myself I would bear any broken bone rather than let on I was beneath the straw. The horse was led away. Somebody else showed up and paid for his horse's board, talking about the excitement that was to be had the next day. "A hangin'! Well, we're ripe for some fun. Haven't had a fuck or a drunk since the fourth."

When it had been quiet for some time, I rose from under the hay, brushed myself off, removed my coat and collar, and crept out. On the side of the barn was the poster; it was as if my own likeness hunted me. Somebody had come along in the two hours since Coy had spotted me and inked a beard on my likeness.

The three of us, though decidedly shady-looking, seemed so happy together on paper, it was more like a family portrait than a wanted poster. At least we were together. I took it down carefully, folded it, and stuck it in my pocket.

CHAPTER 32

Chin and I made our way back to the handcart under cover of darkness. I needed a rest, I needed to think, and I needed a disguise. Inspired by the bald drunk, I shaved my face, then my head, running my hand over my scalp to find whiskery spots. I drew no little blood with my inexperienced blade, but in Ogallala dirt and blood was par for the course. It was odd, really, to disguise oneself by baring oneself, to mask by peeling one delicate layer. How thin is the means by which we know the other.

Bald-headed and bald-faced, I struggled to find a way to save Curly and emerged from my speculations with one certainty. It was madness to try. The town was rife with bounty hunters. The jail was guarded. I had been spotted and they were looking for me. Even if I had a better disguise than no disguise at all, if I tried to save Curly, if I were to find the backbone and daring enough to make the attempt, it would mean two rather than one would die at the end of a rope. As I had no better disguise, no backbone, no derring-do, and no gun, I also had no choice. Though it sickened me to do so, in the morning I'd throw my bag on Chin's back and we would head north, away from Ogallala. Away from the gallows, away from Curly's last anguished breaths.

Through the night I was tortured by the thought of the distant face in the mine shaft, growing paler and smaller as I was raised to safety. Tortured by it even though I now knew it wasn't Curly who had been watching me rising out of the mine shaft, maybe tortured *because* of it. What had happened to that child? Was it my fault that I'd fallen for a mother's chicanery?

Had I chosen the right child to save, perhaps I would now be buying books for my Yale education. I would be plotting my life instead of racing to escape a horrible end. If I had chosen correctly, perhaps Phaegin and I . . . Instead, all was in ruins. That should have made it easier to decide to move on and leave Curly to his own bed, but it did not.

I was not responsible for Curly, I told myself over and over. He had released me with his confession. Perhaps it was justice for the child left behind by Curly's charade, but every time I closed my eyes the two children, Curly and the boy in the mine, merged into one, and cried out, "I jus' don' wanna *hang*."

It was a cold night. I didn't dare light a fire, and the weather, having been nudged toward winter so early in the season, now seemed to want to hightail it right to January. I shivered and shook for some time before Chin walked over, blowing vapor into the moonlight, and lay down, coming close to crushing me on her sweeping roll to the side. Once I pulled my blankets out from under her, however, she made a fine sleeping companion, her deep oceanic breaths finally taking me home to the Connecticut shore, back to when I was Edward Turrentine Bayard III, my mother, father, and grandmother sitting on a blanket watching me watch the waves, and in my mind the world was good and hopeful and forever mine.

I forsook Dawbs's cart to the wilderness, tossing the blankets and my bag on a strangely acquiescent Chin before dawn the next morning, and attempted to push Curly from my mind. We headed due north, Chin plodding along beside me, and I comforted myself with the gruesome. I told myself Curly's fears of a long painful strangulation were unfounded. Hanging was a quick end, one that many would wish for instead of waiting out a crippled old age or chronic illness. A snap to the neck, and it was over.

Chin stopped, looked behind her. I pulled at her mane and we continued on.

Sure, a heavy man would drop and his weight against the rope would make that noose snap and tighten. The trouble was, Curly was barely a hundred pounds and hardly out of childhood. His bones might still be stretchy on top of it all.

Chin stopped again; I pushed, cajoled, cussed. She would go no farther north but turned and, once again, faced the way we'd come.

I stared with her at the crushed trail we'd left, blunt green against the gray-rimed grass. How could I leave Curly to his slow strangulation, eyes bugging against the tight rasp of the horse-hair rope raising its weal? I could not. Though by going to him, I was almost certainly meeting my own death.

I leaned my head against Chin's haunch. And what would that matter? I was tired of the tack my life had taken. I had grown weary of loss and goodbyes. I did not like this world, as it came. Sick as I was of the greed and the viciousness, the cowardice, and all the sorrow that continued to build and build, death did not seem so bad in comparison.

Regret was going to have to do for backbone. I would go to Curly, do what I could, meet what I need meet.

The sun peeked from the horizon.

In an instant the entire expanse of prairie blazed from one edge of the blue sky bowl to the other, in a brilliant, shimmering, blinding spangle. I put up my hand as shield and in awe. Then at its brightest, the zenith frost capitulated to its moment of heat, and the prairie lost its luminosity. Chin sighed deeply beside me.

Having decided to meet death if that's what it took to save Curly, I didn't travel that path courageously. More than nervous, I trembled, I cramped, repeatedly stopping along the trail with gastric distress. We passed where the cowboys had made their camp two long days ago. There was no sign of them now, only that they once had been there: crushed grass, a mountain of cow pies, and the blackened leftovers of night fires.

I caught a glint in the grass, almost dismissing it as remnant moisture. It glinted again and I strayed from the path to investigate. My pistol. I checked the chamber. One bullet.

If I'd had even a moment of shoot-'em-out fantasy, the singular slug ended it. I put the pistol in my belt and we trudged on. The cloudless sky was now spoiling with an uncanny cumulus fleece, great round mountains of vapor, which at their highest reaches shredded in a heavenly gale. I worried over the churning clouds not at all. There were greater storms ahead of me.

In Ogallala the population had doubled overnight, and with the hordes of hanging-hungry citizens, looking like hell itself was on holiday there, it seemed even less probable I could do anything to help Curly. The crowds sparked with anticipation: not only for the neck stretching, but with the possibility that the rest of the "dwarf's gang" would make a showing as well.

I made a desperate visit to an overflowing privy after seeing the ramshackle gallows that had been raised, three lawmen with rifles standing alongside, and then vomited in reaction to the outhouse. Leaning on one knee and wiping my mouth, I spied

Coy Hayes, a veritable armory on his belt and in hand, keeping guard at the jailhouse. He swept his gaze from side to side across the crowd, looking like a murderous mechanical toy. I would have no words with Curly while he was sentry.

I wandered through town, searching for a means of rescue, waiting for an idea to grow in my panicked head. Every time I turned around there was some ragtag pinhead with a deputy's badge on his chest. Coy must have brought a crate full of the tin stars with him on his trip across country.

I sweated buckets threading through the crowd, head down, desperately hatching one impossible scheme after another that died at the first blink of reason. The mob around me was agitated, like a herd of cattle shying at the oncoming storm. Indeed, the day bruised with an eerie purplish light. I could feel change stirring, a collision of tensions that buckled the still air into a panting breeze.

Voices raised against the bluster of wind. I tripped on someone's foot and was hauled up from my hands and feet by a leviathan grip. I was tossed back into the crowd, almost colliding with three soldiers from Fort McPherson. One of them had driven the wagon loaded with roused compatriots and Tilfert so many rainy days ago.

I lurched away, pushing deeper into the coil of strangers. I was nearly trapped by elbows and bellies when a holler mounted from the throng.

Curly was led out of his lean-to prison and through the crowd. His hands were tied before him, legs hobbled by a figure-eight rope. He shuffled to the gallows, staring at the ground before him like an old man on his last legs. He looked up at the gallows and stopped.

Coy struck Curly in the back with his rifle barrel. Curly took the stairs awkwardly, stumbling on the last, and stood under the rope.

With renewed vigor, I pushed my way through the crowd, I elbowed people aside, rammed them with my head, I shoved, heaved, thrust, kicked, and clouted, and only moved forward six yards. In retaliation, I was punched, spit on, slapped. A fat man wheeled and roared, "If you don't stop, I'm gonna knock you from here to Omaha!"

I sidetracked his mountainous girth and drove aside the lesser summit of his wife, who piped like I'd goosed her. The mountain grabbed hold of my collar, drove his fist into my kidney, and tossed me behind to a staggering flurry of blind violences committed upon my person.

I staggered with the blows, unable to catch a breath or to escape being propelled backward to the far reaches of the crowd. I struggled to inhale and could not. A prickle of light haloed against my eyelids, my knees buckled. Finally, as light dimmed into one muted speck, I took a tearing breath, and another.

When I finally managed to stand, Curly had the rope around his neck.

Coy boomed from his gallows pulpit, "Does the prisoner have anything to say?"

Curly did not look up from his shoes. He spoke with only a small tremor in his voice. "I jus' wanted to be a cowboy."

I thought my heart would break.

There was a titter along the crowd.

Coy tied a bandanna around Curly's eyes. The wind lashed into a squall and whipped the red cloth loose. Coy cursed, grabbing at the fabric, and attempted a second knot.

"He's a *boy*!" I screamed.

A toothless old woman beside me counseled, "Shut up and let 'em get on with it! Goddamn startin' to rain an' I don' mean to get soaked."

I again struggled forward against thick humanity, shouting through the tempest of wind and spits of freezing rain. "A *boy,* eleven years old! What kind of people hang an eleven-year-old boy?"

A kid beside me said, "I thought he was a dwarf."

I continued my screaming objections. "Will you kill a *child* over dime-novel fantasies?"

Coy Hayes peered out into the crowd. Around me people were murmuring nervously. "Is it true? He's only eleven years old? Is that right?"

I kept moving forward. "*I just wanted to be a cowboy.* Are those the words of a cold-blooded killer?"

A woman took her husband's arm. "Hank, don't let them hang a child."

I kept up my admonitions, shuffling through the crowd, sowing seeds of discontent. The murmur of discomfiture grew and a few people shouted to the front.

"We don't hang boys in Nebraska!"

And "Take the rope off him!"

The rivulet of unease roiled into protest. The spirit of the mob turned; the moral center of the crowd became evident. I could feel victory. Curly would be spared. It was going to be all right. I had set a fire of decency.

Then someone shouted, "I came here for a hanging, and I'm gonna see a hanging."

And so the back blaze began. Half the crowd shouted for blood as the other screamed clemency. A fistfight broke out beside me and grew quickly into battle royal. I ducked and scrambled amid shouts and screaming. I inched closer, caressing the pistol at my waist, the knife in my pocket. I would take Coy with my single bullet. I'd slice the ropes. Curly and I would escape through the melee.

Then Coy caught my gaze. I could see recognition behind the scarlet fury on his face. He shouted above the din. "There is the other one! The other anarchist, the bald man! *One thousand dollars reward for his apprehension.* Whoever collars the murderer is a rich man!"

The people farther back continued to shout and throw punches, not hearing Coy's pronouncements. But those in my vicinity gave me hard looks.

I put up my hands. "He's *crazy.* I'm one of you, you *know* me, I homestead not five miles north of here." A woman wearing a threadbare dress nodded. "That's right. I seen 'im afore."

The wind whipped Curly's hair; the red kerchief flapped and this time escaped into the air. Curly, clearing from his fog of terror with the slap of the crowd's turmoil and brace of rain, caught sight of me. His piercing voice carried across the low pitch of roister. "Save yourself, Ned! Run!"

I still do not know how I escaped. A din of voices claimed my reward. A fury of hands grabbed my jacket, my arms, my ears with such violence it seemed I was being dismembered, disrobed, blinded, and flayed. I reacted like a madman. I bellowed, I howled furiously in a crazy hair-raising pitch. I erupted into a kicking, punching, flailing assault. I twisted like a snake, leaving behind my coat and a goodly amount of skin. I kicked balls, poked eyes, and might have bit someone's finger clean off. Finally, I dove through the chaos of legs and crawled like a coyote toward open air. All the while I could hear Curly's pipe. "Run, Ned, run!"

When I got to the far end of the crowd, I stood and looked behind me.

Coy kicked the lever. Curly plunged through the trap.

I raised my pistol, sighted Curly's jerking form, and sent my last bullet through his temple.

CHAPTER 33

With the blast of my gun, there was no time for sorrow or thought, only to take what little advantage the stunned recoil of the people around me afforded. I took a last look at Curly, now swinging peacefully on his rope, feet yearning for earth, and was visited with the image of Curly crouched by the pigs in the cold car. "Hope the end were quick, brother."

I ran through the tightening coil of wind and into the labyrinthine alleys of town, rolled under tent canvases, opened doors and ran through shacks, jumped through windows, pushed between tethered horses. Behind me a growing posse; eyes on the lookout, mouths shouting directives that were snatched by the storm so that there was no telling what direction they'd come from. I zigged and zagged through a vortex of rain, in a panicked run for the livery and Chin. I was not two feet away when a fellow shot out of the stable. We collided, staggered apart, I tripped and fell into the freezing mud.

He yelled, "What the hell! Watch where you're going!"

The voice was familiar, and when the stars cleared and I dredged the sleet from my face I saw it was Tennessee. He didn't help me up, just stared as I struggled to my feet. I shouted through the icy downpour, "Tennessee!"

He shouted back while shaking his head, "One thousand dollars!" But he made no move to stop me and, after looking at him pleadingly, I dashed past him and into the barn where Chin waited.

The crowd was close behind. Someone screamed, "In there, in the barn!" But it wasn't Tennessee. I felt a rush of gratitude. I was sure as hell done for, but at least it wasn't a friend who did it.

Shots were fired. Bits of pine burst from the wall. Cringing and ducking, I wedged the bar across the door. I yelled, "Back off or I'll shoot!"

Coy's voice swept through the door, every other word lost in the blow of wind. "Come . . . now or . . . won't . . . easy on you!"

I peered through a crack in the wood. Though it couldn't yet be ten o'clock, it was almost as dark outside as it was in the gloomy barn, the sun obliterated by the coiling masses of cloud and the sleet turning quickly to a hurricane of snow. The liveryman yelled from just outside the door, "It's *my* damn barn, the money's *mine*."

Someone else claimed *he'd* been the one to force me in. I ran from one side of the barn to the other, hunkered down against the occasional bullet. The barn was surrounded, the barn's walls shuddered in the blow. Chin whickered, frightened, from one of the dark stalls.

"Burn him out!" someone shouted. "That'll warm things up!"

The livery owner shouted not to touch his barn, goddamn it, but once the idea'd come on, it was impossible to stop. Someone threw a lantern against a stack of straw. Someone else grabbed a pitchfork and scattered burning straw along the east wall. A refuse pile outside the door crackled. Smoke billowed.

Horses kicked and screamed as fire licked along the walls. I stooped down, arms over my head in a useless shield, and searched for Chin through the smoke, the fire growing at an unbelievable rate, one side of the barn a conflagration in seconds.

The liveryman threw open the barn doors just as one wall collapsed, pieces of burning wood already exploded into miniature conflagrations onto the adjoining buildings. Panicked horses ran out the door, one with its mane on fire, another collapsed screaming under a fallen timber.

"Chin!" I shouted, and suddenly she was there. I tried, ineffectually, to lead her out the door, hoping that in the smoke and panic we might, somehow, get through without being killed, for the folly of the blaze was dawning on the townspeople.

"The whole town's going!"

"Get the buckets!"

Someone shouted, "Good God, the saloon!" The shriek of the storm and howl of the crowd were overshadowed for some minutes by the thunder of exploding alcohol barrels.

Chin reared as another timber fell and still she would not go through the door. I coughed uncontrollably, my lungs searing, my eyes burning. I crawled up onto a smoldering hay bale and from there leapt onto Chin's back. There was a sharp pain in my thigh, but I held tight, flat against Chin's neck, breathing filtered air through her dusty mane, and kicked with one leg. "Yaw!"

Chin rounded on the smoking back wall. She charged and jumped, breaching it even as it burst into flame. We galloped into the smoke-blind crowd, where anyone who had a gun seemed to be firing hopefully into the inferno and anyone with a bucket was throwing ineffective splashes of water on the consuming blaze.

As bullets sang, Chin barreled crazily through the combusting timbers of Ogallala's mercantile center, through the rim of outbuildings and residential shacks, past the incandescent banners of the now-burning tents. The blizzard dissolved into rain in the heat of the conflagration. My back was soaked, my face awash. The fire sizzled and hissed in the melted downpour, but the flames had reached such heights, the wild precipitation was no match against them.

A hundred yards out, however, Chin and I entered the full fury of the storm, a train confronting an accelerating tunnel of frozen air. I kept my head down and could see nothing but Chin's hooves coming into view, then disappearing into the thick curtain of snow, with each great stride. She hurtled across miles, her sodden mane and my clothes freezing stiff on our backs. The only warmth was at the junctions of my ass on Chin's back, my chest on her arched neck. My leg, once hot with pain, had gone completely numb.

The booming roar of the fire and the screams and shouts from the town collapsing around itself were muffled, then lost, as we charged blindly on, my world reduced to the gray hide of Chin's neck at my cheek. The only sounds were the yawl of wind, the draft of Chin's breathing, and the boom of her great heart in my ear. The howling downdrafts were so severe, the whiteout so intense, I could no longer distinguish ground from air.

After a heroic length of time, Chin slowed from gallop to trot, and then to a walk, pitting her weight against the squall as if it were a burden to which she was harnessed. I clung to her, a monkey's child, the terrible noise of not only the wind but my own sobs and the memory of the crowd against Curly's piping cry thrumming through my head. I had no idea of the time that elapsed in the cloister of storm. I mumbled nonsense, my words lost in the squall, trying to stay astride and awake.

"We're gonna be fine, girl. Just keep going. We'll take our share of winter here, this one day, this one time, and then we will give up this cold, turn our back on these uncordial days. It's you and me, girl, heading for the sun. Dawbs had the right idea. You and me. Mexico, or maybe swim the Pacific all the way to Polynesia. Not every horse could do that, but *you* could. I'll make a raft, and when you're tired, you can lay your head on the stern, and I'll row. We'll get there and eat coconuts. You step on 'em, I'll curl the meat from the shell, the only storm we'll ever again know. And there won't be anyone else to lose or ruin. We're gonna be fine."

I drifted away and back, and still Chin kept on. But now she struggled. Her breathing ragged, a gargled inhalation and grating exhale. She slowed into an ungainly plod. I rasped into her neck, "What is it, Chin?"

She stumbled. My hands, too numb for grip, failed. I slipped, landing in the snow beside her, my leg giving way at impact.

I looked up at Chin incredulously through the blowing veil. She towered over me, a mountain. She swayed, then slowly, unbelievably, went down in the blowing drifts, a mountain giving way, a tsunami of snow exploding around her.

"Chin! Oh, God, Chin!" I passed my hands over her. A dark stain high on her neck to a river of red painted her giant chest, sprayed across her front legs and back onto her belly. I looked at my own pants, iced with Chin's blood.

Her breathing was sporadic. I hefted her head onto my lap, flakes stinging, the wind carrying my voice to nothing. "Oh, Chin, no. Jesus. Don't do this, don't go. Stay with me, please, please stay with me." I laid my face on her forelock and whispered, "I'm sorry, I'm so sorry. Please, Chin. You're all I've got left."

She blinked her big eye at me and didn't take another breath.

They wouldn't find us. When the snow let up, we'd resemble no more than a crest of sagebrush, maybe a cottonwood trunk, under the white blanket. Certainly not a failure of a man and an epic horse. The wolves and coyotes would find us first, have their fill, and scatter our bones. Maybe so far as to keep our demise a secret. And maybe it was for the best.

I stroked Chin's nose, as wind hove ice and snow into a vortex around us. I could have died of a gunshot wound, could have been hanged. At one time I was sure my own physical weakness was going to be the end of me. Another time, Phaegin's brothers. Instead, it was weather that would provide the killing blow as icy flake upon flake descended and buried me in cold. What a Westerner I turned out to be. What would Avelina say? Tilfert?

Caught in a blizzard? Clean out the gut and crawl in, they're a goddamn dugout! Room and board. What more can you ask?

Love killed him, but Tilfert would have lived through a snowstorm.

I got tired, then tireder still. Tilfert whispered in my ear, *Crawl in the gut.* Then he shouted. I shook my head. I wanted to sleep. The top half of me was ready, but from the waist down, where my legs and lap were under Chin's head, it hurt like hell. Legs pricked, they stung and burned. The more tired my head got, the more the pain below intensified and wouldn't let me go.

Finally, Tilfert chanting, *gut, gut, gut,* in my head, I dragged myself out from under Chin's head. I kissed her muzzle once, then took out my knife.

Back in Nebraska, another buffalo. A job to do. Cut from chest to belly. The blood heat reviving me to work at a furious pace I had never before achieved, cutting and scooping entrails, loosening the lungs from the esophagus, pulling the engorged stomach and intestines, the shimmering liver, the enormous heart into a steaming purple and red pile.

With the last of my strength, I spread ribs and fit myself inside the cavity, knees drawn up, arms crossed. When entirely in, the weight of Chin's body closed the poultice ribs around me. Silent and dark, damp and hot within the odd embrace, my hands thorned with the thaw, my nose on fire. Too tired to think, to feel, Tilfert finally silent, I fell into thick sleep.

I awoke to a welt of gray light and a strange snarling. My first thought was that I was found out: Coy had tracked me through the snow. But the snarling wasn't human. I pushed at my confines. The cage of ribs would not budge. Chin had frozen solid around me.

The snarling intensified. To my horror, a set of slavering teeth savaged Chin's belly and pulled a strip of meat from the carcass.

I struggled mightily against my confines and cramped muscles, but I was good and trapped. A gouge of flesh was ripped from the ribs, offering a small window out. Wolves attacked Chin's corpse, a toothy muzzle not six inches from my face.

I screamed, *"Yeeeeaww! Git outta here!"*

The wolf yelped and sprang away.

For a moment it was silent. Then came the growling. The wolves seemed to be circling, reevaluating their find. I shouted again. They came closer. Every time I shouted, they seemed to figure more certainly that the noise was less something to worry about than something to eradicate. I gave up vociferation and spent all available energy trying to free myself. The writhing of Chin's corpse effected the wolves' all-out assault, however: snapping and howling, growling and barking, the savage biting and tearing, nightmarish. I struggled; Chin careened; the wolves went mad.

I freed one arm, took my knife from my belt, and brandished it out the ribs. One of the wolves bit at it, yelped, sprang back. Another did the same, but took hold of the skin of my hand as well, tearing it open. I jerked back and lost the knife.

I peered through the rib window. Six wolves circled, fur plastered with Chin's blood. One pawed its gashed muzzle. I gave a tremendous yell, stretched my arms, arched my back, pushed with my legs, and wrenched Chin's ribs open with a crack.

The wolves danced back, growling and yipping. I rolled from her belly. The wolves scattered.

I was more stiff than I thought possible. Attempting to stand, my legs spasmed. My feet like ice, I could not make them work. On torn hands and cramping knees, I crawled through the drifts toward a tree.

The wolves reconvened. They crept closer.

I reached the tree as one of the wolves made a run for me. I grabbed for a low branch and in terror and desperation stood. The wolf stopped short, as if for the first time recognizing I was humankind. I raised my arms and shouted. The entire pack bolted.

CHAPTER 34

Covered in blood, weak, and wanted, I was also alone and had no idea where. How long had Chin run through the blizzard? In what direction? I gazed around me. Cottonwood tossed gently in a warming breeze. A small creek alongside. Scrubby juniper dotted the piebald plains, snow already melting into mud. I could be anywhere in a hundred-mile radius. My bag lay beside Chin. Miraculously, it hadn't bounced off. I washed my face and hands with snow, stood trembling in the sunshine, with my face raised to the light and little heat. I checked my leg. The bullet wound I'd suffered the night before, although deep through the calf, was only a flesh wound.

Chin was unrecognizable as the beautiful horse of yesterday, her face brutalized by the wolves, her ribs peeled and white. Mournfully, I dragged my fingers through her mane. The pile of offal had been dragged about, Chin's big heart glittered with frost underneath a twisted cedar.

I retrieved my knife and freed Chin's heart from the lungs, then plunged the knife into the half-frozen dirt and began digging. The first inch or two was leaves, grass, duff, scat. Below that, clay, and below the clay, crumbling slate. I dug until I'd made an elbow-deep hole and had scraped into shallow rock. I sat back on my heels, panting, gazing at the monition that was Chin. Like a vanitas painting, she cautioned: Things will change.

But will they? I picked up a fragment of a belemnite from the pile of soil. Is what we call change the tiniest whisper along an emaciated moment, barely lighting on the surface? Then we dig down to the heart, dig down through the soil and rock, dig down to what is hard and real.

I pushed some snow into the hole, then placed Chin's frozen heart on the white blanket and filled the hole with rock and clay and sand.

Hearts, once curious and reaching, solidify into an unforgiving form. Not so much a heart as the record of one, and a poor record at that. Closed, hardened. Rock.

I began walking. I headed for the crest of the hill, hoping to get some idea of where I was before the damp of my clothes, my exhausted state, and loss of blood gave me up to the wolves I was sure waited impatiently out of sight.

I slogged through the drifts, warming to slush, my bag slung on my back, until I was wheezing and dizzy, my old ailments haunting me once more. My leg bled; I limped and swayed forward; with nothing in my belly, my head swam.

I crested the rise surrounding the small basin I'd been in and stopped, amazed.

Chin had brought me home. The Republican shimmered in the distance. Lill's place was a mere half mile beyond.

In an hour I was skirting the house, peering in windows, searching for some sign of Lill, of Osterlund.

There was no sign of Ry, but Lill worked at the kitchen table, rolling crust for pies, singing to herself or to the child asleep in the cradle. She was round with the new pregnancy, red-cheeked from heat emanating from the stove. She looked up at the window and, catching sight of me, went white as a sheet. I called through the thin glass, "Lill, it's me, Ned."

She sat down hard on a chair, then immediately stood again and opened the door.

"Ned, my God, what's happened to you?" She ushered me in, then stepped out and looked right and left before coming back in. She led me to the table. I sat down. Pastry was sliced into lattice on the floured surface.

I backed my chair up. "Sorry, your pies."

She gathered the dough up, mashing it into a ball and throwing it into a bowl on the counter. "Pies!" She ran her hands over my face, down my arms. "What has *happened* to you? I thought you were dead, the hanging, in town."

"You heard about that?" I looked at her more carefully. Her eyes were red and swollen.

She nodded. "Of course." She touched my bald head. "Scalped on top of it? *Where* has all the blood come from?"

"Most of it isn't mine." I pointed at my pants leg. "Only the leg."

She attempted to check, then shook her head. From behind the curtain she pulled out a tin hip bath. Put the kettle on, then pumped water into a bucket and poured it into the bath. "First thing, we've got to get you cleaned up."

"I can't stay. They'll be looking for me."

She poured another bucket. "They're not looking for you, Ned. The word is, you're dead. Burned up in the fire. Ry told me last night that the reward's petitioned to Coy Hayes. Man's got gold for eyeballs."

I slumped back, waiting to feel some relief. They thought I was dead. They thought I was dead. But relief did not come. Curly was dead. I was free, but Curly was not. "Phaegin."

393

Lill poured boiling water into the bath. "Some innkeeper in Missouri says you strangled her and left the body in his shed."

I put my hands up. "Of course not."

She tightened her lips. "I would *never* have thought so, Ned." She motioned toward the bath. "Clean yourself up. I'll turn my back and work on these pies or Ry will wonder what I've been up to."

I eased myself into the water. It felt like stepping into heaven. The water pinked around me. When I was submerged to my chin, my mind finally came to. "You were in Omaha. What happened?"

Lill didn't say anything for a while, cut a slice of bread and ham and handed it to me, then slapped dough on the table and rolled it energetically with a bottle. When she'd placed the dough in the pie plate she dusted her hands. "I waited for you to show up and rescue me from my poor decisions. But you didn't come."

I shifted in the water. "I'm so sorry, Lill. I—"

She laughed shortly. "Don't say that. I'm the sorry one. I waited in Omaha for two weeks, having paid for two days, expecting every moment to be turned out of my room. I was desperate, pregnant, hungry, humiliated, sneaking up and down back steps like a thief, though the landlord never said a thing, as if he had absolutely forgotten I owed him rent. But it was Ry. Ry followed me to Omaha. Paid my room. And after a time, he knocked on my door.

"I was never so glad to see anyone in my life, no matter what I had coming. I thought he'd be mad, maybe divorce me, and I would beg him to take me back. Instead he told me to come home and write my poetry if I needed to."

She shook her head. "And I told him no. It wasn't enough. I told him I despised him. I couldn't bear to cook another potato. I told him I wouldn't waste another moment on his tedious life."

I stuffed the last of the meat and bread in my mouth, then slowly scrubbed the dried blood from my arms as she continued. "Oh, Ned. His face: wounded. Every word out of my mouth: a mirror." She slapped the dough on the table. Rolled another crust with energy. "Plus, I'm not *stupid*. What else was I going to do? So I came to my senses and apologized. I came home."

She shook her head and filled the pie with sliced apples. "It hasn't been bad. I would never have chosen this life for myself, but now . . . Ry adores Lucy. Watching him adore her"—she smiled—"like rivers on a floodplain, all into one. So I have that, pies, and poetry."

"Are you happy, Lill?"

"At times. But more, I am . . . *content*. I never felt that before, and it's good. Very good." She exited the room and came back with a set of Ry's clothes. "Get out of there so I can take a look at your leg."

Lill didn't ask questions, not about Phaegin, not about Curly. She didn't ask about the bombing, or my expectations or sorrows. I understood she required a distance between us, from now to forever. She'd made peace with her life and didn't need mine.

She salved my scratches, wrapped my leg in cotton sheeting, pulled the pant over the bandage, and regarded me. I could not read her face.

The baby commenced crying and she picked the child up from the cradle. The cradle had a looping *L* carved on it. Rhylander must have made it. Lill cooed into the baby's neck, kissed her cheeks. "Isn't she beautiful, Ned?"

The baby, while hardly beautiful with a moon face and wispy hair, *was* wreathed in smiles. Lill blew indelicately into her neck.

I smiled. "I've got to get going."

Lill looked sad. "It wouldn't do you any good to be raised from the dead, would it?"

She pulled a jar off the shelf, pulled out a couple of coins and some papers. She put a number of the envelopes back in the jar but tucked the coins into the bib pocket of my overalls and handed me a fat envelope. "This came for you, weeks ago, forwarded from Fenton's Boardinghouse."

Mother Fenton had sent on the packet from the weasel-faced clerk. I turned the brown envelope over, weighing the artifact of the late Ned Bayard's hopes, then pushed it into my pocket as well. I thanked her and fished for the coins. "I can't take your money, though."

"You certainly can. If you don't, I will worry that much more. Do me a favor and save me from it."

I kissed her on the cheek. She smelled of flour and spice. The baby squirmed and grizzled over the proximity of a stranger. Blue-eyed, towheaded—if I hadn't known better, I would have sworn her father was Osterlund himself.

I hightailed it from the little house, avoiding the congregation of new homesteads, and searched out the emptiness of beyond.

Once I felt well and alone, I stopped to consider my next step. It began to sink in: I was a free man. Freed from all identity, all past, free of all responsibility. All ties had been severed, my debts forgiven. I was as light as a babe.

I finally had a moment of euphoria, unparalleled by any experience I'd ever had or, honestly, that I would ever have again.

But no one is ever truly unfettered. As soon as joy buds, the rose begins to fade: memory like time on those tender petals. I would not repeat my litanies of loss, refusing to think of all whom I had known and would never know again. Instead I set my jaw against the loneliness of unfettered life and attempted to draw again that moment of joy by reminding myself I now owned any number of possible destinations. The world was mine alone.

But it was not true, nor did I want it to be.

I pointed myself toward Utah, making haste until the sun had long set and I could no longer see the ground in front of me.

I pulled a blanket from my pack, wrapped myself against the cold, and took out the packet, peering at the writing on the front. I could do little more than make out my name, but I thought I could discern a faint whiff of Mother Fenton's sweet apple pie. The homey perfume eased me into sleep.

When I woke I tore open the envelope. Inside, a dozen or so crackling documents, many charred on the edges, stinking of smolder. The first leaf I drew out was a note written in a spidery, nervous sort of penmanship.

Dear Mr. Bayard,

I am a clerk in the offices of Alan and Jamieson. I found these documents partially consumed in the fire one morning, and as the business they concerned was transacted within the last year, I felt compelled to save them. When I heard the conversation between my employer and Montgomery Elias, I knew I had been right.

I am sorry to have taken so long to track you down, but a clerk's life is one of continual labor, and Mr. Elias (understandably) was loath to be of help. I, in turn, could not risk giving him too much information, not assured of his loyalties. In any case, I hope this collection of papers yet proves helpful to you.

I must say it would be disastrous for me to lose my job at this point. However, as I believe law is about justice and not about money, I assure you I will provide any aid I can to make sure that justice is indeed met.

Yours truly,
Daniel Ritter

Next, I drew out a receipt, paid in advance by my grandmother, for six months' care at the Gravenhurst Sanatorium in McPherson, Nebraska, for Edward Turrentine Bayard III. The sum on the receipt was $800, the amount that Cornelius Pierce had lent the estate. I was warmed by the thought that my penurious grandmother would have paid out such a sum for my care. I also wondered about Mr. Pierce's place in all of this. The sum paid out of the estate did not seem to include any interest or fees. Perhaps the old man was not a part of the plot at all, but merely the curmudgeon I'd thought him to be, enjoying a vigorous carping session as much as Grandmother did.

Four envelopes that once held pleading letters I sent to my mother spilled out next. The letters were missing but I discerned embossing on the return address. Someone had traced my name, perhaps to forge my signature.

Next, a health file on Edward Turrentine Bayard's health. A sheet listed types and doses of pharmaceuticals, from opium to Sneefit's Pectoral Drops.

Something about the writing on these forms gave me pause. I stared at the sharp crowns on the *p*'s and *h*'s, the overlong tails on the *g*'s, until it hit me. The writing was that of my private physician, Dr. Bateman.

Bateman continued his false file with an accounting of my time at Gravenhurst. I had supposedly arrived at the sanatorium near death and been given emergency pneumothoracic surgery to puncture and rest the left lung. I wavered on the brink of death for three weeks before rallying, making great improvements on a diet of milk and radium water. Two months after my arrival I relapsed, after receiving news that the family home had been sold and my mother was involved with a tradesman. I suffered labored breathing and night sweats and was coughing up bloody sputum. The Gravenhurst Sanatorium doctors unanimously agreed that the patient should receive no more correspondence until his health had been fully restored.

Apparently my mother complied and Gravenhurst reported I was bled to good effect and, over the next months, improved on heliotherapy and a nostrum called Kickapoo Sagwa. Finally, "curing" wrapped in dressing gowns and blankets on the hospital's wide porches put the shine on my restoration, and I was released in glowing health nine months after I'd arrived.

Discharge papers rounded out the file. They stated I left the sanatorium with a month's supply of pectoral drops and instructions for deep rest, good food, gentle exercise, and constant vigilance against depression and morbid thoughts. It seems I shook my physician's hand and thanked him for saving my life. I refused to leave a forwarding address, claiming my mother had thrown away my estate and honor, and so I would make my own way from this day forward, a man without a name. It was signed *Edward Turrentine Bayard III.*

I laughed at this unbelievable document, laughed until I had to stretch out on the cold ground and wipe the tears from my eyes. I reclined, stared at the milky mare's tails galloping across the sigh of blue above me, until the beauty primed sorrow, and I cried for being lonely and lost. Blue days are short, and it is a dark night we blunder through, evil intent at every turn. I sat up and traced lines in the dirt, thinking. Though there was evil, I supposed good luck had its hand as well.

I had not been meant to live. The morning of my departure, Dr. Bateman had bled me until I was barely conscious. Then, he'd administered a tincture of arsenic. But instead of experiencing the usual light-headedness, I became nauseated, delirious, and could not make out my mother's face. Had there been a hypodermic? Of what? And what was in the nostrum he had dribbled into my mouth after he'd seated me on the train? Whatever it was, Dr. Bateman figured I would not live long enough to report that there was no sanatorium and no miracle cure.

Bateman and Jamieson would have expected to be called by the railroad and be given charge of the body. I thought of the old attendant nodding at Bateman, acknowledging the doctor's name in my pocket and a fiver in his. That the call never came must have cost the scoundrels some worry but, as it turned out, made no difference in the end.

Jamieson and Bateman had certainly split the proceeds of the auction between them and, when it was done, tried to burn the incriminating evidence that Daniel Ritter providentially rescued. The thieves and would-be murderers had gotten away with it by taking advantage of my mother's gullibility, her ignorance of our affairs, and by feeding her hopes on reports of my growing health. However, these men certainly made a grave mistake.

My mother would never believe my repudiation of her. The instant they had tried to make her believe I had been so low as to forsake my mother because of bricks and mortar, or because she loved a man of a different social class, she would have known they were villains and alerted the authorities.

It was a chill comfort in these circumstances, but a comfort nonetheless, to know there was likely an investigation into the offices of Alan and Jamieson under way now. I only hoped the good Daniel Ritter escaped being tarred by their brush.

As I sat mulling the justice I'd like to see come to bear, I heard the clatter of a wagon. As I quickly stuffed the papers back into the envelope it occurred to me that the mention of the tradesman indicated that the pickle man did actually exist. I could only hope it was so and that my mother had indeed gone to England with him, never to hear that her only son met his end in a burning barn, pursued by the law, a murdering anarchist.

When the wagon overtook me, an old black man wearing a threadbare version of the farmer's swag I had on leaned from the buckboard seat, evincing his own poor hearing by shouting. "Give you a ride, if headin' this way. Slow goin'! Freak storm mudded ever'thin' up!"

I climbed aboard, noting the grindstone, tin, and hammers in the wagon.

His name was Amos Even. "*Almost* Even, they call me. Snoos runs down one side of my chin, not t' other." A tobacco stain marked the left side of his lip and colored his white beard. "What's *yer* name?"

I had a moment of panic and fell into a spate of coughing while I grabbed for a moniker. I shouted back, "Tom Piper."

"Tom, Tom, the piper's son?" he shrieked and cackled while I kicked myself for the choice. "By God, that's a good 'un. Yer ma musta had some sense of humor."

"Almost as good as yours."

"Yoop. Thank God fer wimmin with good humor. Whatcha doin' out here?"

"Looking for a good-humored woman—well, *sometimes* good-humored. Met her on the trail and haven't been able to get her out of my mind."

He nodded. "Hope you get to her in time. Women're like candy out here. No matter how bad they are for ye, everybody wants 'em."

Amos exhausted his conversation after ten minutes of shouting and fell into silence, working his chaw with a slight smile on his wrinkled face.

The silence was fine with me. I was in the infancy of my new life, with much to feel and little to say.

We traveled companionably along the South Platte for two days. Every so often he would break into a spate of loud conversing, exhaust himself yelling, then retire back into silence, apparently ruminating on the last conversation, for after a stretch he'd add on to it.

"Speakin' of wimmin. Knocked on a door las' month, house in the middle of nowhere. Woman answered th' door, little brown bird. Had three plain sisters. I stayed a week sharpenin' knives and patchin' pots." He shook his head. "No sign, no paint, no light, no lace, and still, musta been thirty men found their way there in that time, sniffed out those harlots like they was pies on to cool."

Hours later Amos added, "Speakin' of sniffin'. Ever et a skunk? Wouldn't recommend it."

The next day he offered, "Speakin' of stink. I used to play the harmonica. Fella took it from me in Ohio. Said it was his duty as a citizen. Miss it somethin' awful."

On the third morning he shouted, "You were yellin' *Turpentine!* las' night. Why was that?"

I glanced at the old man. He showed no sign of mistrust or even true curiosity, for he hardly waited for my response.

"Speakin' of turpentine. If they make maple syrup in heaven, turpentine's made in hell. Thought I's a free man after the Civil War, workin' for a wage. I scraped sap from the suicide forest— southern longleaf pine, yellow pine. It were another slavery, black men an' white." Amos shook his head. "Vagrants, debtors. The prisons let the convicts out to die working that timber."

"Why didn't you leave? You weren't a slave any longer, but working a paying job."

"Oh, sure, was against the law in the new South not to pay us. An' we all spent our wages in the camp commissary. The more you ate, the more you owed, see? Then the *other law* kicked in. A man didn't leave camp until the debt were paid"—Amos patted his pocket, drew out a twist of leaf tobacco, and wrenched a bite from it—"less'n he were dead.

"Worked tobacco most my life. It were *bad,* but it din't compare to that sin. Sometimes I dream I'm distilling, wake up afire."

He held out an arm, sleeve up. The black skin was mottled pink and puckered. "Still can't smell nothin' no more, 'cept turpentine." He laughed. "Guess maybe tha's why I never sniffed out a woman."

"How did you get out of it?"

He grinned. "I died. And then I went t' heaven." He gestured expansively. "Gits colder than I thought it would, but it sure is purty."

The Rockies loomed like blue rebellion ahead of us. Amos pointed.

"Speakin' o' purty!" Then he shifted his sight to an upcoming settlement and bellowed, "Hell's Gap! End of the line, Tom! Me an' this wagon both ain't stupid enough to reckon those mountains this late in the season. You got sense, you'll wait for spring t' have your sweet. Stay with me, if you care to. I'll teach you to patch tin an' you'll never want agin."

I shook hands with Amos and thanked him, but he and I both knew I'd be pushing on, no matter the white peaks shimmering in the thin air.

I'd search out the Hell's Gap mercantile first. This would be my last chance to stock up for a while. I'd stretch Lill's money and what I had left of the bone cash. I'd buy as many matches, beans, and bullets as I could afford and get on with the journey.

I was careful to keep my hat low, anxious to keep my anonymity for the rest of my life, if possible, hoping it would be a good stretch after all this. I meandered along the singular avenue of Hell's Gap, a town roughly twice the size of Philip, with what looked like a saloon, a livery, the mercantile, a dozen houses, and a school building. From outside of the saloon came a call. "Cal! Cal Morton! Tis me, Will Smith!"

404

Will teetered on the edge of the wooden walkway fronting the saloon, apparently having abandoned the wagon train for an inebriated life.

I nodded and headed his way. "Will Smith! What are you doing here?"

He lifted his bottle. "Fell off'n the wagon. Wagon, heh, that'sa good 'un!" He laughed, then lost the hilarity like a mask. "*Pushed* off. One mistake too many." He peered at me. "Where's lil' Ben?"

"Where's Ph— Alice?"

He bent his head and slurred conspiratorially. "There was trouble."

"What kind of trouble?"

Will crossed his arms unsteadily and looked decidedly smug. "Turned out Alice had a few weaknesses of her own. Now I know you liked her and all, but she were sure hard with me on *my* sins for someone who liked tobacco the way *she* did."

"What happened, Will?"

"She were concealing smokes, got found out, and *wouldn't give 'em up*! Instead of jus' takin' her punishment, made a stink like a polecat, screamin' and yellin'. *Blasphemin'* like all git out." Will smiled beatifically at the memory and took a seat in a weathered chair. "She give 'em what for, did some eye-blackin' and nose-bleedin' for sure when they took 'em from her. If it had been one on one, she'd be sittin' back havin' a good smoke right now."

"*What happened?*" I was more than nervous, all the stories of cannibalistic Mormons suddenly seeming reasonable in light of sweet Phaegin.

"She shoulda let 'em go. They was nice see-gars, but—" He

blew out his breath and shook his head. "Between her trouble and my tipplin' it didn' go well fer either of us."

I grabbed hold of Will's shoulder and shook it. "*Where's Alice now?*"

"They put us out." He looked mournful. "Fer good."

"Here? Alice is here?"

"Nah. They put us out *there*. Folks headin' to the Dakota Territory took her on. I did what I allus do—followed the wagons, beggin' an' whinin' like a puppy at weanin'." He looked sad again and swiped at his eyes. "Thought they'd think better of it an' lemme back in. But no, ten year invested an' they gave it up in a minit." He sighed, leaned down from his chair for his bottle, and, after offering it to me, tipped it back. "Nothin' to do but wait fer what comes next."

I took my leave of Will, pulled out my map, and charted a new direction: the Dakota Territory, due north. I figured the wagon Phaegin was on must be headed to Deadwood or Sturgis. It would take me well into winter to walk there.

I'd had enough weather to last me a lifetime, but I would not hesitate. All in all, I considered my luck astounding. First to have heard of Phaegin's whereabouts at all; second, to be spared crossing the Rockies in what would almost certainly be more winter than I'd live through; and most of all, that Phaegin was free of the Mormons. A dozen winters were sure to be less a challenge than one tenth of a husband.

I'd find a ride; there would be a way. In a terrific hurry, I counted my coins and went into the general store. I picked up a hunk of hard cheese, beans, cornmeal, and matches. I went to the counter and asked for ammunition. Sliding payment across the counter, however, I saw something that took the hurry out of my sails right away.

The mercantile noticed my stare. "See something you like in there?"

"Those cigars."

"Yep. Good ones too."

"Where did you get them?"

He smiled. "Now that's a story. You know them Mormons up the way? Why *they* had 'em I couldn't tell you. Cost me a pretty penny too. Like I said, they're good ones, Georgia rolls."

"How much?"

He eyed me. "Too rich for a farmer's taste, I can tell you that."

"How much, both boxes?"

The merchant laughed. "You wearin' gold underwear, son?"

I dug through my bag and pulled out the silver pistol. Slid it across the counter. The shopkeep nodded. "So?"

"Trade straight across."

He made a face. "Bunged up, don't guess it even works."

I checked behind me in case my luck faltered and Coy Hayes had stopped in for dill pickles. The shop empty, I confessed. "You know the fella that was hanged and the anarchist who burned to death? This is *their* gun. I found it out where the horse theft happened. The thief threw it in the grass and the cattleboys couldn't find it. I came by the week after and there it was, shining in the sun."

The mercantile perked up. "Yeah, yeah. I heard about them boys looking for it. You sure it's the anarchist's?"

"Sure as shootin'."

The mercantile gave me the eye again and shook his head, frowning. "Wait a minute there. Hold on." He scrabbled through the cubby below the counter. "Whar's that poster?"

My heart leapt into my throat. I was caught. The damn cigars were finally going to be the end of me. Heart pounding, I picked the empty pistol off the counter while the shopkeep was scrabbling for the wanted poster. I ran my hand over my whiskery scalp, swallowed hard while eyeing the boxes of ammunition a prohibitive distance behind the counter. I was going to have to bluff. I took a step backward, pointing the gun at the man's head.

The shopkeep straightened, looked at the poster, looked at me. Spoke quietly. "Wouldna believed it, in *my* establishment, what's the likelihood a that?"

I cocked the gun.

The shopkeep swore before I could speak. "Fuck!" He leaned over the counter and jerked the gun from my hand in sneering disgust.

It was for the best, I told myself. I didn't figure I had enough fight for another run.

The shopkeep peered at the gun, muttering. "Greenhorns can't handle shit." He peered at the paper, then murmured, "Yup. Sure as hell fits the description, all right." He put his hand out again. "You got yourself a deal. I'll put this baby in the window with a sign."

Stunned, I gave him my hand. He shook it and pulled a cigar box out of the case.

I laughed in relief and then, not so much out of greed as of not wanting him to ever know what was in the cigars, I demanded, "*Both* boxes."

"Now, that's too steep." He crossed his arms and stared at me.

Smiling, I retrieved the pistol and threw it nonchalantly into my bag. "Hate to have to wait for smokes, but if I must, I'll manage." I put my coins on the counter, the crackers and meal in my bag, and tipped Ry's cap. I was halfway to the door when the shopkeep called me back.

CHAPTER 35

I unwrapped one cigar and bought a palomino mare, a little lacking in personality but she behaved admirably. I got breakfast, a heavy coat, new boots, mittens, a thick woollen bedroll, a canvas tarp to keep the snow off, and a brand-new Winchester rifle. I rode out of Hell's Gate with a full stomach and ham in the saddlebag, and—finding comfort in Laramore's pronouncement of big country but few roads—I set out to find Phaegin.

When the sun began to set, I made admirable camp, feeling stronger and more hopeful than I had for ages. The fire burned companionably. I drew out the ham for dinner and found the Alan and Jamieson envelope adhered to it, translucent with grease. I peeled it free, cut my ham and contemplated throwing the oily papers away, but decided I might yet find the documents of use. I mopped the envelope, then took out the papers in a lump. With them came a small piece of paper that I almost threw away as a bit of rubbish. It was a poem.

> *I've not seen palaces*
> *worn jewels or drunk fine wine*
> *but I'm rich as any man*
> *because you are mine.*

It was a silly verse, and for a moment I was embarrassed for Lill, thinking she'd fallen so far to have written it. But it could

410

not be. Other than the date, the letters were print, the characters as blocky as the hand that penned them. Osterlund had written the verse, a love letter to Lill. It was a testament to her life that she had so stirred the stolid man, a *yup* or a *nope* often the extent of his conversation, into this. Contentment her gift, indeed.

I smiled and carefully refolded the poetry back into Ry's pocket. One day I would return the verse to its rightful owner. In the meantime, I wiped pork fat from the smoky testament of phantom treatments and imagined pharmaceuticals, and from the envelopes that once held pleading letters for my mother. Through a greasy spot on one, I saw there was a pale blue sheet inside that I'd missed before. I pulled out onionskin stationery. On it, as familiar and dear as her own face, my mother's handwriting.

Mr. Jamieson,

Thank you for your continued time and correspondence, especially as I haven't the resources to pay you as you deserve. I rely on your good nature most fully. However, while I believe your advice is well intentioned, I cannot give up on my child. I did expect that Edward, faced with the many losses he has incurred in the last months, no less with the humiliation of my situation, would be angry. I believe, however, he will rise above my abasement, and as his grandmother always predicted, he will make anew his fortune and his name. When he has done so, he may well forgive me.

Because of this belief, I implore you not to discontinue your search for my son. When you locate him, assure him my new husband is a good man, and that I am well and happy but for missing my Edward.

Liesel (Bayard) Meaney

411

I was incredulous. How could she have believed it of me? She should have known better than to think I would be angry about name or money or social position, and because she was faithless she had allowed these men to cheat us of everything! I crushed the missive and threw it down. After some time I picked it up, smoothed the thin paper.

The nameless person I now was felt incredulity.

Ned, however, had been hurt.

Further, I had to acknowledge, Edward Turrentine Bayard III had been furious over the loss of his name, his supposed standings, before he'd even had any inkling of what actually happened. He had desired more than anything to wear the facade of gentility, even nobility, once again. The fault of our estrangement was dual, laughable, and most horribly tragic.

I turned the letter over.

But perhaps not permanent.

> *Mrs. Aldus Meaney*
> *Drift Cottage*
> *Hammonasset, Connecticut*

Hammonasset. A tiny fishing village not forty miles from New Haven. All that time, my mother had been two long days' walk from my hand.

That night, I dreamed of Curly's mother: now in a higher office, with sweeter cakes, and a sweet belief to salve her loneliness: that her son no longer delved into the poisonous throats of the coal mines. Then I peeked into my own mother's life: she walked the salt marshes of a Connecticut beach with a good man, collecting indigo mussels, the great gray Atlantic booming and sighing, ever tethered by its imperceptible chain to the moon.

The following days were clear, my horse swift and sure-footed. There were no bandits, no Indians, no distressed pilgrims to slow my way. Prairie dogs dug their holes off the road, the frosted grass was high and of the type my horse favored, creeks easy to find and easier to ford. My only hiatus: to the postal office in the tiny settlement of Lookout, Wyoming.

There I drew a perfectly articulated chicken's skeleton on the back of the clerk's letter, a heart visible through the wishbone at the breast. I wrapped that and the rest of the Alan and Jamieson documents in brown paper and, for a thirty-cent Hamilton stamp, sent love and apology and, I hoped, comfort to Mrs. Aldus Meaney at Drift Cottage.

Within two weeks, I came in sight of a freight wagon pulled by a brace of oxen. Beside the wagon walked one man and two women.

I rode up behind the wagon and a fellow inside the wagon leaned out, a rifle on his arm. The man walking turned and gave me a scowling once-over. The women did not glance up. I was taken aback by their gaunt demeanor, sticklike fingers clutching blankets at their necks. Though they looked like nothing I had ever seen, there was something about one of the women that seemed familiar to me. I came closer and the man in the wagon cocked his firearm. I swept off my hat. "Good day."

413

The walking man demanded, "What's your business?"

I got off my horse, frost crunching underfoot. "On my way to Dakota Territory."

I stepped lively alongside and shook the man's hand while trying to get another look at the woman.

Apparently I didn't seem a threat. The rifleman put his gun away and the man with whom I'd shaken hands looked a little abashed. "We've had troubles. Robbed two weeks back, and we'd already strained our supplies by"—he hiked a thumb toward one of the women—"picking that one up. So if you're hungry, we can't help you."

I patted my saddlebag. "I've got ham here, some meal, coffee. Be glad to share."

The woman stopped. Turned slowly and let the blanket fall from her head. It was Phaegin—or what remained of her. She was a virtual skeleton with sallow cheeks and hollow eyes, her tattered dress hanging from sharp shoulders. Still, Phaegin stirred my heart.

She stammered, "Is it you?" She didn't wait for a reply but launched herself into my arms. "Don't ever leave me; never leave me again!"

I held her, all knotted rope and stick limbs, and whispered, "Alice?"

"Bessie. Bessie Dalton."

I got down on one knee. "Would you consider, Bessie Dalton, becoming Mrs. Tom Piper?"

She squeezed my hand tighter than I would have bet she had strength for.

"I don't have a ring right now, but as soon as we get settled."

She smiled through tears. "I don't need a ring."

"You'll get one. Until then"—I drew out a box from the saddlebag—"cigars?" I opened the box and watched her face bloom into wonderment. And if those who witnessed Phaegin dancing across the frozen grass thought her reaction to cigars was an odd thing for a lady, we knew better.

AFTERWORD

Dear Grandad,
Could this be the same Lill Martine you told us about? Tom
said all your stories were yarns.

Love, Neddy

A lifetime later I've often thought of who I have been, and how often I have been remade. Sometimes the remaking was sweet. My mother eventually came west for me; I reincarnated as a fourth cousin, twice removed, of the good Aldus Meaney. The Piper family enjoyed the Meaneys' loving company for two decades after and, notably, inherited money from Mrs. Meaney's recouped fortune. Half of that inheritance went, anonymously, to Daniel Ritter, once lowly clerk but eventually the only honest judge on the state supreme court of Connecticut.

Phaegin and I did, of course, marry, and blissfully did I become a husband. Soon after, perhaps too soon after, I was made a father, and certainly too quickly I became a grandfather—many times over.

Often, the changes I experienced were merely mundane. I have been a freighter, an innkeeper, a baker, an illustrator, a poor electrician, and—what eventually brought me a comfortable retirement—a seller of automobiles.

Sometimes the change was traumatic, identity stripped from my person like the hide from a stunned rabbit. Phaegin and I lost our second daughter and I have never recuperated from being cheated of my place as her father.

As must be, fortuitously or not, all of my personages—from Edward Turrentine to Turpentine to Tom Piper, aristocrat, anarchist, salesman—were temporary. Sadly, even my reign as husband. Which is why, I believe, we love the past.

Never is being so permanent as in yesteryear, when, like a Paleozoic squid, soft memory solidifies into story and, in that solid form, rejects the anguish of reality. So found my friend Amos Even, who died to retreat from the cruelty of the South, or Frank O'Hare Junior, who left a brutish father to become a washerwoman in wild Nebraska.

Yet as the past is relegated, one steps closer to the fact that the end and the beginning are much the same. Eventually no one owns identity. If we exist at all after we are gone, it will be as a story, as a symbol, as something in thrall to *another's* life. You will be a mere cautionary tale, an inspiration, a shame, a way to make someone laugh, a means to learn about that abstraction called history. You will become a fossil through which no blood courses, the shape of which you cannot choose.

I read today Lill Martine died. An old woman on her deathbed, attended by four daughters and seven grandchildren, an old man at her side: Rhylander Osterlund, a figure of estimable constancy and a sometime poet.

There was no mention in the obituary of Lill's miraculous skill with the rifle, of her vividness, of the passions she excited, the murder she committed, and her reason for the flight west, no breath of the name she had been born with.

Lill had been tamed in print, her many facets and colors pushed to one side, and where I might at one time have found fault in that, I would not presume to do so now. It was in the everyday she found joy as we all eventually do, given time enough to grow wise.

I imagine I will be tamed as well. That I lived a full century may find its way into my obituary alongside my being named the first dealer of Ford motorcars in the Middle West and Rocky Mountain region.

But if I could choose, I'd ask to be remembered differently. Therefore, I record not only my adventures, but also how entirely I enjoy a cup of strong coffee, what raptures I feel when faced with a drink and a friend, and how the light of my life came from Phaegin, in early mornings in bed, before children had roused and we were in so many ways naked.

I am often lonely, with Phaegin gone years before, my own children aged, my grandchildren grown, and my great-grandchildren so numerous as to be anonymous and exhausting. Yet in these quiet years my adventures, bottled and stored, have grown agreeable with age: one of the few pleasures left to an old man.

The delight that was missing in adventures filled with pistols and promises, hangings, bombs, coffins, and sorrow I've found in their memory. And now, being beyond both redemption and punishment, I finally reveal the canvas of my experience, tell my stories. I bear the weight of my entire life and feel it settle around my shoulders like a buffalo robe from long ago. It is a comfort and it is warm and will keep me until I, too, am gone from this earth.

ACKNOWLEDGMENTS

I was raised in Wyoming and want to thank my parents, Robert and Mary Streeter, for that, for the stories that their Wyoming upbringings lent them, and for the stories that they in turn lent me. Additional thanks to my sister, Summer, and brother, Nathan, who have also enriched my days and letters.

Having come to writing late, squeezed from a tube of paint, I thank my friends and teachers, often one and the same, for giving me a hand up time and time again: David Matlin and Gail Schneider who embody the creative life and encouraged me to take my first writing class, Gary Snyder who taught me much about language and vision and who introduced me to Carol, thanks to my secret agent Alan Taylor (a life-long appointment), Emily Albu who is even more polite than I am and is still a superstar, Kathy Olmsted who offers sharp historical perspective, and Bill Ainsworth, who reassures me about the promise of red ink.

Thank you to my teachers at UCD: Lynne Freed who says what she thinks, and to Clarence Major, Pam Houston, Jack Hicks, Alan Williamson, and David Robertson. Thank you to the Ucross Foundation for the inspiring place and time in which to write.

Thanks to Carol Kirshnit for miles of bicycle and running therapy, and to Eileen Rendahl, author extraordinaire, for jogging at my speed, for fielding so many crazy calls about everything in the publishing world, and for making me laugh no matter what.

Thank you Shawna Ryan for reading the work time and time again and for allowing me to read your extraordinary prose. May we birth many books simultaneously in the years ahead. (And may the labor be shorter next time around!)

Many friends have read drafts of my work, and plied me with alcohol. Joby and Ted Margadant, who threw me my first author's event, Pablo Ortiz and Anna Pelufo, Chris Reynolds and Alessa Johns, Jaana Remes and Andres Resendez, Ari and Lesley Kelman, Melissa and Ken Franke, and Sally Madden, Web master. Extra thanks to Sally McKee and Allison Coudert, who insisted I send my work to Laura.

Thank you Laura Gross, a wonderful agent and a source of moral support at all the right moments. I am so fortunate to be represented by you.

Thank you John Lescroart for superb advice and the prize that made this possible, and Karen Joy Fowler for her astute support and kindness.

Thank you Morgan Entrekin and Andrew Robinton for all the effort put into making this book happen. Working with you has been a pleasure.

Thanks to my sons, Jesse and Sam, for handmade pizzas and sweet tea, for understanding struggle, and for being so creative, intelligent, and kind. I have to work hard to make them believe we're related.

Mostly, immeasurable gratitude to brilliant and beautiful Louis, for conversations with good whiskey in warm bars, plotting book projects, and untangling literary snarls. You make my life wonderful.